BLOOD IS PRETTY

●

The First Fixxer Adventure

BLOOD IS PRETTY
The First Fixxer Adventure

It's the late 1990s—and Hollywood wants to take over the world!

What those in the know in Hollywood really know is that if they need a dark deed done, if they need a sticky personal or professional problem "fixed," they can call upon the mysterious and dangerous Fixxer. With wit and aplomb, he works the fruitful fields of Hollywood, fixing the sins and correcting the stupidities of the denizens therein.

"Steven Leiva not only promises but delivers. Beautifully written. Bravo"— **Ray Bradbury.**

Blood is Pretty is a wonderful read, a highly entertaining and impressive debut novel." — **Richard D. Zanuck, Academy Award-winning Producer of *Jaws, Cocoon & Driving Miss Daisy.***

"Steven Paul Leiva takes a dash of James Bond, the ghost of noir, a splash of Hollywood and stirs it into *Blood is Pretty*, an adventurous, fast-paced first novel." — **Melodie Johnson Howe, Edgar-nominated author of *The Mother Shadow*.**

"The Fixxer has the mystery of the Shadow, the sophistication of James Bond, and the street smarts of Sam Spade." — **Stuart Nulman, Book Banter/CJAD, Montreal.**

"Fixxer is a fascinating character. Intrigue, murder, mayhem in a fast-paced action-filled adventure." — **E. V. Le Roux, Silver Moon Magazine.**

"*Blood is Pretty* is set in Hollywood; it's funny, it's kind of dark, and has a lot of biting things to say about Hollywood. I urge people to check it out." — **Jeff Cannata, DLC Podcast.**

Praise For

STEVEN PAUL LEIVA

"The author's true strength is in storytelling."

— **Ricky L. Brown,** *Amazing Stories Magazine* —

"Leiva has such a vivid imagination."

— **Stuart Nulman,** *Montreal Times* —

"Leiva is witty and engaging, stylistically striking."

— **Areyon Jolivette,** *The Daily Californian* —

"Steven Paul Leiva is a master wordsmith able to take on any genre or blend them."

— **Jean Rabe,** *USA Today* **Bestselling Author** —

"In a wry and oddly affecting voice Leiva manages to encase his ruminations in an amusingly Monty Pythonesque carapace."

— **John Billingsley, Doctor Phlox on** *Star Trek: Enterprise* —

"Leiva's immense gifts for mystery and suspense are matched only by his wry biting wit."

— **Paul Provenza, Comic, Author of** *¡Satiristas!*

BLOOD IS PRETTY

The First Fixxer Adventure

Revised Edition

Steven Paul Leiva

Magpie

Press

ISBN-978-1-7352985-7-3

Library of Congress Control Number: 2023908166

Cover Design by: J U A N   J O S É   P A D R Ó N   www.jcovers.com

Author Photo by Miranda Leiva

DEDICATION TO THE 2013 EDITION

For my mother
Beverly M. Leiva (1916-1993)
This she would have understood.

DEDICATION TO THE 2023 EDITION

For Mr. Razzleberry Underfoot
Despite his insistence that I
Remove my laptop from my lap
And reserve my lap
Exclusively for him.

CONTENTS

AUTHOR'S NOTE & ACKNOWLEDGMENTS

There is a particular theory of consciousness—of how the brain gives us reality—which I have used as a basis for a significant element in this novel. As reported in the *New York Times*, the theory's strongest proponent is Dr. Rodolfo Llinás, a professor of neuroscience at New York University. I am indebted to him and the excellent New York Times science reporting for the inspiration. However, the technological extrapolation I spin off this theory comes solely from the reality of my brain, and neither Dr. Llinás nor the *New York Times* should be held accountable for it.

I want to thank Lee Smith, Certified Public Appraiser extraordinaire, who generously gave me a guided tour of Lake Arrowhead and opened the doors of the great houses surrounding that beautiful body of water.

I should thank several people who work in Hollywood for their inspiration. But if I did, they would probably sue me.

And, most importantly, much love and gratitude to the Great Girls in my life: Amanda and Miranda, wife and daughter—bright smiles and dancing eyes both. And Nanette, the first child I authored (in collaboration, of course) whose love of books was my greatest gift to her.

CHAPTER 1
DISCRETION IS THE BETTER PART OF VALUE

"The Phone," Roee said to me as I was eating breakfast.

"Yes?"

"It has rung."

"I heard it."

"It's Norton."

"It is rarely anyone else."

"He would like to speak with you."

"Thus, his use of The Phone," I said as I leisurely took another bite.

"I may be assessing this situation wrong, but my guess is that he would like to speak with you now."

"Well, unfortunately, Roee, 'now' is when this plate of Eggs Benedict you prepared for me is hot. And—compliments to you—I am enjoying it. Although I do look forward to the day you lose your faith and chuck off your heritage and slip in some ham instead of turkey."

"So, you want to call Norton back?

"Tell him I am committed to that action and will not be swayed from it."

Roee sighed and returned to The Phone.

xx

Only one outside person, my business manager Norton Macbeth, uses The Phone, a very secure instrument of telecommunication. Norton handles all the top players in Hollywood: Studio heads, the $100 million plus club of directors, and many actors that have become institutions. He also has an unerring instinct for those who will eventually be elevated to these ranks. So he has, as well, a tier of clients who aren't big players—thus big payers—but whom he's betting will get there. He helps them with sound financial advice and management. He also helps them manage other aspects of their lives, from the buying of cars and homes to the solving of sticky career problems to extrication from situations of stark desperation. In the latter two, he has been able to work wonders—by calling on my services.

The fowl Eggs Benedict finished; I went to The Phone and returned Norton's call.

"I have a little job for you, Fixxer," came Norton's cheery voice.

"Tell me about it."

"Young actress. Anne Eisley. She was in a sitcom last year."

"Cobblestone Bay."

"That's right. Great reviews."

"No ratings."

"Yes, but it was really good."

"But it didn't pay the bills."

"Right. But she got a lot of attention out of it. She's poised for the next leap, he-he-he." Norton often punctuates the end of a sentence with this little laugh.

"So what's the problem?"

"Well, she should explain that. She's really a very nice, lovely girl from South Dakota."

"No upfront fee, huh?"

"I couldn't talk her out of it. She thought the series would be a hit and put all her money into her dream house, he-he."

"That's the problem with dreams."

"Can you arrange to do it on contingency?"

"Will it eventually pay?"

"She's a client of mine, isn't she, he-he-he? Very talented, Fixxer, very. Given the right break, she'll be a big star."

"And the problem is something to do with something or someone standing in the way of that break."

"I think I better let her explain. Can you meet her today?"

"Where?"

"Descanso Gardens?"

"Why there?"

"She wants to be discreet, he-he."

"Well, as discretion is the better part of my valor—or, rather, I should say, value—I appreciate that. Time?"

"Eleven this morning. Can you make it?"

"Yes."

"There's a Japanese Tea house on the grounds. She'll meet you there."

I hung up The Phone and walked into the kitchen, where Roee was doing the dishes. "Call downstairs to the garage and have them bring the car around."

"Which one?"

"The 911, I think. Yes, I can open it up a bit on the Two. I'll shower. Tell them to have it washed and gassed in half an hour. And tell them that 'Sir' will be quite upset if there are water spots on my rearview mirror the way there was last time."

xx

I live in one of the high-rises along Wilshire Boulevard in Westwood, one of the little corridors of Los Angeles that suffer from, or glory in, depending on your perspective, pretensions of the urban, especially urbane urban. Each member of the staff of this building knows and addresses me only as "Sir." In the business I have chosen, anonymity is an asset, and they are well-paid to protect that anonymity. No staff member is ever hired for the building without my approval, which I will give only after Roee has done a thorough background check, is satisfied that the individual poses no threat, and is open to manipulation if manipulation is ever called for. How did I get such power?

After all, I don't own the building—just the 15th floor. There is an old saying equating knowledge with power. The old sayings are the best.

My personal staff consists of only one, although his value is numerically well beyond the loneliest number. Roee is sharp-faced and has dusty red hair receding on the sides, leaving an arrow of hair pointing to his nose, which, while not a caricature, is close to prominent. He is gay, a second-generation Israeli, and a failed playwright. I hold none of this against him. I am happily heterosexual myself, but I don't demand that other people be. His being Jewish is only a problem during his holidays. It is a nuisance to suddenly find him unavailable when I need him—especially after sunset. The nuisance is doubled by the fact that his holidays slip all over the calendar from year to year. A surprising bit of sloppy planning from a people of tradition who have added so much to the overall intelligence of our species. As for being a failed playwright, in the American culture of the 1990s, that is practically a badge of honor. Besides his expert preparation of meals, overseeing the cleaning staff of the building, and arranging for the purchase of household needs from groceries to computers, I find helpful the skills Roee developed while a commando in the Israeli Army and, later, an operative in Israeli intelligence.

"Any particular desire for dinner tonight?" Roee asked as I was leaving.

"Something simple."

"Pasta it is."

xx

I left my building precisely a half hour later. I made my way to Beverly Glen Boulevard, then headed north through Westwood, making the quick jag on Sunset to catch the continuation of Beverly Glen that takes you over the hill just east of Bel Air. The Porsche—a 1997 911 turbo, the last of the air-cooled Porsches—loves the winding path of Beverly Glen. On city streets, light-to-light and bumper-to-bumper, the 911 is just another pretty car, and Los Angeles is full of pretty cars. But this car comes alive when the road winds or lays out lonely, flat, and straight ahead of you. With herds of horsepower and a top speed of 190 miles per hour, some would say it's the best-handling sports car in the world. I agree.

The 911 is black. Henry Ford was perfectly correct. Black is the only proper color for a car. White is a waste, and not one car in the world looks good in white. Red is for fire chiefs and fantasists. Gray is the mark of people in suits of the same color looking for power and reading motivational books to get it. Any bright color in the blue-to-green spectrum is an insult to the power of the internal combustion engine. Brown? Brown isn't worth commentary.

I came out of the Glen, crossed Mulholland, and descended into Sherman Oaks. Like many such "cities," Sherman Oaks is just a section of greater Los Angeles in the sprawl known as "the Valley." It's the poor man's Beverly Hills—or the rich man's Van Nuys if you are aware of that dedicatedly dull area of the Valley. This is especially true south of Ventura Boulevard, where game show hosts, local newscasters, and well-worn character actors live in million-dollar-plus homes. Position on the compass of certain main boulevards seems to define social strata in this town, as the sides—one being the right side and one being the wrong side—of railroad tracks did in the nostalgic nightmare of small-town America. "South of the Boulevard" is a desired selling point in real estate ads hawking homes in Sherman Oaks. If the home is North of the Boulevard, only the fact that it is in Sherman Oaks will be mentioned. Those in the know ascertain its position relative to the Boulevard by noting the failure of its mention. Next down on the rung of desirability, but one trying hard to hang on to the rung above, is "Sherman Oaks adjacent," which means, of course, Van Nuys.

As I had the time, I took the curve of Valley Vista to Van Nuys Boulevard and stopped at the Sherman Oaks Newsstand for some information. Nothing to be found in the stacks of periodicals, this information would come from Mike, who has worked the stand for fifteen of its 45-year existence. Mike is a show biz fanatic and reads every line of type about "The Biz." But, more important, he has made it his business to know things before they get into type—and some things that never do.

"Mike, what's the info on Anne Eisley?"

Without missing a move in the unwrapping and stacking of new magazines, Mike answered, "Talented—some say with star quality—beautiful, of course—voted best hooters on an under twenty-five actress in an 'unofficial' poll among studio and network execs—hard-working, ambitious, but with a Middle American charm that takes the edge off—on the cusp, if the cruelty of the business doesn't dissuade her." He stopped his work, turned to me, and smiled. "Why?"

"Just curious."

"Yeah, I noticed that about you, Fixx."

Mike is small, maybe five foot three, with a broken front tooth that, combined with his long, overgrown, black-and-gray chin beard and never-off baseball cap, gives him character.

"Did you hear about Andy Rand?" Mike asked.

"What?"

"He's resigning from NewVue."

"Resigning?"

"Yeah, resigning. Do you think Engstrand would fire him? He made NewVue. Money is one thing, but the ol' Golden Gut is everything. They're going to announce it at a press conference tomorrow."

"But they gave you a call about it today."

"You questioning my abilities, Fixx?"

"Never, Mike. Never. You'll find a bonus in your pay packet this week."

I got back on the road, down Van Nuys Boulevard, to jump on the 101 Freeway to connect with the 134 heading east. I got on the phone and called Norton.

"Sell NewVue."

"Sell NewVue? Just like that, he-he?"

"Just like that. And without delay." I knew that if Mike had the information, the buzz was about, and certain others would soon have it.

"Okay. You are going out to meet Anne, right?"

"I'm on my way now."

"Oh, good."

It didn't take a financial genius to know that the news that Rand was leaving NewVue Pictures would practically crash the stock. NewVue had been a phenomenon, founded by Torvald Engstrand, a Norwegian media mogul, if you can imagine such a thing, with loads of money and piles of promises. But, as Mike put it, money is only one thing. It's hard to buy your way into Hollywood because it's hard to buy relationships, which are both the foundation and structure of Hollywood. And relationships are built in this town by dogs sniffing each other's butts to see who is farting success. The company took off only when Engstrand pulled off the coup of hiring Andy Rand away from Paramount to be his president and CEO. Rand's farts have always been particularly sweet because he is believed to have the Golden Gut, that instinctual thing that allows you to pick the winners more often than not. Suddenly all the top dogs wanted to pee on Torvald's tree, which allowed Engstrand to take NewVue public, making both men near billionaires.

That was in 1985. Now, twelve years later, NewVue Pictures is practically a major with an entire studio facility currently being built out in Santa Clarita, just north of the Valley. It also has two cable stations and the beginnings of a television network, things Torvald happily gave up his Norwegian citizenship for—and Marx and Lenin thought *they* would internationalize the world.

Why would Rand willingly leave NewVue? It couldn't have been over money. It was probably because he was not Number One in the company and never would be as long as Torvald held 51% of the stock. When you have great power and wealth, position is the only thing left to strive for. So Rand quits and puts himself on the market. His asking price: To be Number One. Somebody will buy.

I continued east, passing the Burbank Media District and the Walt Disney Studio with its much-too-visible from the freeway new animation building. Ugly enough to be in downtown Tokyo, the building sports the injury-to-insult addition of a tower-like structure over the entrance, a giant version of the Sorcerer's hat Mickey stole to no good effect in *Fantasia*. It's one thing to know where your paycheck is coming from. It's another to burden the rest of us with the revelation. Of course, they probably don't give a rat's ass about my opinion.

There had been heavy rain the night before, but now the clouds had broken, and the rain-washed air was allowing the morning light to strike and illuminate the landscape unimpeded. This gave a clear, shimmering quality to the view from the freeway, with the hills of Griffith Park and the stunted skyscrapers of Glendale standing out in relief against a brilliant blue sky. This is L.A.'s best time—the morning after a storm. This is when it becomes clear—so to speak—why people once considered this place a paradise. But it is also a time to watch where you're stepping. Rain brings out the worms.

Just after the center of Glendale, I took the long, graceful left curve that put me onto the near empty Two heading north and made the "jump to light speed," urging the 911 into joy, then quickly dashing that joy when I had to pull her back to exit at Verdugo and enter the hideaway town of La Canãda-Flintridge. Separated from the rest of L.A. by the Verdugo Mountains, La Canãda-Flintridge is a nice community of 23,500 good people with pretty houses and quiet demeanors. Here, butt up against the San Rafael Hills, is Descanso Gardens, well over a hundred acres of rich man's landscaping now owned by the County of Los Angeles, thus owned by you and me, bub. Despite the multitude of its shareholders, the place is rarely crowded. I would consider that a shame, except I hate crowds.

I paid five dollars to the pleasant senior citizen at the entrance and was immediately hit with that oddly clean smell of wet soil. I took the luxury of a deep breath. Despite the sun, the air had not heated up yet, and the cool through my nostrils was bracing.

I walked over to the Japanese Tea House, hidden from, but just from, the entrance. There, sitting on a little bench built into an elevated wooden patio that jutted out over a Koi-filled stream, her right elbow resting on a concrete table embedded with pebbles, and her chin resting on her right hand as she stared at the flow of the stream, was the most beautiful woman I had ever seen.

CHAPTER 2

BLOOD IS PRETTY

"**Y**ou have not yet found a cinematographer who has done you justice."

Not startled by my statement, Anne Eisley slowly turned and looked at me. "Are you the man Norton said he would send?"

"I am."

"Please sit down. The bench is only a little damp."

I sat and, out of habit, quickly surveyed the area. We were alone except for a middle-aged woman with the look of a National Public Radio listener doing Tai Chi on the bank of the stream.

"You're right, of course. I have never liked myself on the screen. Visually. I've been relatively happy with my performances. I can't wait to get an A-list cinematographer. Do you have a name?"

"Those who become associated with me tend to call me Fixxer."

"Fixxer? Why?"

"I fix things."

"Not toasters and TVs, I take it?"

"That's correct. It's situations, not appliances, that I'm good at."

"Well, I have a situation I need fixed."

"Tell me about it."

"Can we walk? I wouldn't want to disturb her serenity," she said, referring to Ms. Tai Chi.

When she stood up, I could see her beauty in its totality. Not just her face, which was the most perfect face I had ever seen, with everything correctly proportioned over a jawline that was poetry. Her nose was as perfectly formed as Copernicus's Universe; her lips were full and sensual but not overblown and pouting; and her complexion was clear and luminous. It was probably the long winters in South Dakota that allowed little sun in to do its damage. Here, where the sun was but one of many things that could sting you, she obviously maintained her skin's protection through an admirable intelligence. Intelligence also defined her eyes, which were a unique and deep aquamarine. It was a cool intelligence, but intelligence, nonetheless. All of this was framed by gold-blonde hair that fell down the sides of her face in thick, meaningful waves. As I said, though, it was not just her face; it was the full effect of her that stunned me. She wore a baggy sports jacket, but open, allowing a view. Her breasts were the size and shape that made a man think not just of sex but of nurturing. Her waist cried for the clasp of your hands, and her long legs talked of nights entwined in your own. Did she work out to achieve this, or was she just a case of perfect aesthetics?

Could I fall in love with her? Every man asks himself this question when he is face-to-face with daunting beauty. I could have answered this one in a flash—but I begged myself for more time to think about it.

We left the teahouse and walked on the blacktop path towards the center of the gardens, passing the Rosarium and entering a grove of California Live Oaks, the tree that dominates the gardens. Dozens of squirrels darted across the grounds from tree trunk to tree trunk and, above, jumped from one rough, wavy branch to another.

"I come from South Dakota. Grew up in a traditional Middle American town. A town of values."

"Values are very big right now."

"Don't mock me!" The flash of her anger was stunning.

"I'm sorry if you took it that way."

"Are you going to take me seriously?" she challenged.

"Yes. I promise."

She accepted that and continued. "People may find me odd, but I loved my childhood, I loved my parents, and I loved my town. I did not come to Hollywood to escape anything. I was the dream child— the perfect child, but my parents were down to earth about it. They made me acknowledge it as a fact to be dealt with, not one to be flaunted. I excelled in high school. Good grades. Head Cheerleader. Prom Queen. But I enjoyed drama the most. I enjoyed moving people beyond just the visceral reaction to my looks. I liked the control of it. It sounds pretentious, but there, in that town, I was a star."

She stopped to look at me and gauge my reaction. I tried to give her none but continued interest.

"The scale may have been small, but I learned what that term truly means. It's an incredible high. Everybody encouraged me to come to Hollywood. Had it been a simpler time, say the 1920s, I'm not sure I would have come; local stardom probably would have been enough. But these aren't simple times. You can't escape Hollywood."

We turned left onto another path.

"I should have known better, but when I got here, I was shocked how many—this almost sounds elitist—beautiful people there are here."

"It's one of the raw materials this town uses."

"At first, I thought I was just one of many. That I didn't stand out at all. But I decided to stay. I had the quality; I knew it. I did the typical things to get by. I was a waitress. Worked temp jobs as a receptionist. I even worked for a house cleaning service, 'The Mighty Maids.' Then, finally, I got a small part, a whole scene with Steve Martin. I must have called everyone in South Dakota."

I was dying to say that that couldn't have taken long, but I decided against it.

"Then he popped up."

"He?"

"Fred Crane"

I must have made a visible reaction. "Do you know him?"

"Only by reputation."

"Then you won't be shocked by anything I'm going to tell you. He was only the associate producer on this film, but he was very arrogant. Very—preening. He started harassing me, borderline stuff at first during the audition and some early meetings, but then he finally just came out and asked me to 'Do him.' I hate that term. I'd much rather he had just said, 'Fuck me.'"

"What was your answer?"

"I didn't take him seriously at first. It was such a cliché."

"And he was only the associate producer."

"Yeah, I took that into consideration. At first, he pleaded, promising me all kinds of good things for my career. I tried to say no as diplomatically as possible. He turned vicious. Said he would get me fired from the film."

"And?"

"He did. Somehow, he pulled it off. I couldn't believe it."

"Did you protest?"

"Yeah—to deaf ears. So I was waiting tables again, and did temp jobs, and cleaned houses."

"Were you ever sexually harassed on these jobs?"

"Oh, sure, but what was the threat? I would 'never temp in this town again?' Pip-squeaks I can handle. Can we sit here? This is my favorite spot."

We had come to a bench overlooking a fern-covered gully with a waterfall at one end and canopied by the intersecting branches of several large California live oaks. There was no sense of the existence of anything but this. You could believe you were a million miles away from anything Hollywood had to offer—or to threaten you with.

"I kept auditioning, of course. Did some small bits. Inconsequential. Finally, I got another good part in a feature, a supporting role. Crane was there. He had advanced himself. He was now a co-producer."

"And he makes the same threats."

"And successfully carries them out. I mean, I had the role, the director loved me—even the producer loved me—then this little shit gets me fired. How?"

"He had some control over people beyond his title."

"That's what I figured. Anyway, about this time, I got a job teaching drama to kids for a Parks and Recreation program. One of the kid's moms was Ronnie Charles."

"The TV casting director."

"Yes. She's a wonderful person. She cast me in *Cobblestone Bay*."

"And all was right with the world. Until they canceled it."

"The show did me a lot of good. Created buzz. Now I'm up for the proverbial 'role of a lifetime.'"

"And Crane is the producer."

"It's like I'm tied to that bastard with a rotten umbilical cord."

"The role is that good?"

"It's beyond good. This is going to be a hit. $200 million gross easy. If I get this role and even put in 50% of what I can do, it will put me into the 'Club.' Crane says it's between one other actor and me."

"So what's the problem? Fuck him. It's just sex."

"No, he wants more, much more. I can tell. God knows how he's managed to advance this far."

"He's been tapped into some power source."

"Yeah, and that's what I think he wants to make me. He wants a relationship. I don't know, maybe marriage. He wants to ride me."

"I see."

"So sex won't be enough. He wants my life."

"Fuck him, take the role, get the power, and then—fuck him."

"No. He scares me. He will get me if I don't get him first. Can you fix this, Fixxer? Can—can you kill him?"

I almost laughed. "Anne, what did Norton tell you about me?"

She looked at me, wondering, I assume, if she had made a misstep but revealing nothing from those aquamarine eyes that one could stare into all day. Then, finally, she stated, "Miss Eisley."

"What?"

"I'm very old-fashioned. I prefer to be addressed as Miss Eisley."

"Well, Miss Eisley, I am not a hitman."

"Of course not. I shouldn't have asked."

"As you may have heard, the idea is morally reprehensible in several cultures."

"So you can't help me?"

"I didn't say that. I believe I can. It will take your cooperation. And you will have to experience some intimacy with Crane."

"How much?"

"A little. Not enough to start a family with. You'll have to pretend that you're accepting his offer, even that you've finally come to your senses and now realize what a hell-of-a-swell guy he is. Once you lock the role and secure a pay-or-play deal, arrange a romantic evening at your house. I'll tell you the rest once I've confirmed that something I need is available."

"And this will take him out of my life?"

"I guarantee it."

"And the price?"

"I understand that you're cash poor at the moment."

"That's true."

"I'll do it on a contingency. If I succeed, you'll pay me two percent."

"Of this deal?"

"Of everything you earn for the rest of your career."

Her exterior cracked. "What! That's absurd!"

"You pay your agent ten."

"Yes, but—"

"Norton five."

"But—"

"You have a lawyer?"

"Yes, of course."

"You're probably paying him five percent. If I fail, their percentages may be worthless. You're a beautiful young actress, but you only have a small window to make it in this town. You don't have time to waste."

"How can you be sure I'll always pay you?"

I just smiled.

"Trading one pact with a Devil for another, I suppose," she said sadly. She gave me her contact numbers. I told her to contact me through Norton. Then we started to walk back to the entrance. Walking through the grove, I noticed a small brown bundle on the blacktop ahead. I guessed immediately what it was. I tried to direct her eyes away, but she saw it.

"Oh, poor squirrel."

It lay dead on the blacktop, eyes closed. Brilliant red blood had flowed from under its head to form a pool that now held its shape. I tried to move on, but she stopped, fascinated by the scene.

"Do you think it was run over?"

"Except for the tour tram and an occasional gardener's truck, they don't face that kind of threat here. And it's not—I don't know how else to put it—squashed. No, it probably just fell from one of those branches and, unfortunately, found blacktop instead of a pile of leaves under him."

"But they're so good at jumping."

"Even a squirrel can make a misstep. Or they get old."

She continued to stare at it, especially the blood that a patch of sunlight had now fallen on, bringing out its red brilliance even more. "Blood is pretty," she said.

"Yes," I said, for I had to agree. "Until it congeals."

xx

I walked Anne Eisley to her car, then got into the 911 and put a call into The Phone before taking off.

"Talk." It was Roee's standard greeting.

"It's me. Patch me into Petey on the scrambler."

"All right. Hold on a sec."

It was more than a second, but not much. Petey's loud, shouting voice came over the line. It was just the way he talked.

"Fixxer! How are you!?"

"I'm okay for a man in my condition."

"And what condition is that!?"

"The Human Condition, Petey, the Human Condition."

"Ha-ha! I fall for that each time!"

"That's why I love you."

"Hey, don't go all maudlin! You know I cry at Kodak commercials! What's up!?"

"You remember Formula 12-72."

"Oh yeah! I love that stuff!"

"Got any left?'

"Well, gee, let me think! Oh, yes, sure! I've got some in the deep freeze at home!"

"Can you send me enough for one application?"

"Sure. Can you send me ten grand!?"

"What do you think of five? How often do you get orders for it?"

"Oh, okay! You're a wicked negotiator!"

"Overnight?"

"You pay the shipping!?"

"Certainly."

"Done!"

"So, how's every other little thing?" I asked.

"Well, covert ain't what it used to be!"

"No kidding."

"It's better!"

"How's that?"

"It's become truly pragmatic! As opposed, you know, to using 'pragmatism' as a cover for personal agendas! I feel like I'm working for 'the People' again!"

"Should I return?"

"Oh, come on, Fixxer! Charity work ain't your gig no more!"

"Too true, Petey. Stay out of the cold."

"Stay out of the heat!"

The car phone rang when I was blasting down the Two and heading home. I put it on the speaker. "Yes, Roee?"

"I've got Norton on the scrambler."

"Patch him through."

"Did you talk to Anne?" Norton greeted.

"Yes."

"Can you help her?"

"Yes. Call her and tell her to go ahead with what I suggested. She should call me through you when it's set."

"Okay. What did you think of her, he-he?"

"Beautiful girl."

"Yes, he-he, beautiful seems inadequate."

"Are you in love, Norton?"

"Oh, no—he-he—you know me, stable, happily married man. No, just looking out for my percentage."

"Norton, why did you call? You don't usually ask for such quick reports."

"Oh, yes. Paul Hinckley called."

"That third-rate Spielberg. What does he want?"

"He remembers how you helped him before."

"Yes. And I hope the film-going public never finds out."

"Oh, he's not that bad, he-he."

"Norton, he's had the most amazing third-times-the-charm career."

"What do you mean?"

"Track his career. He'll make two back-to-back absolutely awful films that generate appropriately dismal box office. Then his next film will always just break $100 million, saving his ass."

"Well—he-he—he keeps working. Steady commission. Can you see him?"

"He still has a housekeeping deal at Warner Bros.?"

"Yes, he does."

"I'll drop off now."

xx

Paul Hinckley filled in the rather substantial gaps in his talent with pure ego. Convinced that he was better at every aspect of motion pictures than anyone else, he usually demanded to write or rewrite the screenplay, produce, and be the cinematographer besides directing. The only reason he didn't edit his films was that he hated confined spaces, fancying himself a cowboy. But he usually hired first-time editors more than willing not to bother him with creative input—splice-and-dice jobs. So he often made murky films in look, plot, and flow. Then that third one in the cycle would happen, always with a screenplay he now didn't have the power to touch. Some little well-executed gem of a concept that even he couldn't screw up. Boom—he breaks the $100 million sound barrier, and suddenly he has the right stuff again—and the momentary power to get him through two more insults to the memory of Edison, Eisenstein, Griffith, Ford, and even—Christ!—Jerry Lewis. If there were any justice in the world, Paul Hinckley would be directing television movies for a cable channel with a low audience share.

I entered the main gate of Warner Bros., and the guard pointed me to a VIP parking space. They know me at Warner Bros. They know me at all the studios. They just don't know why they know me.

Paul Hinckley's Hondo Productions was housed in a bungalow suite of offices, all the rooms cramped except his own, which still was not as spacious as I'm sure he thought he deserved. Posters of all his movies, even the two out of three dismal ones, were proudly displayed on the walls: Certificates of honor for completing productions.

"That was quick," he greeted me as his assistant ushered me in.

"Car phone."

"Yes. What did we ever do before them?"

"Listened to disco on the radio."

"Ah, don't get me nostalgic."

He lit up a cigarette. Marlboro, of course. He had probably been smoking them since he was a teenager and still thought they made him look cool.

"Sit." He gestured to a couch, chair, and table arrangement, which was not just a conversation bay but also his workspace. He was one of those filmmakers who considered it bad form to sit behind a desk. "I need something fixed."

"Go ahead."

"There's this kid out there, this—film geek—Dave Finch. You know the kind. They do movie reviews for free for freebie newspapers to get free screenings."

"Yeah. The Land of the Free."

"I want you to give him something for me."

"What?"

"A quarter of a million dollars."

"Jesus Christ! He must have given you one hell of a good review."

"He gave me something better than that. And I want him fairly compensated for it." He took a long drag on his Marlboro, smiled, and blew out a stream of smoke prodigious enough to allow a tobacco lobbyist to cloud the issue.

"So send him a check. I'm not a delivery service."

"There's a message that goes with it."

"I'm not a messenger service."

"There's a behavior change on his part that I want you to assure."

"I see. Well, I have been known to affect behavior modification. Give me the details."

"Fixxer, I have been searching for the Holy Grail for a long time."

"I assume you're being metaphorical."

He dragged on the cigarette again and smiled again. It wasn't a smile that lifted spirits. It was the scary smile of a sad ghoul. "The Holy Grail for any filmmaker—for any commercial filmmaker—and I'm very proud to say that I'm a commercial filmmaker—is the Living Concept Movie."

"Otherwise known as a good story?"

"No, no, Fixxer, it's far more complex than just a good story. It is the magic formula—the secret key. By 'Living Concept,' I mean something that can replicate. Something that can bear children."

"Sequels."

"Sequels, merchandising, spin-offs, those are but the mere manifestations. The real children are elements taken from the Zeitgeist, formed into crystal clear universal representations, then sent out through your film back into the Zeitgeist, thereby reshaping it slightly to your will."

"And none of your past films have reshaped the Zeitgeist?"

"Some had potential, but the studios fucked up the marketing."

"And your successful films?"

"The studios fucked up the story."

"But they made money?"

"Sometimes directing is salvage work."

"So I assume this Dave Finch has given you a Living Concept."

"Forced it on me at an AFI seminar six months ago. I told him I could only accept things submitted through my agent, then he started to scream about the elitism of Hollywood and Catch 22's, almost, I swear, foaming at the mouth. I put it into my pocket just to shut him up."

"It wasn't a script."

"No, just a fifteen-page treatment. I forgot about it. Didn't even take it out of my jacket."

"Until?"

"Last Tuesday. First time I had worn the jacket since the seminar. I didn't remember where it came from, so I looked it over. Within three pages, I knew what was there. I had found my Holy Grail."

"And now you want to buy it for a quarter of a million. So what's the problem? Kid isn't a member of the Writers Guild?"

"I don't want to make a normal deal here. I want to be fair—more than fair. A quarter of a million is a hell of a lot for a treatment. I want to give it to him. Then I want him to go away."

His cowboy crust cracked a little bit. His hands shook as he lit another cigarette.

"I see. You want to present this Living Concept as wholly original to your *own* fertile imagination."

"I will, in the screenplay, of course, make it much more than what it is now."

"Nonetheless..."

"It's the concept that's going to blow people away."

"Still, why go through this? Purchase the damn thing, then bury him in the credits."

"No. No, I've got to do it this way."

"Why? You've had some successes. You've made money. You'll keep working."

"Because I want to be anointed. Spielberg, Coppola, Scorsese, those bastards have been anointed. I want to be anointed!"

It wasn't hard to understand. Isn't Hollywood the Mt. Olympus of the modern age? The rarefied air where gods and goddesses reign and for whom sacrifices are made. Graven images of them or their work bring tributes from the masses. They are worshipped with hymns of attention, attention confirming recognition, a recognition which meant, *I am above it all!*

If you don't happen to be a god who can travel to Olympus on a cloud, you can only get there by climbing. Which probably means you'll have to get your hands dirty.

"Half of what you're paying him."

"You want 125,000 for the job?"

"And the amnesia."

"Okay, I'll have Norton transfer it over when I have Finch's signature on this."

He handed me a one-sheet agreement. It read:

I, David Finch, in consideration of payment of Two Hundred and Fifty Thousand Dollars ($250,000), which I hereby acknowledge receipt of, assign all copyright and interest in a fifteen-page treatment currently entitled "V," as well as in all ideas, elements, concepts, and characters contained within said treatment, to Paul Hinckley, and that by doing so Paul Hinckley becomes, for all purposes whatsoever, the author of said treatment and has full rights to take such credit. I agree that any mention of this agreement by me will be a material breach of this agreement.

"I'm not sure this is a truly binding document. When the film is the biggest thing since *Star Wars*, what's to prevent him from taking credit?"

"The contract's just window dressing. I'm counting on the money and your presence to do the real job. So scare the shit out of him, Fixx."

"Yeah, I can do that—and thank you for the compliment—but let's try something else as well. Can I get into your computer?"

"Sure."

I went to the computer, which was placed on a chest-high stand. He wrote standing up—probably in his cowboy boots. I opened a document and typed:

I, David Finch, hereby acknowledge and admit that while I was working at the offices of Hondo Productions as a one-day temp, I made a copy of a fifteen-page treatment titled "V." I took this copy home with me and retyped it word for word and have submitted it to various film production companies and individuals in the film industry, claiming authorship of said treatment. I further acknowledge that the sole author of the treatment is Paul Hinckley.

"This is great," Hinckley said, his Marlboro breath flowing over my shoulder.

"As you said, he's a film geek, but if anybody were to believe him, this should convince them otherwise. You had him sign it for your protection. Then, being the deep-feeling Hollywood liberal you are, you dropped the matter, not wanting to call in the police and ruin the kid's life. He forced the treatment on you. He may have forced it on others."

"I can't believe that."

"Why not?"

"If anybody of power had read this—it would be an announced project."

He gave me Finch's address on Argyle in Hollywood and a cashier's check made out to CASH.

"I'm leaving here at five. I'm going up to my ranch in Paso Robles. Norton has the number. Let me know when it's all done."

"Going to get in some riding?"

"Yeah. Healthy stuff. Fresh air. Sometimes you just have to get away from the stink of Hollywood."

CHAPTER 3
SILLY PUTTY LIPS

I decided to go home and grab a bit of lunch and change cars before going out bird hunting. I don't mind driving the 911 through Hollywood, but parking it on a residential street there would show a lack of caution that was trained out of me long ago.

"Does the name Anne Eisley mean anything to you?" Roee greeted me.

"Much—but most of it is my active imagination."

"Norton said she called, and you should call her."

"Fine. Set it up. What have you got for lunch?"

"Poached salmon from The Bistro."

I ate as I talked to Miss Eisley over the speaker.

"I called him."

"I assume he was thrilled."

"Yeah. I had to wipe off my phone. He wants to go out tomorrow night. Is that too soon?"

"What do you hear from your agent?"

"Oh, yeah. He confirmed it. Got the deal with the Pay or Play."

"Then tomorrow night is perfect timing."

I gave her details of what I wanted her to do.

"And you'll be there when I bring him home?"

"Yes."

"There won't be a confrontation, will there?"

"He'll never know I was there. Just get him to a heightened state of anticipation."

"That shouldn't be hard."

"Actually, it should be, but we needn't go into that now."

I took the Corolla to Hollywood. It's a not-so-nice, dull mid-80s model. Brown. I went east on Wilshire to Hancock Park, making a left on Rossmore, the most pleasant artery into Hollywood, a tree-lined street of old-money mansions, very East Coast in its feel. "Mansions" may be a bit of a hyperbole, but "big houses," which would be accurate, seems inadequate. Being just up the road from the Wilshire District and not that far from downtown, these houses were occupied by bankers and oil company executives, or retired versions of the same, who had bought the houses in deflated times gone by and now found it hard to pay for the upkeep and replace the antiquated plumbing.

The truly fine houses were down the side streets off Rossmore, where you could find the official homes of several foreign consulates and a few old Borsch Belt comedians. Not that some of the houses on Rossmore weren't grand; there just was no consistency of grand. After you pass Beverly Boulevard, you leave the houses and drive by a stretch of old-fashioned, New York-like apartment buildings dating from the glamour days of Hollywood. There's the Country Club Manor, the El Royale, and a little further up, before you get to Melrose and Rossmore becomes Vine, stands the Ravenswood—

Was it the El Royale or the Ravenswood where Mae West lived for years until her death? I used to know. Damn! This was going to bug me all day.

Past Melrose, you run into the bland ugliness of lower Hollywood, passing the Musicians Union hall, post-production companies, sound recording studios, and various fast food/convenience store corners, eventually reaching the fabled but faded corners of Sunset & Vine and Hollywood & Vine. You could say that Hollywood proper is not very glamorous. You would be more correct to say it is not glamorous at all. Except for a hint of the long gone at the corner of Hollywood & Vine, due solely to the pre-war buildings still standing there. The old Broadway Building on the southwest corner no longer houses that department store. The Hollywood Taft Building across the street to the east, full of offices that one can imagine were once occupied by legitimate and reputable talent and casting agents suddenly scrambling to find actors with good speaking voices. The Pantages Theater, just down Hollywood Boulevard, once the home of glittery premieres and the Academy Awards, is now a stop for road companies of old legit

Broadway musicals. If you look up at these buildings, you can get a feel for the Hollywood that was.

But look down to street level, and you are too rudely handed the Hollywood that is: a tourist trap with very unappetizing bait.

They say they are going to recover Hollywood. Who knows? It could happen. They're doing a number on Times Square; maybe they're waiting to see how that turns out.

I passed Hollywood Boulevard, went one block, made a right on Yucca, and then a quick left onto Argyle. Dave Finch lived on the 2000 block, the last block before Argyle curved to the right and became Hollymont Drive, then twisted its way up to join the wavy roads of the Hollywood Hills.

The old apartment buildings along this stretch of Argyle, including the romantically named De Mille Manor, showed the effects of time in their rundown condition and their faded beauty—a Hollywood tradition, after all. Others showed the impact of the times in their surrounding thick barred security fences with their "airlock" entranceways. The fences never match the aesthetics of the buildings, but aesthetics is probably very low on the list of residential concerns in this neighborhood.

I found Dave Finch's building by surmising the address it lacked in any visible form from the posted addresses on the building just before and the building just after. It was a two-story quasi-Spanish building needing a new coat or ten of an awful pink paint and replacements for the faded green bird-shit-splattered awnings over the windows. Neither improvement was likely to be made soon by the look of things. The "front" of the building was its side relative to the street, with all the apartment doors facing the north side of the De Mille Manor, which towered over it by half. Between the De Mille and the pink building were two or three large overgrown trees that formed a cave-like entrance into what a patriot might call the courtyard—a long, narrow slab of concrete before the apartment doors and the outside stairs in the center that took you to the second story. Between the De Mille and the trees, sunshine had probably not penetrated this area for decades. Finch's apartment number three was on the second story.

I figured it would be useless, but I tried the doorbell. Nothing. I knocked.

"Yeah! Hold on a minute!" came a slightly high voice, followed soon by the door opening. "Yeah?" said the skinny and nervous ferret of a young man who opened the door. Dave Finch was maybe twenty-three. His hair was brown, short, cut haphazardly, with no particular point of view. His eyes were intense focal points of glazed-over attention that suspiciously never left you while fronting a mind totally self-absorbed. His lips seemed to be pinched out of Silly Putty.

"Dave Finch?"

"Yeah?" He was suspicious but curious.

"I have something for you from Paul Hinckley."

"Reeeally!?" He stretched out the word, showing his excited amazement yet a total lack of questioning that Paul Hinckley would have something for him.

"Can I come in?"

"Yeah, sure."

He opened the door, and I entered. His apartment was a cluttered mess of a single with a small kitchen area crammed into an alcove; a Murphy bed, down and littered with not clean laundry from the smell of it; books and magazines piled up here and there, probably by a system of his own; and two tall bookcases wholly filled with black video tape boxes, neatly labeled, indicating that he was a major offender of copyright law. In one corner was a 20" color television on a cart whose lower shelf held a Go-Video dual deck VHS machine (the instrument of his criminality); in another was a small desk upon which sat a Macintosh Performa and a small personal printer. These items indicated where whatever money he made went, as opposed to, say, nourishment. The walls were covered with old movie poster one-sheets, lobby cards, and 8x10 production stills, all unframed, just push-pinned for permanence. There was *The Seventh Voyage of Sinbad*. There was *Star Wars*. Not the original poster, but the neater second version for the reissue. And there was, of course, a reprinted poster of an Orson Wells film, *The Magnificent Ambersons*. *Citizen Kane* must not have been available. "So—so did he finally read 'V'?"

"He read it."

"I'd only been calling him for months."

"You've been calling him?"

"Yeah. His—his assistant, Gina, really nice, very—lovely girl—uh—said he got all my messages, but, you know, he would be on location or vacation or scouting or something. Did—uh—did he like it?"

"Yeah. A lot."

"Reeeally. Oh, wow! I knew it. You see, he needs, he really needs a good script. He's—he's very underrated by—by the mainstream critics, they just—they don't see his superb handling of just pure, raw cinema, of the whole—the whole composition/movement/light package of information as it hits us through the tunnel—the tunnel of our optic sense to the visual cortex to mingle with nets of our own experience, even—even to inform those nets with new manufactured experiences." He paused and bobbed his head in short, rapid movements as if one side of him vigorously agreed with the other. "But—but he's always been a stinker of a writer," he concluded.

"Yes, well..."

"I could start on the screenplay right away. I mean, I've got commitments, you know, to the papers, lots of reviews to do, and—and my continuing exploration of the films of Michael Powell, but I—I could, you know, start tomorrow. So, what should I do? Should I—should I get an agent?"

"I think we can handle the negotiations right here. Don't you?"

"Uh—well—uh—yeah—sure, but, well, you know, I don't want to be taken advantage of. So isn't it better if I have an agent? I mean, I know I've got to get at least Writers Guild minimum, but I would like, you know, a little bit more than that."

"Would this suffice?" I handed him the cashier's check.

"Oh wow!" He looked up at me. "Reeeally? Wow!"

"There are conditions. You must sign these."

I pulled out of my coat the two agreements. Finch took them and studied them intently, reading them at least twice each, as if the first read made no sense—or no sense he wanted to accept. Then the anger hit like a baseball bat to the face.

"No way! This is shit! This is shit, man! It's like what everybody says; they just want to fuck you!"

"Quarter of a million dollars is a hell of a fuck."

"I don't care! Shit! It's my story! I don't want to—fuck! I dreamed of working with this bastard, now look what—"

"Hey!" I had to stop him. Or the shrill of his voice would soon be calling dogs. "What the hell do you want out of life, kid?"

"I want to make movies, that's all. I—I know everything. I—I understand film in a way no one else can even touch. I mean—I mean, shit..." One tear from each eye started a slow race down his cheeks. "I've seen every great film ever made, I've memorized them practically, every shot, every light angle, I can just—I can just close my eyes and see the shots I want to make. But you got to have a break, you know, shit, you got to have that break. You see, to write this film—it's going to be a fucking big hit—that's my break. It's my story—mine. People have got to know that, you know."

"With $250,000, you can certainly buy yourself some time to write a few more good ideas."

"No! No! This one! And fuck the money! I got money coming in. I'm going to have plenty of it. Tell Paul that, tell him that!"

I decided it was time to make him approach life as the existential, nihilistic wonder it is. "Listen, kid. You're very low on the scale of humanity. You are a film geek, a creepy, unattractive, not well-bathed fantasist living a Kafka-like black & white existence but without the political overtones. You are so enamored by film that you are practically celluloid yourself at a time when everything else is going digital. You are nearly useless, except to make a few other poor bastards feel better that they are at least not you. Whereas I am a fucking angel who has come down from heaven to offer you manna well beyond your means. Do not be ungrateful and turn this offer down. The consequences are unthinkable."

I had gotten quite close to his face for the emphasis it provided, which was unfortunate—he started to sputter, splattering the surroundings.

"Pl—pl—please just go. I—I—I can't, I won't. Hey—hey—just tell Paul that—that I'm going to show 'V' to Andy Rand, and—and fuck him!"

"If you could get to him, that would be nice—but useless. He's resigning from NewVue tomorrow."

No shock, no surprise, not a second of thought. "Fuck NewVue! I'm going to be a partner with Andy Rand. What we're going to do—man—fuck!"

That was a quick comeback, even for a fantasist. Something was wrong.

I am not one to believe that money answers all concerns, but Finch should have accepted the money. The amount, the intimidation, good sense, or any combination thereof should have dictated that response. But something else was at play here. Before going further, I decided it was well worth finding out what.

"All right," I said. "Can't argue with artistic purity. I'll inform Mr.

Hinckley of your decision."

"O—o—okay."

I walked to the door. "One last thing. Which apartment building did Mae West live in? The El Royale or the Ravenswood?"

He started to answer, then stopped. "Shit! I—just—it was just on the tip of—shit! I'll look it up!" He leaped for a pile of books.

"Never mind," I said as I left.

After leaving Finch's place, I made a quick stop somewhere where I thought they might know him. The Hollywood Book and Poster Company has long served the needs of people who can't just go to the movies, eat some popcorn, and leave it at that. These people must have pieces, slices, and hunks of the films themselves to adorn household shrines to various seen and unseen gods. Some celebrated the sleaze in movies, the cheap, the B, the camp, and the inept. Others worship the "masterworks," as they called them, of various directors that got under their skin. For others, it was genre decorations—Sci-Fi, Film Noir— and for others, like Dave Finch, their fervent love was all-encompassing.

The posters, lobby cards, and 8x10 publicity shots in Finch's apartment had to come from somewhere. Logically, this Mecca, a short walk from his apartment, would be the place.

I walked up to George, who owned the place and whose services I, on occasion, had called upon.

"Oh, hi," he said, greeting me somewhat nervously. Certain people in town always welcome me that way. It's the money.

"Do you know a Dave Finch?"

The name quelled the nervousness and replaced it with attitude. "Yeah, unfortunately."

"You don't think much of him?"

"I try not to think of him at all. But you know what he's like? He's like one of those—uh—you know, like when you get a song, some stupid song stuck in your mind, and it keeps popping up. That's Dave Finch. He keeps popping up."

"Has he been a good customer?"

"Oh, yeah. He gets spurts of money from his Dad. Dad's a car dealer in Hawaiian Gardens. He supports Dave while he's trying to be a film critic or something. Been going on a long time because I don't know of anybody who's actually paid Dave to write."

"What do you think of his reviews?"

"Oh, he has insights on occasion. But, you know, his writing is pedantic and too aware of itself. Lot of these guys write about film that way; they take it too damn seriously. And he thinks, uh, he thinks his opinion is the only opinion, you know. He's convinced that films are quantifiable, and only he can place them on the scale of good to bad. I remember, once, we went to a screening together. It was this silly sci-fi film made by NewVue before Rand got there. It was a fun film. I mean, it was a stupid, dumb, cheap sci-fi film with some unintentional laughs, but, you know, it was an okay eighty-eight minutes in the theater. Well, the movie's over, he asks me what I think of it, and I said just that, stupid but enjoyable. And he blew his top. He went crazy. He started screaming at me right there in the middle of the theater. He told me that if I thought this film was any good, I had no right to own this store or be involved in the film business in any way, shape, or form. And that, basically, I was, you know, dog shit that had been pissed on. I mean, it was amazing! The fire in the guy's eyes was incredible."

"Maybe that was the spark of divine madness."

"Maybe it was the fucking fires of hell."

"So you wouldn't guess he's the kind of film freak that could develop a good concept for a film and build a story around it?"

"Shit, I wouldn't think so. I mean, he's like a sponge that has soaked up everything that's been done in films, so he can throw it back out at you. But, no, I mean, he's never had a life; he's—he's not that clever."

"Okay. Thanks for the info."

I started to walk out when he stopped me.

"Say—uh—can—can I ask you a question?" He was nervous again.

I smiled. I understood what it was taking to get beyond that and ask. I nodded my head.

"Have you ever heard of a script called *Malice Towards None?*"

"The one you sell bootleg copies of?"

"Uh—yeah."

"The script considered the best unproduced script ever written in Hollywood?"

"Yeah."

"Well, obviously, I have. Why?"

"They say..."

"They?"

"It is said that you wrote that script."

I smiled. I walked back to him. I put my hand on his shoulder and allowed it to move to the back of his neck. I squeezed—just enough pressure to make a painful point. "Do I look like a man who would write something called 'Malice Towards None'?"

"Uh—actually—no."

There was sweat—but then the place was not well-ventilated.

"Do you have an original poster of Fritz Lang's *Metropolis*?" I asked.

"Uh—yeah. Mint condition."

"German?"

"Yeah, of course."

I gave him Norton Macbeth's card. "Send it there with the invoice."

"You—you know, it's..."

"I know the price. Send it."

Then I left, with the whispered word, Fixxer, trailing after me.

xx

I called Paul Hinckley, greeting him with, "I don't think he's a songbird."

"What are you talking about?"

"Finch."

"What?"

"I don't think he wrote 'V.'"

"You're kidding. What makes you think that?"

"Intuition."

"Well fuck intuition. The kid gave it to me; his name is on it."

"So do you want to give him a quarter of a million dollars and have someone else throw a plagiarism suit at you?"

"Sure! Yeah! Then we call it a nuisance suit. Spielberg gets them all the time. As long as whoever it is never had contact with me, then it's just one of those ideas-as-pollen-in-the-air kinds of thing. So just get Finch to take the deal, and I'm covered."

"How well do you know Finch?"

"What do you mean? I told you—"

"Yeah, I know. The AFI Seminar. You knew him before that, didn't you?"

"Well, yeah, okay. He wrote a really nice appreciation of my films about a year ago in *L.A. Week By Week*. So I called him up. He then pushed himself on me, hoping to get a contract to write a book-length study."

"So you saw him on several occasions. A relationship would be easily proved. I now see the value you have put on this deal."

"Yeah, okay, I'll try not to lose sleep over it. Just get Finch to sign and take the money."

"He refuses."

"What? He wouldn't take the money?"

"No. He was quite offended by it."

"That's why he'll never make it in Hollywood. So what do I do now?"

"Double my fee, and I'll find out who the true author is."

"Double your fee!"

"This is assuming that when I find out who wrote it, I can get them to accept the deal."

"Shit! This is starting to cost me."

"Hey, what do you think? You can get anointed on the cheap?"

"Okay, deal. Do it. How long do you think it will take?"

"I can't give you that estimate."

"Well, try to make it quick. I want to start pitching this to the studios."

"I thought you had a first look with Warner Bros."

"Oh, fuck 'em! They haven't the brains to appreciate this one. Hey, did you hear that Rand is resigning from NewVue?"

"I heard."

"You heard! You probably made it happen."

"Now, why would you say that? How long are you going to be at the ranch."

"I don't know. Two, three days."

"I'll be in touch."

I drove home, pulling into the underground garage and up to the valet. A young kid in a green outfit opened my door. An Iranian Beverly Hills High senior nicknamed Joe, new on the job and eager to please.

"Good evening, sir."

"Good evening, Joe."

"Should—should I have the car washed, sir?"

"Joe, it's a ten-year-old brown Corolla. It lives for dirt. It's the only thing that gives it character. Wash it and, 'you'll keep your Christmas by losing your situation.'" I enjoy quoting Dickens.

"Oh—okay. Sorry."

He got in the car and drove it to its stall far more carefully than the car deserved.

Once home, I settled in the library with a vodka tonic, lemon twist—never use lime; it insults the grain—and the sounds of the Fletcher Henderson Orchestra featuring Louis Armstrong—yeah, antiquated 1920s jazz. But combined with the lift from the vodka, the comfort of my chair, and the soothing lack of light provided by closed eyelids, I find it bracing. I love waves of nostalgia for times before my birth. Where would I be if I opened my eyes and suddenly found that this was a contemporary recording I was listening to? New York, maybe Chicago, in a penthouse suite with much higher ceilings than this one, where the power was, where power's not always happy sister, money, was. Great towns—New York, Chicago— vital, aware, and interesting from low life to high life. If I open my eyes, though, it will be the 90s, and if it is the 90s, then this must be Los Angeles.

Play on Fletcher. Play on Pops.

"Penne with Moroccan lamb and mint."

I opened my eyes. It was Roee announcing the "simple" pasta dish he had prepared for dinner.

"Did the lamb really come from Morocco?"

"It's not the lamb that's Moroccan; it's the sauce. Which should include Zucchini, but as I know how much you hate Zucchini..."

"Your indulgence of my dislikes is appreciated."

"And I know you are not a wine lover, but I have found a rather nice Chenin Blanc that I would deem a tragedy for you to pass up."

"Well, if you can indulge my dislikes, I can certainly indulge your likes. I will have a glass. And after dinner, I would like you to join me for a little job."

"Oh." Disappointment was expelled with the word.

"You had plans?"

"I was going to watch a videotape of *Waiting for Godot*."

"Can it wait?"

"I have borrowed it from a friend."

"Can he wait?"

"It is Beckett directing Beckett!"

"Well, he's dead. I suppose waiting is not a problem for him."

"Fine. I will wait."

Roee began to leave as a commentary on my request.

"I met Beckett once."

Roee turned back to face me, as I knew he would. "You did not!"

"In the bar of the Hyde Park Hotel in London. He autographed a book for me."

"Which you have conveniently lost."

"No. You'll find it in the Bs."

Roee went over to a bookcase. "Which one?"

"Small blue book. *Ends and Odds*, I believe."

Roee pulled the book out and opened it up. His eyes widened slightly.

"With your background, this could be a forgery."

"Yes, but for what reason? The only person it has ever impressed is you."

Roee looked at me, raised his eyebrows, nodded his head, and closed the book. "Let's have dinner."

"Good idea. I'm starving."

CHAPTER 4

BUCK'EM

The lamb was excellent. I firmly believe one should eat a cute, fluffy, or furry animal at least once a week. It's essential for good health—mental if not physical.

I filled Roee in on the Paul Hinckley situation over dinner.

"So you don't believe this kid could write a film script?" Roee asked.

"Oh, sure. Anybody can write a film script. And just about anybody does. It's writing one that excites even a mediocre talent like Hinckley that I don't think he could do."

"So he ripped it off from somebody."

"That's the only answer. And where is that, somebody? These drippy-ear wannabes all hang out together and possibly show each other their work for comments. But why would Finch think he could get away with it? If it were the work of another aspiring screenwriter, wouldn't he expect that writer to be trying to submit the piece? And if Finch were to sell it, did he think the other guy wouldn't challenge him? No, it's got to be some other situation. Something more than just casual."

"So tonight?"

"Tonight, we'll visit his apartment and look for clues."

"How mundane."

"I know you hate grunt work, but I could use your help. Be sure to bring the bag."

I was referring to our Bag o' Tricks, various goodies of a helpful nature amazingly packed into a case just slightly larger than the standard attaché.

"Are we just going to break in?"

"Yes. But we'll go as cops. A parked black & white and two cops nosing around are not unusual sights in that neighborhood."

"And Finch?"

"I'm betting he will be out at a movie."

xx

In preparation for our night's errand, I called the Captain.

"Good to hear your voice, Fixxer. How's things in the upper world?" he asked.

"Fine. You ought to try it."

"No thanks. I'm happy as a dedicated public servant."

"There should be more like you."

"What? Taking my glory? Forget it. What's up?"

"I'll be out in the b&w tonight."

"Oh. Anything I should know about?"

"No. Pure Hollywood ego scenario."

"Where will you be?"

"Argyle. 2000 block."

"Okay. Officers Saunders and Hough?"

"Yeah."

"Okay. I'll let the locals know that a special unit is in the area on a hush-hush assignment."

"Thanks."

"Don't mention it. Just pay the invoice."

We drove the 911 to a garage I have just off Wilshire by Sixth and St. Andrews Place. We changed into uniforms, left in the LAPD black and white, got onto Rossmore, and headed to Hollywood. After making a slow trip up and down Argyle for show, I parked just across from Finch's building. Sure enough, at about 7:30, we saw him come out, go up the street, get into a late model Chrysler—probably what his father sells—and drive off.

"Okay, Officer Hough," I said. "Let's go."

We walked around poking our flashlights into dark areas, finally making our way to Finch's building. If anyone saw us, no one was willing to bother us. We went up the stairs. Roee expertly picked the lock. We entered. Roee quietly opened the Bag o' Tricks. He pulled out and set up a powerful, battery-operated small red light, much like those used in darkrooms. This allowed us to see where to step in Finch's maze of piled books, magazines, and haphazardly left dirty plates and glasses without sending noticeable illumination to the outside world.

"What a dump!" Roee said, very Bette Davis.

"Not bad. Can you do Katherine Hepburn?"

"The Calla Lilies are in bloom."

"Work on it."

"Yes'um, boss."

"Now cut that out!"

"What are we looking for?" Roee asked in so normal a voice that I almost didn't recognize him. "And how in the hell can we ever find it?"

"Well, this is where the beauty of the information age comes in. You can't leave your dirty socks lying around inside your computer." I turned the Mac on. It dinged and showed its friendly face. "Let's open her up and see what wonders are contained."

Roee sat at the keyboard and looked at the files on the hard disk. "Son- of-a-bitch. He has Internet access. High tech in low places."

"Daddy buys the toys. Do you think you can log on?"

"What's his name again?"

"David Finch."

"And it notes here that his screen name is birdman."

"Makes sense."

"So what would be his password?"

"Burt?"

"Too short."

"Lancaster?"

"Too obvious."

"Frankenheimer?"

"Too long. Plus, although not as obvious as the actor, the director is obvious enough."

"I'm out of suggestions."

"Why don't we try—"

Roee typed as he spelled it out "—t - r - o - s - p - e - r."

"Trosper?"

"The screenwriter."

"Ah."

"Beautifully obscure. Perfect for a password." Roee clicked the mouse, and we were welcomed into Finch's Internet portal. "How did you know about Trosper?"

"That quirky memory training they gave me."

"Oh."

"Lot of e-mails here. He must save them all."

"A young man looking out for his legend. Open one up. Let's read it."

It was a diatribe against a Jim Cameron film, scolding the poor bastard at the other end of the correspondence for giving it a good review.

"And I thought the Jewish God was a vengeful god," Roee said as he closed the document.

"Look," I said, noticing a statistical fact. Most of the correspondence was to and from the e-mail address *yorkport@aol.com*. We started opening them up in chronological order, the first one having been written about a year back. They were correspondence with a Craig York. We could quickly gather that York and Finch were old friends who had gone to high school together in Portland, Oregon. It was chitchat, philosophical discussions on film, and bitching about Hollywood and its lack of ethics, fair play, and purity. Finally, the pertinent one showed itself. It was from York, dated about eight months previous. It read:

Dave—

Here's the treatment I told you about over the phone. I call it "V." I think it's pretty good. It just suddenly flooded into me. You'll see that it's sort of based on my work with Jim. Why didn't I think of it before? Guess I needed some time back here to wash the L.A. shit off me with clean air, clean water, and clean minds. Anyway, read it and see what you think. And do me a favor, don't show it to Jim or tell him about it. He'll just go all nuclear again, so, Buck'em—

"What is that do you think? A typo?" Roee asked.

"What?"

"Buck'em," Roee said, pointing to the word on the screen.

I had automatically read it as the more obvious. "A typo or a euphemism.

He seems to be a 'clean' person."

"Maybe it's an Oregon thing."

"Maybe." We continued to read.

If there is any way you can get it to any "powers that be" like you offered, feel free to do so. You can kind of be like my manager I guess, so I'll pay you a percentage if anything happens. Guess who I may get to show it to? Andy Rand. He's going to be up here for the Creativity Conference. Of course, Johnny doesn't want people bugging the rich and famous with scripts and such, but I read in Premiere *that Rand is a fishing nut, so I figured I could offer him a fishing trip on the houseboat and get some time alone with him. Way cool, huh? We'll see what happens. Ran into your mom. Will you please write her? She just winds up bugging me.*

Craig

"What a schmuck this Finch is!" Roee said. "He plagiarizes his best friend while worrying about the lack of purity in Hollywood."

"*No one knows the ease of the blade between the shoulders, as the man with his hand on the hilt.*"

Roee looked at me with questioning admiration. "Did you just make that up?"

I had, but: "It's a well-known literary reference. Look it up."

"Seneca?"

"Nope."

"But one of the ancients?"

"I have far too much admiration for your intelligence to give you a hint."

"I know that I know it."

"I'll tell you if you can tell me where Mae West lived. The El Royale or the Ravenswood?"

"Oh damn! I know I know that too. Uh...Damn! Well, it's one or the other."

"Not good enough. Anyway, listen, check for two things. See if Finch has addresses in here. If so, get Craig York's in Portland. If there is none, we'll trace it later through our contacts at AOL. Then look for any other reference to this Jim, especially any letters and an address."

Roee found everything. Jim turned out to be Jim Skinner, another Portland buddy, now a graduate student at Caltech in Pasadena. Finch and he e-mailed a lot, mainly debates about film and science fiction, plus near pornographic renditions of what they called "Dream Dates" with various women of celebrity status. Strange what technology can bring. Two high school buddies living twenty miles apart, they could be talking on the phone, they could jump on the freeway and visit each other. But instead, they choose the near-extinct, almost atavistic form of personal written correspondence. Why? An inordinate love of the missive? I doubt it. It was probably more the case that it was "way cool" to communicate in this new, high-tech manner. It will be a boon for academics in the 21st century. THE PERSONAL E-MAIL OF BILL GATES: CHARACTER REVEALED IN CYBERSPACE. I can't wait for the audio chip version.

"So, anything else?" Roee asked. "Should we rifle his drawers?"

"I wouldn't advise it. Not without rubber gloves."

"To prevent fingerprints?"

"To prevent contagion."

As we were leaving, Roee hesitated.

"Forget something?" I asked.

"Is there any chance you would let me have a little fun here?"

"I can't imagine how you could have fun here."

"The door's got an inside chain lock."

"So?"

"I could use the Henson and—"

"Roee, that is just plain mean-spirited."

"No, no! I would call it being no more than charmingly impish."

"Churlishly childish, more like it."

"Oh, come on! You know this guy. Don't you want to contemplate the look on his face when he unlocks his door?"

It was an appealing idea. And no harm would be done except maybe to the door.

"Okay. I suppose one must be sophomoric on occasion."

"Great!"

Roee took out his invention. The Henson is a collapsible armature with an articulated metal hand electronically connected to an arm-length glove. The armature rests at the end of a telescoping pole. Built into the palm of the "hand" is a miniature snorkel video camera. Roee put on the glove. He then closed the door to where there was just a crack left and slid the armature through the gap, snapping it once to connect its joints. He turned the device on, held the armature by the pole in his left hand, and then, watching a small video display screen, he manipulated his gloved right hand, which controlled the armature. Then, very simply, he latched the chain with this clever tool. Then he withdrew the Henson and closed the door.

"I hope he likes mysteries," I said.

"Who doesn't like mysteries?" Roee replied as he replaced the Henson into the Bag o' Tricks.

XX

The following day I took the Alaska Airlines 6:55 a.m. flight to Portland. I traveled under the name of Bob Hopkins, one of fifty-two identities I can assume by simply going into a special file room I have and pulling out the required documents, whether something as simple as a driver's license— all I would need on this trip—or something more elaborate such as a passport, birth certificate, government agent identification, or even diplomatic credentials. Of the fifty-two identities, sixteen are of foreign nationals. The rest declare me a U.S. citizen, although not always one who could run for the presidency. I even have several histories that peg me as an ex-con of rather dangerous leanings. Those are often the most fun. One of the fifty-two is who I truly am. Although I'm not sure if I can remember who that is.

The plane landed on time at 9:08 a.m., and I quickly rented a car and headed towards downtown Portland.

Lovely city, Portland, a dash of sophistication among the redneck wilds of the rest of the state. Like Seattle and Canada's Vancouver, a desirable place to live. Except for the gray skies and rain. You have to like that. But the weather is never as bad as outsiders think it is. Nor as good as the natives would pray for if they thought there was a hope in hell their prayers would be answered. On this day, it was not bad. It had rained in the early morning, but as I drove from the airport, the sky featured huge cumulus clouds broken by patches of vibrant blue sky. They were still rain-filled black at their bottoms but white and sun-catching as they towered up high—mountains on the wind. It provided a dramatic backdrop for the compact group of skyscrapers that marked downtown Portland, a manageable downtown exuding a pleasant, non-threatening urban feel.

According to his address, Craig York lived at the marina on the Willamette River, which cuts through Portland and connects with the larger Columbia River. He mentioned a houseboat in the e-mail, so this did not surprise me. However, I was surprised by the houseboat. Not commercially built, that was obvious; it was a big, gorgeous craft, with spacious decking at the stern and large living quarters in the center that, I assumed, extended below deck and was topped off with a wheelhouse. The bow had the mock look of an 18th Century British

Man-O-War, complete with a figurehead of a woman well-endowed and fair of face. The boat's name was *Buck'em*, although the B was suspiciously square in its graphic rendition.

I could see all this from an area above the marina, surrounded by a chain-link fence. There was only one access to the rows of slips housing mainly pleasure crafts of various sizes, from the practical to the ostentatious. It was a gangway leading down to the docking. It was gated and locked. I was about ready to call York on my cell phone when I saw a young man come out of the cabin of the *Buck'em*.

"Hello! Craig York!"

The man was somewhat startled but began looking for the shout's source. We made eye contact.

"Ye - yes?"

"Mr. York, can I speak with you? I have something for you!"

"Uh—well, yeah, sure, I guess."

York walked off the houseboat and headed towards me. Like Dave Finch, he was a skinny individual, but he had none of Finch's nervous, ferret qualities. He moved, though, with hesitation, as if never sure of his next step. He was about five-foot-nine and wore old, faded blue jeans, white deck shoes, and a green pullover shirt. The straw-blond hair on top of his long, oval head was cut short and brushed straight forward. His complexion was pale with a tinge of red as if he was permanently embarrassed. His eyes were the faded match of his jeans.

He reached the gate and stopped. He made no move to open it.

"Can we go to your boat?"

"Oh—uh, yeah, sure. I'm sorry."

He opened the gate and let me through. Then, hesitantly, he took the lead, and we made our way to the *Buck'em* and boarded.

"Fascinating craft. I don't think I've ever seen anything like it."

"Oh—uh—thanks. My dad built it. When I was about ten. I helped him, you know, but, uh—yeah, it was his—it was his dream. He designed it—uh—"

"Unique bow."

"Uh, yeah. He was a great fan of the Hornblower novels. Uh, we should go in, maybe." He gestured to the inside of the cabin.

"Thank you," I said and entered.

The cabin's inside featured an economy of design that led to a very comfortable, settled-in feel. The wood furniture was all built-ins, and although the upholstery was well-worn, the hand-worked wood had the lush look of constant care and seemed to have suffered no weathering. The one odd piece was a metal unit bolted to the floor with a rather impressive computer setup. Not a basic Performa like Finch's Mac, but the newer and more elaborate 8100 Power PC with two color monitors, one of which I was sure was high definition. It was more of a professional setup than a personal one.

"I see you live on the boat?"

"Yeah, uh, li—like I said, since he built it, Dad and I lived on it. My mother died when I was young."

"And your dad?"

"Oh, he died a little over a year ago."

I allowed a quiet space to replace any false statement of compassion customarily expected.

"Generous quarter-deck. Fish off it?"

"Uh, yeah, Dad built it so we could take fishing parties out. That's how he earned his living. That—that's kinda what I do now."

"Interesting name, Buck'em."

York laughed just slightly. "Well, uh, yeah, Dad was, uh, he was, uh, well, not a very social guy. Didn't get along with most people. His basic attitude towards everybody was, you know, sort of Buck'em with an F, so that's what he wanted to name the boat. And he did! That was the first name he put on the boat. But everybody, you know, everybody at the marina and everywhere got kinda upset over it. So, we changed it to Buck'em. And he started using that, in fact, and it sort of became— sort of became his catchphrase. So—so you said you—you had something for me?"

"Yes, I have something for you from Paul Hinckley."

"The—the film director?"

"That's right. But I need some answers from you first to certify that I can give you what Mr. Hinckley has for you."

"Well—well, what would a Paul Hinckley have for me?"

"Did you write a film treatment called 'V'?"

There was that instant I was looking for. Was he surprised to hear me mention 'V'? Or was he, once I had mentioned Hinckley, anticipating—or dreading—it as logical? But the instant was just that. It passed before I could read it to my satisfaction.

"How did you know about that?"

"Mr. Hinckley has a copy of it. He likes it very much. He would like to purchase it from you."

"Uh—oh—gee I, um, I don't know how he could have gotten that."

"It seems your friend, Dave Finch, gave it to him."

"Dave? Oh..."

"And the thing is, Mr. York, Dave Finch told Paul Hinckley that he wrote it."

"Oh. Uh—he—he shouldn't have done that."

"No, obviously not. It's called plagiarism. Not a nice thing for a friend to do. Assuming you are friends?"

York did not answer right away. He may have been in shock, but there seemed to be too much activity behind his pale blue eyes for that.

When he did answer, he said, "Yes. Yes, best friends, kind of. We grew up together. Went through high school together. Gee—I don't—I don't know what to say because I'm not sure—uh..."

"You're not sure of what?"

"Well..."

Another silence. York seemed to have fallen in on himself, thinking very hard. Finally, I had to break it. "Let me show you how much Mr. Hinckley wants to pay you." I stuck the check under his nose. It had the desired effect.

"Oh—oh my god! Gee, this is, you know, this is a quarter of a million dollars!"

"Yes. And this is a cashier's check. You can put it in your bank today and draw on it immediately. There are, though, certain stipulations. You better read this."

I handed him the agreement drafted by Hinckley, redone by myself to reflect York's name. The other agreement, the one I had drafted, I felt wasn't necessary just yet. He read it over. But his mind seemed stuck on something else. Not that he wasn't taking in the information in the document, but I could perceive that he was also pursuing another line of thought. I assumed that the two lines intersected. But I couldn't begin to guess where. Then, finally, he spoke up without taking his eyes away from the document.

"Well—this—I would have no problem signing this."

He did so, quickly grabbing a pen and signing in a rush. He left the document on the table and stood up, leaving me to retrieve it. "If that's— uh—all you need. I need to take the boat out and meet some guys."

"Do you have a moment to satisfy a little curiosity?"

"Uh—well..."

"Don't you have any Hollywood ambitions? Credit is often as important as money. You just signed yours away."

"Oh—well—no, not really. I—I hate it down there. I lived there while at Caltech."

"You went to Caltech?"

"Uh—yeah. But—um—I came back a little over a year ago."

"When your Dad died?"

"Uh, yes."

"Why didn't you return to Caltech?"

"Why? Uh—well—I guess I'm a little bit like my dad. I'm not—I'm not very social, and I found that, you know, in the science world there, it's all politics. I—I don't have a mind for that kind of thinking, but—but that kind of thinking gets you your grants so you can, you know, do the kind of thinking you thought you were trained for."

"Practical or theoretical?"

"A little bit of both. Theoretical can be more reclusive, but practical can be more, well, you know, practical, I guess."

"So you've given up science?"

"Well—the boat was being left unattended. I hated L.A. Noisy, dirty, crowded. I mean, I graduated, it was just getting into the whole graduate studies thing—and—and I just thought, hell—I like to fish."

"That seems an elaborate computer set up just to do a little fishing."

York looked at his computer, shocked, as if he had forgotten it was there. I decided to give him some rope. "I suppose it's for soundings to find schools of salmon?" But he did not take it.

"Oh no. I use this for graphics. Computer animation stuff."

Guileless? Was it natural or practiced?

"What kind of animation? Talking mice or something?"

"Depends. I freelance for a computer film company.

"So you are an artist as well?"

"Well..."

"What was your field in science?"

"Oh—uh—how do I explain it? Physics. I mean broadly. But also—well—brain function, on a molecular level, and—and information processing."

"Sounds esoteric?"

"Well..."

"Do you know Jim Skinner?"

He seemed surprised. "Yeah—uh—sure. Jim—I went to high school with Jim too. Jim, Dave, and I, we were sort of—uh—inseparable."

"Did Jim have anything to do with 'V'?"

"Uh, no, not at all. I wrote it after I returned home."

"But I assume it has something to do with your science?"

"Oh, only in a—a minimal way."

"Nothing to do with Jim's work at Caltech?"

"No, nothing."

"So you can assure me that you are the sole author of 'V' and did not just commit fraud by signing this document?"

"Fr—fraud? No. I wrote it. Just me. Uh—uh—look..." He jumped to a desk drawer, opened it, and pulled out a sealed envelope that had been mailed. "I have this." He handed it to me. "I read to do it in a writer's magazine. It's the treatment, mailed to me and left unopened. The postmark establishes..."

"Only the date that you mailed it."

"Yeah, but..."

It was dated about a week before he had sent the e-mail to Finch. Not final proof by any stretch. But it was so sincerely what an amateur would do. "Can I keep this?"

"Oh—sure—yeah. No extra charge."

I chuckled at his little attempt at humor—now we were friends. "Okay. Then I think Mr. Hinckley would be pleased to have me hand you this check." I did so. He took it; looked at it a second; then folded it and placed it in his shirt pocket as if it was not much more than the address of a recommended chiropractor. I was still curious. "So, Craig, you truly don't want a career in Hollywood?" Maybe I had lived in Hollywood too long. Perhaps it had become too much the center of not just my universe.

"No, that's Dave's ambition."

"Then why did you write the treatment?"

"Oh—well—I mean, I like film. We—we all did—Jim, Dave, and me. We were movie buddies. Every Saturday matinee we went together as kids. And we talked about film a lot. And Dave got me into it and got me excited and was always talking about writing something together, but—but we never did. But after I was back up here, this idea came up, so I—uh—did it up, and—and I sent it to Dave because he was saying that he was meeting people in the industry. And, you know,

I thought if I could sell it, it would help me, cause, you know, I'm not making much money on the fishing trips, and, so, I thought, if I could sell it, you know, I would have some money, and—and, hey, it worked." He patted his shirt pocket. "But, as to getting—sucked into that world—uh—no."

"Did you get to show the treatment to Andy Rand?"

"Uh—what? Excuse me?"

"I believe you were going to see Andy Rand at the creativity conference."

"How—how did you know about that?"

"Did you give the treatment to Rand? Did you take him fishing?" My guess was that he hadn't. But if he had, I had the second agreement in my pocket.

"Uh—no—I didn't. I mean, I was too shy to approach him."

It was an apology. But for far more than the lack of action it referred to. Although inundated with the same film and television images that have made the Man-in-the-Street such a slick commodity, Craig York seemed to be one of those individuals who couldn't keep pace with the onward rush of civilized humanity to all be as smooth, well-spoken, wise and knowing as the next guy, especially the next guy on camera. It's not just Warhol's fifteen minutes of fame. It's a lifetime of being "On the Air." Craig York had to live on the river, be among nature, and dwell inside abstract thoughts. Craig York had to get out of the way of the rush. Otherwise, he would be pegged dysfunctional—our modern world's eighth deadly sin— and be trampled underfoot.

"Okay, Mr. York. Enjoy the money. I imagine the cost of living up here is manageable. Spend it right, and it should last you a good long time."

"Oh—yeah—it will be great. I mean, this is real, isn't it? It's not a hoax?"

"You put that money in the bank, and you'll see how real it is. Also, you put that money in the bank then we have a contract—a contract I expect you to honor. So I truly hope you are repulsed by Hollywood and never want to come near it. If you ever try to communicate with Paul Hinckley about anything, he will not respond. I will. Do you understand?"

"Oh, yeah. Don't worry."

"I never worry, Mr. York. Because I master any situation." I turned and started to leave.

"Oh—and—and what was your name?"

I stopped, turned, and looked at Craig York for what I assumed would be the last time. His embarrassed hesitation had never left him. I was not about to let him get comfortable now. "Goodbye, Mr. York," I simply said, then turned and walked off the houseboat.

CHAPTER 5
FORMULA 12-72

Paul Hinckley was one lucky bastard. It's not everybody who gets to anoint themselves—especially with the blood of such a willing sacrificial lamb. It could have gone the other way—he could have gotten a real bleater.

But then, if you can't have talent, you better have luck because Hollywood is a town that loves luck. Possibly because it is filled with people who either don't have talent, have just enough talent to be truly dangerous, or have talent but are so insecure that they attribute their success to luck anyway. And then, of course, there are those who don't trust luck and strive mightily to make their own, an admirable quality among the talented but the cause of chaos otherwise.

Was it worth the half million Hinckley would wind up paying? Certainly.

If V was even half of what he thought it was, he might be able to sell it to a studio for that alone. But, more importantly, if a studio wanted it bad enough, given Hinckley's sometimes success, he could probably negotiate a comfortable back end of gross points from first dollar. Then, if his limited talent didn't get in the way of the film, and if the film was a huge success, he could wind up realizing 30 million or more in profits. Two big 'Ifs,' of course—two big 'Ifs' Hinckley wasn't even considering in his plans.

I thought these thoughts while flying home from Portland, munching peanuts. Short commuter flights are the only time I ever munch peanuts. I don't like peanuts. I like cashews. You would think the intense competition for the flying dollar would have led the airlines to upgrade to cashews. I began to calculate the cost of maintaining a private jet.

We had just reached our cruising altitude when the CNN business news came on the various monitors spaced throughout the cabin. At the top was coverage of the resignation of Andy Rand from NewVue Pictures.

"Filmland wunderkind Andy Rand has shocked Hollywood by resigning as president and CEO of NewVue Pictures, the budding but hugely successful entertainment conglomerate founded by Norwegian media mogul Torvald Engstrand. In twelve years, Rand has taken NewVue from an upstart foreign film company to a Hollywood studio in the truest and most old-fashioned sense of the word: one with an actual physical plant of sound stages, recording studios, and post-production facilities. Not that Rand and Engstrand have ignored the new-fashioned worlds of cable television and interactive media. It was, everybody in Hollywood thought, the dream job. Everybody, it seems, but Rand."

The well-manicured French garden face of the thirtyish female news anchor was replaced by a shot of Rand at a hotel podium.

"It has been a great ride, and I am very proud of what Torvald and I have accomplished in these past twelve years. But the time comes when one must reassess his world and his position in it. Therefore I have decided, effective immediately, to resign as president and CEO of NewVue Pictures to make such a reassessment. Torvald will take over my duties until he appoints a new president. I leave not without regret but with unwavering confidence that excitement and challenges are waiting for me in the future. Thank you."

Reporters shouted out questions, but Rand made a smooth and quick exit.

The anchor returned and gave a brief history of Rand, then turned to an entertainment business analyst for punditry. The analyst assumed what I had, that Rand was putting himself on the market with the price tag being power. And that NewVue's stock would drop.

"Pork belly futures."

"What?" I said, turning to the man in a blue suit sitting beside me. He was an obese man, and I had been contending with his left elbow the whole flight.

"Business news used to be nothing but reporting on pork belly futures. Now they report on *show biz*. Used to be *show biz* was covered by the same reporters who covered crime."

"Failed actor?" I asked.

"Successful salesman. Which is acting on commission." He thrust out a big, pudgy hand. "Mac. Mac McCarthy. Dinosaurs."

"Dinosaurs?"

"Plastic; stuffed; with flesh; without flesh; build your own; already assembled; battery operated; purely kid powered; realistic; cute. The only thing I don't carry is life-size, ha-ha-ha! Name and biz?"

"Bob Hopkins. Dried Fruit."

"Dried fruit?"

"It lasts."

"I see," Mac said, looking at me with questions forming. I suppose somebody from the exciting world of extinct animals found it hard to relate to a mundane man of dried fruit. But not for want of trying, "Well, at least you're not in *show biz*, where the pandering prostitutes of Hollywood are bringing down our culture and corrupting our morals by spewing out their despicable lowest common denominator entertainment."

"Oh, I don't know," I said. "Personally, I have nothing against lowest common denominator entertainment."

"You don't?"

"Would you rather have the people it entertains bored and on the streets?"

"Well—uh..."

"Don't answer now. Just think about it."

He took my admonition to heart and returned to his in-flight magazine and an article on "The Top Ten Easy Listening CDs of All Time."

xx

Roee picked me up in the Town Car, a good and comfortable passenger ride.

"Roee?"

"Yes."

"You're fully certified on jets, right?"

"Yes. Why?"

"Just something I'm giving some thought to."

"If you're considering buying, I can get you a discount."

"What? You have an uncle in wholesale?"

"Please, Vaudeville does not become you. I happen to know that my old employer is upgrading and will be putting some used ones on the market."

"Well, I wasn't looking for a fighter. More something to commute in."

"I know what you want, Fixxer. My old employer has diplomats as well as soldiers, you know. Lot of secret shuttle stuff between the Children of Moses and the Devotees of Allah."

"Good buys, huh?"

"Please! And with my connections, I can ensure they don't strip out the special electronics."

"All right. Make some inquiries."

"Will do. Here." He handed me a package. The return address stated: Uncle Al's Live Spider Farm. "From Petey."

"Oh good." Reality suddenly became the face of Anne Eisley. I settled back in my seat and caressed the vision as best as possible. It was at times like this that I wished I could draw. To put pencil to paper and form a beauty your inner vision only tenuously held onto would be a god-like joy.

"Should I put in a call to Paul Hinckley?"

I was not happy to have Hinckley upstage Miss Eisley. "What?"

"I assume the trip was successful?"

"It was."

"Shouldn't you inform Hinckley?"

"I should. But he's up at his ranch. Let him be anxious for another day. Do him good." Then home for some rest before what I assumed would be, at the very least, an amusing evening at Anne Eisley's.

xx

Anne Eisley had used her TV money well. She had purchased a very secluded, if a small, house on Elusive Drive, a private road reached via Lookout Mt. Road off Laurel Canyon Blvd. It had a commanding view of the hills surrounding it that stretched onto a vista that took in slices of the basin. On a clear night, the diamonds-on-black velvet feel of L.A. probably made it worth the price. Anne had sent a key to Norton, and I told her that when she returned with Crane from their "date," I would be in her bedroom waiting. She was to offer Crane a drink, get him settled in the living room, and then come into the bedroom to "Get into something more comfortable." However, I had requested that she not use that cliché.

"Don't worry. I won't," she assured me.

I got to her house about an hour before she and Crane were due.

Being alone in someone else's house can be uncomfortable or interesting, depending on your nature. Those made uncomfortable usually find the intimate details of another person's life a bad fit. They are the ones who always find other people's tastes, loves, and interests unfathomable and—in what surely must be a genetic mishap—insulting. Others—and I count myself among these—can't pass lighted windows on an evening's stroll without being deeply curious about what the occupants have done to make a house a home and what it might say about them and their march, or stumble, through life. Add to that my training, and I'm sure you won't fault me for my casual walk through every room in Miss Eisley's house, my poking through, and my ruminations.

The house was wonderfully female in its look, colors, and smells. Not in that exaggerated or caricatured manner that some single women adopt, turning their homes into something close to a Seventeenth Century seraglio, but in a subtle style of simple beauties, pleasing shapes, and calm colors, all of them very well matched, but not regimented. The walls featured very tasteful posters from the world's leading museums, with a particularly interesting one in her kitchen from the Detroit Museum of Culture announcing an exhibit called "The Automobile in Toys." It was bright and colorful and showed a Barbie doll in her pink Cadillac convertible, smiling her killer smile and waving to all the happy folks of the 1950s. It had, intended or not, a sharp, ironic twist about it, and I was willing to bet that Miss Eisley placed it on her wall, understanding that twist completely. That was heartening; if anybody could claim to have made Barbie's plastic body flesh, it was Miss Eisley. Barbie was empty-headed, of course, which is to be expected of a doll, whereas Miss Eisley's head seemed full of thoughts. Some, I assumed, were direct, energetic, and commanding. While others crouch in dark recesses. Not in fear. In waiting.

Her bathroom was of interest. Besides its mundane functions, it was a staging area for her public "self"—the one she would allow the world to experience. She did not have a jumble of cosmetics cluttering up the counter, but a neat row of one brand, the various matching bottle, jars, and tubes laid out, I would guess, in the order of their use. This was a woman rarely at a loss.

I settled in her bedroom. It was simple and functional, with a grouping of an easy chair and ottoman, a good floor lamp, and a side table with a stack of magazines and books being more the rationale for the room than the bed itself. Her reading was eclectic. The Hollywood trades, of course, *Time Magazine*, some fashion magazines, respectfully popular fiction, and Hollywood biographies of strong women who fought the system. Nothing dumb—nothing excessively intellectual.

I heard a car pull up. By the sound of the engine, it was a Mercedes SL 500. Two door slams, some laughter, and then the front door opens.

"Come on in," I heard Miss Eisley say.

"You're sure it's not too late for you now? I can go home," came Crane's mushy, accent-less voice.

"Fred, you've been chasing my ass long enough that you shouldn't have to be coaxed."

"That's what I like about you, Anne; you're very upfront."

"And do you like what I have up front?"

"Sure. It's not just your ass I've been chasing."

"Fred, you've been an absolute charmer all evening."

"I'm glad you've finally noticed."

"I was a fool, I'll admit it."

"I suppose I had to get to a certain level of power before you could 'see' my charm."

"No, Fred, that was certainly not it. I was—I was in love with someone else."

"And what happened to him?" Crane said with no hiding of his cynicism.

"He died."

It was a beautiful line reading. And even without seeing, I knew it sliced through Crane's guts. And that, he immediately saw an emotional opening he could crawl into.

"Oh. I'm sorry."

There was an appropriate moment of awkward silence. So much of acting is timing.

"I can feel your compassion, Fred. Thank you. Maybe later, I'll tell you the story when we know each other better. I would like to share it with someone. But—but later."

"I'll always be there for you, Anne."

"I know. But, speaking of stories, I was fascinated by your life story."

"Well, it has been interesting."

"And your whole take on this town and all your plans. Very—very stimulating."

"I don't hide my ambitions, Anne. I fully intend to take over this fucking town. So we're talking about a lot of power and money. I wouldn't mind it if you found that attractive."

"Fred, what I find attractive is that even though you talk like a shark— you retain your boyish charm.

"Yeah. A killer combination, huh?"

"Would you like a drink? I know you had a lot at dinner, but, you know, one last one."

"One last one would be just fine."

"Good. The bar is right there. Make yourself one. Make one for me, too, whatever you're having, and let me—"

"Slip into something more comfortable?"

"Please, Fred. No clichés."

She entered the bedroom and found me sitting in the chair, a *Time Magazine* open on my lap. She wore an attractive dress with a tee-style top, mesh from the cleavage up, form revealing spandex below until a metallic taffeta skirt took over until mid-thigh. She wore dark hose and spike heels, precisely what you would wear to an expensive restaurant in the company of a man of power, real or imagined.

We, of course, had to talk in whispers.

"This better work," she said, tossing a fur coat on the bed. "I've had the most boring evening of my life."

"It'll work," I said, standing up.

"Okay, what do you want me to do? You said I had to get intimate with him?"

"That's correct."

How intimate?"

"I assume you have no objections to cunnilingus?"

For the first time, her control slipped. "You want him to eat me!"

"You and a little additive I've brought." I produced a small silver metal tube. It had no label.

"What's that?"

"Formula 12-72."

"And you want me to put that on my—"

"Person. Yes, you have the idea."

"And he...?"

"Eats it."

"And then he...?"

"You'll see."

"I don't know." She was beginning to feel the fear of the enterprise. "Miss Eisley, I told you, I am not a hitman."

"Well, whatever it will do to him, won't it do something to me? Won't it get in my system?"

"It only works in tandem with a minimum level of testosterone. Otherwise, it is completely harmless."

"Don't women have some testosterone?"

"Miss Eisley, unless there is something you should confess to me now, you don't have enough."

"But—but won't he smell it? Won't he taste it?"

"It's been flavored. Chocolate."

"Chocolate? But—but what if he doesn't like chocolate?"

"Miss Eisley, have you ever met someone who doesn't like chocolate? And anyway, even if it's not his favorite flavor, I'm sure he'll like the container."

"This is very—very strange."

"I could go. He's falling in love out there. I'm sure you two will be perfectly happy together."

"No, give me that." She grabbed the tube. "How much do I put on?"

"All of it."

"All of it?"

"Apply liberally."

"I have the drinks ready, Anne," Crane's mushy voice announced from the living room.

"Uh—all right! I'll be out in just a moment."

She went into the adjoining bathroom and then soon came out. She was wearing a sheer plum-colored chiffon gown with a matching robe. She wore it proudly.

"It was warm," she said, referring to the formula.

"I was sitting on it."

"Oh. I suppose you will be in here listening the whole time."

"I never leave until a job is completed. But don't worry about me. There's plenty here to read if I get bored."

"What happens if he wants to do more than—"

"He's not going to want to. Trust me."

"Trust you? You're a man without a name who will have a two

percent slice of my butt for the rest of my life."

"That's why you should trust me."

She looked at me with her deep aquamarine eyes. They questioned. Mine must have answered well, for she ended the look with a smile and said, "Okay." Then, she headed for the door.

"You look beautiful, by the way," I said.

She turned to me, her unsupported breasts whispering through the chiffon, her nipples: dark accents that thrilled. "Yeah. Thanks." She opened the door and left to rejoin Crane.

"Oh my god!" I could hear Crane exclaim.

"Anything wrong?"

"Nothing. You're just so beautiful."

"Yeah. So I've been told."

"Here's your drink."

"Thanks. Oh. Very strong, Fred."

"Well, we're both adults."

"Yes, we are. Should we go relax on the couch?"

"Yes, that would be fine."

"A little music? What would you like? The theme from '*Jaws*'?"

"What?"

"Just a little joke."

"Oh. I'm going to get John Williams for this film, you know."

"Oh, that would be lovely."

Then, softly, I could hear Billie Holiday making a plaintive musical statement:

It costs me a lot
But there's one thing that I've got
It's my man
It's my man.
He's not much on looks
He's no hero out of books...

Miss Eisley's devil irony? It pleased me to think so.

Not knowing if Crane was the kind of producer who liked to cut to the chase, I picked up the *Time* and began reading a detailed analysis of the current interest-raising actions of the Federal Reserve Board. It helped my mind mask the sounds from the living room, although Crane's declaration of: "Chocolate! My favorite!" did sneak through.

Soon after, Miss Eisley returned to the bedroom, somewhat agitated. "He—he's fainted."

"Well, that's not exactly the clinical term for it, but if I know my Formula 12-72, he has lost consciousness."

"He just suddenly looked up from down there with a shocked expression."

"That's because his erection suddenly de-erected. I've been told it's like having a chair pulled out from under you."

"Then he complained of fever and dizziness."

"Perfectly natural—so to speak."

"Then he just—collapsed right there into my—"

"Was that the Decca recording?"

"What?"

"Of Billie Holiday?"

"I don't know. It was a gift. Are you going to explain this formula to me or not?"

"Don't you think we should go make Crane comfortable first?"

"Oh, I laid him out on the floor. He's comfortable."

"Nonetheless, let me take a look at him."

I did more than that, of course. I had brought a medical bag containing the instruments needed to take Crane's temperature, check his heart rate, and take and analyze a blood sample. This told me Crane was reacting as expected to Formula 12-72 and would suffer its intended effects.

"Here's what you do in the morning—"

"In the morning? Aren't you going to get him out of here?"

"No. He has to wake up here in the morning."

"Why?"

"Do you think we've gone through all this just to slip him a rather pleasant Mickey to keep him from consummating his desires? How would that help you? He would assume he had food poisoning and be back at you in days. You pegged it, yourself. It isn't just sex he wants. He wants your life to aid his plan to 'take over this fucking town.' One bum night would not stop him."

"So Formula 12-72...?"

"Let's make a pot of coffee. Then I'll explain everything."

xx

As the coffee was dripping, Miss Eisley changed into something more comfortable. Flannel pajamas with a simple pattern of tiny blue flowers and a colorful ankle-length flannel robe. She also washed and scrubbed her face. Nevertheless, when she returned to the kitchen where I had been waiting, her beauty had not altered, and her entrance was grand. This woman would become a star.

"How do you take your coffee?" She asked.

"Black."

She gave an approving look. "Good boy." From anyone else, it would have seemed condescending.

She brought two mugs of coffee to the kitchen table and sat. It was hot, truly black, and deeply appreciated.

"Excellent. French Roast?" I asked.

"Yes. I get it at a little place in the Valley on Ventura, Coffee, Etc. They roast their own, of course."

"Part of a chain?"

"Please!" She mocked umbrage and then took a sip. "Should we now discuss the weather? Local politics? Any operations we've had?"

I smiled and quickly wondered if there was any way to make my life more "normal." I just as promptly doubted it. "Formula 12-72?"

"Formula 12-72."

"A simple compound—but it causes a very complex reaction. It was created to combat South American Communist rebel leaders. It was assumed by certain powers-that-were that, being Latino, these rebel leaders put an inordinate value on their manhood. And that if you could take away their manhood, you would demoralize them, and they would become ineffective leaders, and their 'movements' would fall apart.

"Did it work?"

"Well, it was only used once. The formula worked to expectations; the rebel leader was sufficiently demoralized. But nature, as you know, hates a vacuum, and he was replaced by another who was a far more brilliant military tactician and now the democratically elected leader of his country."

"And the guy who got 12-72?"

"He's now their Minister of Culture. You know, ballet, opera, that sort of stuff."

She gave me an incredulous look.

"Actually, he's now an activist trying to save the rainforests."

"And his manhood?"

"Someone steered him to a doctor who could help."

"You?"

A smile was my only answer.

"What's going to happen to Crane?"

"He's going to wake up in the morning feeling awful. He'll have a moderate to high fever, no appetite, and dizziness. You will be an angel of mercy and nurse him throughout the morning. Insist on it. Show great concern. Eventually, not getting better, you will drive him to his doctor. The doctor will be baffled. He will hospitalize Crane, where he will stay for six weeks. During this time, he will have no desire to even think about work, leaving everything up to his line producer. You will start work on the film and turn in a wonderful performance. It will make you a star. After six weeks, the mysterious disease will abate but linger. Crane will also notice another aspect of the disease. He will still feel sexual passion; indeed, he will feel a heightened sexual passion, true horniness like he hasn't felt since he was an adolescent boy sneaking peaks at *Playboy* at the local liquor store—but it will be impossible for him to achieve an erection. This will, of course, distract him further. He will pay very little attention to the film or you. He will just about be ready to agree to an implant to prop up his precious member when his doctor— who, by this time, should have published a paper on the mysterious disease now named after him—will be contacted by a doctor in Brazil who will claim knowledge of the disease and offer a therapy that should cure it. Crane will jump at the opportunity and will spend the next three years in Brazil going through a rigorous regime of diet, exercise, meditation, and injections of what he will think is a miracle drug."

"But will actually be?"

"The antidote. Given out in minimal doses over an extended period. But eventually, Crane will experience a complete cure. By then, he will probably fall madly in love with a Brazilian beauty and get himself involved in the local television industry, or he'll come home. But you know this town—three years out of the loop, and he will have to start again. In either case, he will be in no position to threaten you."

"Amazing. Truly amazing. Should we be concerned about the morality of what we have done?"

"I don't think so. What Crane was doing to you was a form of rape. What I have helped you do to him was self-defense—and a kindness. In the next three years, he will have the opportunity to reassess his actions. He might come out of it a more humane person, less prone to using people. Then again, he might not, but that is not our concern."

She thought about this as she sipped coffee. Both concept and coffee went down smoothly. "What is the significance of 12-72?"

I smiled. It was interesting that she assumed it had significance and wasn't just a notation of rank. "Stands for December 1972."

"When the formula was created?"

"Nope. When man last went to the moon."

"So it means...?"

"Yeah. No more shooting the moon."

xx

It was very late when I got up to leave. It was fascinating, the things we found to talk about. I had left my coat in her bedroom, and she made an offer while we were there to get it.

"You don't have to leave if you don't want to."

"I think it would be best, Miss Eisley."

"And you don't have to call me that anymore. It was just a little joke anyway."

"I'm sorry to hear that. I enjoyed taking it seriously."

She smiled. "You are strange in more ways."

"Some believe the world is going to hell in a handbasket, to use a hoary old cliché."

"Cliché or not, I'm not sure I don't agree."

"Well, if true, do you know when it started?"

"Tell me."

"The day parents stop demanding that their children call adults by Mr., Miss, and Mrs. It was the death of respect. Courtesy took on a rather pallid complexion at that time as well."

"Well then, with the deepest respect, Mr. Fixxer, please don't leave."

"Not meaning to be discourteous, I really should."

"Really?" There was a satisfying amount of disappointment in her voice.

"Really."

"Well, you know, the thing is—Crane wasn't, you know, all that bad, and—and he only just got started when—"

"I understand. But the other thing is—your field is still mined."

"Oh, yeah. How long?"

"Twenty-four to forty-eight hours. Don't shower; take baths for the next two days."

"Will you come back in two days?"

"Why? The job is over."

"Maybe just because you're the typical tall, dark, and handsome type."

"That's not my fault. It's genetics. My mother was tall and handsome. I always wanted to be short and dumpy."

"Why?"

"Because if you are short and dumpy, people underestimate you. That would have been quite an asset in my business."

"Well, for my immediate purposes, I'm happy you're tall, dark, and handsome, Mr. Fixxer."

She put her arms around my neck and kissed me. I knew I couldn't let it go on forever. But there was also no reason to cut it off short. We parted in a mist that had to be dispelled.

"But, hey, someday, give a short dumpy guy a try," I said.

"Not unless he has lots of power."

"Far more than Crane?"

"Far more."

"That's hard of you."

"It's not my fault. It's genetics."

It had been a good day. I had earned an easy $250,000 in the morning and untold riches in the evening. I was looking forward to a long sleep, a lazy day, and a nice quiet evening to savor these facts.

CHAPTER 6
UNTIL IT CONGEALS

People try to understand dreams. I think it's a mistake. If you have a bad one, just shudder and forget it. If you have a pleasant one, enjoy and be grateful for the complexity of your neural pathways. I had a particularly pleasant dream that night. Its focus—a very sharp, tactile focus—was Anne Eisley. Grace Kelly was in it as well. She was, I gather, passing the torch to Anne, who was accepting it with—quite naturally—grace. I, I believe, was positioned to be her prince consort, and I was pretty happy about that. Anne was giving me the most wonderful smile and meaningful look when Roee's voice rudely intruded.

"Wake up. Norton's on The Phone. He's got Paul Hinckley on the line, who's very angry."

As disappointed as I was, I did not linger in sleep or the dream. Training tells. I swung out of bed. "What time is it?"

"Just after ten. Figured you would want to sleep in."

I went to The Phone and picked it up. "Norton, explain."

"I can't even begin to. Hinckley's on; he's raving. Won't explain things to me. You better talk to him."

"Hold him one second." I turned to Roee. "Do you have fresh coffee on?"

"Naturally, I'll get you a cup."

"Okay, Norton, patch him through."

Paul Hinckley's voice came through like a raging river.

"What the fuck did you do? What the fuck did you do?"

"Calm yourself. What's the problem?"

"What's the problem? What's the problem? What the fuck did you do? What the fuck! God damn it to hell, I asked you to fix the goddamn thing, but I got a call from the fucking police at four o'clock this morning, at four o'clock, Fixxer! In the morning! From the fucking police, Fixxer! Of course, I couldn't get a hold of you 'cause you can't get a hold of you until business hours. Now why the fuck did you off Finch? You better have a good explanation for this because I think you've gotten me into a hell of a lot of trou—"

"Shut up, you talentless toad!"

"What? What did you say?"

"I called you an amphibian absent of anything but ambition. But don't take it personally. Now tell me the problem."

"Finch is dead."

It was information. Shaded by Hinckley's delivery. "Interesting."

"'Interesting'? They found him in his apartment, sliced and diced like a goddamn carrot with a Ginsu knife! There's blood all over the place!"

"Why did they call you?"

"Because—because my name—there's correspondence—there's things, and—and, you know, I'm a famous name. What the hell did you kill him for?"

"I did not kill him," I said, achieving, I believe, the proper chill in my voice. "If I had, there would not have been even a drop of blood."

"Oh."

"What are you worried about? You're up at the ranch, aren't you?"

"No—no, I decided not to go. Too tired to drive up there."

"So you were in town when the murder happened."

"Yeah."

"And they've made a connection between you and Finch."

"Yeah."

"Where are you now?"

"Home. But the police have been here. Questioning me."

"But they haven't arrested you?"

"No. Not yet."

"If you're innocent, you have nothing to worry about."

"Yeah? Tell me another fairy tale, Mother Goose."

"Your real problem is facts about 'V' coming out."

"Yeah! Yeah!"

"I'll see what I can do."

"You better."

"By the way. I found the real author. He has signed off and accepted payment."

"All for naught if this thing blows up in my face."

"I'll fix it."

"You—"

"I said I'd fix it. Once I say that, all I require from you is silence." I hung up. I picked up the phone again and called the Captain. "I would like to visit your crime scene on Argyle."

"It's the 2000 block."

"I know."

"Yeah, I know you know; that's why I bring it up."

"If I had had anything to do with it, would I want to come over?"

"Returning to the scene of the crime?"

"What bad books have you been reading?"

"Just police procedure manuals. You know what? You're not covered in any of them."

"I might be able to help."

There was a slight pause. "I'll meet you there."

"I'll be Jack Nichols."

"The independent forensic expert?"

"Yeah."

"Okay, he'll do."

I showered, put on a wig of very short brown hair of no particular style, applied a neatly trimmed mustache, then dressed in a pair of Sears polyester brown slacks, a white dress shirt, a large striped tie, and a brown corduroy sports coat with leather elbow patches. I called the garage and told them to prepare the 1992 Chevy Cavalier. Then I went to the file room and retrieved the Jack Nichols driver's license and employee card from Formosa Forensic Labs, Inc.

"Roee, call Petey and give him my thanks. Tell him the spiders were a delight. Then call up Marcel's in Beverly Hills. Have Marcel send Anne Eisley a basket with his best selection of bubble baths, bath oils, and anything else he thinks appropriate. Have the card read...."

"Yes?"

"Well, I suppose, 'Go soak your head' would be appropriate, but hardly the tone I mean to set. How about, 'Relax. The world is yours.' Unsigned, of course."

"Of course."

I drove very businesslike to the 2000 block of Argyle. The Captain was already there and greeted me as I got out of the car.

"Jack, good of you to come."

He held out his hand, and I shook it. "Captain. What do we have?"

"A rather grisly murder, I'm afraid. Be prepared."

I grabbed my forensic kit from the back seat and followed the Captain's lead to Finch's apartment. We were greeted at the door by Lt. Johnson, a bulky man with the demeanor of a high school football coach on a losing streak. He was not happy when he saw the Captain. "What the hell is Internal Affairs doing here?" Johnson said, both puffing out his chest and shrinking back.

"Oh, I was here before. You were on your break. This is Jack Nichols from Formosa Forensic."

"What the fuck is Formosa Forensic?"

"It's an independent—note that word, Johnson—forensics lab. They have a contract with the city."

"Does this have anything to do with the fact that we have been unable to remove the deceased, or any part thereof?"

"Do you have the cold packs on?"

"Yeah."

"Then what is your concern?"

"I'm tired of stepping over the parts," Lt. Johnson said as he entered the apartment.

Inside, the world was dark red. Blood was everywhere. In pools on the floor with congealing skin surfaces, as splatter streaks and dots covering the walls, the computer, the television and video machine, the stacks of books and the piles of video cassettes now all on the floor, the bookcases that had held them having been tipped over. Even the Murphy bed was soaked deeply in red.

"Pretty sight," the Captain stated quietly.

"Someone recently told me that blood is pretty."

"Really?"

"Yeah."

"Well, I think I prefer a nice seascape." He pointed me to the doorjamb and the ripped-out area around the chain lock. "Forced entry, as you can see. So he wasn't killed by a friendly visitor."

I didn't quite know how to tell him that Finch himself, trying to get in after Roee and I had left the other night, had probably done the damage. I knew I would eventually have to tell him, but not right then, I decided.

"Come over here," the Captain said. "And watch where you're stepping. Try to avoid the blood." The Captain moved to a corner and pulled off a heavy covering from a bulk shape. It was a nude human torso—only a torso. Viscera was spilling out of one end. The other end featured three raw sections where Finch's two arms and head had been attached. There was a small, less than half an inch wound just slightly right of the center of the chest, and up where many people think the heart is, where they put their hand when the flag goes by. But the heart isn't there; the aortic arch is. That accounted for the blood—it wasn't a death blow. The heart kept beating, pumping blood out through this hole in the dyke. This brought up the question—was Finch dead when the dismemberment started?

"Now over here." The Captain moved to the bed and pulled off another covering. Two legs, still attached to the pubic area, which was almost unidentifiable due to being solidly covered with dried blood, much of it matted in the pubic hair. "And over here." We went to the small kitchen area. The covering was on the floor. The Captain pulled it off, revealing Finch's arms. Weirdly, the hands were clasped as if in prayer.

"And the head?" I asked.

"Oh, yeah. The head." The Captain walked to the bathroom. Inside, it was almost pristine compared to the rest of the apartment, with only a trail of blood leading from the door to the toilet, upon which sat a covered lump. The Captain removed the cover. It was Finch's head— eyes open, hair a mess, his silly putty lips forming an angry expression as if someone had just praised a movie he hated.

"Some kind of humor, huh?" Lt. Johnson said. "Putting the head in the head."

"Yeah. Bathroom humor. Always gets a laugh." The Captain said as he covered the head.

"See what you make of this." The Captain led me back to the main room and focused a desk lamp on the wall where the bookcases had stood. There was on the wall a crude painting, done in blood, of a devil's head sticking out his tongue. The tongue was in the form of a strip of film. "Now, what the hell do you think that means?"

Lt. Johnson already had an opinion. "It's obvious. It's the portrait of a film critic. That's what this guy was."

"That's a good guess," I said, speaking as I've always imagined Jack Nichols sounds when he lectures on forensics. "But as basically useless a function as film criticism is, and thus, as basically useless as a film critic is, eradicating one as a representative of the whole, in this particularly radical manner, seems—well—overkill. No, I think the image is meant to convey a more ideologically based point of view. I would hazard the guess that the image means: Film is the tongue of the devil. A sentiment that I'm not completely sure I disagree with."

The Captain gave me a look. Then he moved the lamp back to its previous position. Something caught my eye as the light tracked across the room.

"Wait a minute. Shine the light over there, will you, Captain?" He did so, shining the light into the corner I pointed to. Some tiny flecks on the floor again caught the light. I went over to them, kneeling to get a closer look. I identified them immediately and was shocked by what they meant. It made sense, but not as this scene had been played.

"What is it?" Lt. Johnson asked.

"I don't know. Little flakes of something silvery. Probably nothing, but I'll take a sample to the lab."

"Did our boys find any of this?" The Captain asked Johnson.

"No. Despite this being Hollywood, we don't usually look for glitter at a murder scene."

"Jack, we'll need a sample too."

"Of course." I handed the Captain a small plastic tube containing some of the flakes.

"Johnson, excuse us for a minute," The Captain said, gesturing Johnson out of the apartment. He wasn't happy about it, but he went.

"Do you want to tell me about this?" The Captain held up the tube.

"I would rather analyze it first."

"Some new kind of dope?"

"No, I'm quite sure it's nothing like that."

The Captain paused. I could tell he wanted to pursue the line, but I had cooperated and gave him a sample. He would also analyze it, and if that did not shed any light, he would be back at me like a pissed-off Doberman. He decided to follow another line instead. "You were doing a fix for Paul Hinckley."

"That's right."

"We haven't arrested him. But he is our prime suspect."

"Now, why would Paul Hinckley do something like this?"

"You were trying to buy this kid off. Over something called V."

"I give my clients the guarantee of confidentiality."

"You're not a damn doctor, and you're not a damn lawyer. Hell, you're not even a reporter."

"No, but I try to be a man of my word, as antiquated a concept as that is."

The Captain frowned. I wasn't sure whether in agreement with the sense of what I had just said or as a comment on my naiveté. "Come look at this." He went over to the Mac computer and hit a key. The computer had been left on "sleep," and a document was immediately displayed.

"This is a letter faxed to Hinckley over the modem."

I bent down to the screen and read.

You fucking shit, Hinckley! How dare you send that goon to buy me off? "V" is mine! I was doing you a favor by asking you to direct it. Your career is not what we would call stellar. I'm the only one I know who even likes your films. Together we could have done great things. But you needed me, you bastard. Instead, you try to treat me like some kind of an insect. You idiot! You just wait till I tell the world what you tried to do! You never thought you would hear this from the likes of me, did you? YOU'LL NEVER WORK IN THIS TOWN AGAIN!!

"This is your case against Hinckley?" I asked.

"Listen to this." The Captain hit a switch on Finch's answering machine.

"Finch, this is Paul Hinckley. If you ever—ever write me such a letter again, if you ever dare to threaten me again, I'll come over there, slice your fucking balls off and fry them up for breakfast! Do you understand me, you little, pathetic geek? I know the truth, Finch; *V* isn't even yours. You stole it; you pile of shit! And I have all the facts. I don't ever—ever—ever want to hear from you again!"

"What do you think of that?" The Captain asked.

"He sounds angry."

"Yes. Now, this." He called up another document on the computer.

"Another fax from Finch to Hinckley."

Read the next issue of L.A. Week to Week—and weep.

"Does Hinckley have an alibi?" I asked.

"Home in bed, he says. The murder happened between eleven p.m. and one a.m. His wife and kid in the house but asleep. He could have left while they were asleep, came over here, got back before they awoke."

"Are you going to get a search warrant? If he did this, there's got to be some blood somewhere around him."

"We're thinking about it."

"But?"

"If there were no attempt to make this murder seem like a new Charlie Manson did it, we would have his ass downtown right now. But I don't think Hinckley would have gone to this kind of trouble. The trouble he would have taken would have been getting rid of the letters to him on the computer, but there are a lot, not just these. And he certainly would have erased the answering machine. So maybe it is just a weird Hollywood murder by some cult that thinks movies are frying the brains of people in the skillet of hell."

"Captain. That was almost poetic."

"Yeah? Thanks. I'm taking a UCLA extension course in creative writing."

"There's another point in Hinckley's favor."

"What's that?"

"Finch's balls were one of the few things not sliced off."

xx

We walked outside. Lt. Johnson was down in the courtyard with two uniformed representatives of the Coroner's office.

"Pack him up," The Captain ordered.

"Gee, thanks. Come on, guys." Johnson and the two went up the stairs.

The Captain walked me to the Cavalier.

"Any neighborhood witnesses?" I asked.

"One old guy downstairs in Finch's building said Finch and another man were arguing heatedly around eleven. But he said Finch was always arguing with guests, usually about movies. The old guy said he was quite used to it, and, as he could turn down his hearing aid, he thought nothing more of it."

"So he heard no screams?"

"No, nothing like that. Just Finch ranting and raving."

"Who called the police?"

"Finch's next-door neighbor. Bartender. Returned home at about 2:30 and slipped and took a big spill in front of Finch's door. He slipped on blood. Fell against the door, which opened. Found the mess."

"So, despite your personal feelings, Hinckley has to be the prime suspect."

"That's what Johnson thinks. I'll hold him back as long as I can."

"Thanks. I need one other favor."

"Keep it out of the press?"

"Exactly. Especially any information about V."

"It may not be easy."

"I have confidence in you. Call me if any cop or reporter becomes a problem. I'll take care of it from there."

xx

I called Hinckley from the car on the drive home.

"What? Tell me. What do you know?"

"Well, you are the prime suspect."

"I didn't do it, Fixxer. God damn it! I swear to God; I didn't do it."

"Yes, I'm aware of that. For a fact."

"You can prove that somebody else did it?"

"I don't need to. All they have on you is circumstantial evidence. The worse you would go through is some heavy questioning downtown—and the attendant embarrassment of the publicity. Assuming you can be embarrassed by publicity."

"What?"

"Never mind. I've put a stop to that."

"Okay. Okay, good."

"By the way. Why didn't you tell me about the angry fax/answering machine exchange between you and Finch?"

"Oh, uh—well, you know, this morning I was pretty upset, and—"

"Don't ever hold back information again. Understand?"

"Yeah, yeah, sure."

"That exchange is the real damning evidence here."

"Yeah. Yeah, I know."

"I've got a guy on the inside who will do his best to protect your position. But, it may cost you."

"Oh, what the fuck? I'm into this thing a half a million as it is."

"Then I'm authorized—"

"Spend what it takes."

"Okay."

"So, Fixxer, what was all this? Just a weird coincidence?"

"No. I'm convinced that you and I are—at least in part—

responsible for Finch's death."

"What?"

"Although I haven't yet figured out exactly why that should be."

xx

Finch had been a useless member of the human community. He produced nothing anyone was willing to pay for, and like it or not, making something someone is willing to pay for is the mark of usefulness in human society. Whether it be the border crossing illegals, who come up to pick the leafy vegetables we are no longer willing to stoop over for, or the comic with the guts to fight off flop sweat to make us laugh—something at least as nourishing as lettuce—those of us who can command a value for what we do are those with something to contribute to the tribe. Those who cannot command a value are useless and might as well be dead for all the good they do. But to say that someone might as well be dead, a repugnant sentiment to many, is far from wishing—and light years from accomplishing—the death of such a useless entity. Dave Finch did not deserve to die. Useless or not, he did not deserve to have his remains so brutally violated. He deserved nothing more than the anonymity that was already his. I could not grieve for Finch. You cannot grieve for waste material. But I could be, and was, angry that somehow my passing by his orbit may have caused the perturbation of his death. To be the author of another person's death is—the pun is unavoidable—a grave responsibility. It is one I have never welcomed and one I have, of late, studiously avoided. But when mine, it is one I have never taken lightly. It was not that I was consumed with a desire to avenge Finch's death—I was consumed with one to make it intelligible.

xx

I returned home and immediately took the flakes I had found in Finch's apartment into our lab. I handed Roee the tube. "Tell me if these are what I think they are."

Roee took the tube and prepared a slide. Then, he put it into the microscope and brought the magnified image up on the screen. "Do you think they are fish scales?"

"That was my guess. Salmon, most likely."

"What does it mean?"

"It means you're going to book us on the next flight to Portland. Pull some salesmen IDs for our persons and some Federal agent IDs. Secure them in the Bag o' Tricks. Let me get rid of Jack Nichols. I'll be ready to leave in ten minutes."

We took a limo to the airport. I explained the scene at Finch's apartment.

"Jesus!" Roee said. "I mean that in a most non-religious manner, of course."

"Of course."

"Could Craig York have done something like that?"

"I'm not sure Craig York could murder. And I'm positive he couldn't murder in this manner. But he was there. I'm sure he was the visitor the downstairs neighbor heard Finch arguing with at eleven, most likely about Finch's theft of V. But why was he so upset that he had to fly down to confront Finch? With Finch's plan foiled and $250,000 in my pocket, I would be prone to let bygones be bygones."

"But they were close. Best friends. Don't you think a sense of betrayal could have driven York a little mad?"

"To call Finch up and cuss him out maybe, but to kill him? No, the person who did this to Finch likes to kill. There was no anger, just an odd joy in how the body parts were dispersed. That could mean some 'Charlie Mansonite,' as the Captain put it, but I don't think so. I think the killer was a professional with the proper tools. Dismembering a body is not an easy task. But I do believe it was calculated to make the police jump to the conclusion that it was some murderous, anti-film cult nut case."

"Well, if York didn't—"

"York didn't. But, it was done because of York and something to do with this damn treatment. A stupid film treatment; I don't care how good it is, I don't care if it's going to be the basis of the first five hundred million dollars domestic gross picture; this kind of crime is not logical in relation to it. Something else is attendant to all of this—and the only one who can tell us what that is, is Craig York."

CHAPTER 7
VERITAS

Although it was twilight when we got to the Portland marina, it was nearly dark. It had rained recently. A lot. Only if the still solid covering of deeply gray clouds broke up would this evening's full moon illuminate the scene.

The marina was quiet. The pleasure crafts in their slips were dark and deserted as they gently rocked. A dim light from the living area of the *Buck'em*, though, indicated that York might be there. When we got to the marina gate, Roee examined the lock, snorted a lack of respect for its design, and had it opened within seven seconds. We walked down the ramp quietly and along the docking to the houseboat. No sounds were coming from it. And no sense of movement to it besides that provided by the river. We quietly slipped aboard and made our way to York's living area. We found him on his bunk, on top of the covers, fully clothed, asleep.

"Sleeping the sleep of the innocent?" Roee asked.

"Look at his face. His dreams are not pleasant."

On the table beside him was a small plastic pill bottle. I picked it up and held it under the small lamp on the table. "Sleeping pills. From a local pharmacy."

"Overdose?" I could feel Roee stiffen, preparing himself for action if needed.

"No. A prescription of 25. And there are at least 22-23 in here. He just wanted to be senseless, not dead."

"Should we wake him?"

"Not yet. Open his computer. See what's in it of interest."

Roee went to the computer and turned it on. He was immediately disappointed. "Damn!"

"What is it?"

"There's a lock on this. And it's not a commercial one. It seems to be homemade. Very clever—very goddamn clever." He turned from the computer in frustration. "What now?"

"Let's take her out."

"What?"

"When we wake him, I want him to be down the river, floating in the black. No lights, no landscape in sight, and no reference points. Except for this little cocoon of his—and us."

Roee threw off the lines. I started the engine, piloted us out of the marina, and headed downriver. The houseboat was a dream to handle. It had been exceptionally well crafted. York's father must have been brilliant at what he loved. I cruised slowly. I was in no hurry. I took her well away from the center of Portland to just after Elk Rock Island. We dropped anchor. York remained undisturbed. We drew up chairs around his bed and began to talk about nothing in particular in loud voices, entering York's dreams in this way and confusing them. Soon his eyes opened. He saw us. He would have screamed if his reflexes were not busy drawing in a deep breath of fear.

"Wh—what are you doing here?" We stared at him. We said nothing. He pushed with his legs to raise himself up the wall behind his bunk, which he then used to sit against.

"Do—do you want the money back? It—it's over there—the—the check. I haven't even cashed it."

"Yes, I know," I said. "You've been too busy flying to L.A. and back. How's David?"

His eyes went wide. He jumped off the bunk and ran for the door. We sat unmoved. He screamed when he came face-to-face with the black of the outside.

"There is nowhere to hide, and there is nowhere to run," I said loud enough for him to hear. "There is only the black night, the cold river, and my friend and I to talk to."

He came back in. His head began a slight back-and-forth rhythmic movement. His mouth hung slightly open. It was as if he was a machine stuck between functions. "I—I didn't mean to do it."

"Do what, Craig?"

"Kill—kill David."

Roee gave me a look. I would have given myself one if it had been possible. "You killed David?"

"We argued. He—he was like really mad. Crazy. He—he hit me. Pounded me. It was weird. He wouldn't stop. But I had to stop him, didn't I? I—I saw his letter opener. I thought if I waved it at him, he would stop. But he just got angrier. Threw himself on me. Lunged at me. We fell against a bookcase. Fell to the floor. I got up. Da—David didn't. 'Get up,' I said. I said, 'Get up! Get up! Get up!' But he didn't. He just lay there on his stomach. Then—then suddenly—then he turned around, and the letter opener was in his heart, and he just looked at it, wide-eyed, you know, he couldn't believe it, I guess, and then he grabbed it and pulled it out, and then, my god, it was like—it was like a fountain!"

Craig stopped talking. His breathing was rapid and shallow, as if the scene was still playing in his head.

"Sit down, Craig," I said." My friend Roee here will make you a cup of coffee. Do you have any food? Are you hungry? I want you to be comfortable, Craig, and then you can talk some more. You'll want to do that, and Roee and I will be happy to listen."

Roee fixed a fine cup of coffee. They have some excellent coffees in the Pacific Northwest. York and I sat on green leather benches in the built-in dining area, facing each other across a Formica-covered tabletop. Roee stood about, hovering like some large bird with sharp claws and a tearing beak. York drank his coffee in disturbing big gulps. He asked for a second cup. Roee obliged. Then he began to talk.

"I—I was angry. David—David shouldn't have done it. It was screwing everything else up. So I... No—I mean, you know, so I had to fly down there and talk to him about it."

"A phone call wouldn't have sufficed?" I asked.

"No, no, no, I had—I had—you know, in person. I mean, selling V as if it was his? Screwing me like that? I mean, we were supposed to be friends. Friends don't do that. At least that's the way the world used to be, uh? So anyway, I flew down there. And I went to his apartment. And I confronted him about it. Why? I asked him. I mean, it was just a simple question: Why?"

"And what was his answer?"

"Well, then, he just—he just—well, then he just went nuts. And— and— and started screaming at me at the top of his lungs that I was denying him his opportunity, that he could be the greatest filmmaker ever, and that V was his. Somehow, he was really convinced that he had given me the idea for V and that—and that it was his ticket, or—

or—or something, to prove how—how—how to make a good movie. He started screaming how everybody was screwing it up, how nobody knew how to make movies anymore, like—like the great masters of old, that only he knew how to do it, and that—that all he was trying to do was get the opportunity, that—that—that he would have shared the money with me, but that he had to get that opportunity."

York stopped and took a quick sip of coffee. "And so he's screaming how that 'fucking Hinckley' wanted to take it away from him, and I wanted to take it away from him, and everybody was working against him, and everybody was after him, and they were afraid of his talent, and they were afraid of what he knew, and—and—and he just kept screaming, and—and then he beat at me, he clasped his hands together and started to beat at me. I thought—I thought he was going to kill me—I thought he was going to kill me! So I just—like I said—you know, I—grabbed the letter opener—and then—God. He was dead." York's eyes went glassy, peering well below the top of the table. "God—dead. I've known him since we were kids. We—we had done so much together."

"Then what did you do?" York did not answer. "Craig!"

"Huh? Oh, well, the blood was, you know, spurting out, so I guess I just panicked, and I ran. I got back in my rental car, went back to the airport, and came home."

"Craig, if the blood was spurting out, David was not dead."

"Wh—what?"

"His heart was still beating. Why didn't you try to help him? Why didn't you apply pressure to the wound?"

"I—don't know—I—don't know about that stuff. I stabbed him in the heart; he had to be dead!"

"You did not stab him in the heart but in an artery. He might have lived if you had helped him."

"No!"

"Why didn't you call the police?"

"Uh—li—like I said, I panicked, I just panicked, so I ran, I just panicked."

"Craig?"

"What? I told you."

"Craig?"

"I panicked, I told you."

He took another sip of coffee. As it passed over his tongue, I screamed: "Craig!" It had its effect. York jumped at the shout, spilling coffee, gagging on what had been in his throat. Once he got over his amazement at being orally slapped, I continued. "You didn't call the police, but you did call someone. Whom did you call?"

"I didn't call anybody! I told you; I ran!"

"Whom did you call?"

"I didn't call anybody!" He poured his eyes into the muddy brown of his creamed coffee.

"Craig, listen. Listen to every word now. Are you listening?" I snapped my arm out and grabbed his head, clutching onto the handle of his left ear. I twisted his ear as I brought his head up close to mine and forced his eyes to look directly into mine. "Someone came in after you left and mutilated the body of David Finch! Are you listening? They cut off David's head!"

"No!"

"And they cut off David's arms!"

"No!"

"And they separated David's legs from the trunk of his body."

"No."

"And then they did a lovely mural on the wall of a devil's head in David's blood to try to convince the police that David was killed by some cult weirdo—instead of his best friend!" I jerked his head violently at each of these last words and then threw it back to him.

Then, with all the disgust I could convey, I said: "They violated David's body to protect you."

"No!"

"Whom did you call? Who wants to protect you?"

"Ah—ah..." The pain was searing. That was good. "My—my partner."

"Your partner?"

"My—my investor."

"Your investor?"

"I—I—yes—I was scared, so I just called this man who—who's investing in something."

"Who's investing in something you created with Jim Skinner at Caltech."

"No, no! It's mine! I mean, it's—it started with Jim, yeah, but it's mainly mine, and—and my investor has given me a lot of money and—

"And your investor told you to fly down to Los Angeles. You called him and told him of my visit. Of Paul Hinckley. Of what David did. And he told you to fly down to L.A. and take care of David. Why? Why was David Finch important?"

"Well—well, because we needed him to do something."

"You needed him to do something with Jim, or to get to Jim, because you and Jim weren't talking anymore, weren't getting along, were you?"

"Yeah, well, you know, David still talked to Jim."

"He was still friends with Jim, and you weren't, and you needed him to get close to Jim to do something."

"Yeah."

"But then I told you that he had given V to Paul Hinkley, and you, maybe just your investor, did not want V to be seen by anyone. Is that what you meant when you said, 'It was screwing everything else up'?" York stared at me, offering no answer. "What is 'everything else'? And why is V so crucial to it?"

"Oh—oh, it really has nothing to do with V."

"Yes, it does!" I slammed my hand against his coffee cup, sending it crashing against a porthole. "V has something to do with what you created at Caltech. Doesn't it? V reveals what you created at Caltech, and your investor did not want that information out. Right?"

"Well—well, it really just sort of hints."

"It must detail your creation. Or at least your investor must think so. So he told you to take care of David. Did that mean he wanted you to kill him?"

"No—no, just talk to him. Get all copies of V."

"And what about Hinckley?"

"He—he said he could take care of Hinckley."

"So you went down to L.A. to talk to David, ask for copies back, and watch him dump the V file from his computer. But David went nuts, and David attacked you, and you killed David."

"It was an accident!"

"It doesn't matter! You killed him! And then you panicked but didn't run; you called your investor, and your investor told you to go back to Portland, and your investor said he would take care of it."

"Yeah—yeah."

"And your investor took care of it by savagely mutilating the dead body of your best friend."

"I didn't know he was going to do that. I didn't ask him to do that."

"I don't doubt you. I'm sure he didn't need to be asked. But he did it nevertheless."

York started to cry, trying to hold it in, wanting to let it pour, upsetting the rhythm of his breathing over the conflict.

"Who's your investor, Craig?"

"I—I don't—I—I can't tell you."

"Craig, who's your investor?"

"I promised not to tell anybody."

"Craig! Your investor mutilated the body of your best friend! Your investor is not a person you need to owe loyalty to! Who is your investor?"

"I can't tell you!" York shouted out, then buried his head in his folded arms, now more angry than scared—angry at being scared.

"Okay, Craig. I'll find out. Indeed, I'm sure I already know who it is. Tell me this, though, what does V stand for?"

"Nothing," he said in a muffled voice. "I mean, really, nothing. It doesn't stand for anything."

"What does V stand for?"

He raised his head to plead. "It's meaningless. Really, it's meaningless."

"Craig, does V stand for virtual?"

York started to laugh, an involuntary chuckle kind of laugh that had a history behind it. "That's what you would think; that's what they may all think, but no—no—you stupid bastard! V doesn't stand for virtual—it stands for Veritas!"

Like the sting of a rebuke, I suddenly knew what he meant. "Of course—"

Thump!

You wanted to believe it was some strange knocking, but it wasn't. It was an explosion, obviously located at the bottom of the boat, in the stern, as the rear of the *Buck'em* raised out of the water, throwing Roee forward to fall against the computer setup, and smashing me into the edge of the built-in dining table, knocking the wind out of me as if I had taken the good, solid punch of a heavyweight. York was pushed against the back of his bench as my coffee cup smashed into his chest.

Thump!

There were hardly three seconds between the first and second explosions. It was another underwater explosion, which accounted for the muffled sound of the shock, and it came from the bow this time.

York was thrown out of his bench and onto me, which did not make my efforts to recover my breath any easier.

Roee was the first one to get his wits about him. "The boat's sinking!"

"What? What?" York said as he clamored to get off me. "Where are your life jackets?" Roee shouted.

"In a chest. At the stern."

Roee ran out. I got myself up.

"Wh—what happened?" York wanted to know, needed to know.

"Somebody just blew holes in your boat. Unless this area of the river is mined."

"Who would do that?"

"We'll go through your Rolodex later. But right now, we've got to get off."

Roee ran in with the life jackets, throwing one at each of us. I caught mine and quickly put it on. York let his hit him and fall to the deck. "No, my boat, my dad's boat."

"Craig put on the jacket. Let's go!"

"No, the computer!"

I ran to grab York when the third explosion hit. Not muffled like the first two were, this one was piercingly loud, accompanied by a massive fireball. The engines in the stern were blowing. The boat was suddenly on fire. I grabbed the Bag 'o Tricks and tossed it at Roee. "Go! I'll get York." Roee was out and gone. I heard a splash. "Come on, York!"

"Wait!" York was at his computer, grabbing a stack of gold TDK CD-R recordable compact disks and stuffing them into a bag. "I've got to get these."

I grabbed him, scooped up his life jacket, and dragged him onto the deck. Although the light of the fire was invading the deep black of the night, I could see nothing but the immediate cold water of the river, which was almost at our level. "Get this on!" I pushed the jacket at him.

"Wait, I'm missing a disk." He was staring at the CD-Rs. "I've got to get—"

"Forget it! Grab this! Jump!"

"No!" He screamed as he broke away from me.

Then, from out of the dark, a graceful loop of rope fell over him and cinched around his trunk. Then, with a yank from nowhere, York flew off the boat. I heard a splash and could see York, like an inanimate bundle, being dragged across the river.

I followed the line of the rope pulling him. At its end, I could just make out, coming like an apparition into the illumination of the fire, a tall, lanky man in a cowboy hat standing on the bow of a small cabin cruiser. He was pulling the rope hand over hand as he smiled. A spot of gold in his mouth glinted in the firelight. I jumped. The shock of the river's cold might have rendered me senseless if I had not had as much adrenaline flowing as I did. I swam fast—the houseboat was just about ready to sink, and I did not need to be pulled down with it—and in the opposite direction from the cabin cruiser.

Responsibility for all this lay with it, I was sure of that, and I did not want to meet its crew under these conditions. I swam hard in a direction I felt would bring me to a shore, but I was disoriented and had no idea if it would be the near shore or the far shore. Then, a bright beam of light hit me. A powerful engine started up. The cabin cruiser was after me. I swam harder and harder. The sound of the cruiser expanded in my head like a balloon. I didn't dare look back, and it was hard to fight the back-of-the-neck fear that the boat would soon be cruising over me, cutting me off from precious air and sucking me into its propellers. A rope slapped the water as it fell over my head. I couldn't throw it off before it tightened around my neck with a violent jerk, which flipped me over on my back. In that position, I cut through the water as I was pulled quickly to the cruiser.

I clawed at the burning rope, trying to break its grip and open a passage for air. I was becoming light-headed. Into my increasingly spot-filled vision soon came the upside-down, cowboy-hatted head of the smiling man. I noticed the gold teeth again as he said, in a thick East European accent trying for an American West twang, "In right over head, ain't ya pardner?" Then the smiling man and all that surrounded him dissolved to one last glint of gold, which quickly dissipated as if washed away with black, black water.

CHAPTER 8

MERDE!

I woke up to the smell of straw and human excrement on the cold stone floor of a dungeon in a castle I knew—I did not think, I did not guess—I knew to have been built in the 14th century.

Worse still, I was convinced that I was in the 14th century.

14th century France, to be precise.

It was disconcerting to be so precise as I lay there, shivering, trying to ignore stiff joints and sore muscles. I raised myself to a sitting position. A sudden memory invaded. I threw my hand up to my neck. It was not raw, burned, or sore. But it should have been. The wet rope had cut and burned as it had choked the life out of me.

That was a point.

Was I dead?

And if I were, why would either heaven or hell (it's debatable which I qualify for) be 14th century France?

I looked around and saw various sizes of freestones mortared together to make up the gray walls that surrounded me. A small amount of light came into the dungeon from a slit window about seven feet up the wall. I was wearing the clothes of a nobleman, although they were filthy and stinking, and my left leg was manacled to a long chain that ran along the floor and up the wall behind me to a large round iron fixture embedded in stone about five feet up from the bottom.

Some part of my brain struggled to wonder why I was not assuming that I had been thrown onto a movie set. Empirical evidence would have killed the assumption: These walls were made of real stone, not Hollywood's wood and fiberglass mockings. Nor did the walls show 600 years of wear. These stones were fresh. If fresh is a word you can apply to rocks. My struggle failed; the assumption was never made. I accepted quickly that this was real. That this was the 14th century.

Mark Twain's *A Connecticut Yankee in King Arthur's Court* came to mind, but that was satiric literature, and this was—truth? Also, Twain's hero was confused when he woke up; he did not know where he was—geographically or temporally. I knew both.

That was important. I *knew* both.

"*Monsieur? Monsieur?* I can hear you stirring up there. I know you are awake."

It was a weak voice. Coming from the dungeon's floor—or rather, from just below the floor.

"Have they brought you water? Any water? Please, *Monsieur*, may I have some? Can you get some to the grate and pour it in?"

In one corner of the dungeon was a small recess. Within, there was an iron grate on the floor. Beneath the grate was the *oubliette*, a coffin-like cell within this cell. There was an unwanted prisoner lying in there, someone to be forgotten, someone to be allowed to die a "natural" death of neglect and starvation.

"Who are you?" I asked.

"Just Philippe, *Monsieur*. An assistant cook."

"I see no water, Philippe, so I'm afraid I cannot oblige."

"A pity, *Monsieur*, a pity. Thirst is a hard thing."

"Why are you here, Philippe?"

"Oh, a mere trifle, *Monsieur*, nothing so grand as your offense. I stole some food from the kitchen for my brother's family, just a little, but he broke his leg and could not provide. What else could I do, *Monsieur*? I ask you, what else?"

"And what is my grand offense?"

"Oh-oh, still claiming innocence, are we? At least I have had the courage to confess. And I am but a *Villein*, not an elevated noble, such as yourself. But then, a little bread, a little meat, what's that to spying?"

"Spying?"

"For England. How could you? The uncultured, filthy pigs!"

"Philippe, you are little better than a slave who is going to rot in a hole in the ground. Snobbery does not become you."

"See, *Monsieur*, this is your undoing. No patriotism. If we do not believe that even a French slave is better than an English lord, then how will we raise ourselves out of the feudal system?"

It was bad enough that the situation was surreal, but now the conversation was getting that way. "Shut up, Philippe. You are but a figment of my imagination."

"Tell that to my thirst, *Monsieur; it* might help."

With difficulty, I brought myself to a standing position. Was this difficulty a figment of my imagination as well? It certainly didn't feel like it. The stiff and sore essence of the difficulty felt quite real. But like Philippe's thirst, if I could convince my imagination of it, maybe it would help.

"*Aaaaaahhhhhhh!!!!!*"

The cry came from the outside. Deeply curious, I squeezed my hands onto the bottom ledge of the slit window and painfully drew myself up to look out. I held on for no longer than five seconds before falling painfully to the hard stone floor. But I had gotten an eyeful and now had a memory retention of what I had just seen that was not only clear and detailed—but in color. I had but to close my eyes and could see it all again, as if in playback.

It was a view of the lower bailey, an open-air section of the castle. It was busy with workers who were tending the horses in the thatched roof stables attached to the inside castle wall; tanning animal skins; making bate; sharpening swords on a huge grindstone being turned by one man while another sat up on a platform a good six feet high and held the blade to the stone; stacking—

How did I know about bate? A combination of water and dog excrement used to soften animal skins. I may have read about it once, but how did I know without hesitation what the man at the rear of the bailey was doing as he stomped his feet up and down in the big wooden tub?

And the cry of pain...? In thinking about it, I instantly heard it again. It came from the blacksmith at the forge in the center of the bailey. It seems he had dropped a red-hot horseshoe on his right foot. He was hopping up and down on his left. Several people couldn't help themselves; they were laughing uproariously at this bit of cartoon humor. The blacksmith continued to hop, his back to me—or my memory—slowly turning toward me.

This bit of cartoon humor, I thought again.

The blacksmith turned full face toward me.

How bizarre it was.

The blacksmith was Daffy Duck.

I shook my head violently.

Whatever was going on, whatever seemed to have control of my perceptions, I figured I should just sit and wait it out. That was my thought. But my feeling, a strong, obsessive feeling, was that I had to escape.

That was my duty. I had to escape.

"Philippe, any way out of this dungeon?"

Came the weak voice from the floor: "You are, *Monsieur*, I think, asking the wrong man."

"Yes, I can see that."

"But my dear Papa always told me, 'A chain is but as strong as its weakest link.' He was, of course, speaking of his particular profession."

"And what was that, Philippe?"

"He was a sausage maker, *Monsieur*."

Theft may not have been the only reason they had to throw Philippe into the *oubliette*.

But he had a point. I started to inspect the chain that bound me, looking at it link by link, and, sure enough, at about three-quarters of its length from my ankle to the iron fixture embedded in the wall, was a link whose solder point was separating. I gathered up the chain in a tight grip and pulled and hung all my weight on the one weak link. The effort was hard; sweat flowed quickly, and the deep breath I had to take after each try seemed to burn with the smell of excrement, which I now noticed was piled in a dark, moist corner. Finally, the link separated wider. I stopped and tried to slip the link below it through the separation. It did not quite fit. I made one more deep-pulling effort, failing to mute the loud grunt I was compelled to sound out. Finally, the link gave, and I fell to the floor, a bundle of sweat and pain.

The door swung open, and a loud, deep voice exclaimed: "That you are a pig you have proven by your acts. But must you grunt like one too?"

I looked up through stinging sweat and saw the jailer. He was enormous—or so he seemed from my lack of advantage—and faceless. Literally. I blinked. The jailer had a curved white slate for a face. I blinked again. The white slate began to vibrate like water in a cup sliding across a table. At the same time, hate as raw as I have ever known surfaced in my mind, and screamed just as the vibrations coalesced into the smiling face of the man on the cabin cruiser, that gold tooth son-of-a-bitch!

I leaped at him with murderous fury, wrapping the chain around his neck. He started to call out, but I cut it off with a jerking pull on both ends, tightening the chain around his neck as the wet rope had tightened around mine. He threw his body back, trying to get me to loosen my grip, but I just fell with him and landed on him, still pulling, still straining to squeeze, to smash, to pulverize into pulp the skin, the flesh, the arteries, the ligaments, and the cartilage of his neck. It was not about cutting off his air. It was about cutting off his head.

Then the body stopped its struggle and lay there, a quiet sack of flesh and other organic material.

"I don't believe that murder is so bad. It's whom you murder that counts on the tally sheet of morality."

It was an old voice reverberating from somewhere outside of this 14th Century France. An old voice that once had been very important to me that—

The face! The smiling, gold-toothed face melted—or faded—or vibrated away back to the curved white slate!

"Help! The spy escapes! The spy escapes!" It was Philippe, screaming from under the floor, expressing an admirable sense of French patriotism. I looked for a way to shut him up quickly. There was only one. With my un-manacled foot, I slid a nice pile from the dark and moist corner over to—and over— the *oubliette*'s grate.

"Merde!" Philippe gagged out.

"Exactly," I said as I ran for the door.

Escape. It seemed almost a physical concept, and it battered me. I jumped up the stairs beyond the door, grazing my right shoulder as I made the sharp right turn to continue up, finding at the level of the squint—the small peephole that looked into the dungeon—another faceless jailer. Without thinking, I kicked him in the groin and smashed his egg-like head into the wall. Up more flights of stairs, then I burst into the jailer's room, which was empty. I opened the door to the outside and ran into the lower bailey. It was empty, utterly devoid of people, animals, and everything. Yet the sounds of bustle were there, movement, voices, and the grind of the grindstone. I closed my eyes. There! There was everything as I had seen through the slit window, but in replay again; again, Daffy was hopping on one leg, dancing to the slapstick tune of his pain. I opened my eyes. Sound. No people. I ran for the gates that led to the drawbridge. There were a few guards in place, but so in place, they were like mannequins, lifeless and still. At least they had a face—the same one on each guard.

Run! Escape! The feeling was overwhelming. I ran to the

drawbridge, which was down. I looked out over the country, down the gentle green slope that led to a river and the woods beyond it. I ran across the drawbridge. Make for the woods, was my thought. In my panic, I dropped the chain I was still attached to, and just as I was hitting the dirt path, I tripped on it and fell hard onto the transparent, super-glass floor of the commute tube connecting the main living quarters with Labs 3, 4, and 5.

I looked down through the floor. A massive school of fish was passing beneath me, caught in the illumination of the tube. I got up, no longer stiff and sore, feeling energetic and—and serious. But I was still wearing the dirty and stinking clothes of a 14th century nobleman. I was still manacled. Then, as I inspected these facts, the clothes seemed to unweave before my eyes, the manacle and chain faded to nothing, reweaving began, and soon I was in a clean, comfortable ocean-green jumpsuit.

It was 2026. I was at the Cousteau Oceanographic Institute somewhere in the depths of the Pacific Ocean.

A klaxon! A warning!

"We have had a cetacean breach of the security perimeter. We have had a cetacean breach of the security perimeter. Evacuate all commute tubes! Evacuate all commute tubes!"

There was no time. I saw the giant blue whale just as it entered the illumination from the institute's complex—a flash of massive. Then it slammed into the commute tube about 50 yards ahead of me, neatly taking out a section. I lost my footing in the quaking, but that mattered little as water rushed towards me, then engulfed and caught me in its cold liquid determination to replace life-sustaining gas. The commute tube was jettisoned from the main living quarters—part of the safety measures— and the water rushed me out of the disconnected end. I had grabbed a last-minute breath, but how much good was that going to do me? I'm a strong swimmer, but could I reach any of the airlocks in any of the structures before...? Without a wetsuit, I was quickly becoming numb. My eyes stung; I could not see. My chest was beginning to burn. Part of me knew this could not be real, so I could not die. But it was not a part displaying any robust control. Death seemed inevitable.

I was suddenly nudged with urgency. I opened my eyes. Of course, funny what panic will make you forget. It was one of the rescue dolphins. Qwerty, I would guess. I grabbed the left-hand hold on his rescue suit, and then he sped for the closest airlock as I grabbed the mouthpiece of the attached oxygen tank and took a welcomed breath of wonderfully metallic-tasting air. I relaxed. I knew Qwerty would do the work from here.

The cold remained, though, frigid, frigid cold. "Frozen stiff" were words that invaded my thoughts. I tried moving a little to prove those words wrong and eased into the glow and warmth of the fireplace.

"Isn't that the greatest rug?" she asked as she brought over our drinks. "Vodka tonic. Lemon twist."

"Thanks. It is a nice rug," I said as I accepted the drink and leaned back upon a big bear's head.

"My grandfather shot it."

"Self-defense?"

"Oh, no. He loved hunting. He hunted once with Theodore Roosevelt and Ernest Hemingway in Africa."

"On the same safari?"

"Of course."

"Highly unlikely. The old Rough Rider was dead by the time Papa got to Africa."

"Reeeally?"

"Really."

"Uh—uh."

She seemed stumped. So she sipped her drink, which was amusing to watch. Like the dungeon guard, she had a curved white slate of a face. The glass went up to it and was tipped, but no liquid ran down her lack of visage.

"Well—so—uh—you want to fuck?"

Despite her look, it was hard to think of her as an egghead. Her cute, Kewpie doll voice and general lack of historical grounding worked against her here—although she did fit comfortably into the idea of an empty shell. It was a lot to put up with to get warm. So I decided to concentrate and see if I could make a change. Whatever this was I was in, it had a quick response time. Almost immediately, the curved white slate of her face began to vibrate. It was a distinct pleasure to soon have Anne Eisley before me, now wearing the plum chiffon outfit she wore for Crane, although it was no longer a gown. It was very short.

"Don't drink too much," she said in Anne's exciting voice. "I want you emboldened, not embalmed."

I looked her over with great appreciation. "I don't need a drink for that."

"Are you calling me an intoxicant?"

"Well, you raise the level of something in my blood."

She smiled. "How sweet." She fell to her knees very slowly and with great control, keeping her back straight and her breasts riding high under the sheer chiffon. I don't know if you would call them proud—but I certainly was.

She smiled at me with her aquamarine eyes, tracing and stroking my face with looks alone. "You are the most handsome man I have ever met."

"You've led as cloistered a life as that, huh?"

"Don't joke with me. Other women may say they want a man with a sense of humor. But I want a man with a sense of musk."

As if to prove her point, she gently laid her hand on my right thigh and smoothly parted my silk robe, which I just then realized I was wearing. Then her hand approached my now bare thigh and graced the follicles of hair and the most outer nerve endings on my skin with the very tips of her fingernails. An urgently demanding effect was derived from this cause. Finally, she sighed (I couldn't have said it better myself) and leaned into me, closing her eyes and parting her lips as I prepared...

Then she froze. As did, I noticed, out of the corner of my eye, the flames in the fireplace. And, sadly, all the sensations I had been feeling. Only the vision was left, and that soon spun like a whirlpool into a strange diminishing, leaving behind the concerned, possibly welcomed face of Roee.

"Fixx? Fixxer? Are you with me? Are you okay?"

I looked beyond Roee. We were in a warehouse space. Empty and cavernous except for some furniture, including the chair I sat on, desks, a computer, and other electrical equipment. It was cold. Dry but cold. I looked back at Roee. He was holding a strange pair of glasses in his right hand, trying to get my attention by rubbing my cheek with his left.

"Whatever this is that I've been in," I said, "if you could just get me back there for, say, twenty minutes more, I promise, from now on, to eat my zucchini."

Now my neck hurt. To move it even slightly was painful. Roee examined it immediately, not happy with the mess. "I need to clean and dress it," he said. "There's infection." He grabbed the medical kit from the Bag o' Tricks, pulled out a small bottle, and poured its contents onto a sterilized pad. He approached my neck. "This is going to sting."

I stopped his hand on its approach. "Roee."

"What?" He was slightly piqued.

"Do you remember when we were prisoners in Syria?"

"Of course."

"Do you remember those horrible hemp ropes they tied our hands with?"

"Yes. What?"

"Thirteen days of rubbing our wrists raw."

"Thanks for the memories."

"Remember that medic who dressed our wounds after your people rescued us?"

"Ariel."

"Ariel."

"Yes."

"He told us it would sting."

"Did he?"

"I didn't need to be told then. And I don't need to be told now."

Roee just smiled and applied the pad.

"Ouch!"

"Told you," Roee said with some satisfaction.

"Fill me in?" I said, feeling better after Roee's ministrations.

"I jumped off the houseboat and swam hard to get some distance from it. Good thing I did because the dark hid me from the other boat. I saw the whole thing. I saw them rope York and drag him up onto the boat. He knew them. He started shouting at them about his boat. They told him to shut up, handed him a blanket, and forced him below deck. Then they got you. I thought you were dead when they pulled you up onto the boat. The roper, by the way, was Zhelyu Batsarov."

"The Bulgarian Cowboy?"

"That's right."

"Makes sense considering the lasso. Not much otherwise."

"Well, he was the leader. Gave the orders. The boat started to head to shore."

"What did you do?"

"Grabbed the mini-grapple from the Bag o' Tricks and got a shot off. Latched onto a rail on the stern."

"So you got towed along."

"Yeah.

"Where did they dock?"

"Close to where we are here. We're in one of a series of warehouses by the railway yards."

"The Northwestern Dock, most likely. Hell of a trip for you."

"The coldest, wettest trip I've ever made—but it will make me much more appreciative of the aridity of my homeland."

"Go on."

"When they docked, I got to the starboard and watched them come down the gangplank. There were four of them besides York. One carried you down fireman style, so I knew you were alive. The only other one I recognized was Paddy O'Shane."

"Ex-IRA."

"Yeah. York was now wearing a gray running suit. You also."

I hadn't thought about that. I looked myself over, and, indeed, I was in a thick, gray sweat suit.

"I watched them take you to this warehouse. Then I got on board their boat."

"What did you go on the boat for?"

"I wanted to get one of these snazzy running outfits. I was cold and wet. I found about a dozen, all sizes. They must buy in bulk from Sportswear for Thugs. Anyway, once dry, warm, and with a couple of slugs of the J&B they had on board in my belly, I sauntered to the warehouse to see what they were doing to you."

"You sauntered?"'

"I hadn't heard any screams."

"I see."

"Anyway, I got here, and the door was open. I didn't even have to pick the lock. These are very confident people. So, I could sneak in and see what was going on."

"Which was?"

"You were sitting in this chair with this pair of glasses on, this computer setup running, with York at the controls. One of the thugs I didn't recognize was watching this medical monitor."

"Let me see the glasses." Roee handed them to me. They looked like an ordinary pair of eyeglasses. The lenses, though, were thick, dark, and opaque. I tried them on. There was nothing to see. The other unusual aspect about them was that inside both bows were metal contact points placed where the bows touched the head at the temples and behind the ears. "Was I moving at all while I had these on? Jerky movements, like I was trying to run, or struggling movements?"

"No. You were completely still. Almost, I would say, paralyzed. Batsarov was giving York orders. York wasn't happy about it. He was still upset about his houseboat."

"What kind of orders?"

"Well, 'Do the Castle program' was one. Then he ordered him to shift to the Cousteau program. Then they got a phone call. I couldn't hear any of it, but Batsarov, York, and two others left because of it. They left Paddy O'Shane behind. Batsarov told him to go ahead and have some fun playing more video games with your head, but once he got bored—to kill you. After they left, O'Shane gleefully jumped to the keyboard and punched some keys, changing the program again, I assumed. Then he did something strange."

"What was that?"

"He moved this reading lamp towards you and directed its beam towards your crotch."

Roee looked to me for a possible explanation. I offered none.

"Anyway, it was soon after that, that I subdued him, took the glasses off your face, and saw you regained consciousness."

"Not regained."

"What?"

"I had been conscious for quite a while, I think."

"You didn't look conscious."

"Did I look like I was in a deep sleep?"

"Yeah."

"Nonetheless, I was conscious."

"Well, if you were conscious, can you tell me what was happening inside your head?"

"I can, but later. It's the key to this whole affair, however. Right now, we've got to get out of here. Let's take these glasses, and grab any CDs you find especially gold ones, and disconnect that black box from the computer; we'll take that too."

"What do you think it is?"

"My best guess? You'll notice these glasses aren't connected to the computer by wires. The box is probably an infrared transmitter of some kind."

Roee gathered everything up and put it in the Bag o' Tricks. Then we started to leave. That's when I noticed Paddy O'Shane sprawled on the cold, cement warehouse floor. I bent down to examine him. "Roee?" I said with some surprise. "His neck is broken."

"Yeah. He pissed me off."

"Well, jeez, Roee, he may have been a thug committing God knows what criminal acts, but still, to him, he was just doing his job."

"No, he pissed me off in 1986. He sold guns to Arab bad boys back then to raise money for the IRA."

"Ah. Situational ethics. Always handy."

CHAPTER 9
PRANCING PRUNES

In canvas deck shoes from the boat, we made our way out of the Northwestern Dock and across the train tracks, eventually finding the Sailor's Haven Hotel, a small daily, weekly, or monthly establishment overlooking Overlook Park. The desk clerk was not surprised to be facing two men wanting two rooms at two in the morning. As the name indicated, this was a hotel that catered to sailors, which the clerk assumed we were, and sailors arrive in port, or come off drunks, at all hours.

I quickly climbed into bed. Exhaustion had hit me the moment I saw it, sagging though it was. Nonetheless, as my head hit the pillow, it sped up with the urgency to make sense of the events of the past couple of days.

I now knew what this game was about. York was right. There was little that was virtual about the realities I had been put through. Veritas, York had called it, Latin for truth. I had been absolutely convinced of the truth of the experiences I was having, even while maintaining an opinion that they could in no way be true. Although obviously not perfected, it was a technology far advanced from today's computer graphic virtual realities, as my 911 was from a Model T—but for what purpose? Name it, anything from entertainment to brainwashing and everything in between—if there is anything in between.

A commercial item then, a very commercial item that would not just comfortably compete with the competition; one that could—some would assume—annihilate the competition. With a patent on this technology, you would have a 17 to 20-year monopoly, depending on the outcome of certain legislation in Washington. Enough time to profit greatly and establish real expertise in both the technology and in the creation and improvement of software for the technology. It was the Big Score, El Dorado, a license to print money. Think of it how you may; it could be a compunction-punching goal for certain individuals.

Certain individuals like Zhelyu Batsarov.

What was he doing here?

Batsarov, "The Bulgarian Cowboy," was well known to Western Intelligence. He had worked for them while serving his other masters in the State Secret Service during the last years of Communist rule. It was not so much that he had been a double agent as he had been a happy reporter of any convincing information that Communism was dying which would encourage the West to encourage the situation. He was—paradoxically it seemed at the time, for it meant the end of his state-funded career—anxious for the "New World Order" to begin. It was not the West and the joys of representative democracy he loved; it was the "Wild West" and the joys of sudden, unfettered Capitalism. Wide-open spaces for entrepreneurial thuggery were what he was looking for. Batsarov saw himself as a cowboy. Not a cowpuncher, a dirt-encrusted driver of cattle to market, but one of the red-bandanna-wearing outlaws known by that name who crossed six guns with the likes of Wyatt Earp, who was himself a bit of an entrepreneurial relativist regarding the Law of the Land. Batsarov had a six-gun, a Colt 45 he claimed Cole Younger had used, and a lasso that he was well known for the amusement of his rope tricks. He was also well known as the Bulgarian bore who would ask every American operative that he encountered, "Do you know Clint Eastwood?"

Once Communism fell, Batsarov set up shop with Krassimir Indzhova, a former Olympic wrestler, to form VeriGroup, ostensibly a legitimate commercial group controlling real estate, oil, mining, and agribusiness. But it also had an array of security services offering "protection" to all the new businesses, large and small, flourishing in the New World Order. This was Batsarov's main charge. It was assumed it had made him happy, rich, and settled.

So what was he doing in America involved with film/computer geeks? Maybe it had something to do with the fact that the "security guards" he oversaw became known by the whispered nickname of "Wrestlers" instead of "Cowboys." A territorial fight perhaps? One he lost? So, in the grand tradition of the Old West, did Batsarov leave to find new territory out west?

But how did he get involved in this little affair? It was a question I couldn't answer by just musing away in Sailor's Haven. But I did know this: His involvement did not cause the death of David Finch. Finch's own greedy ego being sideswiped by the greedy ego of Paul Hinckley was the cause, indirect though it may have been. But Batsarov was certainly the cause of the violation of Finch's body; that was certainly something Batsarov would think of and quickly carry out. And the destruction of York's boat—that would have been second nature to Batsarov.

Were there any potential outrages on the horizon?

I made a mental note to get in touch with Jim Skinner at Caltech first thing in the morning.

Was Batsarov the main ingredient in this stew? I doubted it. I had a suspicion about who might be, but to find the tracks on the trail that would lead to that person, I had to question a couple of people first, including a man in Portland who was best known for revealing the delights of prancing prunes.

xx

Roee came into my room and woke me up. He was dressed in his own clothes, which were freshly laundered and pressed. He put a pile of my clothes, similarly recovered, on the foot of my bed.

"How did you get this done so quickly?" I asked.

"Please!" He admonished. Sometimes I forget that Roee does not like his miracles questioned. "Your shirt is in good condition, but I suggest you wear this." He threw at me a store-wrapped turtleneck pullover. I reached for the bandages on my neck. It was a good idea.

"What time is it?"

"Ten-thirty."

"Damn! I should have gotten up earlier. We need to call Jim Skinner." "I've already tried. His home number is unlisted, but a friend at the phone company—"

"George?"

Roee smiled. "Yeah, George. He got it for me. No answer, only a machine. I called Caltech. They would not connect me with his lab. They would only take a message. I guess it's his standing order. I could literally 'hear' the operator's eyes go to the top of her head. I think her patience has been worn thin by eccentric scientists."

"I'll call the Captain, then, give him an update, and ask him to check out Skinner."

xx

We took a taxi back to the marina and found our rental car undisturbed, except for a parking ticket.

"I'll call the Captain on this." Roee said. "He might have friends up here."

I shook my head and took the ticket. "Always pay parking tickets, Roee. It builds up good Karma for when you really need to get away with something."

We drove to the animation studio of Johnny Lynton on N.W. 24th Avenue. Lynton was an interesting character. Originally, he started as a high school art teacher who became frustrated in trying to get to his students. He soon decided to communicate on a level they understood— film. So he lobbied for and got the funding to start an animation class. Clay was the easiest medium for beginners to work in, and soon he had a group of students sculpting strange little creatures and making them do—usually—violent, adolescent, yet funny, actions. After 10 years of this program, he was named Portland Teacher of the Year but denied a raise. In protest, he quit and formed a small animation production house staffed by the talent he had trained over the years. At first, they did raw, funny clay animation TV commercials for the local market, work that got seen at film festivals. Soon major agencies were asking him to bid on national spots. At this point, he named his studio Johnny-on-the-Spot Productions and started churning out very distinctive commercials. His biggest hit was a series of spots for the Prune Growers Association of America, in which anthropomorphic long-hair prunes with cute faces sang and danced to the tune of "Let the Sun Shine."

Let the Prunes in
Let the Prunes in

The Prancing Prunes were a big hit. They were credited with bringing more regularity to America than three hundred years of Sunday sermons. But clay, despite being highly moldable, was limiting to Lynton and he soon branched out and became one of the first explorers in the possibilities of computer animation. His work, at first, was not slick, but it had something most computer animation lacked at that time—spontaneity, humor, and life. His company, now renamed Johnny Lynton Productions, grew beyond commercials, moving into music videos and the occasional TV special. It became one of the most publicized success stories of Portland, and Lynton became a major figure in Portland society. Then he tried to break into features. It was tough going. Wildcatters can produce commercials and TV oddities but features of any great scope are really the product of the Hollywood based. Lynton hated that. He decided to promote his studio and himself by sponsoring an annual Creativity Conference, bringing up major players from Hollywood to sit on panels and impress the locals.

There was something of Mohammed in Lynton.

"I'm Special Agent Herrington, and this is Special Agent McNally," I said to the receptionist as we displayed our Federal IDs. "I apologize for not having an appointment, but it is important that we see Mr. Lynton now."

Lynton's office was on the second floor of his studio, which was a lavishly converted warehouse. The ground floor, we saw as Lynton's assistant guided us, was taken up with computer workstations, displays of past work, and a glass-encased conference room. The employees were mostly young, casually dressed, very Pacific Northwest types— lumberjacks melded with hippies. Lynton himself was a man of medium height with thinning brown hair poorly cut and combed with his hand. He had a face wide enough to support the broad grin he greeted us with. "Please sit down. I'm really intrigued. Why would Federal Agents want to talk to me?" he said in a voice not high nor low, but in that in-between, soothing, windy type usually called pleasant.

"Mr. Lynton," I started, "we are investigating a fairly sensitive matter, and we would like to ask you a few questions about some individuals you may know."

"Who? I can't imagine?"

Roee played his part and looked to scribbles in a notebook he held. "Craig York. Jim Skinner. David Finch."

"Oh. Huey, Dewey, and Louie."

"Excuse me?" Roee confessed confusion.

"You know, Donald's nephews. That's what they called themselves. Although part of the joke was that they would never reveal who was who."

Roee was still confused. "Donald who?"

"Well, Donald Duck, of course."

"I see," Roee said, although I doubt if he did. Walt Disney Comics had not been the preferred reading on the kibbutz.

"Does this have anything to do with Jim's work at Caltech?"

"We can't say," I said.

"Because I didn't think he was doing anything for the government. I mean, the last time I talked to him, he was really clear about not taking any Federal funding. Got into a big fight with the people at Caltech, I understand. But what could they do? He had his own financing."

"How's that?"

"He created the Prancing Prunes. He was thirteen years old, working for me on a work permit, and came up with the idea of the Prancing Prunes when we were bidding for this contract. The characters were a wonderful design. I knew we had something the second I saw them. When the advertising agency flipped and wanted to go for it, I said fine, but I retain the copyright on the characters. They had no problems with that. They thought it was just going to be a one-shot special for the Super Bowl. Damn things turned into an industry, and I controlled it. But I gave Jim 50% of all the profits. He's made a fortune off them."

"That was unusually generous of you," I said with an air of cynicism, playing the part.

"Yeah, sad comment though that is. I would like to think that it was just usually fair of me. To be honest with you, had Jim been an adult employee I might have just let work-for-hire throw all the profits my way, but he was a kid, delighting us with his precociousness. My decision was probably hormonal-based."

"With such an early success, why didn't he stay in this field?"

"Oh, mere entertainment is much too small a thing to intrigue his mind. Only science could do that. Physics and biology especially, but he has never been bad at anything. Jim Skinner is definitely a genius. In the old fashion sense, you know, before the word got corrupted. He sees where no one else can see. He thinks things no one else has thought. He's a bit scary that way."

"People like that rarely have friends. Much less good friends," Roee said.

"Ah, but genius was the glue that bound Huey, Dewey, and Louie. You see, Jim is a genius and knows it. Craig is a potential genius, but you would never be able to convince him of it. And David thinks he's a genius, and you can't convince him otherwise, although, believe me, otherwise is the fact."

"And they were friends from childhood?" I asked.

"Inseparable. Thus, Huey, Dewey, and Louie. They were geeks, of course, who had banded together. Jim was a very intense child. Could read by two-and-a-half. Had to have special tutors because he was so advanced from the other kids. And his genius is wide, right brain, left brain; hard subjects, soft subjects; science, art. Like I said, scary. He was called to my attention by the school district because he was making these neat little animated films on his own with just an 8mm camera, and they felt he needed access to more sophisticated equipment."

"What about Craig York?"

"Craig is a different situation. Very advanced also—had some of the same tutors as Jim—but painfully shy. Lost his mother when he was young, which was, as you can imagine, traumatic for him. Grew up with his father on a houseboat, spending most of their time on the river. His dad became his hero. A bit of a character was Sam York. Rugged individualist. Somewhat common around here, but he stood out anyway. He was a little paranoid, in a survivalist kind of way. Man's sort of man; hunting, fishing, sports, that sort of thing. This made his relationship with his son really special because Craig was skinny, weak, and bookish. But Sam, I've got to say to his credit, was always tender with him. Nurturing, really. Took on the 'Mother' role, I guess. Never really understood Craig, though, and I think that affected Craig. Craig worked for me too. Brilliant at whatever he was asked to do, but not an initiator of things like Jim."

"We understand Jim and Craig had a falling out recently."

"Yeah—but it was a long time coming."

"How do you mean?"

"Well, if you can believe this, despite being the same age, Jim thought he was worthy of being a father figure to Craig. Not just a pal, you know, a friend, but a father figure. But then Jim was born old. The problem was, of course, Craig had a father, and one that he worshipped. Jim was jealous. He considered Sam York a redneck and couldn't understand, literally, what Craig saw in him."

"He couldn't understand the ties of family?" Roee asked.

"Family is not an intriguing enough concept for Jim. He has little need of love."

"Is he homosexual?" I asked, receiving a shutter-shot glance from Roee.

"Who? Jim or Craig?"

"Either."

"Neither. Jim especially. Learned early how sexy intelligence mixed with confidence could be. He's had lots of girls. Emphasis on the word, 'had'."

"And Craig?"

"Had a steady girlfriend in High School. Lost her when he moved to L.A. to follow Jim to Caltech. Which continues the story. Craig did not want to go to Caltech. He did not want to leave Portland, his father, or his girl. He was content to go to college locally and maybe become a science teacher. Jim insisted. Said he had to have him at Caltech. Jim's a very powerful individual and accepted the entreaties and full scholarship from Caltech, only if they would give one to Craig as well. How could Craig pass that up? So they went to Caltech, and Jim quickly became a star."

"And Craig?"

"Became Jim's very bright, high-tech dogsbody. Anyway, they finished four years' worth of studies in two and a half, then went on to graduate studies on some project of Jim's. Don't know what. He and Craig would never talk about it. Then Sam York died of cancer. He had kept his illness from Craig, who, you can imagine, felt pretty guilty after he found out. At the funeral—which, by the way, Jim couldn't take the time to attend—Craig broke down so bad they had to call an ambulance. While recovering in the hospital, he found out that his dad had taken out loans on the houseboat to pay his medical bills. He refused Medicare and Medicaid. Said it was because of his Libertarian principles. Given all that, Craig couldn't go back to Caltech. He was going to work the houseboat to pay off the loans. That boat is like the family farm to him. Jim was furious. He flew up here, and they had a big fight. Jim even offered to pay off the loans. Craig refused. It was his bid for personal liberation. I know all this because Craig came to me to pick up extra work; the houseboat fishing trips weren't really paying. He also needed to talk. So I gave him the time. I've always liked him. Jim, you're in awe of, but you can't really like."

"Did you give him work?" Roee asked.

"Oh, yes, of course. I set up a computer workstation on his boat and fed him assignments. But I told him what I would really like is a neat idea for a feature film. He was always a science fiction buff, so I told him to come up with something that would really take advantage of our computer work."

"Did he come up with something?"

"He said he did, about a year ago. But so far he hasn't shown it to me. Keeps telling me he's not done yet."

"Do you think maybe he gave it to Andy Rand?"

Lynton thought about that. He smiled a small, embarrassed smile and ran his hand through his hair. "Huh! You know, that could be. Rand was up here last year for this creativity conference I sponsor. Of course, I allow no one to approach people with scripts and such, but I did hear that Craig took him out on his boat. Rand's a fishing nut, I guess." Lynton sat there somewhat amazed. "Gosh, I wouldn't have thought Craig would be that way."

"What way?" Roee asked.

"You know, 'Hollywood.' Doing an end run around me and giving the idea to Rand. I'll bet you Dave Finch had something to do with it."

"We haven't talked much about Finch."

"Not much to say. He was a barnacle on the butts of Jim and Craig. He's a real obnoxious shit."

"Who happens to be dead."

"Really?" Lynton displayed no shock.

"He was murdered early yesterday morning."

Lynton sat there for a second or two, his face in his right hand, his mind processing the fact. Finally, he said, "I'm not surprised."

xx

Before we had gone to Lynton's studio, I had gotten a hold of the Captain.

"You're calling from Portland, no doubt."

"Figured that out, did you?

"I do work for a very professional outfit, Fixxer. I've got two men flying up there now. Do you, by any chance, have Craig York in hand?"

"Sorry. Your guys will not find him here."

"Dead?"

"Snatched."

"What for?"

"This whole thing has complexities best discussed when face to face." "But York did it?"

"He killed Finch, yes. But it was an accident."

"What did he do? Slip while chopping vegetables?"

"He is responsible for the wound to the chest only."

"Oh."

"I told you—complexities."

"You know, you should just turn this whole thing over to us now."

"Practicing for open mic night at the Comedy Store, are we?"

"Fixxer, someday..."

"After you retire, we'll have plenty of laughs. Right now it is imperative that you get in contact with Jim Skinner at Caltech."

"Finch's other correspondent?"

"That's right. He may be in some danger."

"I have no authority in Pasadena."

"See the limitations of your outfit."

"Ha-ha. All right. Get in touch with him and do what?"

"We will be flying home in two hours. Get him to agree to see me. Anywhere he chooses. Then cover his back."

xx

We settled down in an Alaska Airlines MD80 for the flight home. Roee was pensive and was making notes on a pad. They served drinks, we both ordered coffee and as I was just about to grumble a complaint about the bag of peanuts the stewardess tossed onto my tray, Roee reached into his pocket and pulled out a small can of cashews. I looked a question at him, and he responded with:

"Please!"

"If I was gay, I would marry you," I said in all sincerity.

"If you were gay, you would be serving me," he answered, then turned back to his notes for a moment, then back to me. "I assume that the really important information gathered from Lynton, besides the histories of Huey, Dewey, and Louie, fascinating as they were, is the fact that Andy Rand has entered the picture."

"That's the confirmation I was looking for, yes. I had a suspicion that York had lied to me about not connecting with Rand during the Creativity Conference."

"A motion picture executive with a golden gut, a former Communist intelligence operative, currently operating as a thug—a strange combination."

"Yes, well, you wouldn't think hot dogs and cottage cheese would combine well, but I once knew a man who ate them every day for lunch."

"Hot dogs and cottage cheese?"

"He would slice up the hot dogs, then mix them with the cottage cheese."

"Hot dogs and cottage cheese?"

"Hebrew National was his favorite."

"Hot dogs and cottage cheese?"

"He got hooked years ago when a high protein fad diet was on the market."

"Canned peaches I can see."

"Hot dogs and canned peaches?"

Roee just sighed and turned back to his notes.

"Batsarov did not recognize me," I stated, returning to the track.

"Of course not. You're the only one I've ever known who's managed to stay out of the files of the various agencies."

"Not true."

"Not true?"

"I've been in the files of three nations. Well, two nations and one rather sophisticated liberation movement."

With great and touching sincerity Roee said, "I'm shocked!"

"Of course, I did manage to eventually exorcise those files of all information pertaining to myself."

"How?"

"I'll tell you if I ever have to do it again. The point is, what did Batsarov make of me?"

"He expressed no opinion that I heard. He may have thought you were just the go-between representing Hinckley, the one York reported to his investor—I think we can assume that to be Andy Rand?"

"Yes, I think so."

"Maybe a private investigator. Or an agent or lawyer; someone inconsequential like that. To him, of course, you became a guinea pig, advantageously there to do some tests on."

"The medical monitoring."

"Exactly."

"They will have returned by now," I said. "Found the dead Paddy O'Shane, and certain precious items missing.

"This will piss him off."

"No longer inconsequential."

"Their only choice will be to get information from Hinckley," Roee warned.

I took out a credit card and released the airphone from the back of the seat in front of me. I called Norton, gave him certain instructions, and then asked him to patch me to Hinckley.

"You'll never guess the phone call I just got," were Hinckley's first words.

"A call from someone you never heard of before, but who hinted that they represented Andy Rand, who further hinted that Rand is setting up an exciting new company backed by more money than God would have if he needed money, who told you that they are aware of V, love it, and want to make a preemptive offer for the rights and your services to write, produce and direct. He further hinted that their offer would be far more money than you have ever made on any one picture."

The other end of the line remained silent for a minute. Then: "You know, Fixxer, you're one scary but fascinating fucker. Why don't you come up to the ranch this weekend? We could spend some time together, and get to know each other better."

"I'm sorry, I don't—bond."

"Oh."

"They want you to meet?"

"Tonight."

"Don't. Call Norton. He will send a limo for you. You and your family will be leaving town. Enjoy your time off."

"Hey, wait a minute, I—"

"It's either that or be dead by tomorrow morning."

"But—"

"Just do it. I owe you no explanations when I am saving your life." I hung up.

"Do you think he will follow your instructions?" Roee asked.

"Absolutely. In a shoot-out, he's the kind of 'cowboy' who would pee before the bullet hit him."

Roee did not laugh. There may have been the hint of a smile, but that could just as well have been gas. "I assume you are going to bring

Rand to justice."

"Or justice to Rand."

"Not what you have been paid to do."

"Call it a hobby."

"Dangerous."

"Possibly—not at all if it was just Rand, of course. What could he do? Put me into turnaround? But with Batsarov... Like Escobar, he probably has a framed picture of Al Capone."

"I wouldn't discount Rand."

"You wouldn't?"

"May I wax philosophical?"

"Well—it's a short flight."

"I believe there is a constant complaint that Hollywood makes films that are too violent."

"From certain quarters, yes."

"Hollywood defends itself by saying it would rather make only high-quality dramas exploring facets of the human condition, but that the audience wants destruction and death, not instruction and depth. And it is, after all, called Show *Business*."

"The standard line," I agreed.

"And one, we must admit, supported by box office receipts. Nevertheless, it is, essentially, bullshit."

"Bullshit?"

"Hollywood does not provide fantasies; Hollywood acts them out. They make the films they do because ripping flesh is in the bones of film executives. All film executives have a strong capacity to kill. It comes from a vengeful streak in them brought on by the indignities they had to suffer on the way up. Their basic jealousy and envy of the creative, and their putrefying mortification over the fact that they will always only be able to bask in the light of talent and glamour and never be able to produce any of their own, have an effect as well, I'm sure. Luckily, this capacity to kill is diluted and made weak by the laying down of cinematic carnage—catharsis before the fact. But, give film executives enough motivation, show them a goal worthy of a Roman general's triumph, and I'm sure they are capable of less frivolous, more serious, devastatingly destructive tendencies."

I considered this. I considered Roee. "Are you sure you've never written and submitted a screenplay?"

"I wouldn't give them the satisfaction," Roee snorted.

CHAPTER 10

CHOO CHOO CH'BOOGIE

Your Mr. Skinner is one arrogant son-of-a-bitch," the Captain said as we slipped into his car at LAX.

"Yes, well, that's the problem with giving life forms consciousness," I responded. "It goes to their head."

"What?"

"Captain, will he meet us?" Roee said, getting to the point.

"Hey, that recipe for Baklava?" The Captain said to Roee, straying from it.

"Yes, sorry, I will send it to you."

"Thanks. Mr. Skinner, speaking through the laboratory door he was not willing to open for one of my men, informs us that he will be taking his usual late lunch at three PM at a restaurant called Sorriso in Old Town Pasadena. If we wish to see him, we can do so at that time. Otherwise, he refuses to alter his routine. You said he might be in some danger?"

"That's right."

"Good."

"Captain, please. You're a public servant."

"Yeah, I'd like to serve him on a bed of rice. Now, shed some light, please."

"The murder was accidental, a heated argument between two old friends that got out of hand.

"That's not an accident. That's manslaughter."

"Well, I'll let you work out the technicalities. Everything else, which York was unaware of, was an attempt by certain parties to keep the authorities away from York."

"Why? What's so special about York that he needs to be protected?

Not to mention 'snatched.'"

"He is in the position to make a credible claim to be the inventor of a process known as Veritas, which could revolutionize and dominate several industries, such as education, medicine, and entertainment, including pornography and the drug trade."

"What do you mean, 'claim'? Is he the inventor or not?"

"I don't know. He was certainly there at the creation, though, and maybe, at the least, the co-inventor."

"This Skinner being the other co-, I take it."

"That's right."

"And this Veritas is potentially worth...?"

"Over the life of the patent? A trillion or three."

"Whew! I'd whistle if I could."

Roee whistled.

"Thanks," the Captain said.

"Don't mention it."

"Well, the old cynicism wins again: Money is the root of all evil."

"Yes," I said. "But it produces such a nice big tree with plenty of shade."

"So, who are the certain parties?"

I explained about Batsarov and asked the Captain to check with Immigration and find out if he had entered the U.S. legally under his own name and, if so, when and how. Then I detailed my suspicions about Andy Rand.

"Well, from what you tell me, we could put on the heat to get York. We could arrest him for manslaughter, at least. Batsarov, if he's here legally, we could get him on obstruction of justice, kidnapping, if that's what it really was, and the Oregon authorities would want to talk to him about the arson of the houseboat. Assuming we could prove any of this. If he's not here legally, we can deport the sport. As far as Rand is concerned, you haven't got anything but a supposition that he's involved. He's in a perfect position to plead ignorance over the not-so-nice things that have happened. He's just an investor, after all. Not shaping up to be very exciting."

"Give it time, Captain. The plans of Rand have been frustrated, and frustrated men do stupid and dangerous things."

xx

The Captain dropped us off at home to pick up the 911. Then we drove to Pasadena. It was a depressing drive through socked-in pollution. All color was dulled and barely deserved the appellation. Distance could not be perceived when we were speeding along on the 134, leaving little visual evidence that urbanized life was to our right and a mountain range was to our left. Is it any wonder most people in L.A. have tunnel vision?

We pulled off the freeway at Orange Grove, slipped onto Colorado Boulevard, passed the Norton Simon Museum, traveled down to Fair Oaks, turned right, and left on Green Street to park in the city parking structure.

We got out of our cars, and I headed towards the stairway exit to the south.

"Hey!" the Captain shouted, pointing north, "The elevator over here is closer to Colorado."

"But then you miss seeing the Castle Green." I continued quickly, leaving the Captain and Roee no choice but to follow me. We descended the stairs and pushed out the narrow door at the bottom to face the old Castle Green.

"What a weird building," the Captain said.

"Yes," I said. "Weird and somewhat wonderful."

I don't know if one could categorize the architectural style of the six-story Castle Green. There was a hint of the Moroccan in its towers and decorations and Spanish in its facade, mixed with a touch of Colonial Revival. California Hodgepodge might best describe it. Built in 1898, Castle Green's most interesting feature, among several, is an elevated covered bridge that runs from its entrance—which was set back quite a way from the street—to the sidewalk, where it abruptly ends, as if sliced off. Originally the bridge continued across the street and connected with the main building of the now long-gone Hotel Green, of which it was once an annex. Slightly decrepit looking, although under refurbishment, Castle Green now leads a very active life as condos; an old-world romantic place for weddings; a unique spot for corporate functions, and, of course, a dress-able location for the shooting of film and TV. It's a bit like a sprightly old lady in clothes old enough to be antique. There is wit there and an I-don't-give-a-damn attitude mixed with a mild patina of sadness.

"Gentlemen," I said to the Captain and Roee with a formality influenced by the view. "When you find an architectural and historical oddity in Los Angeles and its environs, you must pay homage to it. For they are few and— this being Los Angeles and environs—very far between."

"Fixxer?"

"Yes, Captain."

"Write the guidebook later. Let's get back to the very serious matter at hand."

I turned to the Captain and thought it odd that I had never noticed how thick his eyebrows were. "You're suited to your badge, Captain." He took it as a compliment.

The Captain probably wouldn't have appreciated my thoughts about Old Town Pasadena, how I considered it the most refreshingly un-Los Angeles-like spot on the local map. It was just plain downtown Pasadena in the 1920s, built like most of the average size American cities of that time, with dominating 5-to-10-story brick office buildings with retail shops on the ground floor—a nice, solid Babbitt look, possibly dull when conceived, but now charming and nostalgic, and, most importantly, substantial. Unlike most of L.A., which is just a swathe of flat and smooth interlocked suburbs blistered now and then with commercial districts made up of one and two-story box buildings of no particular architectural interest. This stretch of three blocks down Colorado Boulevard had become a slum for a while, a sad disrepair of these grand old buildings; empty, boarded-up shops; the Le Sex Shoppe adult bookstore being the only highlight. But gentrification came in, money wanting a pleasant place to attract more money, and the area was recovered. Now it has the required restaurants, pricey handcraft stores, upscale movie multiplexes, and fancy bookstores to entice people happy to be among the relatively attractive with disposable income. Le Sex Shoppe is still here—but it's been given a classy facelift to mix well with its neighbors, including a window you can window-shop through.

We entered Sorriso, a Cucina Italiana, as they liked to say. It's a pleasant space designed like many of today's trendy restaurants, with a two-story-high ceiling and the ventilating system hanging out for all to see. That's okay; there is nothing obscene about a ventilating system. And it allows the high ceilings, and high ceilings, as the builders of cathedrals long ago learned, give people a pleasant, elevated sense of insignificance.

The restaurant was virtually empty. In the back, at a small table with no other chairs surrounding it, sat a young man in a stark white long-sleeved shirt, barely faded jeans, and Timberlake hiking shoes. His face featured a high forehead that his thin brown hair fell forward on; bright blue ice cube eyes; a roundish nose; a mouth most natural when sneering or snarling, and pretentious dark fuzz that he probably called a beard. I had no doubt this was Jim Skinner.

"May we speak with you?" was my introduction.

Skinner looked up from American Physics Review and addressed me. "Are you the police?"

The Captain pushed forward and showed him his ID. "I'm the police."

"Then who are these two?"

"Two who wish to speak with you," Roee stated.

He looked at us. Carefully. As if his science was not physics but physiognomy. Are you good guys? He was wondering. Are you bad? Should I care? Finally, he said, "Speak."

"Let's move to a larger table," I said.

Dismissing the thought, he said, "I never sit anywhere else," and returned to his journal.

"Oh," I said, not surprised and not impressed. Then I grabbed his table—while smiling, I'm sure—and jerked it violently aside. It and his food crashed to the floor.

"Hey!" He started to rise.

"Sit!' I yelled. "You never sit anywhere else, so sit!" Then I grabbed a large, empty table and dragged it to Skinner as Roee thrust several hundred dollars into the hands of the management and asked them to please replace Mr. Skinner's meal and bring the rest of us coffee. We put chairs around the table and sat. I stared at Skinner and said, "If a man is a genius, it is safe to assume he is smart enough to know it. I assume you know that you are a genius, and I assume that knowledge combined with your fortunate youth has led to your supercilious arrogance. That is fine. I have little tolerance for humility. The truly talented have no right to it, and everybody else with so much to be humble about shouldn't be flaunting it. But for these coming moments, you and I will live in a vacuum, a pure state of question and answer. I will ask the questions, and you will answer in a generous spirit of information sharing. Now, I see a little sliver of fear has crossed your right eye. Put it aside. I will not ask you to reveal exactly how your device works or how you get inside a person's head and collaborate with the information already there to create new realities. But I will ask you about your motivations, I will ask you about certain personal history, I will ask you about the present and the future, and you will answer, and answer well, or that little sliver of fear will grow into a huge, massive, sharp stake that I will drive through your eye and into your head. There it will lodge, impeding all other possible activity."

An incredibly apprehensive waitress brought Skinner's meal and our coffee. I sipped mine. "Excellent. Jamaican Blue?"

"Uh, yes, sir," the waitress said.

"I'll take three pounds. Whole bean."

"Uh, yes, sir."

She left. Skinner smiled while twirling some pasta primavera onto his fork.

"Coffee is not good for you."

"In a world where mothers give birth, as Beckett said, astride a grave, coffee is the least of my worries."

Skinner took his bite of pasta primavera and chewed slowly. He was savoring it. That was good.

"You know that David Finch is dead?"

He nodded while swallowing, then said. "His father called me. Jigsaw puzzled to death, as I understand it."

"Black humor over your friend's death?" Roee questioned.

He shrugged. "I guess it's my way of handling grief."

"Did you consider him your best friend?"

"David was not best at anything. But he was amusing with his intense, almost religious need to be right about movies. He was fun to argue with because the outcome of the arguing was meaningless."

"Unlike a conflict in science?"

"Very unlike."

"Craig York killed him."

That stopped a forkful of pasta from rising. "Craig? Craig couldn't kill. He's the weakest of the weak. And as good as he is at gutting fish, he certainly couldn't dismember a body. It's a thought that would never occur to him."

"You're right. The murder was accidental. Others accomplished the dismemberment."

"Who? Butchers in training?"

I took the Veritas glasses from my pocket and placed them on the table. "People who want to exploit these."

Skinner looked at the glasses. Then back up at me.

"Is Craig dead too?"

"Might as well be. He has sold his soul to devils."

Skinner picked up the glasses. "The prototype. I spent $35,000 developing a better pair. I thought I had safely stored these away. But, obviously, Craig stole them."

I put the gold CD-Rs down on the table.

"Copies of my programming and software, I take it." "Yes."

"And he would have been able to build a transmitter. Basic child's play."

"Do you call it Veritas?" Roee asked.

"Yes, that's what I call it. Did he steal that too? Craig is highly intelligent but has the originality of a fruit fly."

"So what are we talking about here?" The Captain asked. "Virtual reality?"

"Virtual reality? Virtual reality sucks!" Skinner declared. "What I have created far outstrips something as clunky and inelegant as VR, which is nothing more than bad computer animation slammed through to your optic nerve combined with rudimentary sound design screamed into your ears to impress your auditory nerves. But if they can yank you out of equilibrium, no matter how crudely, they think they're giving you something close to reality. It's a con game. What is reality? Not the three dimensions of your surroundings, but the four dimensions of your surroundings as processed by your brain. Reality is what we perceive it to be in the moment, combined with what we have perceived it to be in the past and what we are assuming it will be in the future. Reality is what our brain makes out of all of the input from our senses, not just sight, and sound, but all of our senses providing information that runs the gauntlet from abstract data to silly pleasure to excruciating pain. The key to a manufactured reality that is Veritas—truth—lies in directly manipulating the brain rather than manipulating the senses through "virtual" renditions of reality. If we have a direct link with the brain and know what to communicate, if we can "mock" all the senses instead of just piggybacking on two of them, then the brain will cooperate with us in perceiving a reality worthy of the name, Veritas. VR is like chiseling pictograms on stone. Veritas is the elegance of fine literature written on the breath of life."

"So these, uh..." The Captain picked up the glasses. "These glasses aren't like little video screens, then?"

Skinner laughed. "Absolutely not. In fact, they are in the shape of glasses as a little personal joke." Skinner reached over and took the glasses from the Captain. "The right 'lens' is a receiver collecting information from an infrared wave. The left 'lens' is a transmitter sending back information to the home unit."

"And the metal contact points in the bows are your direct link to the brain," I guessed.

"Yes."

"On some kind of an electrical level."

"You might say that. But, assuming a singularity, the question is: what level?"

"And the information, depending on exactly what it is, visual, aural, neural, cognitive, is somehow routed to the proper area of the brain for processing. And the brain, thinking this is actual, sensually delivered information, processes it into—reality."

"Very good. You've had a science background."

I smiled and asked, "How were you inspired to create Veritas?"

"Oh, let's just say I dreamed it up."

"Of course. You mean that literally, don't you? You woke up from a dream one morning and said to yourself, as we all do on occasion, 'That was so real.' Then it hit you. If you could get inside the brain, you could create and control dreams."

"You have a multiplex of levels to your thinking. Congratulations, Mr...?"

"Those I allow, call me Fixxer."

"A nickname? Perhaps you are related to the character actor Paul Fix, who co-starred as the sheriff in *The Rifleman*, starring Chuck Connors and Johnny Crawford?"

"It is more designation than name. I am known for fixing things."

"Really? I have nothing that is broke."

"Veritas has been in the hands of some very dangerous people."

"But it no longer is."

"That will not stop them."

Skinner shrugged. "Well—a rapist can't do much without a prick."

"Rape is not a crime of sex, but a crime of violence," the Captain said.

"Don't you believe it," Skinner snorted. "Rape is the gene survival strategy of losers."

I took a good look at Skinner. He was a young man in his early twenties, with a face hardly worn. And yet his ice blue eyes darted about to be both everywhere at once and to dodge incoming slings and arrows. "You perceive yourself to be surrounded by rapists, don't you?" I asked without accusing.

Skinner thought for a moment, playing with this metaphor. He smiled. "If you equate intelligence with manhood—what other perception could I have?"

"I have experienced Veritas."

"Really?" Immediately he became genuinely interested. "And did you enjoy it?"

"Oh, yes, I love the smell of feces and urine."

"Ah, the Castle Program."

"Not sure I enjoyed the panic of drowning."

"Based on one of my favorite science fiction novels. And the enjoyment comes when you are saved."

"The bear rug, though..."

"I take no credit for that. Craig insisted on it, but then—he needed it."

"I found things missing, and my memories did not always successfully fill the gap."

"You experienced an early version. I'm much closer to perfection now."

"And when it's perfect, what will you do with it?"

"You know the power of what I've created. Do you know how often science has created power only to see it abused? I kept trying to explain that to Craig. I had to sketch out a whole scenario of abuse that could happen. Sketch it out like a movie to get him to understand it. What am I going to do with Veritas? I'm going to do with it, as I will. I'm not going to let the rapists have it."

"You're very confident," I said.

"And you would like to mock me because you know that that confidence comes from the independence of wealth. Wonderful country, isn't it?" He smiled. "You can draw a set of anthropomorphic prunes and make a fortune."

He dropped the smile. "You underestimate me. The prunes did not do it alone. I've taken that money and rolled it over a thousand times. Yes, isn't he amazing? He has another talent. I play—no, I *work* the stock market. I'm up every morning at three-thirty. I'm at my computer at four. I make or lose between 200 and 350,000 dollars by 8 A.M. I've been fortunate to make it more often than lose it. I need no one. Not the government. Not private investment. I am the most enviable man the world has ever seen."

"Have you recently been approached by anyone unaware of how enviable you are?"

"A man with a foreign accent tried to—initiate a discussion."

"And you told him...?"

"I told him to fuck off."

"Well, a genius may not necessarily be smart. If he tries another initiation, would you cooperate with me and be more pleasant to him?"

"No."

"Why not?"

"Because I'm not convinced that you're not a rapist."

"If we don't get these people, you will come to harm. As will others."

"I cannot come to harm."

"Why?"

"Because the 21st century is going to be my century."

I took a large swallow of coffee, took a moment to enjoy it, and then said, "Young master Skinner, you suffer from the greatest folly of youth. You think you're immortal. Unfortunately, you now have adversaries that disagree. I can help you."

"Why?"

"Because I choose to do so."

"To be polite, I should express appreciation for your concern, but politeness takes time, and I have little to spare. I am so close to perfection; I must return to it." He stood up and gestured towards the glasses and CD-Rs. "May I have my property back?"

The Captain looked at me. I shook my head. He turned to Skinner and repeated the action. "Evidence in a murder case, but I can give you a receipt."

"No, never mind. I trust you. Thanks for picking up the check."

I stopped him before he could walk out. "Just two more questions." He turned with a sigh. "Yes?"

"Do you know any Hollywood trivia?"

"It's a hobby I shared with Dave and Craig."

"I've been trying to remember for days. The apartment building on Rossmore that Mae West lived in, was it the Ravenswood or the El Royale?" He started to open his mouth, then stopped. He chuckled.

"Well, on rare occasions, my genius fails me. I can't remember. You had a second question?"

"Yes—which one were you? Huey, Dewey, or Louie?"

The ice-blue eyes dulled. They stopped their darting. A mild sadness crept in. Jim Skinner turned and left.

xx

We had another cup of coffee. The Captain put in a call to his contact at Immigration. There was no record of Zhelyu Batsarov having entered the country. So he was here illegally and undercover. We gave the Captain a description, and he said he would put out an APB, but we knew it would prove useless. He said he would try to keep some men detailed to Skinner, but with the manpower problems of the LAPD, it would not be easy, and he hated to call in the Pasadena Police on something so full of conjecture.

As Roee and I traveled home on the 134, just outside of Pasadena, just into Eagle Rock, a sound that might have been a sonic boom interrupted our conversation.

"What? Is the Space Shuttle landing at Edwards?" Roee responded casually.

"No," I said, "The shuttle always causes a double boom."

Out of instinct, I checked my rearview mirrors. The cause of the boom, or rather its effect, was rising high into the slate gray sky in the form of a black tunnel cloud. The height it was reaching indicated an immense explosion. "Turn on KPCC."

Roee did so. A fine example of "Classic American Music," as KPCC bills its fare, was on the air.

Choo choo, choo choo, ch'boogie!

Woo woo, ooh ooh, ch'boogie!

Choo choo, choo choo, ch'boogie!

Take me right back to the track, Jack!

"Hey, we've got to interrupt the music here to report that that big boom you just heard if you live anywhere here in the San Gabriel Valley seems to have come from Caltech, which is practically right next door to us here at Pasadena City College, so you know we've been pretty shook up here. Nonetheless, we will get all the information we can on it. It sounded like an explosion, and our general manager reported a black cloud rising from the Caltech campus. Now this follows right on the heels of the sniper incident that we reported before going to the last song. We

don't know if the two are related, but—"

Roee turned the radio off.

"Well—I guess the 21st Century will just have to do without Mr. Skinner," I said as the freeway curved us up towards Glendale, and I lost sight of the black cloud in my rearview mirror.

CHAPTER 11

SCIENCE KILLS

What a fuckin' mess!" the Captain declared over the phone.

"Deaths?" I asked as I settled back into my chair in the library.

"Sixteen, including Skinner. Shot by sniper fire or killed in the explosion."

"Lay it out for me."

"At about three thirty-seven, two individuals, both male, it is assumed, from the roof of the Millikan Library, at ten stories, the tallest building on the Caltech campus, began firing high-powered rifles. One fired west down onto Bechtel Mall and Wilson Avenue and the structures across the avenue, like the Geological Survey and Financial Aid. The other shot east into the campus along an area of heavy foot traffic heading towards the Athenaeum Faculty Club. The shooting was random but precise. They were mostly shooting people's kneecaps off. But Skinner, they shot right through the heart. They had a perfect view of his parking space and got him just as he got out of his car. He was the first shot. Just before the shooting, two huge banners were unfurled, one on the west and the other on the east. Both said the same thing: SCIENCE KILLS."

"A ruse, of course."

"Knowing what we know, of course, it was, but as you may have gathered from the news, everybody else is taking it seriously."

"Let's make sure that remains status quo. It can only help us."

"Agreed. The Pasadena PD SWATs got there quickly but were powerless as the library towers over everything, and there was no way to get a shot at the snipers. As for helicopters, you probably heard what happened to the KTLA news chopper."

"Portable surface-to-air missile, I assume."

"Absolutely—most likely a sidewinder. It was just a warning.

Smashed the anti-torque rotor. Great fuckin' pilot, I'll tell you, he managed to set the chopper down on the athletic field. They proved their point. No police chopper could get close."

"The explosion was centered in Skinner's lab, of course."

"Yes, in the Bridge Laboratory, on the south side. The building faces the library on the north side."

I was quiet for a moment. So was the Captain. He knew when I was thinking. Finally, I said, "Yell out if something doesn't make sense. Batsarov took a crew of thugs to Caltech with the single purpose of breaking into Skinner's lab and stealing the Veritas glasses and software. For two reasons: One, they lost the prototypes to me and probably got into trouble for that blunder. And two, Skinner couldn't be bought, which I'm sure York kept telling them would be the case. Also, knowing from York what security measures Skinner had—serious ones, I assume?"

"Yeah. We talked to the Caltech administration about that. All put in at Skinner's expense. It was state-of-the-art."

"I'll bet. And knowing that, they knew they couldn't be subtle about breaking in."

"So they needed a diversion to get people's, not to mention the police's, attention focused away from Skinner's lab."

"Yes. Some anti-science political snipers are a rather radical diversion, but Bulgarians are a melodramatic lot. Not to mention film executives. They smashed their way into the lab, not caring about alarms, found what they came for—York either told them where it would be or might even have been dragged along to guide—then they planted the explosives, to be set off by remote control or a timer, doesn't really matter. Then they left the lab, melding into the hysterical crowd."

"Why such a huge bomb?"

"To make it seem just part and parcel with the snipers' political action. I'm sure they hope the authorities will assume the location of the bomb was as random as the sniper fire. The snipers got away?"

"Yes."

"I'm sure they posed as air conditioning maintenance men to get up there and geek science students to escape while the explosion became the diversion."

"A diversion to cover up escaping from a diversion. Very slick."

"Yes. Sick slick."

"Why did they kill Skinner? I mean, he was obviously targeted."

"It was imperative. They want no challenge to their patent application. Plus, look how neat the plan was. The first shot kills their intended target and starts the mayhem for their diversion."

"Two birds—one stone."

"Hell of a deadly stone."

"Well, the Pasadena PD will do a thorough investigation."

"And we will not get one piece of evidence that will lead to Batsarov. I know the kind of training he's had. But worse still, there will be no evidence to link Andy Rand."

"So, assuming you are right about Rand, how will you get him?"

"Wish I knew, Captain. Thanks for the report." I hung up. I thought. I cursed. I picked up the phone and punched Roee's extension.

"Yes?"

"Get to the computer. I want to see everything, absolutely everything, on Andy Rand, including all press accounts, pros and cons, rumors, hearsay, and verbal indiscretions people have made to us regarding him. Then call Norton. Have him arrange a meeting for me with Torvald Engstrand at NewVue. Then make up a big pot of that Jamaican Blue. We have some late-night reading to get through."

"Well, that all sounds to be just incredible fun, Fixx, but may I make the outrageous, but I think not irrational, suggestion that we can put that off until tomorrow? It's been a rough few days. Sleep beckons me, and I'm sure it has you on its shortlist."

"Carnage has been committed today, Roee. Death of innocent *Homo sapiens*."

"Yes, and if by any chance Mr. Rand and Batsarov persist in that direction and finish off the rest of humanity tonight, well, at least it will be good for the snail darter, the spotted owl, and the cute-as-a-button mink."

What could you do but think about it? "You are, Sir, a philosopher of rare depth."

"Thank you. Go to bed."

The Phone rang.

"You are unavailable," Roee instructed me.

"See who it is first, please."

There was a pause as Roee dealt with it. Then he came back on. "Norton has Anne Eisley on the line."

"Oh. May I talk to her, Mr. Roee, sir, please?"

"All right. Then it's spit spot off to bed with you."

Her voice came on—pleasant tones of molten gold. "Thank you for the bath goodies. I am taking advantage of them right now. How did you know Marcel's was my favorite?"

"Elementary, my dear wet-one."

"How so?"

"They're the best. I assume you settle for nothing less."

"How true. When am I going to see you again?"

"Do you have more work for me?"

"No. I've got the role. Crane is in the hospital and very grateful for my nursing and my agreeing never to speak of the circumstances. I do costume fittings next week and start filming in three. I'm thrilled, and I'm happy. So, I have no work to offer. And, in any case, I was somewhat thinking more about play. You said 48 hours. It's been 48 hours, nearly. You said to take lots of baths. This is my fifth. So I was think—Ow!"

"Is anything wrong?"

"Uh, no. Something just—slipped."

"Oh."

"That should teach me. Besides the best, never settle for less than the real thing. Busy tomorrow?"

"I'm afraid so. Unfortunately, my time right now is not my own."

"That's very disappointing. I will be in the same situation once we start filming."

"Well, then, in these next three weeks, I will strive mightily to find, steal or make time to play. But I can promise nothing. Except to make the effort, of course."

"Not the most soothing news, but enough to hold dear. Good night."

"Good night."

She hung up. So did I. Sleep awaited. I was looking forward to it being sweet.

xx

I woke up early the next day to find all the information on Rand I required in a neat file on my desk in the library. A carafe of Jamaican Blue was being kept warm on a burner, and Roee entered with a hearty bowl of steel-cut oatmeal.

"It'll stick to your ribs, as the old American phrase goes. Although I've yet to figure out the benefit of sticky ribs."

"Keeps your heart in place."

"Really? Never thought of it that way. Much to my credit."

He left. I sipped the hot coffee, letting it excite my tongue and thrill my senses. "Ah—a drug," my body gratefully said. My body, I feel, has always been somewhat disappointed in my long-term and steadfastly square attitude toward drugs. Except for caffeine and alcohol, it has missed out entirely on all the less traditional yet well-circulated drugs and intoxicants of the era. But to listen to your body is to listen to a poor advisor, one who can lead you into the arms of your enemies. And everyone is your enemy until they prove otherwise.

My reading and thinking took me until noon, interrupted only once when Roee informed me that Norton had scheduled my meeting with Engstrand for three-thirty. By that time, I had a clear picture of Andy Rand.

He was born poor in Nebraska. "Mr. Middle America," he liked to call himself as one explanation for his golden gut. Went to a state college in Lincoln, shooting for an MBA. Bored to tears, he founded a campus film club to bring some light—all of it projected—into his life He screened the old classics and became a bit of a campus celebrity when he managed to get actors and directors from the bygone days to make personal appearances. He soon realized, though, that there was too much past tense in the word "classic." He had decided that movies were the business for him, and as movies were a business of the moment, it was people of the moment he needed to attract to the plains of Nebraska. So he did. Nobody of any real importance, of course— this was, after all, Nebraska—but people important enough to wave it in the little Nebraskan's face and tell him to call if he "ever came out to the Coast."

He quit school and went to the Coast. He is quoted as saying:

I knew then that distributing intellectual property would become the leading industry in America. Oil was dead. Steel was dead. The Japanese were poised to wipe our rears with small cars. Aerospace was downsizing. Europe and the Pacific Rim were becoming real competitors in all areas—except filmed entertainment. Only we in America seem to know how to make the common man laugh and cry and gasp at stunning action and mind-boggling effects. If I was going to be in business, I wanted to be in the growth industry of the future.

Whether this brilliance existed in the foresight of his actions or the hindsight of a victor writing history can best be answered by tracking what he did next. When he came to Hollywood, he did not call all those who had said to call. He first got himself a job in the mail room of one of the smaller talent agencies, one of the ones that did not demand an Ivy League diploma to become a shit-toting, shit-taking, shit-loving slave. *Then* he called them, putting in a friendly call, a call not saying, "I want something," which is a call no one in Hollywood wants to take, but a call saying, "I'm here, I've got something, so I'm not desperate, I just wanted to say hi," which is the kind of call that alerts the person on the other end—he's a comer; keep an eye on him. This brilliance, more instinctual than intellectual, was the brilliance of foresight.

He soon jumped from the mailroom to a "desk," handling an agent's calls, correspondence, and appointments, listening in, not speaking, learning that the Biz was the deal and the deal was the Biz. But he also learned that he did not want to be an agent. The only flesh he wanted to peddle, the only career he wanted to look out for, was his own. Now he called his Nebraska-visiting "friends" again and soon became the personal assistant to a newly-hot producer of volatile temper and loud mouth who, mentally and near physically, abused Rand, constantly screaming at him in front of others, calling him names not often heard on the plains of Nebraska. Rand eventually escaped to one of his other contacts, a young female producer who had her first hit—a simple-minded independent film about an autistic boy who asks the world's leaders the simple-minded question, "Why not peace?" —and a first look housekeeping deal at MGM. He became her director of creative affairs. Then he left her for a better offer at a director's production company, becoming his vice president of production.

Then, after two hit films for the director based on screenplays Rand found, he became the company's president. The director became the "A-List" director of the moment, giving Rand a substantial power boost. He used the power wisely, making friends, targeting enemies, and cultivating favors. After the director had an embarrassing flop film that Rand had begged him not to make, Rand took his first studio job. He did not fit in well. Studios were now parts of conglomerates with claustrophobic corporate cultures that tended to diminish all but those at the top. And even then, it was like the military: It was the uniform, not the man, that was saluted. You were you because of the company; the company wasn't the company because of you. Nevertheless, he stuck it out, suffered indignities, fought for films and lost, and spent hours getting to know and build loyalties with actors and writers not yet proven. When one of them, a good-looking hunk who could do comedy, found himself in a hit sitcom, Rand found him a feature vehicle, shoved it into the hands of the head of the studio, pushed hard to cast this "TV kid," got the green light, kept the budget minimal, and smiled as all the other studio executives ran for cover because he knew it would be a hit. It was. The other executives had ducked so deep that none could find a way to take any of the credit. Rand got it all. The film helped the studio squeak into the black that year. It won no Oscars. But no one held that against him.

Then the studio was taken over by an even more massive conglomerate. There was the attendant massacre of the studio executive ranks. It ultimately passed Rand by, who, it was rumored, may have provided the takeover company with vital financial information the studio had done its best to camouflage. He became the president of production. But he was not as happy as he could have been. He thought he deserved to become president of the studio. It meant more time to wait. It pissed him off. But he made hits. His guts were gold, everybody was sure of that, and it made their normal organic guts miserable. But what could they do? They had to love him. So Paramount grabbed him and made him president of their studio. But not an officer of the parent company, Gulf & Western. He thought he deserved to be and resented it. Again, there was more time to wait, and again it pissed him off—but he made hits for the conglomerate, hits for the board members, hits for the stockholders.

And he was a defender of the faith. Congress became concerned about violence in movies. Rand gladly testified:

Movies reflect the world. Movies aren't the world. Movies are but puffs of entertaining smoke trying for some semblance of verisimilitude. If that means we have to put violence in our movies, it's because there is violence in life. I quite frankly resent you, Congress, the makers of our laws, the guardians of our society, pointing the finger at movies. Gentlemen, use your power to remove guns from the streets, to put more cops on the beat, to end poverty and hunger, to make this a better world, and I guarantee that movies will reflect that. You give us peace; we'll give you peace in movies. I mean—to use the vernacular—Get real. Did the movies invent the atomic bomb? Do movies pollute the air? Are movies decimating whole populations of species? Gentlemen, movies don't kill. Science kills...

Ah, yes. Science kills...

Rand was well-paid and famous; he was wearing a prince's crown. But you know what every prince wants. And it's not just a princess. Then Engstrand came along, an outsider with a minor concern, but he offered Rand the opportunity to make hits for just Engstrand and him. Rand would be the president and CEO of NewVue. This was just when "CEO" became a magical designation as the Eighties began deifying business. Everybody wanted to become a CEO. The owners of small companies in Hackensack printed new business cards and dubbed themselves "President and CEO." It looked so—so *Barron's*, so *Business Week*, so *Forbes*. It appealed to Rand, who, golden gut or not, was still human and susceptible to petty vanities.

And now he has suddenly left NewVue...

And who was Rand the man? As differentiated from the business man? He was short, five foot six, but people swore it didn't affect him, and he carried himself like a tall man. Nevertheless, corporate America is a tall culture, which may have influenced this MBA student's attraction to show business. Show business has always offered opportunities for the disenfranchised: Jews, Gays, Gals, and Blacks, as they used to be called. Do you think it's an insult to include short men in this list? Try walking in the shoes of a short man some time. Besides pinched feet, you'll know what it means to be low to the ground.

There was a lot of whispered talk that Rand had ingratiated himself with the Hollywood powers of the Eighties by finding and exploiting the best sources for cocaine. An old girlfriend, one of his more intelligent ones, once told me that he was "addicted to addicted personalities. He finds them fascinating in their malleability." If the law ever got interested, they never got close. The talk never rose above a whisper.

The old girlfriend also told me that no matter how busy he was, and he was always busy, he would schedule—literally schedule—in sex. Not so much because he enjoyed it—although he was fascinated by beautiful women—but because he took it as an accouterment to the job. She was sure that when he didn't have a trophy girlfriend on hand, he paid for trophy whores.

His charity and cause—another accouterment of the well-heeled Hollywoodite—was Nouveau Internationalism. "More important now than ever," he is quoted as having said. "With the old two-power rivalry gone, the world is fracturing, breaking into little pieces of ethnic strife. Now, more than ever, we must promote the idea of world citizenship. I am an EarthPerson." His charity was EarthPeople, and it funded conferences and educational tools promoting World Citizenship as a vehicle to solve problems feuding governments couldn't. It was a private United Nations, making Rand a "worldly" guy.

Roee collected me at one for lunch, a delicious cold seafood salad accompanied by his homemade bread.

"When Norton called to confirm the Engstrand meeting," he said as we sat down, "he warned not to expect him to be very cooperative."

"Why?"

"Couldn't understand why he should talk to you, a person Norton couldn't even explain or give a name to."

"He has not heard of me?"

"He has not heard of the Fixxer legend, no."

"But Norton did his best."

"Well, he got the meeting. Engstrand made it clear, though, he has very little to say about Rand. Somewhat hurt over Rand's abrupt move, Norton thinks. Engstrand also suspects you're a writer doing a book."

"Well, we must find a way to put him at his ease."

"I think I already have. I called a friend in Norway. He faxed this to me. Makes a nice little file."

Roee slid a file folder over to me. I opened it and glanced at the areas underlined by Roee. "Well," I said after digesting it, "this will hardly put him at ease."

"No, but it should open his mouth."

xx

NewVue Pictures had offices in Century City, but Torvald Engstrand would only agree to meet on the construction site of the studio he was building in Santa Clarita, a community up the 5 freeway north of Hollywood with a film history as a location for westerns.

The site was stunning. Massive, behemoth sound stages under construction, giants of steel and concrete that existed mainly to enclose and control space, to create and maintain environments not necessarily native to the location or the moment. I've seen many sound stages. These would be the biggest in Hollywood.

"Impressive, aren't they?" Engstrand said to me. "But then monuments should be. Yes, monuments, monuments to filmmaking. Practical, usable monuments, yes? But monuments to stir the soul nonetheless."

"Too much, too late?" I asked.

"I don't understand?"

"Don't you think digital scene simulation will eventually eliminate the need for huge sound stages? After all, if you can recreate Rome in a computer, why build the Forum on a sound stage?"

Engstrand, a man about 55 years of age, tall, silver-haired, with an elegant, aristocratic bearing, snorted. "You sound as shortsighted as Andy Rand. He was against this; he thought it was a waste of money. But there is something indefinable in the creation of movies, in playacting, that you will miss if you just have actors and directors work in a big green room. If you want to stir souls, you must have on the screen souls that are stirring. How are you going to do that in a big green room?"

There was a breeze, focused and tunneled between sound stages into a nearly silent, just whispering wind. Quiet because outside the guard at the gate, we were alone. It was a holiday, one of those nondescript government holidays well-loved by Federal employees and union members. We walked from the sound stages that were nearly completed to those that were still skeleton-like, including a giant among giants, one with a deep hole.

"Our tank stage. I could re-make "Jaws" in there for less than what it originally cost."

Engstrand was proud of this little kingdom he was building and proud to show it off. Even to me, a stranger with motivations he was unsure of.

"Now, please, tell me why you take up my time on a holiday?"

"You seem to be working anyway."

"I never abandon my child. Now, what is it you want?"

"Some information on Andy Rand."

"This is the film business. Andy Rand has been a media darling and a media victim. Surely you could get all the information you need from old press accounts."

"No, I don't think so."

"Who are you? Are you a reporter?"

"No."

"Lawyer?"

"No."

"IRS agent?"

"No."

"Drug dealer?"

"No."

"Then what could you possibly want information about Andy Rand for?"

"I'm afraid that is information I must keep to myself."

"Then I'm afraid I must keep any information I have on Andy Rand to myself."

He huffed, turned, and walked toward his trailer office. "You know the way out, Mr. No-name," he shouted back dismissively.

"How's your father?" I shouted after him.

He stopped. He turned around. "Why would you inquire after my father?"

"I know he's still in Norway. I believe it's a nice home you have him in. By all accounts, he's a sharp old man. Still opinionated on politics, though."

"He is more interested these days in his bladder than in politics. But I'll be happy to inform him that a stranger asked after him. Good-bye." Again he tried to turn and dismiss me.

"Does he ever talk much about Vidkun Quisling?"

Again Engstrand turned back to me and stared at me, wondering, I'm sure, why he must have both Andy Rand and his father mixed in some stew this stranger was preparing. He looked down. I did not see what he saw there until he quickly bent down, grabbed it, and rushed toward me.

The 2x4 slammed into my raised right arm and was deflected, but not without some pain. Engstrand pulled back and tried again, but I was on him like a madman, jumping at and gripping his two hands enclosed around the wood as I slammed my right knee into his belly. He collapsed as if an off switch had been pulled. We were far from the front gate; the guard had not seen the struggle, so Engstrand knew there would be no reinforcements. He held up a hand to beg surrender. I gave him a moment to get over the loss of breath. Then I helped him up and sat him on a pile of lumber.

"Vidkun Quisling was the head of the Nazi party in Norway," I told him, although he knew it very well. "He was instrumental in paving the way for Hitler's invasion of Norway in '39-'40. Your father was one of Quisling's secret operatives—"

"That is not true," Engstrand said, still feeling the pain in his belly.

"No, it is true. But you and your father have always done a marvelous job covering it up, especially with the help of the CIA, his employer after the war. They, shall we say, appreciated your father keeping an eye on the Russian activities along the Scandinavian border. Your father has never been less than a dedicated Nazi and a fervent anti-Communist. And a real hater of Jews, of course, but that goes without saying. A feeling, I believe, you share, even if you keep it quiet in this town."

"So? What of it?"

"So? So nothing. Just facts. Just history. Nonetheless, this is not a town that likes Nazis, paranoid and now out-of-date anti-Communists, Jew-haters, and upstart rich foreigners who think they can compete in Hollywood by just throwing money around."

"I came to America to compete."

"Yes, I know you did. I understand the frustration of being an entrepreneur in a fairly socialist society. America is the land of opportunity. And Hollywood is the land of the dead who have fallen trying for opportunity. No one sees that, do they? Like no one sees all the dead skin one sheds every day. Except in a case like yours. High profile. Rand gave you acceptance in Hollywood. Rand gave you hits. You no longer have Rand, but you've been here a dozen years; now, you're a part of Hollywood. So much a part that the competition would like to 'kill' you and grab your assets. Your family history, were it known, could only aid them in that kill."

I bent down and brushed off the dirt that had clung to his clothes from the fall.

"Now tell me why Rand quit, what kind of unusual contacts, especially foreign, he's had recently, and what you think he's up to now."

He wanted a drink, so we moved to his trailer. It was an opulent affair, befitting a builder of monuments. After settling down, he began to talk.

"I am totally at a loss as to why Andy quit. I gave him anything he wanted outside of turning over total control of NewVue. He argued with me about this studio, as I said, but he knew how much I wanted it. Then, last week he came in and announced he was quitting. Wouldn't explain why beyond the explanation he gave the press."

"Was his contract up?"

"No, we had no formal contract. We never needed one. The fact that our self-interest lay so heavily in each other was our contract. It was always his option to leave at any time. My first thought, quite frankly, was that he was dying of something horrible and wanted to get out of the public eye."

"Something horrible like what?"

"Oh, you know, Cancer, AIDS."

"AIDS?"

"No, no, of course not, the thought left me quickly. He is very healthy— in all aspects of his life."

"So, what was your second thought?"

"That he was telling the truth and was tired of this business. It happens, but it seemed unlikely. Did something better come along? I asked myself, but what could that be? I have racked my brain to think. Outside of mine, he had the greatest job in Hollywood. Almost total green-lighting freedom."

"Almost?"

"Well, he did have to answer to me. I do own 53% of the company. But I gave him great latitude. I have made my fortune giving him great latitude."

"What do you think of his charity, EarthPeople?"

"I have contributed several hundred thousand to it."

"Do you believe in its goals?"

"What is there not to believe in? We should consider ourselves one people instead of diverse nations and ethnic groups. Sure, why not. Nationalism is an antiquated idea. I changed my citizenship for business reasons. Do I think we will all come together in happy harmony soon? No, of course not. But it can't hurt to try. And it was important to Andy."

"EarthPeople gave him many contacts with people around the world."

"Well, yes, of course. But then so did the film business."

"No, I mean with people not involved in the film business."

"Oh yes. Normal people. Yes, yes, of course, you're right. He liked associating with thinkers, politicians, diplomats, Mother Theresa, the Pope."

"Did he have any particular interest in people in Eastern Europe?"

"Oh, that was new ground for him ever since the Iron Curtain came down."

"Have you ever heard of a man named Zhelyu Batsarov?"

"Batsarov?" He took a moment to think back. "Yes! Yes, I made a payment to a Batsarov. It was an option on a story he had that Andy was very high on, a post-Cold War spy story of some kind. Andy became interested in what would happen to all the spooks, agents, and the James Bonds now that the great rivalry had ended. He wanted to do a movie about it. So he nosed around in East Europe and returned with Batsarov's story. I paid him a much larger than normal option fee, but Andy said it was the only way to loosen his tongue. It was, Andy said, what he was used to in his last business. 'His quote,' as we say in this business."

"Did you ever meet Batsarov?"

"No, Andy dealt with him exclusively, always going to meet him over there in, ah, in...."

"Bulgaria?"

"Yes, exactly."

"When did this all start?"

"Oh, a little over a year ago."

"Did a script ever come of it?"

"None that I saw. Andy kept telling me that the idea hadn't gelled. But he kept going to Bulgaria to work on it with this Batsarov personally."

"Can you recall when Rand's last trip over there was?"

"Two months ago, I think. Yes, we had a Royal premiere in London. Andy went on from there."

"Did Rand take drugs?"

"No! Never!"

"You mentioned drug dealers."

"You asked if he took them."

"True. Have you talked to Rand since last week?"

"No. I've tried, but he's not at home. The maid, of course, speaks no English, just *Senõr Rand no en casa.*"

"Does he have a second home? Vacation property?"

"No. He's a hotel man when he takes vacations, which is rare. He likes traveling on business and grabbing an extra day or two on each trip to rest and see the sights—brilliant. He likes, you see, feeling a part of the world, likes to be in among it, not just a 'tour bus lookie-loo,' as he called it."

"So you know of no way to contact him?"

"No, really, I don't. But, of course, next week is the annual EarthPeople Ball. I can't imagine him not showing up. It's sold out. He's the host. All of Hollywood will be anxious to see him there."

"Can you get me two tickets?"

"Now? Absolutely not! It's impossible."

I gave him an incredulous, questioning look tinged, I hoped, with something dark and asked again. "Can you get me two tickets?"

"Well, yes, all right. Where should I send them?"

"To Norton Macbeth. Now, tell me about Rand and women."

"What is there to tell? He is a very powerful man in this town. He can get any beautiful woman he wants."

"That's a bit of a Jackie Collins hyperbolic cliché, isn't it?"

"Well, any beautiful woman within reason. Reason these days taking into account threats of sexual harassment suits by women who don't know their place in the natural order of things. But still, that leaves plenty of women in this town."

"As long as they are beautiful."

"Very beautiful. Andy has high standards."

"Then why does he use high-priced whores?"

"Because high-priced whores tend to be very beautiful. And he can afford to, which places him well above middle-class morality. And because he didn't have to put up the pretense of caring."

"He's never married."

"He was married to NewVue."

"Until this divorce."

"Yes, until this divorce."

"Did he ever talk about marriage?"

"No, but he once confessed to me that if he ever thought a woman truly loved him—the inner him, as he called it—he would grab her instantly and forsake all others."

"He felt unloved then?"

"Yes. But he worked hard not to let it bother him."

"I'll bet. Well, thank you, Mr. Engstrand." I stood and started to leave.

"Uh..."

"Yes?"

"What we discussed earlier—the information you have, how did you get it?"

"Mr. Engstrand, think of me as a reporter on the soul's condition. I never reveal my sources."

"What are you going to do with the information?"

"Keep it to myself."

"Is there any way I can ensure that you do? Can I pay you something?"

"That, Mr. Engstrand, would make me a blackmailer."

"But—but I volunteer this payment."

"No, Mr. Engstrand, the information is more valuable to me unsullied by a financial transaction. I will keep it safe as long as you remember I have it. I may need your help in the future."

"Yes, yes, of course, anything."

"As you may need mine someday. If that day comes, if you find yourself to have a problem, business or personal, that you can't easily fix, call Norton Macbeth. Tell him you want to talk to me. My prices are not reasonable. But my work is guaranteed."

"And who—and who do I tell Mr. Macbeth I wish to speak with?"

"Ask to speak with the Fixxer. Good-bye."

CHAPTER 12

ONE SICK PUPPY

On the drive back from Santa Clarita, I opened the 911 up and had some fun, slowing down only once when my long-range radar detector, which I have given the pet name of McGee, indicated a public servant was lurking nearby.

We really are stupid at times, we humans. Not getting caught is our greatest joy. For most people, this entails nothing more than sneaking smokes as kids, at least one brush with shoplifting in our teen years, and, as adults, flouting traffic laws in ways often inconvenient to our fellow citizens and dangerous to ourselves. But in aberrant others— individuals and institutions alike without "better angels" in their natures—this propensity extends into darker territories, and that's when it can be dangerous. Not that the aberrant care. If they did, they wouldn't be aberrant. If we—the normal or the aberrant—get caught, then the next best thing is getting away with it, thus the high living standards of defense attorneys. That is our system, though, and few would trade it. One wonders, however, if the incentives were enough, whether certain individuals or institutions would sell it.

As I had to slow down in any case, I put in a call to Norton.

"How was Engstrand?" Norton asked when he came on the line.

"A competent tour guide."

"You got him to talk then?"

"Yes. He seemed pleased to do so."

"Good, good, he, he, he."

"How's the Hinckley family vacation going?"

"Going well. He was not happy, and the family was confused, but they went, he, he, he."

"Good. Keep them amused."

"How long?"

"Can't predict."

"Well, I'll do my best, he, he, he."

I begged off dinner when I got home and asked Roee to prepare a cold pack for my arm instead. He also insisted on redressing my neck.

"How's it looking?"

"Not bad. There'll be no scars."

"Good. I'm getting sick of turtlenecks."

"But you look so good in them."

"Roee, I looked good in leisure suits, but that doesn't mean I would wear one now."

"Turtlenecks are timeless."

"Yes, well, be that as it may, please fix me a very stiff vodka tonic and bring it into the library. I've got some reading to do."

When I got to the library, I opened the top right-hand drawer of my desk and pulled out the envelope Craig York had mailed to himself. Once settled with the vodka, I opened the envelope and pulled out the contents. York had not lied. It was the V treatment. I read what I now knew to be a stern warning from Skinner to York about what "rapists" might do with Veritas adapted into a highly fanciful and melodramatic film scenario with a "high concept" at its core—precisely what would appeal to a studio executive. Unfortunately, I had firsthand knowledge that it was also possible—especially now that a studio executive had read it who may have gotten the idea to step beyond the fanciful and into reality. Or, possibly better stated, a new reality—a very malleable new reality.

The question was, was it an evil new reality? Taken to the extremes the treatment predicted, yes. Even if you believe the universe is amoral, which I do, and even if you subscribe to situational ethics—I have a lifetime subscription myself—the answer was an unavoidable yes.

I laid the treatment aside and got up and put on the stereo some Telemann concertos for the oboe. They help me think. It is partly the sound of the oboe itself, which I have always found the perfect musical representation of the inner mind. But it is also the form of alternating slow movements with those livelier ones that gives a rational order to a train of thought. The slow movements—for example, the second "Recitativo" movement of Telemann's F minor—are contemplative in their deliberateness, as if one step at a time was the binding element of the universe. Then the following lively movements admit to the random, allowing your thoughts to strike more than just the fellow behind and the fellow ahead, causing the possibility of surprising sparks that truly illuminate. If not, the following slow movement puts you back into the process. A series of such pieces can keep you on track nicely.

Power was at the center of the affair. That's a given in almost all evil. Power over people and events, power to be hoarded, not shared, or shared only in a compromise that allows the power. What brand of power was under consideration in this case? Commercial power? Control of Veritas would certainly give Rand that—money, power, prestige, and influence beyond any usually granted to someone from the entertainment business.

Was this a big enough prize to kill for? Yes, for someone like Batsarov, it certainly was. But it was obviously Rand who had gotten Batsarov involved. Why? Because he had an early version of Veritas from York and wanted Skinner's perfected one? Was he even aware that York's was last year's model? Why would York tell him that? Wouldn't he claim that he, with time, could work out the obvious faults in Veritas? If Rand weren't aware, then he would not need to negotiate with Skinner, which York would have told him was fruitless in any case. He did need to destroy what Skinner had, in any case. That was important; otherwise, York could not claim the patent. That's what Rand needed Finch for. Finch was still friendly with Skinner; he was a computer correspondent. Maybe they were using him to introduce, perhaps through an e-mail-delivered file, a virus into Skinner's computer that would eventually make his system crash, wiping out his Veritas software and programs. But a person like Skinner would have backups. No, they needed Finch to get on-site at Skinner's lab.

Finch, I'm sure, promised he could do it. However, Skinner wouldn't have allowed it, not even for a childhood friend. Unless he was using Finch as a Guinea Pig, testing Veritas on him. But assuming not, assuming Finch had failed them, after eight months—eight months in which York had been unable to improve the earlier version of Veritas, maybe now admitting Skinner had a better one—Rand may have had no choice but to pact with the devil to get the job done. The Caltech attack was made imperative when they lost York's version of Veritas, but maybe it was already in the planning; perhaps it would have happened several days before if York had not killed Finch. But was all this done for commercial power? Not that commercial power is to be sneered at, but it has been my experience that such measures are more likely to indicate a bid for political power.

For so many years, political power has been gained by local appeals to nationalism and then maintained by chest-thumping abroad. In a flip of the good thoughts of René Dubos, most world leaders have thought locally and acted globally. Can an appeal to internationalism gain any political power? Communism tried and gained but eventually failed. Rand, though, had a bug up his butt about it. Why? Was it just an excuse to throw fancy fundraisers and be thought an incredibly good, peace-loving guy? Most likely, this is all it was at first—it had networking and image payoffs in the Industry—but what came second? As Rand aged, as Hollywood became more and more courted by the world for its power and influence, what was Rand thinking? What, in the deep recesses of his recognition-loving mind (recognition in the sense Fukuyama has written about), did he really think whenever he stood in the shower and whistled "If I Ruled the World?"

What did those thoughts coalesce into when Rand read York's treatment during a pleasant fishing trip, said, "This is cool," and then had the actual, for real cool demonstrated for him? Yes, what did Rand suddenly realize about a possible destiny he had only contemplated before as a way of—entertaining himself?

xx

I made a series of phone calls.

"Anne?"

"Fixxer?"

"I think we can get together earlier than I thought."

"Wonderful!"

"How about tomorrow night for dinner at my place?"

"Should I bring some bubble bath?"

"A nice thought, but not this time. It's going to be a dinner party."

"Oh."

"I guarantee you will find it interesting. A car will pick you up at six."

"Petey?"

"Fixxer! How'd 12-72 do?"

"Just fine, Petey, just fine. Listen, how much vacation time do you have built up?"

"Oh, well, let's see—two weeks a year for the last, uh, 22 years, that would be..."

"Forty-four weeks."

"Yeah, forty-four weeks. Guess I'll add them onto my retirement."

"Well, sacrifice some of it and get out here; I need you."

"When?"

"Catch the next flight."

"Well, I'll have to talk to—

"I'll deal with your immediate superior. Is it still Duckmeyer?"

"No, Fucky-Ducky's gone. It's Heartburn."

"Really? Hillburn? Even better. Got any new, undetectable body-homing devices?"

"Have you been circumcised?"

"Circumcised?"

"Yes, circumcised."

"Isn't that a matter between a man and his god?"

"Come on, stop kidding with me. Have you been circumcised?"

"Yes, Petey, the good doctor who brought me into the world took my foreskin out of it."

"Good, then I have just the thing."

"Dare we go into the details now?"

"No. It'll just disturb your sleep. See you soon."

"Captain."

"Fixxer, damn it! I'm off duty and trying to have conjugal bliss with my wife."

"Dinner. Tomorrow night. My place. A car will pick you up at six."

"Fixxer, damn it, I resent—"

"Don't keep Mrs. Captain waiting."

"Roee."

"Yes."

"A little dinner party tomorrow night for five. Anne Eisley, Petey, the Captain, you, and me. Six-thirty drinks, seven o'clock dinner."

"Salmon steaks suit your palate?"

"Yes, that'll be fine."

"Good. I've had a taste for salmon ever since our last swim."

xx

The next day Petey arrived in time for breakfast. He came bursting through the door like a tattered tornado, his small frame carrying a proportionally oversized head that he kept unkempt from his deep black hair to his gray spotted beard that seemed to have been trimmed with a hacksaw. His cavernous mouth was the perfect amplifier, and he rarely talked below a shout.

"Roee, what the hell? Turkey in Eggs Benedict?" Petey said upon his first bite.

Roee gave Petey the look of a stern old family doctor. "It's healthier for you."

"Healthy? The fucking sauce will kill me! What do you want to do? Kill the market for Canadian bacon? Hell, you'll be the cause of a border war. How about a Bloody Mary?"

"No," I said. "I need you in the laboratory with a clear head."

"Laboratory? I thought I was on vacation."

"Twenty-five thousand for the week."

"Plus costs?"

"Plus costs."

"Vacations are for the vacuous. But would a nap be out of the question?"

"Didn't you sleep on the plane?"

"I can't sleep on airplanes. Can you?"

"Petey, I can sleep anywhere because I sleep the sleep of the innocent."

"Yeah, sure!" Petey snorted.

"All right. Roee will lead you in some deep relaxation exercises that will give you two hours of sleep that will seem like eight. Then it's to the laboratory until six."

"Fine. What am I doing? Dissecting earthworms and frogs?"

"Nothing so mundane. You'll be dissecting the future of evil."

"Oooh! I don't know if that was portentous or pretentious, but it sure was entertaining."

xx

The Captain, Petey, and I were having drinks in the library when Roee ushered Anne Eisley in. I had told them that one more guest would be joining us, but I had not indicated that the guest would be a woman, nor a woman as thoroughly attention-grabbing as Anne. They were furiously talking at each other—debating some fine point regarding the effective interrogation of a sociopath—when Anne appeared. They simultaneously stopped in mid-sentence, leaving a sweet silence somewhat reminiscent of early morning or the sound of the world just after a thunderstorm.

Anne smiled—the sun breaking through the clouds. She was wearing a mid-calf length black evening dress held up by small straps over each shoulder. The neckline of the bodice was cut to reveal enough to convince that nature could, indeed, produce art. The skirt was made of sheer cotton overlaid by a mad pattern of heavy silk swirls, allowing hints of the radiance of her legs. I walked over to her. I could see that she was nervous. "Welcome to my home, Anne. What a lovely dress—Mizrahi?"

"Thank you," she said in a quiet voice. "Yes, it is. I wore it to the Emmys. I hope no one here remembers."

"I'm sure that will not be a problem. Let me introduce you to the others." I led her by the arm over to the Captain and Petey. Roee accompanied us. "Gentlemen, I would like you to meet Anne Eisley. Anne, this is Petey to your right. He is the developer of Formula 12-72."

Anne took his hand. "Oh, really? How in the world did you ever think up that concoction?"

Petey smiled big. He loved talking about his work. And so rarely can. "Oh, it was easy! I just drew on my natural vindictiveness and jealousy over all the men out there getting laid while I wasn't!"

"Oh."

"I mean, would you want to have sex with me?"

It was a question with an easy answer, but not one easy to answer.

Nevertheless, Anne caught the stream of Petey's consciousness and answered well. "Only, I suppose, if I was blinded by love."

"Oh, well, that couldn't happen! I'm about as lovable as a dried slug on a windowpane!"

"Oh, I'm sure somewhere deep inside you is something to love."

"Oh, yeah! Pure, raw, pathetically pompous intelligence, but few people find that lovable. But if you ever think you might, Fixxer's got my phone number."

It seemed best to move on at this point. "And this is the Captain."

Anne turned her attention to the tall Midwesterner in the well-worn suit. "Captain...?"

"In our association, 'Captain' is enough," the Captain said.

"Then Captain, it will be."

"And do forgive me if you catch me staring at you all evening, but you are a beautiful woman."

"Thank you, Captain. I'll try not to let it unnerve me."

"And, of course, my friend Roee must have introduced himself at the entrance."

"Yes, he did."

"What would you like to drink, Miss Eisley," Roee offered. "I have a wonderful Chenin Blanc, or, of course, various imported bottled waters, both gasata and non-gasata, as the Italians like to say."

Anne looked at each of the four men she had been invited to have dinner with. I think she knew she was "safe" in our care, but it was also quite apparent that something out of the ordinary was soon to present itself. "No, thank you. They sound lovely, but I think Scotch— neat."

The dinner Roee prepared was excellent, the salmon especially, which had been caught that morning in Alaska and flown down in the afternoon.

I thought Petey would appreciate having Anne report exactly how Fred Crane reacted to Formula 12-72. She did so without embarrassment, which was good, for it had been a test of her courage.

After the Captain fully understood what Formula 12-72 did, he turned to Petey in amazement and said, "Petey, you are one sick puppy." Petey loved the designation. Then the Captain got us off the subject to pontificate against the gun lobby. He took the standard police line. Anne nodded vigorously in agreement.

Roee brought out and explained exactly how he had created the dessert, which was far too technical for me. The coffee was good, but for our second cup, I suggested that it was time to move back to the library to discuss the matter I had brought them together for.

We sat in a circle. I positioned Anne across from me and directed my comments to her. Roee and the Captain knew the basics. Petey had experience enough to trust me. It was Anne whose help was essential and whom I had no right to involve in this. It was Anne I had to convince.

"Three nights ago, a young man named David Finch may have been killed by one of his best friends, another young man, Craig York. A letter opener thrust into the aortic arch above the heart was the possible cause of death." Anne's eyes reacted with a slight widening. "It was an accident, the result of a heated argument. At play were desperation and ego, a dangerous combination. After Craig York left the scene, certain individuals he had, unfortunately, become involved with mutilated Finch's body by removing the head, arms, and legs from the trunk. If York's action had not killed Finch, this follow-up would have done the job."

Anne now gave a small, high-pitched gasp. "But, why...?"

"The mutilation was done to cover up any trail that could lead back to York."

"An effort that failed, I take it," Anne said, beautifully keeping the whole picture in her head.

"Thanks to Fixxer's sharp eyes," the Captain offered. "So you're something special?" Anne gave me her eyes to play with. "Well—I enjoy doing a competent job. Anyway, to continue, this murder has been reported on, but, thanks to the efforts of the Captain, it has not been generally noted by the public—just another L.A. murder, no big deal. That cannot be said of another event of violence, the sniper and bomb attack at Caltech two days ago."

"I saw that on TV," Anne said. "It was horrible."

"The two are related. The mutilation of Finch's body and the attack on Caltech was the work of Zhelyu Batsarov, a former Bulgarian intelligence agent turned thug, now residing in this country illegally."

"What—what is it all about?"

"The attainment of profit and power. The motivation for most organized attacks on the sanctity of life."

"That's a fairly general answer."

"I will eventually explain in detail, for I am making it my business to stop Batsarov. And I need your help."

Anne now questioned with her eyes. Doubt as to my seriousness or my sanity must have crossed her mind. Nevertheless, she surprised me by saying, "Sounds intriguing."

"Batsarov, having been well trained in Moscow, is an expert at what he does. He also knows how not to get caught. The authorities, represented tonight by the Captain, have not one shred of evidence linking Batsarov to the crimes. Nor do they have any idea where to find him."

"And you think, somehow, I can help?"

I smiled. It was a question I did not need to answer. I could see she was still intrigued. "I believe I know how we can get to Batsarov, and the beauty of it is, we can get to him through the man he works for, our real target."

"And that is?"

"Andy Rand."

This shocked her. "Andy Rand! I can't believe that."

"Nor would anybody else. That's partly what protects him. That's why I need Andy Rand to fall in love with you—at first sight."

xx

I explained everything in detail. The history of "Huey, Dewey, and Louie;" the creation of Veritas; the split between Skinner and York; York's co-opting of Skinner's nightmare scenario into a film treatment in the hope of getting money to save his houseboat and buy himself a life. I explained my assumptions on how Andy Rand got to read the treatment and experience Veritas. And my guess as to what he made of them. I covered Finch's role and how it led to Paul Hinckley's involvement, my involvement, and Finch's death. Then I had Petey bring out the Veritas equipment, which he had spent the day examining in the lab, and give each of my guests and Roee a demonstration.

When Petey was finished, everyone had a good idea of the power and extent of Veritas.

"Here's everything that everybody's excited about with the 'New Media,'" I said, "but taken to a level that should be—but for the short-lived existence of a particular genius—at least one hundred years beyond today's technology. If Andy Rand patents this technology and monopolizes its use, he will have control over the most powerful, the most profitable commercial entity in existence. Had he paid for the creation of Veritas, that would be as it should be, and our only course of action would be to envy him. However, although he has certainly spent money, he has not paid for Veritas; he has stolen it. And he has murdered, or caused to be murdered, individuals during that theft. This makes him susceptible to sanctions under the law, but that, Anne, is the business of our friend, the Captain, and the people he works for. It is a business I might choose to meddle in, but not one I should ask you to become involved in. I do ask you to become involved, though, because I believe Andy Rand is smart enough to see beyond the normal commercial applications of Veritas to the potential of political applications. Whose politics? Most likely Andy Rand's, or possibly the politics of somebody ready to meet Rand's price; it doesn't matter which. What matters is that it would not necessarily be my politics, yours, or any other person's, and that would certainly stifle free debate. Not that I have ever thought much of the quality of political debates in this country, but I have always appreciated the fact that they have been free."

I stopped to see if Anne had anything to say. This was wildly fantastic stuff to take in when her main concern in life right now was memorizing a movie script.

Anne did, indeed, have something to say. "Having experienced Veritas, I don't doubt what you're saying. I mean, I would love to doubt it, to write you off as just another conspiracy theory nut, but—I know a mind fuck when I experience it. Men do it to women all the time." She leaned forward, presenting herself as ready. Her eyes were bright, shining, and intense. "So what's the plan?"

"The plan is to fill a need. Veritas is imperfect. We know that for a fact with our version. So possibly did Rand. But, according to Skinner, the later model of Veritas, while an improvement, was not yet perfect either. Imagine Rand's disappointment when he brought it home and turned it on. York tells him he can finish Skinner's work, but at this point, Rand does not believe it. He has spent eight months watching York try to perfect the earlier model. He has probably concluded what others have, that, technically brilliant as York is, he lacks creativity, that openness to sudden inspiration, to random connections that leads to breakthroughs. Rand has been spinning dreams of unlimited power and has given up much for those dreams. He has admitted to a capacity for evil and has acted upon that capacity. Now he is sitting somewhere wondering if all his dreams are built on a false foundation. He is fighting a fear that it may have all been for naught. That makes him vulnerable to us."

"Wait a minute," the Captain broke in. "What's so damn imperfect about this Veritas? I've never been through anything like it in my life. It seemed pretty damn perfect to me."

"It's got goobers!" Petey nearly shouted.

"Goobers?" The Captain asked.

"Sticky little problems. Like gaps, blank spaces in the program."

The Captain didn't understand.

"Think back," Petey said. "When you ran into the lower bailey, wasn't it empty, yet full of sound?"

The Captain thought. "Yes, yes, you're right. Yet how did I know it was called the lower bailey?"

"And the egghead people," Roee said. "Not very realistic."

"Those are both goobers," Petey declared.

"Let's look into something else," I said. "You were all given the 'Castle' program. This was just a test program developed by Skinner and York. It has no purpose except to let them fool around with their theories. So, you saw an almost realistic rendition of a world you have never known. You knew particulars of this world, from the time and location to the recipe and use of bate, which was completely artificial, that is, knowledge you had not previously acquired. You were all a prisoner with an overwhelming need to escape, which forced an adventure or game on you. Do we all agree that we shared these experiences?" Everyone agreed. "But what differences did we have? That's the interesting point."

"What do you mean?" The Captain asked.

"Why were you in the dungeon?"

"It seems I was a Captain of the Guard caught taking bribes," the Captain answered, giving me a pointed look.

"And you, Petey?"

"I was an alchemist who had little success turning lead into gold."

"Anne?"

"A traveling player caught stealing—the king's affections away from the queen."

"Roee?"

"I was just a Jew. That seemed to have been offense enough."

"Did the guard become someone you knew, however casually?"

Everyone agreed.

"It is obvious that Veritas works in conjunction with your mind. And the memories, feelings, and sense of self within your mind. Was this planned, or is it a problem? Getting your mind to do some of the work could be an advantage, less to program. This would be fine if Veritas is to be nothing but an entertainment or educational tool. Except for the fact, of course, that possibly there are memories and thoughts in your mind you don't find particularly entertaining, or your mind has things to teach you, you would just as well avoid learning. Such aspects could diminish Veritas' popularity. Also, if Veritas is to do more with indoctrination than entertainment or instruction, you don't particularly want the mind you are trying to influence to collaborate. I'm guessing a perfect Veritas is the one that minutely designs and minutely controls the 'truth' it pumps into your brain. That's the perfected Veritas I believe Rand wants. To get to him, we need to offer it to him."

Anne had been following everything with great interest. It was, after all, dramatic, practically melodramatic, suited to the nature of an instinctually great actress. "How?" she asked, eager to know.

"Ever since Rand announced his resignation from NewVue, he has been hiding. Seclusion might be the more press release-oriented word. In either case, it helps the image that he is off somewhere alone, trying to figure out what he wants to do with his life. All of Hollywood is trying to guess his next move. Will he go off and climb mountains? Will he go sit quietly on a beach or in Tibet, trying to find the spirituality so lacking in his life? Or will he suddenly reemerge with a bid to buy or the financing to create a motion picture studio? A typical set of Hollywood options. I, of course, am convinced that none of these are true. Through thorough research, Norton has discovered that Rand had a huge outlay of cash six months ago totaling ten million dollars. I believe this was for the establishment of a—headquarters. Where this headquarters might be, we have been unable to discover. It could be anywhere in the world. However, it is here that he has based, housed Batsarov, and now houses York and, I would assume, a state-of-the-art laboratory. By sometime next week, I would like you and me, Anne, to be guests at his headquarters. We will be guests because Rand will have fallen in love with you."

"Well," Anne interrupted. "I can see how love might motivate him to invite me. But how do you get to tag along?"

"I will be introduced to Rand as your brother."

"Oh. How am I going to justify bringing you along, then? That I need a chaperone?"

"No. Rand will extend me an invitation."

"You've found out, maybe, a kinky side to Mr. Rand?"

"In a manner of speaking."

"But what if Rand doesn't fall in love with her?" asked the always practical Captain.

"Oh, I've got a little potion that will guarantee that!" Petey blurted.

"Hey, wait a minute," Anne said. "What makes you think I need a guarantee?"

We were all speechless.

"I mean, why did you ask me in on this? Would just any girl do?"

"Well—" I started.

"If that's the case, why don't you just call central casting?"

"I'm—I'm sorry, I just thought..." Petey was shamefaced. A condition I had never seen him in before.

"I'll bet you, and I'll give you good odds, that I can make Rand fall in love with me within five minutes of meeting him. *Without* the use of any— potion." She gave the word a deeply vulgar shade. "Does anybody want to take the bet? Captain?"

The Captain vigorously shook his head.

"Petey? Put your money where your potion is."

"I'm sorry. I said I was sorry."

"Fixxer? You set this up. Come on, let me get some of my money back?"

"No, Anne, I will not take your bet."

"Why not?"

"Because it is a sucker's bet." I smiled. I held my breath. Then I was pleased to see her smile back.

"So you and Anne get invited to Rand's secret hideout," the Captain said. "To get some evidence against Rand?"

"Yes. Evidence. Or a witness willing to testify."

"York?"

"Yes. He has a vulnerable personality."

"Well, you better have a homing device on you so we can give you some backup."

"That's the plan."

"And it better be a well-hidden one. Batsarov is versed in such things," Roee added.

"Petey assures me he has a good one."

"Yeah! I have a great one! You want to see it?"

"Petey, I think that can wait until—"

"No, here, look, I got it right here!"

Petey whipped out of his pocket something two to three inches long, wrinkled, flesh-colored, and floppy. He held it proudly in his hand.

"What the hell is that?" The Captain moved closer for a better look.

"A synthetic male foreskin attachment with a built-in flexible nanoelectronic homing device. It's really great! It has an anti-detection chip built in, so no electronic scan can pick it up, and, as you can see, it is completely non-detectable during visual inspection. Of course, it only works with a man who's been circumcised, but as most men are, thanks to the good, hygienic sense of your people, Roee, we find it applicable to 92.4% of our agents. You see, you attach it with this special glue—"

"Yes, well..." I had to stop him. He was unzipping his pants. "You and I can go over this tomorrow."

"Oh, okay, but I better tell you before I forget. It has one drawback."

"What's that?"

"While you've got it on, you can't take a bath. It might short out. Sponge-wash the penis only."

Anne could no longer contain herself and began to laugh.

The Captain shook his head and leaned back in his chair. "Petey...."

"What?" Petey answered, still proudly displaying the foreskin-homing device in the palm of his hand.

"You are one sick puppy."

CHAPTER 13

12.5 THOUSANDTH OF A SECOND

We ended the evening with Anne agreeing to do anything she could. "Just make sure I'm available for the first day of filming," she said as I escorted her to the door.

"I guarantee it," I said with jaunty confidence, although worry was beginning to gnaw inside. What I would be taking Anne into was not a benign situation. There was danger. There was the possibility of harm, a possibility she had not even raised, which won my admiration, but the possibility was still there. It was unconscionable asking for her help in this matter, but the simple fact was that I needed her. Not, as she had facetiously suggested, any beautiful girl from central casting, but her—for reasons beyond the obvious. "Are you available tomorrow?"

"Yes, where are we going?"

"You and Roee are going shopping."

"Really? What for?"

"With luck, the most gorgeous evening gown currently existing on the face of the Earth."

"Sounds delightful. Why is Roee coming?"

"He has incredible taste."

"And you think I don't?"

"He has incredible taste—and the credit card."

"Ooooh! Lovely—where am I going to wear this dress?"

"To the EarthPeople Ball."

"Wow! I am impressed. But, of course, it is Rand's thing, isn't it?"

"Yes, it should bring him out of hiding, but it's a small window of opportunity. That's why it's got to be love at first sight."

"I'll practice at home in front of the mirror."

"Well... Goodnight."

"No damn 'goodnights' until you kiss me, Fixxer."

I did—but the pleasure was streaked with fear, like scratches down my back, fear of future regret.

Early the next morning, I called Norton and asked him to connect me with Sara Hemmings. Hemmings was an A-list actress but at the bottom of the list. She had been in some box office hits that had pulled in 100 million plus bucks, mainly through their spectacle and special effects. Her presence probably didn't mean much more than a million or two added to the bottom line. Nevertheless, they had put her in the upper stratum. Gilt by association, as someone once said. She was not a great actress or even possessed true star quality, but she was pleasant on the screen and had become reliably professional, which had not always been her reputation. Entering film from the modeling world, she had been nervous, shy, and vulnerable on her first several shoots. She had manifested this through a cold, standoffish attitude that had led to a brush fire branding as "difficult." Combined with this, she was, of course, gorgeous. It set the loins of the men she worked with on fire and their teeth on edge. A gorgeous girl is no good if she doesn't respond to you.

She came on the line. "Is this really the infamous Fixxer?"

"I am known as Fixxer, whether infamous or not."

"Well, I've heard some fascinating stories about you."

"Someday, you must recount them to me."

"Oh, they're probably all wrong. I would rather hear the real stories from you."

"I'll let you know when the book signing is."

"What? Can't I have a private performance?"

"I'm open to discussing it, but not right now. Right now, I need to do you a favor."

"Do me a favor? Under what terms?"

"What I require from you in return is very simple and will take but a minute."

"And what do I get favored with?"

"The opportunity to wreak vengeance on Andy Rand."

There was silence. This had been a titillating game for her, but now I had stirred a dark desire she probably thought she had successfully hidden from all, not the least being herself. And she knew enough of my reputation not to take lightly what I had just said.

"Why—why would I want vengeance against Andy?"

"The film you did for NewVue, *For Richer, For Poorer*—you know you weren't the director's first choice."

"Yes, I'm aware of that. Andy fought for me. So for that, I should want to do him harm?"

"But you also know why he fought for you. The director later confessed to you, didn't he? Rand and his production president, Tom Parr, in finally explaining why they were insisting on you, told the director, quite frankly, that it was because they wanted to prove to Hollywood that, quote, 'We can control the bitch.'"

"How do you know this?"

"Why am I infamous? From day one on that shoot, those two men harassed you and made your life miserable. I don't need to laundry list the details for you. Still, the most amusing incident was when you woke up one morning to find a lawsuit on your doorstep seeking damages for a lost day of shooting, supposedly because you had walked off the set the day before."

"I did not."

"Yes, I know. For his own reasons, the director had changed the shooting schedule, releasing you. Nonetheless, the document was on your doorstep. It was more than upsetting coming on top of all the other harassment, and you lost it. You became challenging to deal with."

"Okay, it was not a pleasant experience. I was angry for a long time afterward."

"The bad rap you got from it as an even worse bitch than people thought almost ruined your career. Especially when the film flopped."

"That's all gone. That's all past. In fact, I owe Andy a debt. Maybe I learned how to be more—professional."

"Oh, come on! He pulled a stupid, macho, little boy's game on you. He didn't do it for your edification. He did it to play with you like he probably played with his pets when he was a kid—much to the disadvantage of their physical well-being. It was a mean-grin form of torture. He wanted to make you suffer. You should feel no shame in wanting to make him suffer in return."

Silence again. Then: "What can I do for you?"

"Introduce someone to Rand."

"That's all?"

"At the EarthPeople Ball. You will be there. You are on the committee."

"Yes, I'll be there. Who?"

"Anne Eisley."

"Oh. She's beautiful. If this will make Andy suffer, I would like to see what you would suggest I do for friends."

"The purpose of all this will become clear in time. When it does, you will be proud of what little part you played."

"So I get to wreak vengeance and be proud of it?"

"That's right."

"I know a lot of Hollywood ladies looking for a Guru like you."

"Anne will be at the ball with her brother. They will be at your table."

"But—"

"Two of your guests will reluctantly have to cancel. Introduce yourself. Then find the perfect moment to introduce Anne to Rand. The more magical the moment, the better."

"Okay, I'll do it, but really because I can't see the harm in it."

"I will make my appreciation apparent at some future date."

I hung up the phone, smiled, and brought up an image of Sara Hemmings, especially as she appeared in *Twilight Time*. I must admit I entertained the slightly evil hope that she would need my services at some time in the future.

After breakfast, I went to the lab to get a report from Petey. I found him perfectly paralyzed, sitting in a chair, wearing the Veritas glasses. A program was running. There was a grin to make a mama scream plastered across his face. I pulled the glasses off.

"Oh—oh—oh," Petey said as he lunged for the glasses.

"Found the bearskin rug program, I see."

"I want a copy! Keep the salary; give me a copy!"

"I'll think about it. So, who did she become?"

"Sally Glasscock. She was a cheerleader at my high school. She would never look at me twice. Twice? Hell, I could have stood in front of her buck naked, my hair on fire, surrounded by the contents of Fort Knox, and she wouldn't have seen me!"

"You are kidding?"

"No, I was that much of a nonentity!"

"No, I mean her name."

"Oh. No, that's absolutely true. Want to see my high school annual?"

"Maybe just before I die to dispel any deathbed regrets. Now, what can you tell me about Veritas?"

"What do you want to know?"

"How it works."

"At this point, I can only give you a guess."

"But an educated one?"

"Oh, the best!"

"Then I'll need competent mumbo jumbo to convince Rand and York that I may have the key to its perfection."

"That won't be easy."

"Nevertheless...." I did not need to say more.

"Well, okay, my guess of how it works is based on a current theory of how the brain works."

"Which is?"

"That the brain is like comedy—it's all in the timing. In a nutshell, this is it: You sit here watching me as I talk. Your eye takes in light that has bounced off me, and nerve cells break that down into fragmented, electrical information about shape, color, contrast, and motion; essentially: what I look like. Your ear takes in the sound waves created by my talking and does the same thing. The nerves on your skin register the temperature in the room, maybe the slight movement of air from the air conditioning fan, and breaks that down into fragments of info. Your nostrils take in molecules from the air that have flowed off my face, and that came, originally, out of a bottle of Old Spice and fragments the hell out of that. Nerve cells called neurons transmit all these fragments into the brain, specifically into an area in the center called the thalamus. The thalamus acts like a clearing house and has these relay stations, one for each sense. The relay stations send the fragmented information to corresponding and dedicated areas of the cerebral cortex, the layer of cells covering the brain's outer surface. You know, the funny, gray convoluted part.

"Now, this is all well and good, but if this is all that the brain did, our perception of the world would be like viewing it as a reflection in a shattered and scattered mirror, which would be damn confusing. But here's where the brain becomes really marvelous. Inside the thalamus is this tire-shaped group of cells called the intralaminar nucleus. Every 12.5 thousandths of a second, this thing sends out a scanning wave of nerve impulses that sweeps across every bit of the cerebral cortex. Think of it like a radar wave sweeping across the top of the brain, passing each area of the cortex corresponding to the senses. Now, the frequency of this wave is 40 cycles per second, which is the same frequency the thalamus uses to regulate the active sensory cells in the cortex. So all this fragmented information is being relayed to and activating sensory cells in the cerebral cortex in a rhythm of the electrical activity of 40 cycles a second, just as the intralaminar nucleus sends a scanning wave across the cerebral cortex at the same 40 cycles. There is a meeting of minds, so to speak, and a coherent wave of messages is sent back to the thalamus, which now perceives all this fragmented information bound together as a whole. Of course, that whole is itself but a 12.5 thousandth of a second fragment of time, but that is so fast these 12.5 fragments of time meld into a continuous, connected flow."

"So it's like film. Cameras document then breaks up movement into 24 frames or fragments per second onto film; the developed film is then run through a projector at the same 24 frames per second and 'binds' those static fragments into one moving image projected onto a screen."

"In a sense, yes. But of course, you are only talking about the sense of sight there."

"Of course. Now, how does Veritas take advantage of this?"

"Well, here's an interesting fact. When you are in a deep, non-dreaming sleep, the thalamic cells operate at only two cycles per second. When you are awake but not paying attention to anything in particular, they operate at ten cycles. When you are fully awake, then it's, as I said, 40 cycles."

"And when you are dreaming?"

"The same 40 cycles."

"Interesting."

"You've got to think of the brain as just an organ whose function is to create perceptions. During wakefulness, those perceptions are controlled by information gathered by the senses and split into fragmented bits, which become the building material of the perceptions the brain creates. At night the perceptions the brain creates are our dreams. What are the building blocks? Probably just the leftover information in the cells, causing the erratic, shall we say, anarchic weirdness of dreams. I mean, you could say that our life while awake is a dream living under a dictatorship. The dictatorship of the five senses."

"And Veritas operates on the same 40 cycles a second."

"That's right. My guess is it simulates the dream state by, one, stimulating neural inhibitors, thus paralyzing the body and numbing, in a sense, all the senses. And two, sending at 40 cycles, sensory information directly to the relay stations in the thalamus to replace the sensory information not being received by the numbed senses."

"Thus creating a dream living under a dictator."

"The dictator of the program in the computer converted into a 40-cycle signal sent by this black box via infrared beam to the glasses' right lens, down the right bow to the little contact points, which directs the signal to the thalamus. The contact points on the left bow monitor the electrical signals of brain activity and send them to the left lens, which is an infrared transmitter that beams the information back to the black box, thereby creating an interactive loop, allowing the program to know what decisions you are making, such as going into the right tunnel or the left tunnel, whether to panic or stay calm, whether to use the missionary position—or not."

"Yes, a heady decision."

"But, of course, Veritas is better than a dream. You know how we always ask, 'Do you dream in color?' Well, do you taste in a dream? Feel cold? Smell shit? You can't really remember, can you? Veritas gives you all that. If truth is nothing but our perceptions, and Veritas can dictate our perceptions, then Veritas is truth."

"And it's even more, isn't it? He's managed to add cognitive information to sense information."

"Yes, that's right."

"How? How has he encoded this information into the computer program?"

"I'm not sure. He was some kind of a genius, that's for sure. But his ambition is what was causing him problems."

"What do you mean?"

"Recreating information from all five senses, plus cognitive information. Overload. That's why pieces are missing."

"And this is where I need the mumbo jumbo."

"Well, if we really don't understand how—"

"Mumbo jumbo, Petey," I insisted.

Petey looked up at me, a worried furrow on his brow, not something you usually see there. But then, in the past few minutes, as Petey had been talking, as he was in his element, the element of ideas—his whole countenance had changed. He became attractive. Not, of course, physically attractive in any conventional manner, but attractive, nonetheless, because he was being his essential self. Gone was the prankster, the loud little guy with self-deprecation as his self-defense. Instead, here was a brilliant man who knew his stuff—and reveled in it. On occasion, *Homo Sapiens* are to be admired.

"Well," Petey said, "Baker at UCLA has been doing some research that might relate, but it would be going out on a limb."

"Explain it to me."

xx

Later that afternoon, after Petey had filled my head with complexities on the quantum level, I was surprised to find that Roee had brought Anne home after their shopping carrying fancy logo-stamped boxes. She was excited and delighted.

"We found a fabulous outfit! Fabulous! Where can I try it on?"

"That's not necessary. You didn't have to come back. Surprise me on Wednesday."

"Fixxer, you're thinking of a wedding dress. This is a ball gown. That you're paying for. I want you to approve of it."

"I have complete trust in both you and Roee."

"Thank you," Roee said, "but I agree with Anne. You better look at this."

"Where can I try it on? Your bedroom?"

"No, I think the library will do."

She gave me a smile and nod, accepting this little defeat.

"Okay. I'll be right back." She grabbed the boxes and went quickly into the library.

I turned to Roee. "Had a good time, did we?"

"We stalked our quarry and bagged it. We ran it to ground in the fourth Beverly Hills store we visited. Had a very nice lunch at Via Rodeo. You know, that fake little European street where Cartier and Tiffany's moved to."

"Yes, I'm aware of the location."

"Speaking of Tiffany's..."

"Yes?"

"I figured she needed a little something for around the neck."

"Yes?"

"So I picked up a little Peretti piece."

"A little Peretti piece?"

"Very nice. Gold link chain, broken up every now and then by diamonds."

"Just every now and then?"

"Not often."

"I see. Beautiful?"

"Exquisite."

"And....?"

"And we can get at least seven times its cost in Moscow later if we want to."

"It's nice to see you haven't completely abandoned commerce for aesthetics."

"I have an ex-apparatchik friend whose wife has got an eye for—"

"What do you think?"

We turned. Anne stood in the doorway.

"Of course, my hair isn't done, and I have on daytime makeup, but..."

It was a fabulous outfit, but it was not what I expected.

It was two pieces: A teal satin double-breasted jacket and a matching long slit skirt. She had on the Peretti necklace, which provided a delicate accent to the trip your eyes could not help but travel from her long, carved marble neck, down the plunge defined by the two lapels of the jacket, to the separation between her breasts, that always exciting bit of space where every man believes the purest of air exists. She stood with her left leg thrust forward, taking full advantage of the slit, and her leg, cut from the same marble as her neck, sang that mysterious song, the song of the Sirens, enchantment leading to sweet destruction. She looked down, assessing herself, and then raised her head. The teal of the jacket was captured in her aquamarine eyes and made them glow.

"It's lovely," I said. "But—"

"But you were expecting...?"

"Something more..."

"Something more Grace Kelly in *To Catch a Thief?*"

"Possibly." Only self-control kept away the embarrassment of having my mind read so clearly.

"I understand. But consider this: Feminine shape and cleavage, combined with masculine tailoring, combined with a feminine color, excites the nerve ends of most males. It keeps them guessing. Is this mine for the taking? Or must I ask respectfully? Dare I? Could I? Should I? Might I? The answer must be obtained. The bold will grab for it. This outfit is seriously sexy."

I considered this. It was an interesting theory.

"From—believe me—an objective position," Roee stated. "What she says makes sense."

"Holy shit!"

It was Petey, just in from the lab. "You should have warned me you were going to be running around here dressed like that! I would have put on my rubberized undies!"

Anne laughed. She is very charitable.

"Well," I said, "who am I to argue with the majority?"

"Good," Anne said, closing this matter. "Now, are there any other preparations to make before Wednesday night?"

"Well, yes, I would like you to come by tomorrow to brief me on your childhood, your parents, and the community where you grew up. I need to have an effective feel for being your brother."

"And where do you intend that we should do that?"

"Here, of course. I can record you and use it for further study."

"I don't like this idea."

"Well, we needn't get too personal. Just atmosphere stuff, a shared sense of where this brother and sister came from."

"That's not what I mean. When I tell a man about my past, it's usually in one of two places: Over a fine dinner by candlelight. Or in his arms after sex."

"Say, I was wondering about your past!" Petey piped up to no response from us.

"So what are you suggesting?"

"Roee says you enjoy Santa Barbara."

"I do."

"Fine. Pick me up in the morning. Not before ten." She returned to the library.

"Roee?"

"You have reservations, Mr. Harrington, at the Four Seasons Biltmore."

"What if Mr. Harrington decides he has work to do?"

"The only thing Mr. Harrington would do, left to his own devices, is brood."

"Brood?"

"Yes, brood."

Well, in this world of 5 billion plus, I suppose it is better to brood than to have a brood."

"A clever but meaningless statement. We have an out-of-town guest with us. It's not fair to subject him to your moods. Vacating the premises is the only courteous thing to do."

"You mean I don't get to go to Santa Barbara?" Petey piped again.

Roee shot Petey a look. "I'll take you to the Santa Monica pier. You can ride the merry-go-round."

"I have to confer with the Captain. We have to book Michael," I protested.

"I will take care of everything. You will relax."

"Why? Why do I have to relax?"

"April 1987," Roee said by way of answer.

It was the right answer.

xx

I picked Anne up precisely at ten the following day in the Bentley. Bentleys, like Rolls-Royces, are not uncommon in Los Angeles, despite being absurd cars for daily driving in the city. Costing about the same as a mid-size condo in Covina, they are nothing more than a swagger on wheels between stoplights. On the open road, though, these "touring cars" are the apotheosis of the internal combustion engine. You can drive one with a complete understanding of the depletion of the ozone layer, but you just won't give a damn.

"Nice car," Anne said as I walked her to it, carrying her single piece of luggage.

"Yours?"

"Mr. Harrington's."

"Who?"

"As far as the hotel knows, I am Mr. C. Lawrence Harrington of Chadds Ford, Pennsylvania."

"Oh."

"Third-generation wealth."

"Must be nice."

"I've learned to live with it."

"What does the 'C' stand for?"

"I don't know. I've never thought to ask myself."

xx

We took Sunset Boulevard to the beach, turning right onto Pacific Coast Highway, or, as I explained to Anne, more popularly known as PCH,

"Sounds like a substance that should be controlled."

"Yes," I smiled. "Yes, it does."

Anne was like many transplants from across America who come to L.A. pursuing one "Show Biz" dream or another and who spend their first several years here sticking close to their new neighborhoods, whether that be West L.A. or Silverlake, Santa Monica, or Hollywood (they usually land in the basin). They immediately assume that the few square blocks around their not-so-well-built apartment *is* L.A. and never get around to discovering the various other parts of it, not to mention the expanse radiating out from L.A., which is Southern California. Anne was beyond that now, of course, had a little bit of her dream realized and had a lovely house in the hills. But she had been working so hard that she was still not locally well-traveled. It was apparent when we started the run-up PCH, heading north towards Santa Barbara, that when she had previously thought of the Southern California coast, she had thought of beaches with bikinis and muscles, both bulging; of bright pink sunglasses, and oiled down, slowly frying skin, and all the little comedies of humans tiptoeing their way back into the font of life. She did not think of a coastline where the continent ends, often sliced off, forming cliffs that meet the pounding waves and surrender just a little more every year in the ultimate battle of attrition. Drama. True drama. She watched the coastline pass as the Bentley glided the continent's edge and was impressed—and delighted. She turned to me and smiled as if I had arranged it. As if I had thought to create this clear evidence of the planet we dwelled on.

We chatted about inconsequential matters: The horsepower of the Bentley and the details of its luxury. Why do people live in Malibu if they will eventually be washed out in floods? Did I surf? No, I said, it wasn't intellectually stimulating enough. Did I really like the outfit she bought, which turned out to be a Galliano, and should she take it back if I hated it? I told her I liked it. She said that she would buy it from me after everything was over. I told her that it would be a gift if everything were successful. No, she insisted, she would buy it. The necklace can be a gift. That would disappoint Roee, I told her. She laughed for the wrong reason. But I did not care to explain the situation. Soon, much quicker than she had imagined, we were in Santa Barbara and pulling into the hotel.

"This is so beautiful!" Anne exclaimed as we got out of the car. Santa Barbara had enchanted her from the moment she caught her first sight of it nestled between the ocean—on this clean, clear day, very blue—and the Santa Ynez Mountains, themselves seemingly blue and rising relatively high and nearly mystical in the landscape. The hotel had a two-story main building surrounded by one-story cottages, all California Spanish-style, with brilliant white walls and red tile roofs. Although the sun was hot, the air was cool coming off the Pacific and stunning with its vibrant ocean smell. The quality of sight in viewing all this was crystal. Facets. She took in a deep breath and, with her eyes, declared her love for all the facets she could take in.

I turned the car and our luggage over to the proper people, and we walked into the quiet lobby with the high-beamed ceiling, Spanish arch doorways, and large ochre tiles on the floor. Bob Hedron, the hotel manager, a man fascinated by my "old money," greeted us.

"Mr. Harrington, so good to see you again. I had no idea you were on the West Coast."

"Just a short trip, Bob. By the way, I would like you to meet Anne Eisley."

"Miss Eisley, a pleasure. I'm sure you will enjoy Mr. Harrington's favorite cottage suite."

"So it's available?" I said, displaying a remarkable lack of presumption.

"Once the call came in from your man, we ensured it would be."

"Thank you, Bob. Thank you very much. It is deeply appreciated."

"Always my pleasure, sir."

Bob loved this old world, old money lack of pretension and genteel courtesy, which was part of my performance as Mr. Harrington. Dealing, as he did, with so many new moneyed Hollywood types who were so aggressive in their joy of suddenly being at the top of the top percentile of American wealth, he found Mr. Harrington a cooling presence, like an early evening ocean breeze, after of period of blistering heat.

We went to our cottage suite and found lunch waiting for us, laid out beautifully on the attached patio: a chilled seafood salad, a light white wine, and a selection of multi-grain bread. Anne, amazed by how delicious each selection of seafood was, responded to the food sensually.

"It's all fresh," I said. "Caught this morning, I'm sure. The dressing, by the way, is made with seven herbs. It's a creation of Roee's, which I have passed off to Bob as an old family recipe."

"Roee doesn't mind?"

"I paid him for it."

"Oh. Well, it's delicious."

"Yes, isn't it? Roee and I once thought of opening a restaurant."

"Why didn't you?"

"The hours are too long. Also, the idea came to us while we were under torture, which is never a good time to make plans."

She looked up into my eyes. "No," she smiled an unsure smile. "I would think not."

Coffee came at just the right time, and over its stimulation, Anne began to tell me certain particulars about growing up.

"I think I gave you some feel for my background when we first met." I nodded assent. "It was a brilliant childhood. Old fashioned, but not out of touch with the times at all. My parents had been antiwar protesters. You know, the Vietnam War?"

"Yes, I guessed."

"They had both come from sprawling upper-middle-class suburbs. Their parents freaked over their views. They met at an anti-war rally, of course, at Columbia University."

"What were they studying?"

"Journalism for my dad. Social Science, of course, for my mom."

"Of course."

"The anger, the rancor they felt the previous generation had for them, simply because they didn't want to see America cheapened by this immoral war, really shocked them, made them very nostalgic for a simpler time."

"The back-to-nature movement?"

"No, not that simple. They didn't join a commune or anything like that. But certainly back to a more manageable America, where democracy was more local."

"So they moved to a small town in South Dakota."

"Yes. Dad became a reporter on the local paper..."

"Eventually becoming its editor."

"Yes, exactly. Very good," she said, impressed.

"And your mom?"

"A mom—and a community activist, of course."

"Of course. Any siblings? I mean, besides me."

"No. I'm an only child. My parents wanted to replicate but didn't want to get carried away. They have never trusted the future."

"A wise point of view."

"Maybe."

"Were you spoiled?"

"No, but I had a lot of attention paid to me and many expectations expressed, but not without encouragement. So I have never had problems with self-esteem."

"Would you have liked siblings?"

"I guess, but Mom, Dad, and I have this special bond. I would not want to have given that up."

"If you had had a brother—an older brother, say, could you have seen him becoming a scientist, say, a theoretical physicist?"

She thought about that. Then said, "Sure. Although Mom and Dad had a suspicion of technology—at least until PCs came along— they've always had a healthy interest in science. Dad has the paper report on it a lot. And we had a great science teacher at the high school. He died just last year. Sad. Anyway, I could see a son of theirs getting turned on to science."

"Good. Next week for a short time, I will be that son. An older brother to you, shy, reclusive, but fascinated, like most current Americans, by this world of Show Biz you have found yourself in. Despite your age differences, you are very close and have a loving relationship."

"So it will not be out of character for sister to hang on to her brother's arm at the ball."

"Not at all. You are proud of your brother and don't mind showing him off."

"Good. That will be easy to play."

We filled the rest of the afternoon with details I solicited from Anne: Names, dates, places of recreation, memorable vacations, childhood diseases, and many facts, most of which I would never need, but I needed to know them; I needed for them to be in the back of my mind as if experience had placed them there.

Then Anne noticed the light changing. "My god! Most of the day is gone, and we haven't been to the beach."

"Too cold to go swimming."

"Oh, forget that. Grab a sweater, and let's sit on the beach. I want to see the sun set into the ocean."

We got to the beach and kicked off our shoes. The sand was still warm and pleasant between our toes. So we decided to walk for a way, Anne being brave enough to dance with the waves, eventually not moving quickly enough and getting soaked to just above her ankles.

"Oh, jeez, that's cold! My toes are numb!"

"Come up here, bury them in the sand."

She came up to me, and I directed her to a place to sit. She dug her feet into the sand. The sun was beginning to touch the horizon.

"God, it's beautiful," she said.

"Not a normal South Dakota vista, huh?"

"Nope. This is almost frightening, edge-of-the-world stuff."

"Frightening?"

"Yeah, like a roller coaster."

"So you might buy a house in Malibu after all."

"Only if it floats."

We stopped talking in order not to distract from the sun's last moments in our view. Then it was fully set. Anne turned to me and, without hesitation, asked, "And you? What do I get to learn about you?"

"Nothing much."

"Why?"

"That's my choice."

"I grilled Roee, you know, without mercy. He didn't give up a thing."

"Roee is a man who has been under torture far greater than nagging questions from a beautiful woman."

"You see, you say things like that."

"Like what?"

"Being under torture."

"A metaphor, maybe?"

"No. Self-dramatizing."

"My mother always accused me of being melodramatic."

"So, you had a mother?"

"Yes, I had no choice. I might have preferred sprouting full-grown in a wheat field, but if the option existed, it was never offered to me."

"You know what I mean."

"What?"

"You have a past."

"Of course. Fifty-two, in fact."

"Yes, that's the problem."

"I have never found it to be a problem."

"No, you like it, don't you?"

"Like what?"

"Being a mystery."

"Aren't we all a mystery?"

"Oh, come on!" She punched me in the ribs.

"Ow!"

"I assume you once worked for the CIA or something."

"You can assume that."

"Fought the good fight against the Communists."

"Oh, yes. I excelled at holding up dominoes."

"You never assassinated anyone, did you? You know, like a South American leader or...." I suppose something suddenly surfaced in my eyes. "Oh. Oh, listen, you're right. I shouldn't ask. None of my business."

If she only knew how much I would have loved to tell her.

"Maybe we should go back," she said.

But I was not ready. "You ask if I love being a mystery. That is a meaningless question. If you ask if being a mystery is an effective tool of my profession, then the answer would be yes. It's very effective."

"But what is your profession?

"It doesn't have a name."

"Except being a fixer."

"Yes, except that."

"Why?"

"I'm good at it. I'm well trained. It pays at a level I demand to live as I see fit."

"So you do it just to buy the Good Life."

"The only good life is a life of freedom. Money often enslaves more than it frees. My life is good because I demand to be free. Money just adds a great deal of comfort to that freedom."

"Well, yeah, of course, freedom. We're Americans; it's our inalienable right. Why are you laughing?"

"You assume I'm an American."

"Aren't you? Surely, you're that, at least."

"And there are no such things as inalienable rights, despite whatever your high school history teacher may have told you."

"Well, I think he heard it from Jefferson."

"A great man. Good writer. Terrific salesman. Freedom is not a right, inalienable or otherwise. If it is, then something is very wrong with the universe, for the vast majority of people during the vast majority of human history have never even come close to it. But freedom is every person's most fervent desire. And desires are rarely met through gifts. They are usually only fulfilled through personal acquisition."

"So grab your freedom, and fuck the other guy?"

"I did not say that, but I am not responsible for the other guy. I can only concern myself with myself."

"You lie."

"I do?"

"Why are you determined to bring Rand down? What business is it of yours? Is someone paying you to do this?"

"I assume Roee has already told you that no one is."

"Roee admires you. I could tell that. Why would he admire someone who is only concerned with himself?"

"You're determined to find something noble in me, aren't you? Women are like that."

"I am only determined to know you. If I cannot know the mundane facts about you, what's left but the tricky issue of your character?"

"Character?"

"Sorry. It's probably a Middle American concept. Very big on the plains."

"I like the concept. But I cannot speak to it."

"Do you believe in morality, Fixxer?"

"Not as such."

"As such?"

"As something imposed on us from above."

"But...?"

"If I told you my moral code, you would find it so simple that it would seem corny to you, and you would laugh."

She looked at me. In the day's diminishing light, she looked at me with an intensity I usually would not have been comfortable with. "It will be hell falling in love with you, Fixxer. It's going to be painful and tragic and full of woe."

"And if I were the kind of man who always lived up to my simple moral code, I would warn you away. I would shun you. I would not allow it to happen."

"But...?"

"But—I sin."

She leaned over and kissed me. It was a long, slow kiss—the kind of kiss where more than just breath was exchanged.

CHAPTER 14
THE IDEA OF MANHOOD

Anne was still asleep when I woke in the morning with a not unhappy aspect on her face. Of course, she could have been dreaming of Mencken, her father's Labrador that she had loved with all the wild abandon a child has for a pet, but I am human enough to have ascribed the cause to something more personally flattering.

Did she snore? As much as I would like to paint perfection here, she did snore. But it was a very charming, delicate snore.

I quietly moved to the bathroom and did the usual requirements. Then I got on the phone and ordered a continental breakfast for two with two full pots of coffee. While waiting, I decided to shave. I ran the water until it was near scalding, then cupped it in my hands and brought it to my face, holding it there, feeling its wonderful sting. Then, just as I was preparing to lather my face, I felt her presence and heard her say, "Oh, don't do that."

"What?"

"Shave."

"Why not?"

"I like a man with a day's growth of beard."

"You and practically every other woman in the world."

"Well..."

"What's the appeal? A full beard, I can see. Clean-shaven, I can see. Scruffy, I cannot see."

"It's not scruffy. It's—"

"Sexy. Yes, that seems to be the prevailing opinion—something 'bad boy' about it. Gotten women into more trouble than not, I would guess."

"Probably. Still—"

"If women had higher standards, the world might be a better place."

"Oh, so it's women's fault?"

"Since the dawn of time."

The doorbell rang.

"That'll be our breakfast. Could you answer it?"

She gave me a stern look and a warning as she approached the door. "Don't shave! Okay?"

"I make no promises."

I heard her greet the porter and direct him to the table she wanted the breakfast on. That done, she signed for the meal and was obviously generous with the tip because the porter's "Thank you" was far more sincere than was the norm for his profession.

"Breakfast!" She called out.

"Be right there!" I called back. A minute later, I came out of the bathroom, crossed over to the table, and sat down.

"You idiot," Anne said with a smile.

"I thought it would answer both our needs."

I had, of course, shaved just half of my face.

"I should make you keep it this way."

"I'm willing."

"Sure you—"

The phone rang. I walked over to the desk and picked it up. "Harrington," I said into the mouthpiece.

"Sorry to disturb you, Mr. Harrington." It was Norton Macbeth. "We have a bit of a problem."

"Go ahead."

"Hinckley and family slipped out, he, he, he..."

"What? Weren't they being watched?"

"Well, not really. I mean, they weren't prisoners, he, he. I thought his good sense would have kept him there."

"If Paul Hinckley had good sense, don't you think his movies would have reflected it?"

"I've never seen his movies."

"Norton, you handle the man's financial planning, and you've never seen his films?"

"I take that back. I saw *Red Dust*."

"And?"

"That's why I've never seen any of the others."

"I sometimes forget your natural wisdom. Okay. Have Roee call the Captain and see if he can track Hinckley down. If so, have the Captain bring him in quietly for more questioning. The fool won't like it, but it's for his protection."

"Okay. Will do." Norton hung up. I turned to Anne.

"You better shave the rest of your face," she said.

"I think it would be best if we get an early—"

"I agree. I'll pack."

xx

I dropped Anne off at her house. Then, after a particularly stimulating goodbye kiss, I said, "You will find a package on your doorstep. It contains certain instructions for tomorrow night. Follow them precisely."

"Okay."

"The next time you see me, I'll be your brother."

"That'll be interesting." She got out of the car. "Hey, wait a minute. What's your name going to be?"

"Good question. What name would you like for a brother?"

"I've always been partial to Tom."

"Then Tom it is. Tom Eisley."

"No!"

"What?"

"Eisley is my stage name."

"Oh. I should have thought to ask. Well, what's our real name?"

"Einstein."

"Einstein?"

"Yes."

"I take it we took a lot of kidding when we were kids?"

"Why do you think I changed my name?"

"And now, here I am, a theoretical physicist by the name of—"

"Einstein."

"Tom Einstein."

"We could say you were named after Edison."

"Oh, thanks. Well, see you tomorrow night, Sis." I started to pull away, back down Elusive Drive.

"Fixxer?" She called out.

I stopped the car. "Yes?"

"Damn, I wish you had a real name."

I could only nod, smile, and move forward.

xx

When I got home, I first asked Roee to get a rush on some ID in the name of Tom Einstein, assistant professor of Physics at MIT. "We can take the pictures as soon as Michael leaves." Then I asked him about Paul Hinckley.

"We haven't got a clue where he is. He hasn't returned to his home in L.A."

"How about the ranch in Paso Robles?"

"We've called up there. No answer."

"Called? Hasn't the Captain sent somebody?"

"He can't justify it."

"God damn it!"

"Fixxer, you've got to remember, he's part of a government organization; he's got procedures."

"Never stopped us."

"Yes, well...."

"Yes, well..." I echoed Roee. It was an old subject with us. "All right. What happened?"

"From what we can gather talking to the manager at the resort, Hinckley got restless. Said something about being cut out of a deal."

"Idiot."

"I thought you said he would follow your instructions."

"I told him to get out of town, which he did. But unfortunately, I forgot to instruct him to stay there until the all clear."

"Plus, you didn't instruct him not to get paranoid."

"Instructing someone in Hollywood not to be paranoid is like instructing a dog not to hump you. You've got to kick the good sense into them. I guess I didn't kick hard enough."

"I don't mean to be unfeeling, but isn't this Hinckley's problem from now on?"

I looked at Roee. I knew the line of my mouth was as straight and rigid as possible. No smile, no frown, just raw reality. "Yeah. His problem."

An hour later, Michael Slayton arrived as arranged by Roee. Michael is one of the top make-up artists in Hollywood, a son and nephew to make-up artists who had done magic on the great stars of the past, a father and uncle to make-up artists who will do magic on the well-manufactured stars of the future. He is a squarely built man with a broad face you must like because it's a face that seems to appreciate all that comes before it unconditionally. Although privy to some of the darkest revelations about stars, some coming from the stars themselves, none have ever diminished his essential love for these people. But then, no artist, I suppose, ever hates his canvas—except when it is blank. This doesn't mean he doesn't relish passing on the information. Gossip is also an art form.

"So, do you understand the assignment?" I asked Michael as he sat me in front of a mirror in my bathroom.

"Yes, Roee explained it and sent over some photos of Anne." Like many in Hollywood, he always used first names, even for those he's never met. "Beautiful girl, isn't she? I would love to do her. I mean, regarding makeup."

"Yes, I understood."

"Now you need two things. To change your appearance to fool a couple of people who have seen you as you are."

"That's right."

"Although, who has really ever seen you as you are?" he said somewhat wistfully for some strange reason.

"No editorializing, please."

"Sorry. And you want your new appearance to make you a credible 'brother' for Anne. Well, the second one is easy. You're not supposed to be twins, and siblings don't always resemble each other; there's always enough genetic mixture from the two parents for diversity."

"Still, it's important that we seem credible as brother and sister."

"Well, your bone structure is similar, and that helps. The nose difference we can assume is a function of sex difference, although I could bring yours in line with an application."

"I would prefer not. I don't know how long I will have to be in this look."

"Okay. Well, how about the first need? How well do these people know you?"

"Not well. One has met me twice, but he's the kind of shy person that averts his eyes a lot. Also, he felt a certain amount of fear on both occasions."

"I can imagine. You scared the shit out of me the first time I met you."

"You had been a bad boy."

"I'm better now."

"Yes, thanks to my incentives."

"For which I will, of course, always be grateful. Now, the second person?"

"He did not see me in the best of conditions. Think of me then as a cat just dragged out of a river."

"Yes, not a true representation of a fully fluffy pussy."

"No, not at all."

"Okay, then, I think simple will be best here. One of your most prominent features is a full head of thick black hair. Anne is a natural blonde?"

"Oh, I hope so."

"Well, if not, who's to tell? We'll make you blond, including your eyebrows, which will make a major difference. As for the rest, I can thin out your hair—a lot—and give you a wispy hair look. Balding, some might call it. If we can't use applications, the rest will have to be in your performance."

"I think I can manage that, but what about this?" I showed him my healing neck abrasion.

"Ouch! Fixxer, what drove you to it?"

"It was not, believe me, self-induced."

"Body makeup will take care of that. Just reapply it often."

"Okay, let's get started."

xx

Small changes, yet a remarkable difference. I have, of course, changed my appearance often for my work, but always for the short term, one day, one evening, and always through wigs, make-up, and applications. They helped me to "inhabit the role," as such things have helped thousands of actors on stage and screen, especially those classically trained. This was different, though, this was nothing but a changed hairdo, and I felt the role inhabiting me instead of the other way around. No wonder women do this. I had to turn away from all reflective surfaces to feel myself again as I talked to the Captain on the phone.

The first words from the Captain were, "Sorry I couldn't help much on Hinckley, but no one here could see the point, and as they are being very accommodating to us concerning the whole Finch murder, I don't feel like pushing it."

"Did I say anything?"

"Did you have to?"

"How about the press?"

"No one has got wind of it. Just another murder in L.A., or worse, a scroungy area of Hollywood where the death of a single, white bachelor of no particular importance is not considered news."

"No one leaked the conditions of Finch's body?"

"I was worried about this assistant coroner. So I promised him five thousand. Hope I can deliver."

"Just call Norton."

"Okay."

"What help can you give me in the next several days?"

"Nothing official, I'm afraid. But I'm taking some time off due me. So I will stick with Roee and monitor the track. You have no idea where you're going to wind up?"

"By a lake somewhere."

"How do you know that?"

"Rand is a fishing nut. If this is where he will base for a while, he would want it close by."

"Why not a river or the ocean?"

"Good fishing at most rivers is in remote areas. Which would seem ideal, but I think it's important for him to be near transportation for a—"

"Quick getaway?"

"Possibly, but I think he's arrogant enough not to worry about that. Just for general purposes, more likely. He likes to roam the world."

"And not the ocean because...?"

"He prefers freshwater fishing."

"Oh."

"Everything is simple when you apply the facts."

"So he could be by a lake anywhere in the world?"

"Well, probably not Lake Victoria, but I wouldn't rule out Europe, Britain, or Canada."

"Really? Well, we better have a jet standing by."

"Roee's already arranged it. You'll be test-driving it for me."

"Okay, so we follow you to the ends of the earth. Then what do we do?"

"Wherever we land, hunker down and monitor. We can't do

anything until I get evidence or a witness."

"And, assuming that happens, what's to prevent him from taking flight."

"Oh, if I come out with evidence or a witness, I'll come out with Rand. I'm sure he'll enjoy my new jet."

"In that event, I'll take a commercial flight."

"Yes, I think that would be best. Just—"

"Get the reimbursement from Norton. Believe me, I will. What if you get into trouble?"

"You and Roee will rescue us."

"Oh great. How are we going to know you're in trouble?"

"I'll take a bath."

"Ouch!"

"If the signal goes dead, find a way to get us out."

"I'm sure Roee has some thoughts on that."

"And Captain?"

"Yes?'

"In any rescue situation, Anne Eisley is the priority."

xx

I sat down to dinner that night to one of Roee's specialties and one of my favorites, an autumn duck salad with French-cut green beans. The combined flavors of orange, cranberries, and pecans, with the delicate taste of the duck and the snap of the braised fresh green beans, are what savoring is all about. Like a cool breeze and the attendant sound of a benign wind's travel through trees; like a quiet moment when you allow reflection to pass through every part of your body and note the glory of the absence of pain; like a brilliant sunset—such experiences need to be minutely embraced until the very second, and only until the second, that they let go.

"Where's Petey?" I asked, suddenly realizing that our houseguest was missing.

"Oh, I sent him out on the town."

"By himself?"

"No." Roee was enjoying his smile of self-satisfaction for a good idea well executed. "With one of Dora's ladies."

"One of Dora's?"

"Tracy, I think. You remember Tracy?"

"Yes, I remember Tracy very well. How biblical of you."

"What?"

"Having the lamb lay down with the lion."

"I thought he was spending too much time with the Bear Rug Program. So consider it a blow against Veritas."

"Petey seems to enjoy it—and if ever there was safe sex—"

"Call me old fashioned, but—"

"Roee, it was a very nice thing to do."

"Maybe, but it wasn't selfless. We could use a night of lower decibels."

"Ah. Yes." I paused to honor the quiet. "That is nice. Thank you."

"For tomorrow?"

"Yes?"

"I don't suppose I could talk you into sneaking some armaments into your luggage."

"Now, what would a geek scientist be doing with a semiautomatic weapon?"

"It doesn't have to be that. A small service revolver."

"Much good that would do me."

"Batsarov is a son-of-a-bitch."

"Yes, but a witless one."

"Which makes him even more dangerous."

"But, like any dumb animal, easy to fool."

"Don't count on it."

"Okay, I won't. I'll count on you as I have on many previous occasions."

"I thank you for your confidence, but—"

"Roee, we have been in dangerous situations before."

"Yes, but we were in the service of something then. What are we in the service of now?"

"Of whatever we want to be."

"That's a meaningless answer."

"I don't think so. What we were in the service of before became— corrupted."

"We went along with it."

"Until the breaking point."

"So, you are trying to make up for—"

"I make up for nothing. I apologize for nothing. I simply live. And I do what I have to do to live in the manner I desire, which you seem to enjoy as well. If, on occasion, I want to do a private job to correct an imbalance I perceive in the universe—that is a right I have grabbed for my own. I will always ask you to participate and pay you far more than any other corrupt entity has, but you can refuse."

"You know I never will."

"Then this conversation is a waste of breath." I stood up. "The duck was fabulous."

I left Roee and went to my room. I read for a while, then went to sleep. You may think, you may very much want to think, that it was a fitful sleep. It was not. It was deep and undisturbed.

xx

The following day I walked into the lab to find Petey staring off into space, a dreamy look in his eyes and a soft, yet potent, smile on his lips. "Good morning," I said quietly so as not to jerk him away from his reverie abruptly.

Petey turned to me and broadened his smile. "Fixxer! Congratulate me! I'm in love!"

"Oh. Well, Petey, you know, Tracy is not really a proper object of love. I mean, she certainly could be, but—"

"Not with Tracy. With the Idea of Manhood! And I used to think masturbation was great!"

"Oh."

"I got to get me a girl, Fixxer! Two, if possible!"

"Well..."

"Give me lessons, will ya?"

"The only real lesson to learn is just to be yourself."

"No, that's never worked!"

"Then I suggest you keep yourself available for the odd job from me so you can afford the likes of Tracy."

"Yeah! That sounds practical! Thanks for the hint! Now sit down, and let's review your mumbo jumbo."

We worked for several hours and then stopped for lunch. I then suggested Petey catch a matinee, preferably a G-rated one, then rested in the library to several symphonies by Walter Piston, nice jaunty, romantic, heroic stuff. Around three p.m., a call came in through Norton from John Walker, who had assisted me once on a job. He's a DP, a director of photography. He told me he was on the current

Bobby Lifton film, shooting in Texas. I congratulated him. Lifton was hot. Currently, the bright boy of film comedy who had had a fantastic string of four box office hits in one year. The previous year he had been best known as the least of ten regulars on a TV sketch comedy show. Before that, he was a standup who worked a lot and a comedy actor who did pilots during pilot season, none of which sold. He was a hard knocks kind of guy. Then he does one low-budget, breakout independent comedy, and suddenly the world can't remember when he wasn't a star.

"Congratulations are not in order, I'm afraid," John said, then went on to explain that Lifton had been a complete madman on the set, making life a living hell for the first-time director on the film, and, in a case of reflected gory, for John as well. Now the director was being fired, possibly deservedly, but it looked like John's head would also roll. Of course, it wasn't fair. His job, as DP, is to support the director, not the star. He appealed to the studio, but that did no good. A DP is a DP is a DP, but a Star is money. "I don't know. I thought of you. I can't afford to lose this picture. Not just because of the money but because it's my first big studio picture. Shit, I lose this, I'll be pushed back to shooting low budgets for foreign and direct-to-video, and they don't even make many of those anymore. I—I don't know what you charge, but—"

"One-half of one percent of your earnings for the next ten years."

"Oh. Ah, okay. Do you think you can do something?"

"I'll give it a try."

We hung up. I turned to my computer and opened Lifton's file.

I scanned through it. I found what I needed and put in a call through Norton to Lifton in Texas.

"Who the fuck is this!" Lifton said, obviously not happy that he was taking a call from someone who would not give a name.

"We want you to know, Mr. Lifton, that we perfectly understand your position."

"My position?"

"Concerning the director that you are having fired. But we believe you go too far in asking John Walker to leave."

"What fuckin' business is this of yours? What are you, the union?"

"Now, we know what a long, hard climb you've had. And how you were abused, browbeaten, cheated, and just plain pissed on by one no-talent asshole after another every step of the way. Never once was it fair or right or proper. Never once did you deserve it."

"Look—"

"Remember when the network would not make a contractual payment to you, claiming some concern that the payment would trigger other payments they were unwilling to pay yet? They knew damn well that wasn't true, of course, did it just because they could, didn't they? Just because it made somebody at the network feel power—no matter how insignificant—throb through their veins."

"How do you—"

"The fucking assholes, right? The goddamn fucking assholes! But now it's your turn, isn't it? It's your turn to be the fucking asshole. Why? Because you can, right? Well, more power to you, Mr. Lifton, but train your guns at those who deserve it. Not innocent bystanders like John Walker."

"How about I train them at you, you—"

"I know your involvement in shutting out certain comedians from the LaughWerks clubs in 1987. If you didn't work at LaughWerks back then, you couldn't make a living on the road, could you? You did it through rumors and innuendo. You just thought of it as pruning to make more room for the likes of you. But, of course, it hurt a few people. Harry King killed himself, didn't he?"

"Look—"

"Wasn't really a crime, I suppose, and who could really peg you as doing anything more than expressing an opinion, passing on things you'd heard? Except for the fact that you planned all this out and confided, in a conspiratorial way, to two other comedians, one of whom just happened to have his tape recorder on, the one he used to rehearse with. I know where that tape is, Mr. Lifton. It's mine for the asking."

"What—what do you want?"

"I think I've made that clear."

"Just keep Walker on?"

"That's it."

"Well, fine. I never really thought of letting him go."

"Of course not."

"Now that tape?"

"What tape?"

"Well, the tape—"

"I know of no tape."

"Look, I've got to have that tape."

"I don't know what you are talking about."

"Who the fuck is this anyway?"

"People I allow, call me the Fixxer."

"Oh, shit—"

I hung up.

There was no tape. But the details of what I had said, told to me by a drunken comedian I once had to rescue from a drug charge, obviously were, judging from Lifton's reaction, perfectly accurate.

xx

At about 6 p.m., just before I was going to dress for the evening, Petey burst into the library.

"Hey, Fixxer, it's time to put on the homing device!"

"Yes, I suppose it is."

"Do you want me to put it on you?"

"No, I would prefer to put it on myself."

"You told me you were circumcised when you were an infant!"

"I spoke the truth."

"So you have no idea how to attach this fake foreskin exactly!" He held it in his hand, its floppy nature a wonder to behold. "I mean exactly how far it should extend from the tip of the penis!"

"I'll try to figure it out."

"That's funny! You know, almost everybody says that! But it's not like a man knows his penis like the back of his hand! So I prepared this little diagram which shows exactly where to attach the foreskin!"

Handing me the fake foreskin, he held up the diagram, which, in simple black-on-white line drawings, showed two penises. One was an uncircumcised penis with a dotted line encircling it about three-quarters down from the tip. An arrow pointing to the dotted line extended from a legend that read, ATTACH FORESKIN HERE. The other penis was an example of what the situation should look like once the attachment was on.

"You can use this!" He held up a little silver tube, just like the one that Formula 12-72 came in. "It's my special adhesive glue! It spreads on easily, so you should have no problem!"

"Thank you, Petey."

"See, the beauty of this thing is, if you have to go through a strip search, they may look up your rectum, but nine times out of ten, they won't play with your penis!"

"I'll count on those odds."

"Take the little tube of adhesive glue with you 'cause it sometimes comes undone! Which is also why you should wear briefs and not boxers!"

"I'll be sure to pack it."

"And remember: No baths! Here!" He handed me a little plastic bag.

"What's this?"

"Skin-tight plastic briefs. Wear them during showers. Then sponge bathe the—"

"Yes, I think I'll know what to do."

"Well, if you've never lived with a foreskin, you may not know proper—"

"Petey, please. I'll forego the instructions and use common sense, okay?"

"All right! All right! It's your penis." He started to walk out, stopped, and turned with one more point. "Oh yeah! You can only put the foreskin on when you are fully erect! Do you think you can handle that?"

"Well," I wasn't sure Petey was aware of his double entendre but decided it was best to assume he wasn't, "I'll have to, won't I?"

"Okay! Well, have a good time tonight!"

"I'll do my best."

"Wish I was going with you!" There was now a hint of charming sadness in Petey's voice. "I've never been to a fancy ball before."

"Well, Petey, that was once the case with Cinderella. And look what happened to her."

Petey brightened up. "Yeah! Yeah! I suppose there is always hope! Well, thanks, Fixxer, for those kind words."

And out he went. A hopeful individual newly enamored with the Idea of Manhood and prepared to believe that his Fairy Godmother— or at least some kind madam with a quality list—was just around the corner.

CHAPTER 15
NATIONS HAVE BORDERS—PEOPLE DON'T

The charitable impulse in humans is always suspect. I have never seen an instance of charity that was unconditional, even if the condition was as seemingly harmless as, "Here, take this charity, this money, this helping hand, this leg up, and in return, give me nothing more than the right to count myself among the humane." Humane as opposed to human, I suppose. To be human is to lie, cheat, harm, steal, rape, pillage, and murder. To be humane is to feel bad about it. The most popular charities are safe charities. Contributing to the recovery from a natural disaster is a perfect example, for unless one is very Old Testament, there is not one chance in a million trillion that the victims of a natural catastrophe deserved their fate. Animals are also good. Animals never offend us with wild opinions of their own. The unborn have been very popular of late for this very same reason. But the poor, the hungry, the homeless, the war-torn, the disadvantaged—is there not in all of us a sneaking suspicion that they may just be deserving of their fate? Certainly, many seem to be offended by them. Still, even they have their charities, and certain people contribute—and feel good about it.

So the impulse may not be pure, so what? The outcome is the same—a helping hand is extended. The person grabbing that hand probably doesn't care what the motivation of the person extending it is. However, it's no stretch to imagine that the person grabbing would like to believe that they have suddenly become the object of pure love.

How did Andy Rand's EarthPeople stack up as a charity? Well, it was more a cause than a charity. Still, Rand always portrayed his theory of World Citizenship as a way towards solutions to those problems of poverty, hunger, and even disease that commanded, on occasion, the short attention span of overnight charities where slews of celebrates and powerful Hollywood executives band together to get something "done about it."

NATIONS HAVE BORDERS—PEOPLE DON'T was the bumper sticker slogan of EarthPeople. An absurdly naive idea, of course, for it is the borders within people that shape the political boundaries surrounding them. Still, even an absurdly naive idea is an idea, and this made EarthPeople a risky charity, for there is always much that can offend in an idea. So Hollywood prefers its charities to be—as Hollywood prefers so many things to be— what has become known in the trade as No Brainers.

Despite this, EarthPeople was popular because Andy Rand was powerful. And the EarthPeople Ball was always one of the top charity events of the year.

I picked Anne up in a gaudy lavender stretch limousine.

"Oh my god!" She said as she opened the door. "You do kind of look like my dad. This is freaky. Your hair!"

"It will grow back, I'm sure."

"I hope so. Otherwise, you're one-third less the man I love."

Anne, of course, was radiant. She stood in the Galliano, the unique diamond pin we had sent over pinned on, her evening make-up glowingly applied, her hair put up in a formal yet soft way. She smiled. If I was not a man who had been trained to have control, I could have become lightheaded.

"Do you have your luggage?"

"Yes, right here."

In the entranceway were a suitcase and an overnight case. I called for the driver and had him take the bags and place them in the trunk next to the two pieces of old American Tourister Roee had found for "Tom." That done, we headed for the Century Plaza Hotel, where the ball would take place. Anne, following her instructions completely, played the role of my sister from the moment she got into the limo, which was one of a fleet from a commercial service that Anne, as part of her instructions, had ordered., The driver was probably an aspiring actor, writer, director, or some combination thereof. Roee had booked a room for me at the Miramar in Santa Monica, and we had the limo pick me up there. We talked about brother/ sister stuff. She asked me how things were going at MIT. Had I talked to Mom and Dad lately? I thanked her for the gift of a place to stay at the beach. She said she was happy to do it. Every landlocked native Dakotan needed to stay at the beach on their first trip to the coast, she said.

We arrived in Century City to join a long line of other limos and Rolls-Royces, Mercedes, Bentleys, Porsches, and the odd Lamborghini that stretched along the curved driveway in front of the Century Plaza and spilled out onto Avenue of the Stars. The parking valets worked furiously to move the cars through and get the guests into the hotel. It's but a few short steps from your car to the entrance, and I knew exactly where to go from there—an immediate right to the narrow escalator that would take you down one level, where you would make another immediate right to jump onto another narrow escalator down to a basement of three ballrooms below—but I acted as if I had not only never been here before, but was being overwhelmed by the glamour of it all.

"Wow, look at that!" I prodded Anne, then pointed past the substantial marble columns to the Lobby Court pit bar directly ahead, filled with celebrity watchers and paparazzi, all being held back by security people, who also directed us to the escalators. I acted somewhat giddy about the popping flash bulbs. "Oh-oh, look, Anne, jeez, it's David Hasselhoff!"

Anne leaned into me and whispered. "Do you really think an MIT physicist would be excited to see David Hasselhoff?"

"You'd be surprised at a depth of his fandom."

"Watch your step," another security person said as we were herded onto the escalator, some women fearing for their full, long evening gowns on the tight squeeze. Down one more escalator to the grand foyer, which served all three basement ballrooms: The Santa Monica Room, the Los Angeles Room, and the Beverly Hills Room. Tonight the movable walls between them would be gone making for one huge "L.A. Basin" ballroom that would, nonetheless, be crowded to the point of claustrophobia. We were ushered by security to a table under the middle of three quasi-Arabic golden domes that were the main feature of the foyer's ceiling and which gave the room a golden glow. Two pleasant young women at the table gathered our tickets and checked them against the guest list. They were in Anne's name. One of the women smiled broadly at her and said, "I loved *Cobblestone Bay*. You were wonderful in it. It broke my heart when they took it off the air."

"Well, thank you very much. That's very kind of you to say," Anne said gracefully as the woman handed us two slips of paper that noted the table we were to sit at.

We entered the expanded ballroom to the sounds of Bobby Baker's Roaring Rhythm Rascals, a band put together by an ex-child star of the 60s that played upbeat, yet offbeat, what they called "New Wavy Wave Dixieland." The five-piece retro hot band also included an ex-member of a 70's Disco group, who performed here as the lead vocalist, and a man who had spent just a little over two years in jail for masterminding a famous Wall Street insider trade in the late 80s. The other two members were just musicians, but three out of five kitsch celebrities weren't bad. The band was performing on a stage and in front of a giant banner featuring the EarthPeople slogan—NATIONS HAVE BORDERS—PEOPLE DON'T— and a monumental painting of the big blue marble view of Earth from space. That motif filled the ballroom: Space views of the earth plastered all the walls and hung, like flags, from the ceiling; flora big blue marble earths sat as centerpieces at each table and, placed at their seats, there was a little gift for each woman of a small round blue bottle, perfect for their favorite perfumes, created and hand blown by craftsmen in Venice, especially for this occasion and donated by Silvio Ramassa, an Italian media mogul who has always been suspected of Mafia leanings, which, of course, he has always denied.

There was the standard buzz of the beginning of such a night and a crowd in front of the bar. Anne took the lead as I made a credible show of gawking as we looked for and found our table. Sara Hemmings was already there with her husband, a director—luckily for them—of approximately the same stature as Sara.

"Hello, Sara Hemmings," she introduced herself as if we didn't know. Then her husband introduced himself. Then Anne introduced herself and me, who stumbled slightly over my statement of how much a fan I was of both of their work.

"' Einstein, uh?" Sara said, being charming. "With a name like that, I hope you're a scientist."

"Uh, yes, actually, I am."

"No! Really? I suppose it was your name that gave you your interest."

"Thank goodness it wasn't Curie," the husband said with equal charm. "Or we might have lost Anne to science." There was a bit of flirting in how he said it.

Others soon joined the table—Sara's agent; Sara's manager; Sara's sister, and all their dates—to give us a full complement of ten. I went to the bar and got drinks, white wine for Anne and beer for "Tom," noticing many people I had dealt with at one time or another, including Torvald Engstrand. No one recognized me. Not so much because my disguise or act was that good, but because at such affairs, only the highly recognizable were recognized. All others float by like flotsam.

When I returned to the table, dinner was being delivered by waiters, and Anne was skillfully participating in several conversations around the table, being funny and bright, but never at the expense of Sara, indeed, in what seemed to be a conspiratorial collaboration with her. They were becoming great friends. I sat down and remained quiet and began to eat the assembly line prepared, yet still quite palatable, sea bass concocted by Jacques du Mont, the currently hot Hollywood chef. It was apparent that in my absence, the story of whom I was had gone around the table, and so I was left alone to Star gaze, the extremely fortunate unimportant outsider that I was.

Andy Rand was nowhere to be seen. His place at the head table was empty. But conversations made his presence felt, for everyone was still intrigued by his sudden departure from NewVue. Our table got into it at one point, and Sara speculated that Andy had possibly left to devote his full time to EarthPeople, and perhaps would make that announcement tonight. Her husband couldn't believe that. "I mean, this is nice, this 'can't we all get along' philosophy of his. But for a man like him, can it be anything more than a hobby? I mean, where's the power in it? I did two movies for Andy. He's a control freak. We got to like each other, but only after some heated arguments from script through editing. Half the time, he wanted to do things one way just because I wanted to do them the other. Still, his story instincts are pretty good, so you must listen to him. But he likes to win the day. That's the main thing. He always wants to win the day. What the hell is there to win in promoting world harmony?"

Later, as the plates sat before us holding slaughtered vestiges of our meal, the host for the evening took the mike to hearty applause. He was a well-liked comedian who had become a respected actor, praised playwright, and box-office-pleasing director. He was also damn funny, skewering certain audience members, the President of the United States, and the current tawdry scandal in the sports world. Then he introduced the surprise entertainer for the night, a country singer with buns so tight he had recently managed to cross over and have the number-one pop song in the nation. The audience loved him, swung to the music, and stared at him with the adoring eyes of people always happy to be in the presence of a moneymaker.

But we had still seen no sign of Andy Rand. It was beginning to cause talk as the dance band was setting up. Had he divorced himself from Hollywood so entirely that he wouldn't even attend his event? Maybe he couldn't get a flight from wherever? He went to Tibet, someone swore. The monks wouldn't let him come home for this. Well, when is somebody going to make an announcement?

Not two seconds after the question was asked, the host shouted into the microphone: "Ladies and gentlemen, the founder of EarthPeople—Andy Rand!

Then there he was, appearing from behind the stage, in a spotlight, to triumphal music from the band and a standing ovation, like the goddamn President of the United States of America, or, at the very least, a presidential candidate in a roomful of party faithful. He strode in smiling, slim, and seemingly taller than his 5-foot-6-inch self, an illusion aided by his extremely well-cut conservative tux. Rand could not be described as attractive nor unattractive, for he looked like a precocious, prepubescent geek kid whose favorite subject was math. This was partly due to the oversized glasses with squarish frames that he wore in imitation of an 80-year-old movie mogul on whom they looked good, combined with his extended high, round, and shiny forehead that had "egg" written all over it. But mostly, it was due to a particular look in his eyes that said: "I'm smart, and I know it. You're not, and I know that too." However, the aspect of his face that was truly disturbing was his large, oval jaw that hung below his long, straight mouth, giving him the look of a children's show puppet. You were convinced that when he talked, the lips would part, go up and down, and never articulate.

The standing ovation continued. Why? Courtesy? Release from the pent-up pressure of anticipation? Or could it have been the well-timed drama of it all? It must have been a combination of the three, but mostly the third—timing is everything.

Rand made that gesture a speaker does to get control of a crowd, as if both patting their heads and pushing them gently down.

"Thank you! Thank you! Please! No, thank you!" The applause died, and the crowd deflated onto their seats. "I'm sorry not to have been able to join you earlier in the evening and enjoy what I understand was a great meal and some great entertainment." Applause made an enthusiastic comeback. "But I was busy counting all the money we've raised tonight for EarthPeople due to your generosity, and I'm happy to report that it is coming in around Six hundred fifty thousand dollars!" There was more applause; like that for the home team. "Thank you! Thank you! Your generosity truly, truly moves me because this organization, which I founded five years ago, is of such importance to me. Now, if I may make a few comments—I know you didn't come here for a speech—uh—, but it's either indulge me for a few brief comments—or receive a rather long memo from me in the morning."

Laughter broke out at this ultimate in-joke referring to a now infamous 20-page inter-office memo Rand had written two years ago pointing out that most of NewVue's competition was ruining the business by overspending on talent. It had been momentarily embarrassing for Rand when it had leaked out, but only momentarily. Hollywood's atmosphere is never pure enough for embarrassment to survive much more than a moment.

As the laughter died down, Rand added one quick, self-deprecating punch, "And I don't want to do that again!" getting the required laughs to close the matter. Now things became quiet. "Serious" was about to invade the ballroom, and "serious" was taken very seriously by these people.

"EarthPeople is an organization built on the simple philosophy that the earth has borders, but people don't. So to us, it is important that people throughout the world communicate with each other about our shared problems. I don't know if you're like me. Still, I've become frustrated over the years watching governments trying to solve these problems, problems of economics, problems of poverty, problems of disease and horrible epidemics, and problems of ethnic strife. I've become frustrated because governments seem to have an agenda that is not always in the people's best interest. Now, I'm not saying, as you know, that government should be thrown out—I'm not an anarchist—obviously. But I am saying that all the people of the earth should take responsibility for themselves." Rand gestured to the banner behind him. "We should all understand that we are all citizens of this 'Pale Blue Dot' and that together, with all the intelligence we have among all of us on this planet, we can come up with solutions to problems and help guide our governments to execute those solutions. Because that's all governments truly are. They're—they're executives. I, for one, know a lot about being an executive." There was laughter, of course. "And I know, as an executive in the motion picture business, that it is the *people* that make it happen. In our case, the people are the—the actors, and the directors, and the cinematographers, and the grips, and the electricians—"

"And the writers!" Someone anonymously yelled out from the back.

Rand laughed with the people. "Yes—yes, of course, and the writers. So this money you generously donated tonight will help us in a continuing effort to put people in touch with people. That's what EarthPeople does. It facilitates a World Citizenship mindset by getting people to communicate with people as fellow EarthPeople, in the hope that such communication will lead to solutions for our shared problems. Now, that's all I want to say, which is, basically— thank you."

Somewhere from the back, before the applause could break out: "Andy, what are your plans?"

More than a few shouts called out, seconding the motion.

"Okay—okay. Before I turn you over to the dance band, I understand you all want to know my plans. Well, I have little more to add to what I said at my news conference." There were, I believe, the beginnings of a tear coming from his right eye. When I saw that, I was convinced that the man in the back who had asked the question was a plant. "Folks, I need some time, I guess, time to be by myself and to just— search my soul. There is much in the world that I would like to do yet, that I would like to accomplish. And believe me; it includes this great business of filmed entertainment. So, I am not leaving you. But I do need this time as a time to reflect and contemplate. So if I seem not to be in communication for a little while, please don't let anyone take it as a slight. I will be thinking of you constantly, my friends, all of you who have been so generous here tonight, all of us who have had fun together in this business. Even some of you whom I may have locked horns with. Because, you know, in this business, we may lock horns occasionally, but we never really mean it, do we?" Laughter again. Slightly nervous, though, bordering on ironic, as if the audience wanted to believe, but...

Rand wrapped it up. "So, again, I'm very moved. I'm about ready to break into tears at your support and your generosity for this cause.

Thank you, thank you from the bottom of my heart, please enjoy the rest of the night's entertainment, and—and—well, how can one be any more eloquent than simply to repeat: Thank you."

Rand gestured to the dance band, and music started to pound into the room; the guests applauded and pressed forward to either get close to Rand or move onto the dance floor. It was a superb performance. And Rand came down from the stage and into the crowd to receive his due from his admirers.

"Wow! He seems like a really great guy!" I said with all the enthusiasm of a man from Middle America, pleasantly surprised by the genuineness of this "Hollywood type."

"Oh, he is," Sara said. "A true humanitarian."

"And very attractive," Anne said, hand on her chin. "In a little-boy-gee-whiz kind of way."

"Well, would you like to meet him?" Sara asked.

"I would love to meet him."

Sara and Anne, like two high school best friends at the first dance of the year, got up—Sara grabbing Anne's hand—and moved swiftly towards the crowd around Rand.

"You know," Sara's husband, the director, said, "If Andy were anything less than what he is on the Hollywood food chain, he would not be described by women as little-boy-gee-whiz, but as little-boy-gee-what-a-little-whizzer."

The agent and manager and even their wives laughed. I feigned a struggle to appreciate the humor to be included as I listened through the tiny earphone Petey had placed in my right ear to the conversation just starting on the other side of the room. The diamond pin mic stuck into Anne's Galliano was working faultlessly.

"Andy! Andy!" Sara made herself known and announced for all others to shrink back.

"Well, hello, Sara." It was amazing how the 5 foot 8 Sara, with added 2-inch heels, bent to kiss Rand without making him seem small. "You look wonderful, as always. I thank you for your help tonight."

"Absolutely my pleasure. You know what a fabulous job I think you're doing with EarthPeople."

"Thank you. Your support means a lot."

What Sara did next was nicely maneuvered. She had kept Anne directly behind her, and now she moved with the slow grace of a parting curtain to reveal her. "Andy, I would like you to meet Anne

Eisley, who also admires your work."

Even with the distance between us, I could see the impact on Rand's face. It's hard to hide a blow to the heart.

"That was a great speech, Mr. Rand," Anne said with a full flow of her golden tones.

"Oh, hardly a speech, just a few comments. And 'Mr. Rand' was my father's name."

I must have grimaced over the cliché because Sara's agent's wife asked me if I was okay.

"Have you thought of going into politics?" Anne asked.

"What?" Rand said, gesturing around him. "And leave the 'Real World?'"

Anne gave a nice little musical laugh I hadn't heard before. She was a brilliant actress.

"No, seriously. I mean, I'm an actress—"

"Yes, of course! Let's see...." He thought for a moment. "*Cobblestone Bay.*"

"Yes, I'm impressed."

"I don't often pat myself on the back, but I have the best casting eye in the business."

"So why haven't you ever cast me?" she teased.

"Could never find material good enough for you."

"Oh, perfect comeback, Andy. I am doubly impressed."

There was a moment of silence. If Anne was doing her job, she was directly looking into Rand's eyes and encouraging him to reciprocate.

"So—so you think I should go into politics?" Rand asked, obviously not wanting the moment to pass.

"I think any man of your intelligence who is as comfortable with power as you are should not pass up the opportunity to exercise it for good."

"An interesting perspective for an actress."

"Andy! That's an almost sexist statement!"

"Oh, I didn't mean it to be. I—" There was real fear in his voice. "I guess I meant to say—"

"Sexist yet true. That's what I was trying to say earlier. I'm an actress, but the world being the way it is these days, I've realized that I can't be just an actress. Even if that hurts my career."

"So, what are your ambitions?"

"Oh, I don't know. Making the trains run on time, I suppose."

It was, of course, an amusingly fascist thing to say. But coming from the lips of a stunningly beautiful woman who had just declared her love of power, it was—for the likes of Rand—sexy as hell.

"I assume you're here with a date?" Rand asked.

"Yes, of course. Why? Do you have something in mind?" It was an intriguing challenge.

"Well, if you were free, I could devise a not unexciting proposal."

"Sound's interesting. If you don't mind dragging along my brother."

"That's your date?" Rand was delighted.

"Yes. He's visiting from Massachusetts. I thought I would show him some Hollywood glamour."

"And your—boyfriend didn't mind?"

"I don't have a *boy*friend, Andy. It's a man I'm looking for."

"Oh."

"Why don't you come over and meet my brother? He's a big movie buff."

"Well..."

"Come on." She grabbed his hand and gently dragged him to our table, an action noted by everybody. Sara, who had moved on to talk to others, left them to catch up. I stood up as they approached us, quickly checking my tux for any food spills, which allowed the slightly nervous "Tom" to hide his eyes.

"Tom, I want you to meet Andy Rand. Andy, this is my brother, Tom Einstein."

Rand was amused. "Einstein? Don't tell me you're—"

"A physicist, yes. Everybody asks."

"Oh, well, I'm sorry to have joined the hoi polloi."

"Tom is an assistant professor at MIT."

Rand, obviously a man who liked labels, was interested. "Really? Well, you know, I have a strong interest in science. What end of physics are you in?"

"Oh, nothing dramatic, I'm afraid. I mean, I'm no Stephen Hawking."

"Oh, but you are an Einstein, so think well of yourself."

I refused, of course, to get the joke. "Oh, well, but, you see, we're not really related. At—at least, I don't think we are. Anne, you're the family historian."

"No, afraid not. Just a coincidence."

"Well, at least you can't be blamed for the atomic bomb," Rand joked again.

"Nor, unfortunately, for the general and special theories of Relativity."

"Nonetheless," Rand said to be kind, "I'm sure you're doing good work."

"Well, it's interesting, anyway, because—do you really want to hear about it?"

"Andy, you should take this opportunity. He never talks to me about his work."

"Well, it's just that I find it hard to put in layman's words."

"Try me. I'll scream if you get abstract."

"Well, what I'm doing is a blend of quantum physics and neuroscience. I'm trying to understand the brain's workings, such as information processing, consciousness, and attention. I'm—I'm making a basic assumption, I suppose, that the brain works on a quantum level in the final analysis, just like the universe works on a quantum level. Deeper—deeper than just the neurons, you know."

"Really?" The ballroom faded for Rand. The noise abated. Anne was a presence he probably couldn't let go of, but other than her, I became the sole focus of Rand's attention. "Fascinating. And where is your research leading?"

"I don't know. I—I do pure research."

"Would it apply to a technology for direct communication with a human brain?"

"Direct communication? Well, sure, yeah, I guess. Understand the mechanics of anything, and then you can build tools to exploit that understanding. But why would you want direct communication with a brain? I mean, we have that right now talking to each other."

"But what if you couldn't talk, or we didn't speak the same language? What if you were in a coma or suffering from a stroke? Or were like Helen Keller, deaf, dumb, and blind. Sorry to be so non-PC."

"Oh, no, that's okay." I displayed extreme interest. "I see where you are going. Yes—yes, some of the ideas I'm developing are in that direction. Especially my experiments in laser encoding of information on atoms. You have an interest in this?"

"Yes, I do. It comes out of the work that EarthPeople has been doing, and I would like to talk to you about it more, but this is not the place. So why don't you both join me for a few days."

"Where?" Anne asked.

"Well, I don't want to..."

"Oh, of course," Anne said, showing proper sensitivity. "Well, Tom and I were going to fly to Lake Tahoe tonight for a few days."

"Tonight?"

"Yeah. We've got bags packed in the limo and a 2 AM flight. It was a mad, impulsive idea."

"Well, get madder and more impulsive then, and come with me now. I've got a helicopter on the roof."

"Well, what if—I mean the rumors? We don't have our passports."

"Hey! I'm a world citizen. I don't deal with passports. Believe me; it will be no problem. The whole world wants to know what Andy Rand will do next. Come with me, and you'll have the privilege of finding out. And the bonus is, if you've packed for Lake Tahoe, you are packed perfectly for where I will take you."

"Well... Tom?"

"Sure. Why not? It sounds exciting. But only if we can talk about movies too."

"Oh, of course. Love to talk about movies."

Anne smiled. "Well, okay. Why not?"

"Great!" Rand raised his right hand, and suddenly a man with a long, passive face was standing next to him. "Could I have your valet ticket?" Rand asked me. I gave it to him. He turned to the man. "Get the bags from this limo. Pay the driver with a handsome tip and dismiss him. Then bring the bags up to the helicopter."

"Leaving now?" The man said in careful English as if trying to hide an accent.

"Yes, I think we can leave now." Rand turned to Anne and me. "Shall we?"

We said our goodbyes to Sara and the rest of the table and headed toward the exit. A little voice in my right ear said, "Be sure to dump the stuff." I scratched my nose in acknowledgment of the message. "By the way, did you recognize long-face? Don't know his name, but I connect him with the Basque ETA separatists."

"Dump the pin," I whispered to Anne as we passed a bus cart from the kitchen. She quickly removed it and put it on top of a half-eaten dessert. I placed my earpiece next to it. Roee, looking very smart in his waiter's uniform, took the cart to the kitchen.

Blood is Pretty

CHAPTER 16
CHATEAU DE LA LUNE-SHINE

Can I be blamed for a bit of smugness? It's always good when suppositions prove correct and plans based on those suppositions run smoothly. But, of course, this had always seemed like a sure thing. Start with a man who's just been the center of positive attention. That man will feel powerful as if the world does indeed revolve around him, as he has always suspected. Place before him a most desirable woman. The man will surely be attracted, but his current powerful state of mind will embolden him to do something about that attraction, not to let this moment slip by. Then immediately place before him another attraction, something possibly more cerebral but no less visceral than the smooth skin and warm presence of the woman: The acquisition of More. More property. More position. More power. Tie one to the other, and the man will think that he is twice blessed, that he cannot lose, that the world is his for the taking, and the man will act to consolidate his spoils, just as you have predicted. Easy—but then I'm only asking for a bit of smugness.

We were escorted, Rand, Anne, and I, by an appreciative hotel representative up a private elevator to the roof of the Century Plaza Hotel. There, warming up, was a spectacular Aérospatiale Dauphin commuter helicopter, its rotor blades spinning powerfully, the noise from them deafening, the disturbed air blowing in a confusion of directions. Rand motioned us to duck our heads and quickly led us to the craft, opening a sliding door to the back seats in the cabin. He indicated the boarding step and offered Anne his hand. She stepped into the helicopter with surprising grace, given the formal nature of her attire. I followed, noting the unusual landing skids the craft rested on. Why customize landing skids? Especially ones that seemed larger than necessary, even considering the size of the craft. I sat next to Anne.

Sitting in his seat on the flight deck, the pilot turned to look at us. It was a hard, Hispanic face that refused to reveal any confusion in his eyes.

Rand entered and shouted to be heard, "I'm taking some guests with me, Miguel."

It must have satisfied because Miguel snorted an "it's your money" snort and turned back to his controls. Then the man from the ballroom, the Basque, came onto the roof with a hotel bellman bringing our luggage, which he quickly stored in the baggage compartment at the rear of the craft, then came around to enter the helicopter and sit next to Miguel on the flight deck.

"All right, let's go," Rand said into his headset microphone, and the craft rose, immediately giving us that combined feeling of lift and hanging by a rope that distinguishes flight in a helicopter.

I had expected the craft to make the ridiculously short trip from Century City south to LAX, where a private jet would be waiting. I had thought a helicopter was a bit more than was required—a limo from and to the airport would have done nicely—but I had put it in the ego column, something ostentatious Rand needed for his self-image. So I was surprised to realize that we were moving not south but east, at a good clip, away from the airport and the city itself.

"So, can you tell us now where we're going?" Anne asked.

"Not far. Not far at all. Have you ever heard of Lake Arrowhead?"

"Yeah. Up somewhere by the Big Bear skiing, isn't it?"

"Big Bear is at 7000 feet. This is a man-made lake 2000 feet below it, about a hundred miles from here; been a resort for years. Boating, water skiing, fishing. Some industry people have vacation homes up there, but nobody who's on the A-list. That's why it was perfect for me. No one would think I would take a house there. They all expect me to be in Aspen or Switzerland or even, God forbid, in some monk's retreat in Tibet. People in motion pictures are so predictable. So I found a hideaway right in my backyard. I'm like the Purloined Letter."

"Purloined letter?" Anne queried curiously.

"Uh, it's from Poe, Anne," I as Tom informed his sister. "A man hides a letter by putting it in plain sight."

"Oh. Anne said. "That's very clever."

"I thought so." Rand acknowledged.

Yes, very damn clever—clever enough to dull my little smugness.

I wondered what Roee was thinking right now as he was facing the disappointment of being unable to test drive the jet.

"I bought a house on the lake through a dummy corporation. Sent out a rumor that it was being bought for an exiled Central American politician. Not a big fish, not anybody infamous, just someone who got away."

"Altering the letter slightly," I said.

"What?" Rand asked.

"Like in the story."

"Oh, yeah. I've never actually read the story."

Rand turned his attention back to Anne. "Cost me 7.9 million. I think you'll like it."

Anne and I turned now to watch the lights pass below us. We were leaving L.A. proper and traveling over Alhambra, El Monte, and West Covina. There was nothing much distinctive about the landscape below outside of the rivers of white and red lights that were the freeways, high school football fields, and the well-lighted masses of the occasional mall. Soon we were over Pomona, and the chopper veered slightly north and headed for the San Bernardino Mountains. The lights disappeared as we came to the mountains, and we were suddenly enclosed in the dark as we swiftly ascended. Anne must have felt it keenly, for she inhaled a deep breath of fear.

"Don't worry about the night flying," Rand said. "Miguel is used to it."

Exactly why, he didn't say. Nor would Anne have thought to ask, but I was pretty sure it was experience gathered in flying guns, drugs, or both, into and out of some inhospitable jungles in Central or South America.

Then, suddenly: The lights of Lake Arrowhead. Most were clustered at the village on the South end, but bright spots peeked up here and there out of the thick growth of pine trees, indicating homes along the lake. We flew over the village and then headed over the lake for two coves at the northeast end. As we approached, Miguel flicked a switch above him, and lights blazed ahead, illuminating a large house on a headland that divided and helped define the coves. Also illuminated was a large dock on the lake about forty feet below the promontory. An orange metal tram and its track ran up those forty feet along a steep hillside, passing between tall pines, allowing access to and from the lake.

"Chateau de la Lune," Rand said. "I swear I didn't name it. That's what it's always been called."

Miguel hit another switch, and there was a sudden and scary combination of sounds: An automatic opening followed immediately by the sound of decompressing air and inflating material. I looked out the window and confirmed what I was beginning to suspect was the need for the oversize skids. They had contained a system to turn the skids into pontoons. There were now prominent, inflated silver bladders extending from the bottom of each skid, allowing us to touch down gently on the lake's surface, just to one side of the dock.

"Oh, wow!" I said, displaying my scientist's sense of wonder. "What are they made out of?"

"A super thick, multilayered Mylar. Very tough," Rand answered.

Miguel maneuvered the chopper to the dock, and the Basque jumped out and secured a line. We then exited, using the Mylar pontoons as a step to get us onto the dock. Rand led us off the dock and to the tram, which was nothing more than a metal cage with padded seats and a simple UP BUTTON/DOWN BUTTON control. Once we were settled, Rand hit the UP BUTTON, and the tram jerked into motion, slowly climbing, leaving behind Miguel and the Basque, who busied themselves securing the chopper and retrieving our bags. When we reached the top, we could see the Chateau de la Lune through a small forest of pines. It was illuminated for glory and did not fail to impress.

"They tell me it's a copy of a chateau in Rheims," Rand said.

"Oh, Andy! It's beautiful!" Anne waxed.

"Wait until you see it in the daylight."

We followed Rand up a path to the house and entered by tall glass French doors that led us into a large living room with a cathedral ceiling, the underside of the gable roof, secured by a series of connecting cross beams, jutting up and coming to a point far above our heads. Hanging from the center cross beam on a long ornamental metal cable was a sizeable ornate brass chandelier, made initially to hold large candles, now fitted with electric lights in the shape of candles. Dominating at eye level, directly opposite the glass doors, was a 14-foot-high fireplace, the giant fire pit large enough for a man to walk into.

The walls were unpainted plaster adding to the antique feel of the place. The furniture, two large sofas arranged opposite each other and several club chairs, was all upholstered in the same red and blue fabric of a fussy design. There were tables where needed.

"Very dramatic, Andy," Anne said.

"Well, don't blame me if you don't like the interior design. Everything came with the place."

"For 7.9 million, I would hope so." Anne laughed.

"Do you need anything, Mr. Andy?" The voice came from the side, from a doorway into what looked like the dining room. A beautiful dark young woman, maybe 18 or so, stood in a servant's uniform. Not a "sexy maid's" outfit, just a plain, dull gray knee-length cotton dress with a demure white collar and a utilitarian white apron. Nevertheless, "sexy" shouted through it, a natural, native, elemental sexy.

"Well," Rand said, "here's where I must admit to a heinous crime. Imelda is an undocumented worker, and I do not pay her social security. Of course, for the excellent service she renders, I more than adequately compensate her. I'm also helping to put one of her brothers through college in Peru, a very bright young man who wants to be an engineer. And I've managed to extricate her other brother from the clutches of The Shining Path rebels."

"Is that Miguel?" I asked.

"No," Rand answered, then left the subject. "So you see, Anne, I could not enter politics, even if I wanted to. This immoral behavior of mine would be found out by the opposition and used against me. Once the public found out how despicably I have improved these people's lives at the expense of the immigration and tax laws of this land, they would flow in massive numbers into voting booths to vote against me." He turned to Imelda. "Yes, Imelda, thank you for staying up so late. There is something you can do. Please escort Miss Anne and Mr. Tom up to the guest bedrooms. Make sure they are comfortable and get them anything they require." He turned back to us. "It is late, and I'm sure you're both very tired."

I yawned. "Now that you mentioned it."

"Good. I will see you both at breakfast then. Nine o'clock. Good night." He turned and left, exiting into a room that seemed to be an office or study from the glance I got of it as he passed through the door.

"Come, please, this way," Imelda said as she turned and led us out of the living room and into the foyer.

"I'm glad I packed my slippers," I said quietly to Anne, stopping her.

"What?" Anne asked.

"Look at the stone floor. Italian, I'm going to guess. Very cold in the morning."

"Oh, right. It's gorgeous, isn't it?" She was sincerely impressed.

"This way, please." Imelda was already halfway up a winding, mahogany staircase. We followed. At the top of the stairs was an arched opening that looked out onto the living room. Here its full effect hit you. It was a magnificent room, a literal sculpturing of space into an aesthetically pleasing form.

"Miss Anne, this will be your bedroom." Imelda was halfway down the hall holding a door open.

Anne went to her and looked inside. "Oh, very nice."

Imelda moved across the hall and opened another door. "And Mr. Tom, this is your room."

"Thank you," I said as I moved to the room.

"Do you need anything?" Imelda asked us.

"Only our luggage," Anne said.

"That is coming."

"Well, thank you, then," I said.

Imelda nodded shyly, then left.

"Well, Andy seems perfectly nice to me," Anne said.

"Seeming is not believing," I answered.

"Are you sure we won't be embarrassed by this charade?"

"No, we will not be embarrassed. We may get killed, but we won't be embarrassed."

"Oh, speak other words of comfort to me, *mon frère*."

"Keep performing as beautifully as you have been, Anne, and everything will be okay."

"Thank you. Positive reviews are always welcomed. Good night."

"Good night."

We turned to our respective rooms—then she suddenly turned back.

"Oh, 'Tom?'"

"Yes?"

"Remember how, when we were kids, and I couldn't sleep, I used to crawl into your bed? If I can't sleep tonight, can I crawl into your bed?"

I smiled. "Sweet dreams," I said and entered my room, shutting the door behind me.

It was like being transported to the 1930s. The room was decorated entirely in the Art Deco style: The bed, dressing table, lamp, and end tables all had that clean, angular, black-and-white feel, not at all warm. You expected Edward Everett Horton to walk in and have something nervously witty to say.

Instead of Mr. Horton, the Basque walked in. I jumped as if startled and smiled nervously at him. "Oh, my bags. Thanks," I said. He snorted—a contagious habit, obviously—and dropped the bags at the door and left.

I picked them up, put them on the bed, and opened them. I always pack my bags in a very distinct way. Although they had tried their best to leave them looking undisturbed, I could tell that they had been searched. Nothing was missing. But then, I don't suppose they would have had any need for my boring wardrobe, two science books, one by Penrose and the other by Crick, and a file folder with student papers to grade.

I went to the window and looked down on a wide stone-paved parking area in front of the house, which faced away from the lake. At one end was a driveway that stretched maybe fifty yards ending at a tall metal gate. To my right were the garages. To my left, I could see that that wing of the house was substantially larger than the one I was in. Satisfied that I had a good grasp of the physical layout of the front of the house, I grabbed my toilet bag and went into the adjoining bathroom, which was decorated in more Art Deco. I took care of the typical needs, then returned to the bedroom and put on a pair of fifty percent polyester Sears pajamas. I then set my watch's alarm to wake me in three hours. I got under the covers, took seventeen deep breaths, and fell into a deep sleep on the seventeenth breath.

Three hours later, my watch vibrated at the precise frequency to wake me fully alert. I got out of bed and put on my robe and slippers. The Art Deco clock informed me that it was 3:42 am. I slowly opened the door, left the room, and headed for the stairs. Before going down, I surveyed the living room through the small arched opening. It was bathed dramatically in the moonlight streaming through the French doors that looked out over the lake. Everything was quiet. And still. I slowly moved down the stairs and passed from the foyer into the living room. I crossed quickly to the door Rand had gone through. The gap at the bottom, between the door and the floor, showed no light. Still, I listened carefully at the door. Then I tried the wrought iron handle.

It pushed down easily. I opened the door and entered. It was a book-lined study with three walls featuring floor-to-ceiling built-in bookcases filled with leather-bound volumes. They were well-dusted but not, I assumed, well-read. They probably came, like the furniture, with the house. There was a door opposite the one I entered, leading, I assumed, to the other wing of the house.

The fourth wall was mainly a large window overlooking the lake. In the middle of the room, seeming out of place, was a five-foot slab of smoked glass resting on two marble blocks about two and a half feet tall. It was being used as a desk, although a strangely low one. Maybe this was predicated by the simple wooden captain's chair instead of the standard plush desk chair on wheels. On the glass slab sat a computer but no printer.

There were no file cabinets, no drawers, and no safe. It was hardly worth getting up for. I turned on the computer. It required a password to get into the files and applications. Here's where I missed Roee. I decided, though, that probably not much was to be discovered on this computer. Rand most likely had it because one is supposed to have a computer these days. If he did anything on it, he probably played video games.

I heard a sudden, deep CLUNK from somewhere outside and the mechanical rolling of metal wheels—the front drive gate, I assumed. The acceleration of an engine confirmed that someone was pulling into the driveway. I turned off the computer and went to the door, took a quick peek, and was about ready to dash across the living room when I heard a noise coming from the dining room. I pulled back, closing the door but leaving a crack to look out of. From the dining room came Imelda, in robe and slippers. She passed through the living room and into the foyer. I could hear the soft beeps of an alarm system being turned off and the front door opening. The engine sound was close now, echoing around the courtyard in front of the house. Then it stopped. A car door opened. I could hear the quick clicking of claws on stone and a voice saying in a loud whisper, "Go Bat, go piss big!" The clicking speeded and faded. "Imelda, get bag!"

"Yes, Mr. Zhel," Imelda said.

Heavy steps entered the house and landed on the stones of the foyer. "Piss Bat! Stupid! Don't smell all trees!" Soon I could hear Imelda's struggle as she re-entered the house. "Is bag heavy for you?"

"Yes, Mr. Zhel."

"Then use two hand, stupid bitch!"

Claw clicking rushed in.

"Come, mangy dog."

Then it began to growl with low throat vibrations of willingness to tear flesh.

"What...?"

Three quick, loud throaty barks and the pounding of paws accented by slamming clicks—the dog was on his way. I closed the door and looked to see if there was any hiding place. A useless gesture, for I could not hide my scent. The dog slammed against the door and began to claw at it furiously.

"Bat! Sit!"

The dog protested but did as commanded. I grabbed a book out of the bookcase. The door opened. A light was switched on. Zhelyu Batsarov—the Bulgarian Cowboy—in blue jeans, boots, a western shirt, and a sweat-stained Stetson entered. He looked at me with white-hot eyes. "Who fuck you?"

"I—I—"

"Get on knee! Get on knee!" he screamed, his two front gold teeth gleaming.

I did so, giving an excellent performance of stark fear.

"Zhelyu, what the hell is going on?"

Rand came through the other door and pulled on a robe.

"I find intruder."

Rand looked at me. He was not happy to see me here, but... "Tom is not an intruder. He's a guest, Zhelyu. Would an intruder break-in in his pajamas and robe?"

"Guest? Why guest?" Batsarov demanded to know.

"I'll tell you in—"

"Why in here? Four o'clock morning?"

That seemed to worry Rand. But he smiled at me gently. "You can get up, Tom." I did. "What are you doing down here?"

I showed him the book. "I—I couldn't sleep. I was looking for something to read."

Miguel and the Basque ran into the room, suddenly concealing guns behind their backs when they saw the scene. They were somewhat silly figures standing there in their boxer shorts and tee shirts, looking like children hiding the stolen candy, an image enhanced by the fact that Miguel had on a tee shirt displaying a group portrait of the Looney

Tune characters in radically hip "Gangsta Rap" clothing, and on the Basque's tee shirt, B.U.M. curved across the chest.

"Go back to bed!" Rand demanded. They looked to Batsarov. He nodded, and they left.

Rand turned back to me and looked into my eyes, which I averted, wondering if I had seen the guns. "Something to read?" He asked for more of an explanation.

"Uh, yeah. I only brought, you know, work-related stuff, and I wanted something—lighter. When you went in here earlier, I saw some bookcases. I—I didn't think you would mind."

"Tom has suffered from insomnia since he was ten."

It was Anne. Everyone turned to her—and their blood shifted gears. She stood there, very casually, in nothing but a chemise made of crinkly cotton gauze. The off-the-shoulder neckline and empire seam shaping just added to the delight. She wasn't even wearing slippers. The effect on both men was immediate, especially on Batsarov. Had he had just a few fewer neurons in his brain, he might very well have happily drooled. As a mental diversion, it was perfect.

"I'm really, really sorry," I said.

"Well," Rand said reluctantly, moving his gaze from the gauze, "why don't we all go back to bed."

"Yes, I think that's a good idea. Come on, Tom." Anne walked past both men slowly and came over and retrieved me. "You can give a more proper apology in the morning."

"Well, I said I was sorry."

We both retreated and passed Bat, the most enormous German shepherd I had ever seen. He growled but made no move to follow.

"Nice doggie," Anne said. "He didn't growl when I came down," she whispered as we exited.

"No, but I bet you he drooled," I whispered.

We made it upstairs, passing Imelda, who was still in the foyer with the bag. She gave Anne a look. I couldn't begin to guess the particulars behind that look. I stopped Anne at the arched opening.

"Hey!" She whispered somewhat urgently. "These stones are cold."

I gestured for silence, then for her to listen.

"What the hell are you doing coming back at this hour?" Rand was saying in a whisper that the good acoustics allowed us to hear.

"I come. I go. When I want. America is land of free."

"I suppose you did a hundred and ten all the way down."

"Sure. Pedal to metal."

"Stupid, Zhelyu. What if you had been stopped?"

"I bribe."

"You know, American police—"

"All corrupt, I know, I see *Serpico*. Who guests? Who girl?"

"I'll explain in the morning but know and understand this now—he might be able to help us advance the project, and she is my guest."

"She looks at my crotch."

"Zhelyu, go take out your frustrations on Imelda, and let me get back to bed."

"Yeah. Sure. But I watch those two."

"Just look, don't touch, and keep a rein on that stupid mutt."

"Bat okay. Tear throat out."

"So you've told me."

The conversation ended. After a moment, I moved Anne back to our rooms.

"Thanks, Sis," I said. "That was quick thinking."

"Was it worth it?" she whispered.

"Nothing was gained, if that's what you mean."

"Should I worry?"

That's the problem with second thoughts. They're persistent. "No. Didn't that little dialog put your mind at ease?"

"Yeah, I suppose—and my heart in my throat."

"Try to get some sleep."

"Yeah. I should have said that to you three hours ago. Night."

"Sweet—"

"Don't waste your breath," Anne commanded, then entered her room.

I went into mine and climbed into bed, and tried to settle into sleep. I took my seventeen deep breaths. Despite the still-flowing adrenaline and the lingering image of Anne in her chemise, it was just beginning to work when my legs suddenly jerked up—the homing device was starting to itch.

xx

When I came down to breakfast at 8:45, Craig York was sitting at the dining room table, his head practically buried in a plate of eggs and sausages, scooping the food in as he read a magazine. I very quietly said, "Hello."

York looked up. There was no hint that he recognized me. "Oh, hello. You're the guest. Imelda said there were guests. I'll finish right up."

"Well, you don't have to hurry because of me."

"No, that's okay. I—I've got to get to work."

"Oh, you work for Mr. Rand?"

"Yeah." He scooped furiously at the eggs.

"I hope you weren't disturbed by the little commotion I inadvertently caused last night.

"Commotion? No, I'm—uh—I'm a heavy sleeper. Well, Imelda will be in, in a second."

He started to leave just as Rand came in, all cheery. "No, no, Craig, stay. I want you here."

"But—"

"Sit, Craig. Have some more orange juice. Good morning, Einstein."

"Einstein?" York asked.

"That's right, Craig. His name is Einstein, but he tells me he's no relation. But he is a scientist—neat, uh? Craig is also a scientist working on my current project. Doing a good job, but a bit—well, that's what we will talk about."

"Good morning."

It was Anne, as radiant as the morning, any residue of fear from last night well hidden.

"I would ask if everyone slept well, but—"

"Yes, I really want to apologize again," I said.

"Forget it. What's wrong with a bit of drama in the middle of the night?

Anne, this is Craig York. He's working for me on a special project."

Anne went over to shake his hand but probably, more effectively, shook his mind. "Oh, are you writing a screenplay for Andy?"

"Uh, no—no, I'm not a writer," York said as Rand laughed.

"No, Craig is a scientist."

"A scientist?" Anne nicely played the confusion.

"Sit. Sit. All will be explained. Imelda!"

Imelda came out of the kitchen. She looked tired and a bit—done in.

Rand did not choose to notice. "Any special breakfast orders?" he asked.

"Just a grapefruit for me, if that's okay," Anne said.

"Sure, sure, anything. And you, Einstein?"

"The eggs and sausage looked good to me," I said, taking advantage of the vacation from Roee's kosher cooking.

We all sat. Anne looked around. "This is a lovely room, Andy."

"Yeah, isn't it? Look at this ceiling."

We all looked up. "Oh, my," Anne said.

The ceiling was made up of light, bleached wood beams interspersed with rows of colorful square tiles. Each one was unique and had that lovely crude look of medieval craftsmanship. Some were abstract, some pictured flowers within an abstract design, and a few depicted scenes of English royalty. Directly above me was a picture of Edward Rex seated on his throne within his castle, talking to two noblemen.

"The first twenty or so Kings of England are up there, they tell me, but I haven't had time to count them."

"Are these originals?" Anne asked.

"Who knows? But let's go ahead and say they are. Then we'll enjoy them more. This whole house is pretty fascinating. When we first inspected it, do you know what we found in the garage—a 1925 Duesenberg with bullet holes in the passenger door. I first thought it was a picture car used for a movie. But no, it was real. It turns out this was the house of a rather successful bootlegger. This area fed L.A. during Prohibition the way the Catskills fed New York. After the bootlegger died—in his sleep, I understand—the title to the house became confused. It sat going to pot for over 50 years. Then, finally, the title was cleared up and wound up in the hands of a distant heir in Canada. He restored the place, and it went on the market just when I was looking to buy. The furniture, everything, it all belonged to the bootlegger. Maybe they should have called it Chateau de la Lune-shine." He laughed at his joke, and so did we, except York. Perhaps he had heard it before.

"That's a great story," I said.

"And this is a great house," Anne said.

"You haven't seen anything yet. This house has special attractions."

The food came, and we all started to eat, chit-chatting about nothing in particular. Then the kitchen door swung open, and Batsarov, wearing the same clothes he had had on at four in the morning, entered. "Howdy," he said in his Bulgarian-Western accent. This was my first good look at him. That night on the Willamette River, my perspective was a bit skewered, and during the recent encounter, I had kept my eyes fearfully averted. Now, though, I faced him directly, if with well-played apprehension.

Batsarov was a tall man. At least six foot five and lanky. You could take him for a real cowboy if he didn't open his mouth. That is, I mean if he didn't speak. Nothing but a silent view of his two gold teeth didn't hurt the effect, as they seemed not incongruous with 19th Century America. His face was all flesh-draped-over-a-bony-head featuring high cheekbones, a broad forehead, a prominent chin, and a massive hatchet nose that must have resulted from limited breeding choices within a small village. His smile was pleasant—in a vicious sort of way.

"And how our guests this morning?"

Rand looked at Batsarov casually and said, "I take it you stayed up to work?"

Batsarov snorted—it was catching. "Work! Yes! Good work."

"Well, why don't you go get some sleep then? A shower, I think, first. And then some sleep."

"I wanted to greet guests and apologize for Bat," he said, staring at me hard, quite clearly apologizing for nothing.

"I'm sure Einstein's not worried about last night."

"Oh, you forgive Zhelyu?" Batsarov stared at me, tilting his head.

"Su—sure. Think nothing of it."

"Good! You make me feel good! I take Bat for run. Bat!"

The German shepherd lunged into the dining room and sat obediently by his master.

"Beautiful dog," Anne said. "Why did you name him 'Bat'?"

"Named after Bat Masterson, great frontier marshal, and sportswriter. Come Bat."

They left. And man and dog.

"I would say you'll have to excuse Zhelyu, but there's really no reason why you should. He's a completely crude individual. But he's the most honest business partner I've ever had, and for that, I value him."

"He's your business partner?" I said with calculated overreaction.

"Yes. Now, why don't we have a fresh cup of coffee while I explain a few things."

CHAPTER 17
THE MAN WITH THE GOLDEN GUT, THE GODDESS WITH THE IVORY SKIN

They say I have a 'Golden Gut,'" Rand started in on what seemed to be a prepared speech. "You know, they're right—and I can tell you the exact place, day, and time I got it. It was in Japan on the evening of April fifth, 1974, at 7:07 p.m. I was new in the business but so enthusiastic for success I literally vibrated to the frequency of 'Make it Happen!' I was at dinner with a lovely young Japanese woman who worked for the local distribution company that was releasing a film of mine in the Far East. We were at the Fujiya Hotel in the mountains above Lake Ashi in Hakone. The hotel's at least one hundred years old. It was the first hotel in Japan built for *Gaijin*—foreigners. At the suggestion of the maître'd, I ordered a special meal to be prepared by the chef just for us, every item on the menu to be at his discretion. It was, of course, a spectacular meal. But the most spectacular item of the meal was—the soup."

"The soup?" Anne said. She had hardly taken her eyes off Rand, even while eating her grapefruit, giving a sense of connection that fed him, that he played to, that made him seem invincible. "How so?"

"It was gold soup."

"Gold soup?" Anne repeated as if stroking his—hair.

"Yes, its base was a clear golden broth—simple enough—but floating within that broth was real gold leaf."

"Really?" Anne said.

Rand nodded. "Can I eat that? I asked the woman. Yes, she said, it would be an insult not to. So I took my spoon and captured some floating gold, brought it up to my mouth, said the only prayer I've ever said in my life, and ate it. It had the most delicate taste and went down slow and warm, warming my stomach. I had a second spoonful, then a third, and then the warmth in my stomach passed into my intestines and became—hot—very hot. I was scared at first. I began to sweat. Had I been poisoned? But then I understood. The gold had become a hot liquid and was applying itself to the lining of my intestines. The broth would pass, but the gold would stay. 'Now I really do have a golden gut,' I told the woman. She didn't know what I was talking about. But it didn't matter. The truth was within me. I had a clear mental image of my gold-lined intestines. That image became my visual mantra.

"From that time, I made no decision on supporting or green-lighting a project until I had meditated with this visual mantra, and always, within that meditation, a crystalline—" he thought for a moment, searching for just the right word. "Perfection appeared. If the project matched that crystalline perfection, I made it a 'Go' project. If it didn't, I sent it away. I cursed it; I banished it.

"Now, you may think this is all just weird shit, and it may be, but my track record is better than anyone else's in the business. If it's weird shit, it's weird shit that works, and isn't that what it's all about?"

"I can believe it," Anne said. "The Japanese, I mean, there are things, I mean mystic things, that they know that we just can't grasp with our rigid Western minds."

Oh, very good, I thought. Well played. At least, I hoped it was play-acting.

"But Einstein doesn't believe it, do you, Einstein? You're a scientist. A rationalist."

"Oh, well, you know, physics blows people away. It's considered magical by most people. That this, uh, visual mantra of yours allows you to focus great mental concentration on what you must focus on is, uh, perfectly reasonable. With that focus, you probably, heighten your instincts, which have proven to be, you know, pretty good."

"Yes," Rand said. "Yes, that could be the explanation. But in any case, the bottom line is, I'm better at my job than anybody else in Hollywood."

"Well, you see, that's factual. Data can prove that," I said, wanting to make him believe that I wanted to believe.

"So why did I quit?" It was a dare.

"Uh, sometimes," I offered, "the best at what they do get bored. No challenges."

"Oh, you can't get bored in Hollywood. Not if you're successful.

Too many people hate you for that. And to have people hate you for your success is always—interesting. But you can begin to think that your life is a little frivolous. After all, what are you doing? Nothing more than constructing little strips of escapism for the masses. That's all. Have you ever noticed how people in the film business are apologetic about what they do? They are arrogantly apologetic, of course, but apologetic nonetheless, almost to the point of nausea. How many times have you heard someone in Hollywood say in an interview, 'Well, what we do isn't rocket science.' Or 'it's not brain surgery.' Or, 'we aren't finding a cure for cancer"? All that is true; filmmaking is none of those things. It's just a frivolous little occupation that pays us millions of dollars so that we can live a thousand times better than the millions of people who give us their hard-earned cash in exchange for 90 to 120-minute samples of our frivolity."

"I—I've always liked movies," I said, somewhat disappointed.

"Yes." Rand looked up to the ceiling. "Yes, me too." Then he looked back down at me. "But put together a list of your ten favorite films, and I'll bet most of them were made before 1980."

"Well..."

"And now the pressure is on to make animation. Animation! Fucking cartoons! Now what kind of a job is that for a grown man?"

"I like cartoons," I rose in defense.

"Do you, Einstein? Well, I like a good fart now and then, but that doesn't mean I want to manufacture them for the masses.

"Masses, by the way, which are suffering one indignity after another, indignities of disease; handicaps; poverty; hunger; oppression. What few people there are who are doing their best to alleviate those indignities are paid next to nothing compared to what we make and are given the weakest of resources. Whereas the world will move mountains to accommodate a Star."

"I can see where EarthPeople came from," Anne said.

"Are you disappointed in me?"

"Disappointed?"

"You were attracted to an aura of power about me, weren't you?" Anne began to protest, but Rand cut her off. "I don't fool myself that you were attracted to my physical presence, but now I have shown you a—soft side of me."

"Men will never understand just how sexy that can be in a man—coupled with that aura of power," she said.

I cleared my throat.

"Oh, Tom, grow up."

"Don't make Einstein nervous, Anne. I need him."

"You need me?"

"Are you a genius, Einstein?"

"A genius? I don't think so, but I'm good at what I do."

"That's good. Because Craig here—Craig is a genius. He has created something that will benefit humankind on an unimaginable scale. Sometimes, though, genius can be blinded by its own light. But, right now, Craig is a blind man—a stumbling blind man groping in the dark—and he very much needs a man good at what he does to guide his way. Don't you, Craig? Don't you need someone who can help you?"

Craig looked up from his glass, now empty of orange juice. He looked up from the tiny bits of pulp clinging and drying on the inside of the glass. "Uh, yeah. Help. I need help."

xx

Rand wanted to show us the grounds. First, he took York aside and gave him some silent instructions. After which, York gratefully scurried out of the room. Then Rand led Anne and me out of the dining room, into the living room, and then out the French doors. The air was cool and brisk with that invigorating snap that belonged exclusively to Mother Nature. The view of the lake through the mini forest of pine trees was all blue with a texture of ripples, giving the body life. Rand rattled off facts and statistics as he led us through the pines. The trees were Jeffrey Pine and Ponderosa Pine. He admitted that they were less lush than the trees in the Pacific Northwest but not bad for being only a hundred miles from L.A. The lake was man-made, created when a dam was built around the turn of the century. It was two miles long and a mile and a half wide. There were fourteen miles of lakeshore. It was all the standard stuff coming from a recently converted resident, the kind of stuff you nodded at in wondrous awe to help friends feel their manufactured pride. Then he told us about the fishing: Trout; catfish; carp; big mouth, and smallmouth bass. Both fly fishing and reel fishing were popular.

"Do you do any fishing, Einstein?" Rand asked me.

"Uh, no, not really."

"What? You, growing up a Middle American boy?"

I shrugged my shoulders and said, "Comic books." He seemed to accept the logic of the answer.

"I sometimes fish down there on the dock. The fishing is great in this cove; they gather here to escape the wind. I stand in a big floppy hat, the lonely, exiled Central American politician." He chuckled. "Sometimes, the locals boat by and try to engage me in conversation. I just stare back at them in my dark glasses and say nothing. I think it pleases them. Brings a little dark drama into their resort lives."

We came out of the pines and stood on the bluff by the tram. The view was spectacular. The sky was big above us, and a blue not often seen in the city. And through the crisp, clean air, we could see in detail the pine-crowded hills surrounding the lake, admitting only occasionally to civilization.

I looked down to the dock. The helicopter was there, as was Miguel puttering away at the engine.

"I notice you don't have a boat at the dock. Don't you do any boating?" I asked.

"Oh, I have a boat. You'll see it. But that's part of the second half of this tour."

"Well, it's all so beautiful," Anne said. "You must be very comfortable up here."

"It's serving its purpose."

"Much nicer lakes in Bulgaria."

Anne caught her breath, startled. It was Batsarov. Rand gave him a look of displeasure. They had not heard him walk up behind us. Yet there was no other approach but over fallen and dry pine needles. Training tells. I, of course, had heard him. Training tells.

"Except they all polluted. Stupid communist fucks!"

"Oh, were you a fighter against the Communists?" I asked, wide-eyed.

"No. I was stupid Communist fuck too!" He laughed.

"Zhelyu, why don't you go down and help Miguel," Rand suggested strongly.

"What I know about fucking copter?"

"Hand him things. Make his life easier."

Batsarov smiled. He jumped into the tram, turned to face us, and smiled again—smiled hard directly at me. Then he hit the down button and slowly descended, his eyes boring into mine, his smile never fading.

Anne shivered. Rand assumed it was from the wind off the lake. "Are you cold? May I?" He removed his jacket and draped it across Anne's shoulders, leaving his arm around her.

She leaned into him, comfortable. "Ooooh, that's nice. I appreciate your warmth."

Rand did not expect that. He may have desired it, but he didn't expect it. Possibly had it been any other woman than Anne, he would have doubted her sincerity, having gotten used to doubting sincerity in his life. But this was Anne. When you looked into those aquamarine eyes, it was too painful to doubt. "Uh, why don't we go inside," he said, returning to business. "The real wonders are there."

"Whatever you say," Anne answered. "We're in your hands."

We walked back to the house, Anne nestled in Rand's arms. Rand, I was sure, was a man in love—but one hoping to control it, I suspected. I walked behind them, trying to ignore the electricity in the air. Like a proper third-wheel brother should.

Rand took us directly to the study and went to the back bookcase. "You want to see something right out of a movie?" he asked enthusiastically.

"Sure," I said.

"See this?" He pointed to one of the many leather-bound volumes. "It's *A Thousand and One Nights*." He laid his index finger right at the embossed title on the book's spine. "Open Sesame," he said with anticipated delight as he pushed the book. There was the click of a latch being undone, and the whole bookcase swung towards us, revealing a dark, concrete stairwell beyond. "A secret passage. Neat, huh? Built by the bootlegger, of course. Come on down."

He hit a switch, and the stairwell was now lighted and revealed to be spiral. It was claustrophobic and narrow; I had to pull my shoulders in to avoid scraping them as we descended. There was a wooden door at the bottom. Rand opened it and ushered us into a large, well-lighted room full of computers, electronic equipment, a chalkboard, and York, at a bench, bent over, scribbling in a notebook. To the right was a series of rooms, none with doors. All but one was empty, and it had just a bed, a night table, and a small dresser. This was York's "cell." I now knew why he did not hear the early morning commotion. One end of the room was wholly occupied with the Veritas equipment.

"Bootleggers are no good unless they have something to bootleg. This is where they brewed the hooch. We found the most elaborate old still, very high-tech for the 1920s. Now, as you can see, we're very, very, high-tech for the 1990s."

I showed a fascination with the equipment, and I looked at some of the calculations on the chalkboard. "What—what are you working on?" I asked, doing my best to show wondering confusion.

"Truth, Einstein," Rand declared. "We are working on Truth. And that Truth shall set the world free."

xx

The hot Mediterranean sun beat down on the harsh landscape of rocks and olive trees on which Athens sat. Funny, standing here on the Acropolis, looking down on my city, I was somehow disappointed. Although, here in 425 BC, Athens was still a relatively new city, having had to be reconstructed a mere twenty-some years ago after the devastation of the Persian occupation, the new council chamber, the new prytaneum, the new homes, the new porticoes, all looked— primitive to me, not as great as I expected, not as grand as I think Rome is—is? Will be? Rome, what and where is Rome? 425 BC? BC? Yes, definitely 425 BC, but that is not a date that means anything to me.

Music—drums and pipes. I am reminded of my purpose. I turn around.

Ah, the Parthenon. No disappointment here: 228 feet by 101 feet by 65 feet, the rectangular temple of translucent white marble from Mt. Pantelakos—as warm as human skin—sits in welcome, bidding me to come, bidding me in.

I walk towards it. It is Athena's feast day, and if my faith is not to be questioned, I must go to her temple to show my reverence. As I approach, I can see physics in the Parthenon; I can see that every straight line is a curve, that the curve—very, very subtle—of the temple steps gives you a feeling of the grace and strength of the building. How lovely that strength has grace. Physics?

I walk up the steps, feeling ennobled—yes—ennobled. And large. I can walk with the gods! In the gable pediment far above me, the birth of Athena in a heroic statuary group reminds me that Athena was not born of woman but sprung in full armor from the head of Zeus, her father. In the metopes, just below the pediment, are panels depicting the battle of gods and giants. Oh, for those days, my heart cries, those days when you could do battle with giants!

I pass the columns before the entrance. Not one piece! Of course, how could they be? Each column is a stack of drums. No mortar. All the blocks in the temple, all the drums in the columns, so accurately squared, cut like jewels, so finely finished, the division between them is nearly invisible. The great doors open! The sun streams in and moves in an instant to the back to fall upon and illuminate the great goddess, Athena, standing 36 feet high, in a robe of gold, with flesh of polished ivory; with spear and shield, and holding aloft in her right hand, the winged figure of Nike, Victory, as tall as myself, offering up a giant gold garland to the goddess. Made by Pheidias, our finest sculptor, but could this truly have been made by the hand of man? No. No, this *is* the goddess. This is wisdom, reason, and purity.

I start to walk towards Athena. I don't want to take my eyes off her.

But they are caught by something. Something frivolous. Colors. Why do the colors surprise me, the bright yellows and blues and reds of the inner frieze? How can I expect them to be white, shorn of color? I, a child of the Mediterranean sky? Is this faithlessness in front of the goddess?

Slowly Nike twists her head down, her face as serene as the goddess' as she first notices me. Then, suddenly, it becomes the face of hell, and she launches herself off Athena's hand, down, directly towards me, her wings beating with a horrible screaming. I am paralyzed with disbelief and fear!

Her expansion mocks my horror as she comes closer—closer.

With a gaping mouth, I allow Victory to dump the vast, heavy garland of gold on me, knocking me to the ground and knocking the wind from me.

The triumphant scream of Victory echoes within the temple. Cut and bruised, I claw my way out from under the giant garland. I cast my eyes up to plead to my goddess, and my mind screams to see no wisdom there, no reason, no purity, but rather the fierce and ruthless battle-goddess our ancestors knew. She steps towards me—thunderous pounding—another step, another, soon she is but a gold and ivory tower above me. She lifts her foot. She means to crush me. She means to crush me for the insect I am. I roll. I roll with pain out of the way. The foot crushes: the wind it causes blows past me. I stand and run. Why, why is my goddess angry with me? The thunderous crashes behind me impel me forward. I shoot out the door. I'm going too fast when I hit the steps. I lose my footing. I fall. I tumble. I strike my head hard twice. I come to rest three steps from the bottom, on my back. Athena crashes through the front of the temple. The front of the temple collapses. Dust. I can see the dust of disintegrated stone billow up to surround my goddess's ivory and gold head.

My goddess who hates me!

I turn to crawl. But—no—more—strength. Blood. My blood is flowing down the last three steps. It is bright red in the Mediterranean sun, bright red against the translucent white steps. Pretty, I seem to recall—blood is pretty.

Dark.

Light!

"So, are you astonished?" Rand said.

York had just taken the Veritas glasses off me. I looked around. There was Rand, hovering above me, eager for a report. I turned my head. Anne was sitting over by the blackboard, watching me.

"Wow!" I managed to make myself say. "That was neat!"

But it was not neat. It was not anywhere near neat. This was the problem with Veritas that I wasn't sure they understood yet. It allows your brain to fill in too many of the gaps. Not gaps in the landscape nor gaps in the faces. Psychological gaps. But this I could not report on. I had to be an enthusiastic convert. "It was—god, talk about sensory overload! I got information. I got facts. No! I didn't get them. I knew them. I saw, and I felt. Then, suddenly, the damn statues attacked me like it was a Harryhausen movie."

"Yeah," Rand said with pride, "I made Craig add that."

"But—but it wasn't—what's the word?—total. You told me when you put on the glasses that the next time I saw you, I would have this memory of being a citizen of ancient Athens visiting the Parthenon, but I knew things I shouldn't have known then."

"That's one problem, among several, that we still have with Veritas. That's where we need help in solving those problems."

"Well, yes," I stood up and started to pace. "Yes, if you can get it right, it has so many applications."

"That's right," Rand said.

"I mean, last night, you talked about helping the blind and stroke victims."

"And more, and more, far beyond that." Rand was glowing with excitement, consciously trying to make it contagious. "Never has my gut been so golden!"

"But—but gosh, it's going to be hugely expensive, right? Would people be able to afford it?"

"Oh, don't worry about that. Veritas will create enough money to support philanthropy."

"How?"

"Simple. Simple to anyone who understands how the entertainment business works. Look, forget for a moment about Veritas's educational and—charity aspects. Just think of the entertainment aspects."

"Yes, well, of course. Games. Experiences. Fly a jet. Climb Mt. Everest. Go to Mars."

"Win the Olympics. Conquer evil." Rand stopped and smiled and subtly nodded towards Anne. "Make love to a movie star. No offense, Anne."

"None taken—as long as I get my residuals."

Rand was too busy being too evangelical to appreciate the humor. "All things most people will never be able to do—couldn't do; don't have the ability to do—but the inclination, yes, they have the inclination; the inclination is there in gross amounts. Why else has there always been a market for manufactured fantasies? Why is everybody investing in virtual reality?"

"Oh, this is way beyond virtual reality."

"Leaves it in the dust."

"Way in the dust, but still, what about the cost? Research, manufacturing? Is it going to be just a rich man's toy?"

Rand smiled with the satisfied smile of a man with the key, the concept, the answer. "Einstein, you say you like movies. What almost killed the movies in the 1950s?"

"Uh, I don't know. TV, I guess."

"No. Government interference. A little thing called the Paramount Consent Decree forced the studios into divesting themselves of their theaters. No longer could they be the manufacturer, the distributor, and the exhibitor. No longer could they pull profits from every stop along the way. It practically gutted the studios. They couldn't support a full range of films, all types, A and B films. No longer could they afford to keep stars, directors, and writers under contract. No longer could they afford—power. The power went to the stars, the A-List directors, or their representatives. That's diffused power. That's almost a form of democracy!"

I don't think Rand meant it as a compliment.

"And then video came along. It saved the studios financially but didn't give them more power, plus videos can be copied. Piracy—the worst crime, Einstein, the worst crime of all, taking my product, making money off it, and not giving me my cut. The worst crime of all."

I really wanted him to—as I'm sure he had requested of many others— cut to the chase.

"I—I'm not sure I'm following."

"Veritas is control! Veritas is power! Look how it's made. Look how it is set up. All I have to sell the consumer is these cheap glasses and a simple infrared transmitter. Everything else is rented, over and over and over. Look, in a few short years, every house in America will receive video on demand through their cable, phone lines, or satellites. They will also receive Veritas. I will rent them the converter box. I will charge them a base monthly fee for the service. I will charge them each and every time they call up and order a particular program. They won't be able to buy a program once, make a copy of a program, and use it repeatedly without paying me again. If they want it again, they pay. That's ultimate and total control. Control is power. Do you understand now, Einstein? Do you get that simple concept?"

I did my best to show wide-eyed understanding. "This thing could be, I mean, like, you know, like being online, this thing could almost be addictive."

"Right!"

"You wouldn't even have to charge that much each time to make a fortune."

"Right!"

"Gosh."

"Right."

"But what about the blind and victims of strokes?"

"Oh, I am going to set up a non-profit foundation funded by some of the profits from Veritas."

"There's so much—so much that could be done."

"And listen, this is the most exciting thing. Don't you now know— no—understand what it is like to be a 5th Century BC Athenian?"

"Well, yeah."

"Understanding. Empathy. Getting into the head of others. What else is going to solve conflicts? Bring people together? Get people to understand the sacrifices they will have to make to solve the world's problems? With Veritas, with Truth, we will set the world free!"

I said nothing. I just considered the implications.

"So, are you astonished?" Rand ask.

"Yes."

"So, can you help?"

"Well, I've got to understand this much, much more. But, just having this experience, seeing your problems; certainly, my research relates."

"So, will you help?"

"Well, my job at MIT."

"How much do you make?"

"Pretty good. 43,500 a year."

"I'll plus it by ten. No, let me round that out to 500,000."

"Half a million?"

"Half a million, and you can do some good for people. How often is someone given that opportunity?"

I started to sweat. I looked at Anne. "Wha—What do you think?"

"Well, I don't even know what you all are talking about, but it sounds good to me. You get to do your research. You can apply it for good. And you can earn enough money to buy me a great and costly Christmas gift each year. So where's the debate?"

"Well, yeah. Okay."

"Great! Great! I want you to get started right away. Sit down here with Craig, and he'll explain everything in detail. Won't you, Craig?"

This whole time York had sat scribbling in his notebook. "Yes," he said, not looking up. "Yes, I can do that." Then he looked up. He looked up at me. "You're at MIT?"

"Yes, I'm an associate professor there."

"Good school," York said.

"Of course, it's a good school," Rand declared. "I only hire the best. Now, let me quickly finish the tour, and then you two can get to work. As for you and me, Anne, how would you like to take a boat ride on the lake? After all this dry talk of men's ambitions in an underground room, you must want some fresh air."

I could see Anne holding back a barb. I could see it in her eyes. But the corners of her mouth shot up enthusiastically instead. "That would be lovely."

The rest of the tour was quick and straightforward. Rand walked us through a door at the far end of the room. As we entered, we could hear lapping waves, the perfect accompaniment to the damp cold air in what seemed to be a storage room approximately 30 feet long. Instead of a far wall, the room ended with a ramp descending to an underground dock.

"This is all a cave?"

"Yeah," Rand answered. "Dug out by the bootlegger, reinforced with concrete. This is how he got the hooch out. Loaded here undercover into small boats, then taken to various points along the lake, where the trucks picked it up. Watch your step going down this ramp."

"Very dramatic," Anne said.

"Yes," Rand agreed. It has that appeal, doesn't it?"

As we walked down, a bank of lights came on automatically. There we could see docked, a 20-foot white, black, and red air trapper powerboat, the kind known to enthusiasts as a "hot boat." Its front sponsons reaching out like pinchers, and its flat platform styling with its simple scooped-out cock-pit, gave it a slick, no-nonsense look.

"You asked about my boat. Here it is. Had it built to my specifications."

"Doesn't look very comfortable," Anne said.

"Not built for comfort. Built for fishing. Got a Lowrance 350A fish finder, three bait wells, a custom aluminum poling platform, rod racks in the side panels."

When someone is going on like that, it is best to feed him. "What kind of engine is that?" I asked.

"That's a Mercury 260 horse 2.5 EFI engine harnessed by a 14-and-a-half inch by 23 pitch Power-Tech four-blade prop. That's a mean prop, I tell you."

"Why is the motor under that canopy thing?" Anne asked.

"That's a hydraulic Land & Sea jack plate."

"That hardly answers my question, Andy."

"It lowers the engine into the water."

"Oh. Can it go fast?"

Rand looked at Anne and smiled. "Instead of facts and figures, let's go for the feeling. Come on." He took her hand and led her to the boat. They climbed into the cockpit and sat on the driver's bench, simply a padded area of the back platform behind the instrument console. Rand leaned back and hit a switch on the jack plate, and the big, black engine hydraulically lowered its prop into the water. Then he turned to the instrument panel and started the engine, then turned to me, standing alone on the dock.

"Get some good work done with Craig, and when I give you a break, we'll have some fun with those babies." He indicated two Yamaha WaveRaider water jets. "Lots of fun." He pulled the boat out. Anne turned around and waved; then they disappeared out a small opening toward the sunlight streaming in.

CHAPTER 18
KILL!

I walked back up the ramp, wondering if there was anything to snoop in here, but decided no; I have my chance with York; I better not waste it. Back in the lab, I found York sitting as he was when we first entered, huddled over and scribbling in a notebook. He didn't hear me enter or was ignoring me, for his eyes never left the notebook, and his right hand never stopped its rapid scratching. I decided not to disturb him and instead moved around the lab, ostensibly checking out the equipment but really looking for listening devices. I found nothing. There was a small FlexCam video camera; it looked like a small white cobra with a perfectly round hood and one mesmerizing eye. But it was connected to a computer that was off and was probably used, I assumed, to scan and digitize images and textures to help "build" credible castles and true-to-life temples. Once satisfied that we were truly alone, I turned to York.

"Well—Craig, is it?—I guess you better catch me up on your development so far. It sure is amazing. I congratulate you. Veritas just floors me."

York stopped scribbling. But his hand still shook. Then he looked up at me. "If you're not a genius, then how are you going to help me? It takes a genius, a goddamn genius, and the goddamn genius is dead."

"Well, possibly I was being modest in front of Rand. But I know my stuff."

York started to talk, without a preamble, running down the history of the research and development he and Skinner had done—without mentioning Skinner—in complex, technical language. But I understood enough to know that Petey had made some good guesses. So I was able to seem intelligent when I asked a few questions.

Questions that disturbed York, not for their content, but for interrupting his flow. Each time he had to backtrack a sentence or two to start again.

Much had happened to York since I had first seen him in Portland a little over a week before. He had become a young man even less connected to his ego than he was then. Sad. Sad flesh and bones bothered by mind. However, this was suitable for my purposes, and I was glad of it.

York suddenly finished as if the text had run out. "Now," he looked at me straight back for the first time, "fix it." It was half a challenge and half a plea.

"Well—well, let me think about this for a moment. It's a lot of information to digest. Can I have some paper?"

York found some and gave it to me.

"Something to write with?"

York found a pencil, a stubby one, and gave it to me.

"Okay?" he demanded.

"Okay."

York collapsed back into his hunched position and began to scribble in his notebook again.

I made a few notes on my paper. Then started to make conversation. "So, where did you go to school?"

"What?"

I had startled him. "Are you all right?"

"Tired, very tired, been—been trying to crack this. Mr. Rand really wants it cracked."

"He seems a nice guy."

York just looked at me. Then began to scribble again.

"Do you ever go fishing with him?"

"No."

"Do you fish?"

"N—no."

"Me neither. So you didn't tell me, what school did you go to?" What school? What school, York? I just wanted him to say it.

"Uh—Caltech." He started scribbling again.

"Really? Awful thing that happened there, wasn't it?" Now I had the key. It was just necessary to open the gates. "I mean, Christ, tragic. 16 dead." York stopped scribbling. "You know, I knew some of the people killed. Well, you probably did too. I had done a conference with

Dr. Thornton. Great guy. What a loss." He tried to start scribbling again. I stopped him. "And those two kids visiting their dad in the bombed building. Shit, what's this country coming to?"

"Don't—don't talk about it."

"Oh, well, I'm sorry. It's just, jeez, why? I mean, why? What stupid nut case would do a thing like that?"

"I—I don't..."

"And that Skinner guy! What was his first name? Jim, I think. Very promising."

"Wahhhhh!" York cracked, ran to his cell, and curled into the fetal position on his bed. His whimpering was loud and loaded with pain.

I went over to his cell. I stood in the doorway. I dropped the Einstein persona. "Guilt. It's like a goddamn fist in your chest, isn't it, York? Like a goddamn fist that's grabbing your soul and squeezing. Hurts. Won't give you any room. Come on, York, give in to it. You might as well. It owns you now."

He started to cry. It was not cathartic. It was encasing. It was a cry that darkened all light.

"Killer!" I threw loud anger, screaming accusations at him. "Coward! Admit it. You killed them all, didn't you? You made a pact with the black devil, and you killed them all! Finch! Skinner! Thornton! Those two kids! But now, I'm here, York. I'm here, and I'm your savior. But you've got to give yourself to me, York; you've got to do as I say, and then we—"

I did not hear. With York's crying and my loud, angry words, I did not hear the heavy, running footfalls of Batsarov as he piled down the narrow, spiral stairwell, burst into the lab, and took giant leaps to reach me. He grabbed me around the neck from behind, squeezed his left arm tight, rabbit-punched me with his right fist in the kidney, kicked my legs out from under me, and dragged me back to the stairs.

"I knew! You fuck! I knew!" I could hear through the pain.

He slammed his fist against the side of my head. Ringing. Again! Stunned. He let go of my neck, gathered me by the collar, and pulled me up the narrow stairwell, yanking me hard against the rough concrete walls when my body would not naturally bend to the curve of the spiral ascent. He got me to the top and into the study, a half-conscious rag doll. He picked me up and slammed me into the captain's chair. I wanted to push out, to attack back, but I couldn't; I could only watch as he forced my arms behind me, pinning them between the curve of the chair's stiff wooden back and my own body. Then he placed his knee down hard on my crotch and slowly applied the total pressure of his weight, putting his two hands flat against my chest for balance. I was helpless. I was at his mercy—what little there was of it.

"Who fuck you?" Batsarov screamed. "Who fuck you?" he screamed again, even louder.

What the hell had happened? How had—Then I saw to the side of Batsarov, the computer on the glass top desk. The monitor was on. It was showing a video view of the lab, empty, but the sound of York's whimpering was echoing. Shit! The FlexCam! He must have had a way to turn the computer downstairs on remotely. And it was linked to this one. Shit! Of course, this was no study; this was a Goddamn guard's station!

Batsarov continued to push his knee against my crotch. He ground it, moving it back and forth over the central member and my left testicle. Weirdly I wondered about Petey's homing device. Could it stand the abuse?

"Talk! Talk!" Batsarov yelled, sending sprays of spit into my face.

I managed to talk. With a growl, I said, "Why don't you go play with your own crotch."

He screamed! He lifted his hands off my chest and shot them around my neck. He squeezed. Tight. I thought, at first, just to get my attention, but, no, no, he intended to kill me; I soon had no doubt about that. The pain in my arms and crotch was excruciating. I couldn't move, but all that became secondary as my whole body took offense to the lack of oxygen, as panic spread, as fuzzy gray dots began to float and dance around the vicious, snarling head of Batsarov, hovering over me—all of Hate come for its due.

Laughter—light, lilting, sweet laughter; Anne's laughter. Anne was laughing at me—laughing at *me!* That was the worst pain of all.

"Zhelyu!"

"Tom!"

It was Rand. It was Anne. They had come back from the lake. But they had entered from the living room. What did that mean? They had docked at the outside dock. I was thinking straight. Why? Oh. Oxygen. Oxygen was flowing again. Batsarov had let go of my neck, but he kept his knee in place.

"He is not who he say," Batsarov claimed.

"What?" Rand demanded.

"He was in there making York cry!"

"Making York...?" Rand was all confusion.

"Look! Look!" Batsarov was looking at his hands, the inside of his left forearm. There was the residue of body makeup on both. He grabbed my head and yanked it back, revealing the scar on my neck. "This man on York's boat!"

Batsarov was feeling triumphant. Rand was trying to make sense of it all. I was a mess. Batsarov knew it and released the pressure of his knee but kept it on the chair, a one-legged man. From somewhere deep inside, somewhere training had taught me to find, I pulled at some strength and pushed my body hard and forward, catching the one-legged man by surprise. He hopped back, off balance. I ran. I told the pain to just fucking leave me alone, and I ran out of the study, into the living room, and out the French doors.

"BAT! KILL!"

The horrid sound of Batsarov's voice came as my feet hit slippery pine needles, and I fell, tumbled, managed to pick myself up, and ran again.

Of course, I had nowhere to go. But that wasn't the point. The point was to show panic, the panic of an amateur. Then they could recapture me, more confused than ever about my intentions. Unfortunately, Bat was not clued into this plan. In all his growling, snarling, steel-muscled, sharp-toothed reality, he was trying to carry out his master's command. KILL! It was not a course of action I particularly agreed with, but my opinion was not being sought. I would have to force it on them.

It was no use trying to turn the forest of pine trees in my favor by trying to dodge the shepherd. Even without the disadvantage of carrying a testicle ground into applesauce, I could never have been competitive with Bat on an obstacle course. And it was no use stopping, picking up as heavy a fallen branch as I could find, and standing my ground, prepared to whack the shit out of the monster— long before I could rise back up and position myself, he would be on me.

So I just ran, ran as fast as I could down the path towards the tram; ran watching out for lose rocks or clumps of pine needles that could trip me up; ran not worrying about Bat's speed, Bat's gain, Bat's hot breath, Bat's teeth; ran straight for the very edge of the promontory, steeling my muscles as if to jump, but suddenly dropping like a marionette cut from its strings instead, dropping hard and painfully, dropping with a momentum I clutched at the ground to stop, dropping to hear the rush of Bat flying over me, to watch him sail down in a graceful curve to awkwardly hit hard the slope of the hill, roll once, twice, three times, slam his back and head into the side of a pine tree, squeal loudly, but continue to move beyond that tree, down, down to the water's edge where he finally came to a rest, his head slowly bobbing with the small waves left over from a speedboat that had just passed, its occupants too busy having fun in the sun to have noticed the last seconds of the now drowning dog.

A boot was placed on the small of my back. A certain amount of weight was pushed there. "He was only friend in America," came the slow, sad voice of Batsarov. "Now I kill you." I heard the cocking of weapons.

"Not now, Zhelyu," Rand said as if to an annoying child. "And certainly not here. Pick the bastard up and bring him inside."

I was forcibly turned around and picked up by Batsarov. I hung there in his arms. I could see Miguel and the Basque standing on either side of Rand discreetly holding semiautomatics—if that's possible. It was unclear if they were trained on me—or Batsarov. I wasn't terribly concerned, as all I wanted to do was lose consciousness—which I managed to do.

Consciousness returned with a chill and two thick, brutish latex-covered fingers up my rectum. I was being strip-searched. I made a groan that persons of limited sophistication might interpret as one of pleasure.

"Feel good, you fuck?" Batsarov rudely asked as he extracted his fingers. "Nothing," he said, not addressing me.

"Well, what did you expect to find up there?" Rand asked.

"Microphone."

"Microphone? You're kidding?"

"Or homing device."

"But all you found was shit."

"Never know."

"Are you finished?"

"Yeah. Finished?"

"Then turn him over."

Batsarov grabbed me by the shoulder and flipped me around. I was half on, half off a couch in the living room. He grabbed my legs and swung them up on the couch. "Least he not fucking Jew!" He sniggered at his joke that referred to my "uncircumcised" state.

I looked up at him. *"A lehben ahf dein kop,"* I said. It was a little Yiddish Roee had taught me. It means "A blessing on your head." But Batsarov did not know that, took it for a curse, and swiftly gave me the stone-hard back of his hand across my face. *"Gey kakn afn yam!"* I spat out, and he slapped me even harder. It was deserved this time. I essentially told him to go shit in the ocean.

"Let's dispense with this, shall we?" Rand, sitting in a club chair opposite me, revealed his impatience. "Get dressed," he ordered. I was happy to comply, putting on my clothes with slow movements to diminish the possibility of further pain, noticing the Basque in a corner, his semiautomatic trained on me.

"Where's Anne?" I asked.

"Anne is upstairs in her bedroom being guarded by Miguel. Who, by the way, may very well be in love with her. I know I was." It was bitter, his statement. "Now tell me what all this has been about. Who are you? Who are you working for?"

"Tom Einstein, Ph.D. Associate professor of neural quantum physics at the Massachusetts Institute of Technology."

"What is that? The equivalent of name, rank, and serial number?"

"It's the truth."

"Do you know who Paul Hinckley is?"

"He's a not very good film director."

"Do you know him?"

"No. It's never been one of my ambitions."

"He cop!" Batsarov said.

Rand looked up at Batsarov and slowly, to make himself clear, said, "Zhelyu, do not say another word or do another action until I ask you to. Okay? Thank you." He turned back to me. "I find it hard to believe you are just Tom Einstein."

"Why?"

"Why would a scientist from MIT go to all the trouble to get involved in my affairs?"

"Well," I chuckled a knowing chuckle, "maybe you have one of the general misconceptions about scientists that we are all just lab-bound geeks, not interested in the material world except to study it for pure knowledge. That's not always the case, Mr. Rand."

"You're after material gain?"

"Oh, yeah! A lot!"

"Earlier today, I offered you half a million dollars a year."

"That's not a lot."

"It is for most people."

"Is it for you?"

Rand did not answer.

"I thought not. You want to understand my motivations? Then judge me by your avarice standards."

"All right. What was your plan?"

"To get in your confidence, turn York against you, and steal Veritas."

"You were going to come here and steal Veritas from me?"

"Would have done it too if that pseudo cowboy son-of-a-bitch hadn't overheard me."

Batsarov went to hit me but was stopped by Rand with a quick, sharp shout, "Zhelyu!"

"How did you even know about Veritas?" Rand continued.

"Skinner. Jim. He had read a paper of mine and knew I was dealing theoretically with ideas that he thought could help him solve some problems. He was stuck, so he contacted me. He tried to pump me for information by talking around the subject, but I finally pinned him down. He demonstrated Veritas for me. I was astonished. I knew immediately that I could help him find the solution. I offered to do that for a fifty percent share in the patent. He wouldn't do it. He went crazy. Called me a rapist. So I started to check around. You know, the science community is relatively small. I learned that York had been his associate but that there had been a not-happy split. So I decided to deal with York, see if we could work together, get ahead of Skinner, and patent a version of Veritas before he could. I went to Portland. I was on his boat when it blew. He had just told me about David Finch, you, and this guy." I indicated Batsarov. "He was very, very scared. Not at all a happy employee."

"Zhelyu, go down and ask Craig to join us, will you?"

Batsarov left.

"Where did you find him?" I asked. "You know, he's almost strangled me twice now."

"Well," Rand said nonchalantly, "third time's the charm. Whereas you killed one of my men in Portland the first time, not something I would expect of a scientist."

"Neither did he. That's how I caught him off guard."

"After which you had a version of Veritas. Why didn't you leave it at that?"

"Because once I looked it over, I knew it was just a prototype, not as good as the one Skinner had shown me, and I still needed York. There were details I couldn't figure out by just looking at the mechanics. Then you attacked Caltech and killed Skinner. I knew you had the real Veritas, as well as York."

"Here he is." Batsarov pushed York into the room.

Everything now depended on this young man, this young man with very little sense of self, and what he did have, had been beaten to a near pulp. But he was my only chance. I would have been dead by now if Rand suspected anything near the truth. My body would have been tied with weights and dragged out of his little cave to be deposited on the bottom of the lake. The lie must hold, or I would soon be dead. So often in my life, I have depended on the lie.

"Craig," Rand said in as friendly a way as he could muster, "have you ever met this man before today?"

York stood there, avoiding all eye contact.

"Craig!" Rand shouted to get his attention.

"What?"

"Come around here and take a good look at him. Have you met him before?"

York moved around and stood before me. He raised his eyes.

Got him! I got his eyes!

Suddenly York recognized me. "Yes, but—but he wasn't blond then."

"He was on your boat?"

"Ye—yes."

"And what was he doing there?"

York started to think. You could see it. He began to wonder, to catalog his options.

"I—I was upset about David. I—I talked too much. I'm sorry."

Good, nice, and neutral, open to interpretation.

"How many times was he on your boat?"

"Wha—what do you mean?"

"How many times! Numbers! You're a fucking scientist; you know about numbers?"

It was the first time Rand started to heat.

York looked at me, pleading. I moved my neck slightly, affording York a better view of my scar, red again from Batsarov's abuse. Then I closed my eyes very slowly. Once.

"Only—once."

"When we blew up your boat?"

"Yeah." York started to cry. "Please, can I go now? I want to sleep."

"Okay, Craig. Go take a nap," Rand said.

"Can—can I have one of the pills?"

"Yes, certainly, Craig." Rand was calm again and compassionate. "Zhelyu, take him down. Give him a pill."

Batsarov grabbed York hard and pushed him out of the room. The Basque shifted his weight. I had almost forgotten that he was there; he was so quiet.

"So you went to Craig," Rand said, "thinking you were just engaging in some scientific chicanery and wound up involved in something much larger, much more dangerous. Whatever made you think you could compete with me?"

"Well, you were just a movie guy." I knew it would hurt.

"Just a movie guy?" Rand repeated as if he had heard it before.

"And I thought, 'Great, my sister's in film. Maybe I can get to Rand through her.' It worked," I said with some adolescent pride.

"So, Anne, is your sister?"

"Of course. What did you think?"

"But why would she go along with this?"

"I convinced her I could get her some major 'Fuck you' money. I know how important that is to you guys."

"So you made up all this playacting to get close to me to steal Veritas?"

"Hey, it was worth the effort. We're talking about a lot of money."

Rand exploded. He leaped from the club chair, his face suddenly, amazingly red. "No, we're talking about something that could aid and benefit all of humanity, and you're trying to fuck it up!"

"Oh, don't give me that self-righteous shit! Do you think I believe any of that charity con game from you? If you're trying to aid and benefit humanity, how come you hang around with guys like this?" Batsarov was back in the room. "No, don't try to fool a man who deals in cold, hard facts. Veritas is a commodity to be sold at the highest possible price. You know it. I know it. If we stay honest, at least in this, then maybe we can deal."

"Deal?"

"Sure. You need me, Rand. Veritas is still imperfect."

Rand sat back down. "All right. I'll up the offer to a million a year."

"Well, it was easy getting you back to the bargaining table. A million a year, uh?"

I made the pretense of considering it quite clear. "No. I want what I've always wanted. Fifty percent."

Rand brought years of making deals in Hollywood to bear and kept his face emotionless. "The thing about greed, Einstein, is that it is a sin, and you must be willing to pay the price. So try this offer: One and a half million a year to prepare Veritas for the market and for continuing service to improve and add to it during the life of its patent—or I let Miguel express his love for your sister just before I let Batsarov vent his rage on her."

"Yeah, I do that good," Batsarov said, and he moved to stand behind me. He bent down and whispered into my ear. "I'll make it quick, only hour or two."

I smiled. "Oh, that's smart. Kill her, and then what have you got to hang over my head?"

There was a crack of frustration in Rand's eyes. "You're pretty bright."

"Well, I am a fucking Ph.D., you know."

Rand shook his head just like Ronald Reagan used to when he wanted to both laugh at and express pity toward an opponent. He stood up and began to walk around the room. "Einstein, you've got me all wrong. Not about the money, I intend to become the richest man in the world with Veritas. But you're wrong in thinking there is no charity in my soul. The world's a mess. Governments don't seem to be helping—"

"So bring everybody together in 'World citizenship,' and 'The People' will solve the problems," I mocked. "Do you really think anybody swallows that crap?"

"Oh, yes. Many do. I did once—but not now. After five years of trying to talk sense to the world, I finally learned that sense could not be talked—it could only be enforced. Still, EarthPeople has been very helpful. It allowed me great access to people and places," he looked over to Batsarov, "and talent. Power, Einstein, power well executed, pure and simple, the power to hand people their fondest fantasies and, in return, receive their souls. The power to get into people's heads, where you can best advise them what to think, feel, and want. That's what we're talking about here. The minute I experienced Veritas, I knew what it would bring me. More power than any man has ever had in the history of civilization. That is a hell of a burden to have placed on your shoulders, but it was placed on mine for one reason or another. It is a responsibility I do not take lightly, and it is one I could not share, even if I wanted to. Now I've made you several generous offers, but I'll make one more: Two million a year. Don't answer right away. I want you to take a while to think it over."

Rand made a slight, almost imperceptible nod of his head.

A dull, ringing shock hit the back of mine.

CHAPTER 19
RED DUST

I woke up to the smell of straw and excrement. Not human this time. Horse—most definitely horse. It was a smell my brain vibrated in recognition of, although it had been a long time since the assigned neurons had had to deal with it. I opened my eyes. Three shafts of bright sunlight streamed through a dusty environment to land on my body in three well-heated slices. It was the one lying across my face that had woken me. I moved slightly to avoid it and discovered I was lying on my side, on pounded earth, with my hands tied tightly behind my back.

Veritas, I thought. Was I again a captive of invented truth?

A horse whinnied. As I turned to look at the creature, everything hurt. It was a whole range of hurt, from the dull ache to the sharp pain. I reminisced for a second. Yes, I could account for every point of pain, and the accounting was all from reality. And unless Rand was being truly sadistic, was reality as well, and not Veritas. I'm not sure that gave me any comfort.

Despite the pain, I looked around some more. I was in a horse barn. That was obvious. Not a clean, orderly, modern one, but one from the Old West, or, at least, from an old Western.

Suddenly there was music. Six sharp, quick notes lead into the expansive open sound of multiple violins painting a picture of wide vistas and America at its most mythic. I thought the Marlboro Man was going to ride in.

No! Not the Marlboro Man. The Magnificent Seven! The music was originally the theme for *The Magnificent Seven!*

Seven men did not ride in. Only two. And they were horseless. There was Batsarov in a fresh cowboy outfit—if that term can apply considering the sweat stains—and with a six-gun strapped to his right leg. If you discounted the incongruous large black boom box he carried, blaring out "The Theme from *The Magnificent Seven*," he gave the perfect image of the ugliest, meanest desperado west of the Pecos. Wherever the hell that is. With him, comfortably carrying an Armalite AR-18 semiautomatic, was a massive fellow about 6'5" with a beer barrel of a belly, a bull neck, and a flushed face that seemed one size too small for his head which was just a few millimeters shy of the size of a beach ball. He wore a short-sleeve checkered shirt and blue jeans that seemed to perilously hang from what hips had escaped from the fall of flesh. He had graying blond hair that had been Brylcreamed into rigor mortis. I figured he was either an Afrikaner emigrant still pissed over the election of Nelson Mandela or an American white supremacist militiaman on a leave of absence. Not that it mattered much.

Batsarov stared down at me. He smiled his not-pleasant smile, enhanced now by a straw of hay clenched between his two front gold teeth. He took the boom box and placed it down next to my head, the music blaring into my face.

"LIKE IT, YOU FUCK?" Batsarov shouted. "*MAGNIFICENT SEVEN*! GOOD MOVIE!" He started humming loudly with the music, bouncing in time as if bouncing on a galloping horse. "GOOD MUSIC! GOOD MUSIC TO DIE TO!" Then he bent down and turned the cassette section of the machine off. Now he whispered. "This not so good." He hit a switch on the CD section. A high-frequency tone screamed out of the box and pierced my ears. I shouted in pain. It was the only thing I could do. With my hands tied, I couldn't cover my ears. I tried to move away, but Beer Barrel moved quickly behind me, placing a heavy foot on my side. Finally, Batsarov turned off the machine. The sudden quiet was a jolt in its way. I looked up at the two men. They were both removing earplugs. "Now you real awake and paying attention," Batsarov said. "That good. I need attention. I need no games. I need no clever crap. Attention. Listen. Answer. Why? Why you do this—Fixxer?"

How? "What's fixer?"

Batsarov sighed and nodded to Beer Barrel. They put earplugs back in, and Beer Barrel turned on the CD. I'm not sure how long they let it run—pain proves the relativity of time. Then it was over.

"Fixxer. Strange name. But that what Hinckley call you."

I now knew where I was: Paul Hinckley's ranch in Paso Robles.

Batsarov pushed the boom box aside with his boot. Then he used it to turn my face, wiping something moist off his boot in the process. Horse manure, I suspected. "You know, you not bad looking man."

"Thanks. You are."

"Yep," he laughed. "Uglier than shit! But you know? It never stopped me getting bitch. Not handsome, girls like, but power, and I always with power. Soon more. Much more. Power and real piece of meat between legs that make eyes go wide, that get you any bitch you want. But I only like nasty bitches. Nasty bitches with dripping—"

"All right," I said, "I will admit to not being Tom Einstein if it will get you to stop talking."

"Not care who you not. Who you are, I want. What kind of name, Fixxer? Hinckley said that's what they call you."

"It's a nickname. Don't you have a nickname?"

"Sure! I am 'Bulgarian Cowboy!'"

"That's the silliest thing I've ever heard."

Batsarov kicked me. Hard. I thought he would have appreciated Marx.

"Now tell me, are you cop?"

"No."

"What are you then?"

"The man who wants to kill you."

Batsarov laughed. "Fine. Good. Go ahead." He spread his arms out as if offering himself to me.

"Can I take a rain check?" I wasn't about to say, "Sorry, a bit tied up right now," although I'm sure I was expected to.

"What rain check?"

"Never mind. I doubt the sincerity of your offer."

"I called Rand. I said, guess what? He not physicist, after all. He just fuck! I kill. Rand said, okay. Okay?"

"I have a vote?"

"No, sorry, do not come from democratic tradition."

"Have you already killed Hinckley?"

"No. This Hinckley place! Would not be proper for guest to kill host."

How gentlemanly.

Then he added the addendum, "Without fighting chance. Come! See!" He indicated for Beer Barrel to grab me, which he did, by the rope that tied my hands, picking me up entirely off the ground and setting me on my feet in a near run as he pushed me toward the doors.

Light, which is supposed to bring truth, brought only pain—although, possibly, they're one and the same. Not that I was being that philosophical at that moment. I was too busy dealing with the purely physical problem of getting my eyes to adjust to the harsh, bright sunlight without the benefit of using my hands to shield them and ease the process. During this momentary sightlessness, I worked with my other senses to get a feel for the place. My feet half ran, half were dragged over dusty ground. The sun pierced my skin with a thousand little flaming needles. The air dried out my nostrils in an instant, and except for the noises we were making, carried no familiar sounds, especially the vibrations of technological life: traffic; distant TV; leaf blowers, jackhammers, lawn mowers; somebody else's choice in music.

Form, dimension, and color finally came into definition just as I was forced up against a wagon wheel and my bound hands were tied to it.

It was a Western town—one street of classic wooden structures fronted by traditional wooden sidewalks. There was a saloon, of course, and a general store. A feed store, a barber/surgeon, horses saddled and ready for ridin', tied to hitching posts, plops of manure beneath them keeping the flies happy, and, at the end of the street, a white church with its white steeple rounded out the inventory.

"Damn, fuckin' great!" Batsarov said. "Hinckley had it built for *Red Dust*. Awful movie. But great town! He told me he made movie studio pay for it, then he kept it and now rent it to more movie. Ha! He would have made great apparatchik."

I looked down the street opposite the church. Beyond it was a landscape of rolling brown hills dotted by California Live Oaks, a typical central California landscape. Not as "Western" as Monument Valley, but pretty "Western."

"Where's Hinckley?" I managed to ask.

"He in the saloon. Having a few belts." He turned to the saloon. "Bring Hinckley out!"

Paul Hinckley was pushed out through the double, swinging saloon doors. He stumbled, fell, and landed half on the wooden sidewalk, half in the street. The Basque came out. He had a thick leather belt wrapped tightly around his right fist, and Hinckley had a discolored, swollen face—a perfect match. Hinckley picked himself up. I could see he was wearing a costume, that of a farmer, a sodbuster. I would hate to have had Batsarov's childhood.

Batsarov picked up a lariat lying on the ground. He started to twirl it. "Hinckley missed our meeting. We look for Hinckley. Hinckley cannot be found. Make no sense." Batsarov formed a large opening in the lasso and jumped through it three times, then came to a stop.

"I would applaud if I could," I said.

"No, that okay. It help me talk. Especially in English." He started a small twirl again. "Why would Hinckley not want big, fat deal from Rand for stupid treatment? But we patient. We watch there. We watch here." The lasso had gathered momentum as he spoke. He brought it over his head, swung it around, and threw it at me. It landed around me. He cinched it tight and walked over to me. "Then, Hinckley, here he is. Good. I drive up. We visit. He has very nice house, right over that hill." Batsarov took the rope off me and then pointed to the rolling hills down the street. I could imagine the house. Spacious, well appointed, and in the middle of 2,500 acres, close to nothing reasonably like neighbors, and so safe from prying eyes—but also helping hands.

Batsarov walked back to the middle of the street and started to twirl again. "We just start to talk. I want to get to know him. Then I get call from hotel. Rand bring back strangers to lake. Strangers? We weren't going to have any strangers. My friends stay to keep Hinckley company. I drive back. Fast. Find you snooping. I never believe you fucking scientist. You man on boat. Or you man giving York money for Hinckley. Maybe you both, but you no fucking scientist. But you fool Rand. Okay. I watch."

Batsarov threw the rope again. It was perfect in its flight toward me. "I catch." He cinched the rope. "You so stupid. I bring you up here, show you to Hinckley. He will tell me nothing. Not loyalty. Maybe greed. But I think he scared of you. I have you hog-tied in horse shit, but he scared of you. Why? We beat him. Civilians can't take pain. You took pain. Now we know. You mysterious Mr. Fixxer. What is that shit?" He walked over to me and again took the rope off. "What are you, some kind of—cowboy?"

"I thought you were the cowboy."

"No. Everybody always had that wrong. I'm outlaw."

Again he walked back to the middle of the street. "Now everything okay. Hinckley not need treatment. You have nothing for Rand. Now—"

"How do you know I have nothing for Rand? I had to get my information from somewhere. I know scientists who could help."

"So? Been telling Rand, Russian physicists! Out of work. I can get those. Cheap! But Rand think I'm only thug."

"Yes, and none of us like to be pigeonholed, but how do you know any Russian physicists have done work in this field?"

Batsarov shook his head in pity. "Typical American. No, you have nothing useful for Rand. Now it's my turn to have fun."

Batsarov gestured to the Basque, who walked over to the saloon doors, reached in, and pulled out a six-gun and holster. He walked over to Hinckley and strapped it on him.

"Wha—what are you doing?" Hinckley asked, startled.

"Gunfight!" Batsarov shouted. "We are going to have gunfight. Lots of fun. You'll see."

Hinckley's eyes went all scared, questioning, and pleading. He turned to me. "Fixxer! Help me?"

"Not much I can do at the moment," I said.

"But—but..."

"He's just trying to scare you. They're prop guns, aren't they? They have blanks." I was hoping I was right.

"No," Hinckley said. "We do target shooting with them."

"No OK Corral? Why you not build OK Corral? I always liked OK Corral better than walk down middle of street. More realistic."

"Batsarov!" I yelled.

Batsarov turned and stared at me with newfound respect. "Oh. You know who I am. Even more reason to have fun." He turned to Hinckley. "It's your move, Hinckley," he said in his best Bulgarian twang.

"You've got to be kidding," Hinckley said.

"No. I give you chance. Fair fighting chance. Code of the West."

"Except that, if by any chance Hinckley shoots you, your friends will kill him immediatcly," I said, still trying to get Batsarov to concentrate on me.

"Not my fault they don't believe Code of the West."

"Pretty cowardly to have a backup."

"Not backup. Spectators get out of hand, like Soccer game. Now, Hinckley, dra—no, wait, I forget. Can't have gunfight without frightened townsfolk. Bring them out!"

Out of the general store came a thug I hadn't seen before. Big, mean-looking, ugly, but other than that, nondescript enough to give no clues as to what local controversy he was a refugee from. Then came a woman dressed like a schoolmarm and a girl about ten, wearing a gingham dress. They both were exhausted and scared and were followed by another thug, a nondescript Black. All the thugs carried the same Armalite AR-18 semiautomatic—volume buying, no doubt.

"Hillary! Joan! Are you okay?" Hinckley started to move towards them, but the Basque stopped him.

"We're okay, Paul," his wife Joan said.

"Okay. Draw, Hinckley!"

"No! No, I refuse."

Batsarov jerked his head towards one of the thugs. The thug spattered three quick rounds from the AR-18 directly before Hinckley. Hillary, the girl, screamed as the dust settled back down to the ground.

"Come on Hinckley. Show kinfolk what kind man you are."

Hinckley looked around him as if he was trying to make a decision, and the answer was somewhere out in the open if only he could see it. "I can do this," he may have been thinking. "Of course, I can do this. It's every American boy's birthright, easy grip on a gun, lightning-fast draw; I've seen it hundreds of times—felt it."

Hinckley went for his gun.

Batsarov drew quickly and shot.

A sudden chunk of red flew off Hinckley's left shoulder as the sound of the gun's report was still in the air. Hinckley screamed. His wife and child screamed and clung to each other, thinking...

Hinckley fell to his knees, disbelieving that he could be feeling such pain, that such a thing could have happened to him.

"Get up Hinckley. You not dead yet!" Batsarov shouted down the street. He was enjoying himself. He was having his fun. He holstered his gun.

"Daddy," cried Hillary.

"Batsarov, that's enough!" I shouted. "If you're going to kill us, just do it."

"I am not, Mr. Fixxer, cold-blooded killer. I am passionate about what I do! Now come on Hinckley. Stand up, you son-of-a-bitch!" He said it just like the mature John Wayne. It was no compliment to Wayne.

Hinckley stood up. He still gripped his gun in his right hand.

"You don't even have to draw again. You got gun, shoot!" Batsarov challenged.

Hinckley looked over to his wife and child. Tears streamed down his cheeks—for his pain or theirs?

It was the child's cries that were heart rendering. "Daddy!" she cried again, and a slice was struck out of my heart, immediately becoming an old wound.

Hinckley screamed, raised the gun, and tried to shoot.

Batsarov drew again and shot Hinckley in the right leg. Hinckley collapsed.

"Ha! Look!" Batsarov pointed to the ground around Hinckley. "Red dust! Ha-ha!"

"Okay, Batsarov, I think you've used up your fun on him. Give me a chance at you."

"Give you a chance Mr. Fixxer? Yes, I can do that. Do you know firearms?"

"I've shot a few in my time."

"Sure. A few. I have no doubt. But not this!" He held his gun up. "Colt 45. Gun for man of skill. You people," he waved his gun at all of us, me, the Basque, Beer Barrel, and the two nondescripts, we were all in the same club, "shoot only semiautomatic, automatic. BLAU! BLAU! BLAU! Spray of death! Easy! No challenge. No Code of the West!"

"Cut the fucking rhetoric and give me a gun!" I screamed, revealing more hate than was necessary.

Batsarov felt it. "All right, Mr. Fixxer." He gestured to Beer Barrel, who untied me.

"Let Hinckley's wife treat his wounds."

"Why? I'm going to kill him eventually."

"Letting him slowly bleed to death is not really the Code of the West, is it?."

"True." He instructed the two thugs to let Joan go to Hinckley. She ran, dropped down beside him, and looked at the wounds. She started to tear at her long schoolmarm dress for bandages. It was like something out of an old Western. Batsarov seemed to like that. The Basque took the six-gun and holster from Hinckley and brought them to me. I put them on and took a position on the street.

What could I accomplish here? If I outdrew Batsarov and managed to kill him, the thugs would let loose their AR-18s on me. I did not doubt that. I could turn, drop to the ground and try for a single shot slaying of Hillary. That way, at least, I would know that the child would not suffer the pain and indignities these bastards would likely cause her. I would be killed immediately, leaving Hinckley and his wife to suffer more pain before death. But that could not be helped. The child took precedence. All children should take precedence. They so rarely do. Or I could try to win Batsarov's respect. Not something I desired, but maybe something I could use to bargain for diminished suffering for the Hinckleys.

"So, Mr. Fixxer, you may draw now."

I did, watching Batsarov's hand move with a blur as it went for his gun, grabbed it, brought it up, and shattered as my bullet sliced through his hand between the middle and third finger. The Colt 45 flew away and behind Batsarov. His eyes went quickly from incredulity to stark raving anger. There seemed to be no room for respect.

"KILL HIM!" Batsarov shouted.

The Basque's head exploded.

Batsarov's jaw dropped.

My brain was trying to decide if it had heard the gunfire.

In quick succession, the two thugs became truly nondescript as their faces became unrecognizable among the bleeding flesh and shattered bone.

Beer Barrel was falling, dead, before he hit the ground with a thud.

Poor Hillary was screaming again. There was a therapy bill for you.

Roee stood up from his prone position on top of the saloon. He cradled his Galil Sniping Rifle. It had been a gift from his father. He loves that rifle.

The Captain was on the roof of the general store, pointing his Remington 700 rifle at Batsarov.

I was beginning to feel like I was in a "Firearms Are Your Friends" promotional video from the NRA.

Batsarov ran, leaving a trail of blood, grabbed a horse, mounted, and took off at full gallop down the street towards the rolling hills.

"Kill him! Kill him!" Hinckley started shouting, which made me feel good knowing he had enough blood left for lust.

"Sorry, he's already in the witness protection program," I said as I ran towards a horse, grabbed the lariat, mounted, and took off, giving chase.

The music would have been excellent here: Bernstein's soaring score backing up the excitement of the pursuit. But as it was, the brown rolling hills, the stark profiles of the oaks, the heat, the dust, they all added up to make the whole venture appropriately atmospheric.

I was catching up. It was a good horse. I swung the lariat above my head, a movement not without pain but necessary to catch Batsarov before he bled all over the hills. He suddenly took a left turn towards a grouping of oaks. I followed. When I got close, I saw an opportunity he was handing me if I could get the timing right: Like comedy, like the brain.

I let the lariat fly just before Batsarov went under an oak branch. It flew over the branch falling to loop around his shoulders just as he passed under. I jerked my horse to a stop. The rope slipped up Batsarov's shoulders. He grabbed for it. I pulled my horse back. The rope slipped again and cinched, forming a noose, catching Batsarov's hand against his neck, and yanking him back. His horse kept running. I secured the rope to the horn of my saddle and dismounted, commanding the horse to stay. I walked over to Batsarov. He was swinging, kicking his legs, pulling at the rope around his neck with his one good hand, creating space for air to pass. He looked down at me. His eyes pleaded. I just looked at him. "Back!" I commanded the horse. The horse moved back, pulling Batsarov up higher. Now it was harder for him to pull at the rope. It would soon be too hard.

"Don't you know," I told him, "that every American is a *real* cowboy?"

His legs kicked furiously. It was time to end this. But I didn't. I couldn't. I heard the screams of Hillary Hinckley again, saw the terror and fear in her ten-year-old eyes, and saw again the love in those eyes for her father, Paul Hinckley, a minimally talented near idiot, but her father, nonetheless. Maybe— maybe I should just let time slip by.

A horse rode up, and Roee was soon at my side. "Fixxer," he said calmly, "Fixxer, you cannot do this. *You* cannot do this."

Fuck you, Roee, I wanted to say.

I pulled the six-gun out of the holster. I pointed it up. Batsarov's eyes widened to the coward point. I aimed carefully. I fired. The rope broke; my horse jerked back; Batsarov fell.

"Pick the bastard up," I said to Roee.

Roee started to.

"No, wait." I walked over to Batsarov and punched him hard in the mouth. "Fucking gold teeth."

xx

As we rode back to town, Batsarov running behind us, tied to the rope, trying to keep up, not to trip and fall, for that would mean a skin-scraping drag over the landscape; three helicopters flew low over our heads bound for the same destination. Two were police choppers; one was a medical chopper.

"Paso Robles PD," Roee said. "They weren't happy about our plans, but the Captain convinced them."

"Good for the Captain. Glad you guys made it in time."

"In the nick of, I would say."

"Yes, if you want to be melodramatic about it."

"Better melodramatic than existential, don't you think?"

"Or surreal."

"Yes, surreal would have been bad."

xx

When we returned to the town, a doctor declared the four thugs dead. Another was taking care of Hinckley. A policewoman was talking to Joan and Hillary. The Captain was on the radio starting the process for an arrest warrant for Rand. We sat Batsarov down in a rocking chair in front of the general store and had a doctor tend to his hand as we talked to him.

"I want to make this clear," I said to Batsarov, who sat there looking in vain for his self-confidence. "You will cooperate with the police and be a witness against Andy Rand."

"Why should I help?"

The Captain walked up and joined the conversation. "You will, of course, be charged with murder, kidnapping, terrorist activities—"

"And not having a work permit for any of that," Roee added. Batsarov didn't get it.

"If you would like to have any break in your sentencing, you better cooperate," I said.

"You declare me guilty? This America, am innocent until proven guilty. So go ahead, spend millions to try me. I get best lawyers."

"The other option, of course," the Captain said, "is to deport you as an undesirable. I don't think that there is any question that you are undesirable."

"Fine. I want to go to Brazil."

"Well, no, we'll send you back to Bulgaria," Roee said. "We were thinking of putting you right into the hands of Krassimir Indzhova" Batsarov looked up at us. It was funny how he tried to hide the fear in his eyes.

"I've been talking with Krassimir," Roee continued. "I guess you pissed him off big time when you left Bulgaria with 3 million of VeriGroup's funds. He said he would love the opportunity to talk to you about it."

"American justice has just become your best friend," I said. "I suggest you give the police full cooperation."

Batsarov said nothing. Then he nodded, closing his eyes to further hide the fear from us.

Sometimes satisfaction is hard to find.

I walked over to Paul Hinckley, strapped to a gurney inside the medical helicopter. I asked Joan and Hillary to give us a moment. Hillary was still crying. I wanted to pat her on the head, or some such useless gesture, to assure her it was all over and that all would be okay—in time. But I didn't.

"Jesus Christ, Fixxer, how could you get me involved in all this?" Hinckley demanded to know.

"Unless I just aced a course in 'Fooling Yourself for Fun and Profit,' I rather think it was you that got me involved."

"Yeah, well... What the fuck was it all about? A stupid treatment?"

"Veritas is real."

"What? Oh, my god! So you have it now? Great! Look, how can I get involved?"

"Shut-up! You're lucky to be alive. Why didn't you stay put, like I told you?"

"Well..."

"You put your wife and child into mortal danger by being just plain stupid!"

"But—"

"I'd cause you pain right now if you weren't already in it."

"Look—"

"And forget the treatment. It doesn't exist."

"But—"

"The two hundred and fifty thousand you were paying York."

"Ye—yeah?"

"It's mine." I walked away, giving him no chance to protest.

Blood is Pretty

CHAPTER 20
THE PROP THICKENS

The helicopters took off with the dead, the wounded, the fragile, the criminal, and the stupid. The Captain, Roee, and I went to Hinckley's house to talk. Sitting near it was the Aérospatiale Dauphin.

"That's how I was brought here?"

"Yep," the Captain said.

"How did you follow?"

"Let's go inside and relax. Then we'll explain."

xx

We had some drinks. My vodka tonic quickly made an impact, reminding me that I had not eaten in over 24 hours. We went into the kitchen and put together a meal. Roee talked as I ate.

"We were surprised when the helicopter did not head for LAX. At first, we thought it was heading for the desert, but when it veered towards the mountains, I figured Arrowhead or Big Bear. We got up there as fast as we could. Once we found out where you were, we looked for a place to observe from. Many of the houses on the lake are unused most of the year. It was no problem finding an empty one we could base at. We set up the observation equipment, but there wasn't much interesting to see until your little run with the dog. That was a neat trick."

"Yeah. Promise me you won't tell the animal rights people."

"That confirmed that you were in trouble, which we suspected when Petey's homing device stopped sending a signal. They found it?"

"Well, let's just say Batsarov zeroed in on it but not out of cleverness. Which reminds me..." I excused myself and went to the bathroom. "Should I save it?" I yelled back out at Roee. "Can Petey fix it?"

"No. He said it's disposable."

After a not pain-free separation of the homing device from the base of my manhood, I flushed it down the toilet.

When I got back, Roee continued. "Luckily, I had taken the precaution to plant another homing device on the helicopter."

"Scuba?"

"No time to get the equipment."

"This crazy son-of-a-bitch swam across the lake buck naked in the dead of night," the Captain said.

I looked at Roee.

"No problem. We did a lot of skinny dipping at the Kibbutz."

"Still, it must have been cold," I said. "You don't like the cold. I appreciate it."

"Thank you. Pats on the head are always welcome. When we saw them take you to the chopper, we could see Anne wasn't with you."

"She's still there, with Rand. Unharmed so far, I'm guessing."

"We thought about going in to get her, but...." The Captain started.

"No. You were right. If they were taking me off alone, you could have only assumed she was already dead or safe for the moment."

"Yeah, that's how we saw it," Roee said. "We headed down the mountain, watching the track on the chopper. I wasn't surprised when it stopped at Paso Robles. We made our way to the 101 and headed up. The Captain cleared the way for us with the CHP, so we made good time. Still, this place is remote. Once up here, we had to approach it slowly to figure out the best way to get close to you. The locals wanted to help, but the last thing we needed was a party. So we asked them to wait off stage with the choppers."

"How did you get on the ranch?"

"On a couple of stealth horses."

"Sounds logical."

"Logical but butt-breaking," the Captain added.

"The locals know all about the Western town, of course. Hinckley's considered a good citizen for bringing in the business. Knowing Batsarov, I figured he would have you and the Hinckleys there rather than at the house. When we got close, we could hear what was going on. I took the saloon roof. The Captain took the general store."

"You had no problem sneaking up?"

"He had no guards posted. From his point of view, he had no need.

He truly did think he was in the lawless Old West."

"That's the problem with hobbies," I said. "They can be self-defeating."

Now we had to prepare to take Rand. I told the Captain that just pulling up in police units with the arrest warrant in hand would not do it. Rand would not give up that easily. He still had Miguel, and who knows how many armaments? And he had Anne and York: A perfect hostage situation. With the international connections Rand had built over the last five years, all he would need would be to get out of the country. Places to live the good life outside our legal reach would be easy to find. Of course, he would take York and Veritas with him and could continue with his plans. All he would need front people: A ready commodity for a free-spending buyer.

"What do you suggest then?" The Captain asked.

"Plenty of cowboy clothes around here. I'm going to dress up like Batsarov. His hat is probably still out by the tree. Roee will pass for the Basque. We'll take the Aérospatiale back to Arrowhead. Hopefully, they'll suspect nothing as we land and come up the tram. With luck, we'll get close enough to make Miguel ineffective before we're recognized. At that point, Rand will be, shall we say, emasculated."

"You know, the Aérospatiale stopped for fuel once on the way up here. The tanks now are nearly depleted."

"Call your buddies in the local police department. See if we can get some fuel out here immediately."

"Okay. What else?"

"Alert the San Bernardino Sheriffs. We'll drop you off just outside of Arrowhead at their pad. Get them to the lake, but out of sight, and prepare them for "the switch," just in case. Add Anne to that."

"Okay. At what price?"

"At what it takes. If everything goes smoothly, we'll signal you, and you can come in with the sheriffs through the front door. Have a rent-a-car available for Anne, Roee, and me to leave in immediately."

xx

I contemplated the passing landscape below as the Aérospatiale Dauphin sped towards Lake Arrowhead with Roee at the controls. Such arrogance man has—to have found ways to lift himself off the ground, to damn the fates of physical realities, and to manipulate the laws of nature to achieve that which any cursory reading of nature seems to inform us is not ours to achieve—such wonderful, inspiring arrogance. Would that all arrogance had such lift.

"Worried about Anne?" Roee asked, mistaking the mask contemplation had given me.

"Worry is a useless emotion. It expends energy best applied to dealing positively with that which you are worried about."

"What if there is nothing you can do?"

"Then it is even more useless. Resignation would be the only recourse in that case."

"But you are concerned?"

"I suppose if you must have some humanizing emotion to tag me with at this moment, Roee, concern is as good as any. But to be honest, I am more curious as to what may have been going on at the Chateau de la Lune since we've been away. And the possible ways to rectify the situation if things have been negative."

"Jesus Christ, Fixxer," the Captain joined the conversation. "You're talking about a beautiful woman who didn't have to get herself involved in this except for your asking."

"Which makes her my responsibility. Worry and concern are false ways to prove to observers that you take your responsibilities seriously. Analysis, planning, and action are ways to fulfill your responsibilities."

"Yeah, well, sure, but—"

"If it will make you feel better, Captain, know that emotions will catch up with me when everything is finished. They always have in the past."

xx

We dropped the Captain off at the San Bernardino Sheriff's Search & Rescue helicopter pad. Things were already in preparation, and the Captain quickly took command of the operation. Then we ascended again. I put on Batsarov's cowboy hat. We eased our way to the lake. It was late afternoon.

"Fixxer?"

"Yes?"

"The pontoons?"

"The switch up there."

Roee hit the switch, and the multilayered Mylar pontoons inflated out of the skids, and we descended and landed on the water by the dock. We got out of the helicopter acting as casually as we could: Roee did some checks of the craft, as would be expected, and I chatted with him. Then we started moving off the dock towards the tram with no perceivable ulterior motivation beyond getting from point A to point B.

"STAY BACK!' came a female voice from the promontory. We looked up. "JUST STAY BACK, YOU BASTARDS!"

There was a smoky disturbance from under a blonde head, then the weirdness of watching a small missile head down toward us. We both hit the deck, and the missile passed over us and slammed into the Aérospatiale Dauphin. The craft exploded with a frightening boom, an orange ball of light, and a rain of debris that only by luck missed injuring us.

"DON'T MOVE. JUST STAY IN THAT POSITION!"

It was Anne. How and why? I was curious to know. I tried to lift my head.

"LIFT IT HIGHER, AND I'LL BLOW IT OFF!"

"Anne!" I tried shouting, but shouting into the wood planks of a dock tends to muffle even your best efforts.

"Do you think she knows it's us?" Roee asked.

"What?"

"Well, maybe Rand charmed her over to his side. The aphrodisiac of power, and all that."

"No, I just think our little ruse is working too well for the situation we find ourselves in."

"Well, in any case, this is a really uncomfortable position."

"Too bad I put this hat on tight. If it had fallen off when I hit the ground, maybe she could see that I'm her 'brother.'"

"That's an idea. Can you wiggle it off or something?"

"One little wiggle, and it will be off all right. Along with my head."

"Well, I suppose we can just wait here for the police to arrive. I could use a nap."

"Good plan, Roee. Unless she is now working for Rand."

"Oh great. I thought it was my job to sow the seeds of doubt. Well, then, how about a quick dash to the tram, assuming her trigger finger isn't that fast, and we can get some cover and her attention before she reloads."

"Good plan."

"No qualifications this time?" Roee asked.

"Time and place for everything. I'm sure we can think of the qualifications later."

"Right."

We jumped up and ran. The explosion was right behind us. This one blew the hat off. But we made it to the tram. "ANNE!" I yelled, poking my blond head out. "ANNE! IT'S ME!"

Her blonde head came peaking over the promontory ridge. "FIXXER?"

"YEAH! AND ROEE!"

"OH GREAT! I'LL SEND THE TRAM DOWN!

Anne was still holding the Sidewinder launcher when we got up to the top, probably the same one Batsarov and company had used at Caltech. She was smiling a big, broad smile. "Where did you learn to fire one of those?" I asked.

"Oh, about three years ago, I did this cheap B-movie for this crazy director about a bunch of models trained to be commandos. I think he got off seeing beautiful women fingering phallic symbols."

"Is it out on video?"

"Yeah. Only."

"So, I take it you're in control of the situation here?"

"Sure. You didn't even have to come back. You could have, you know, just sent in the police."

"Oh."

"Well, what did you expect, Fixxer? A damsel in distress?"

"Uh—there's no safe way for me to answer that question, is there?"

"I think not."

"Is there any chance," Roee asked, "we can know the details?"

"Well, I couldn't have done it without Imelda."

"Imelda?"

"Poor abused girl. Besides cooking and cleaning, she was being used to relieve these bastards' pent-up sexual frustrations, including Rand's. She's just an ignorant peasant girl who thought she had no choice. But we communicated, mainly through our eyes, Especially after Rand found out last night that you weren't my brother. He came to my room ready to take it out on me, I think, but managed to control himself. He just played the popinjay instead, telling me how Batsarov would make your death slow and painful and how he was going to take over the world, so how would I like to be his queen."

"You're kidding?"

"Well, not in those words, but I got his drift. I thought about going along with him, thinking it might be my only chance—seeing how you were going to be dead and all. But it was a role I couldn't play. I've had that problem before, you know. A lack of sycophantic hypocrisy is a real handicap in Hollywood. Rand was—disappointed. According to Imelda, he started making plans with Miguel to get rid of me quietly, something to do with pushing me out of a plane over the Pacific. I think he got the idea from the newspapers."

"No, Miguel probably had the experience listed on his resume."

"Oh. Well, anyway, that's when Imelda decided to do something. When she brought my meal up this afternoon, a steak knife was hidden in the napkin. I used it on Miguel."

"Did you kill him?" I asked, a strange streak of alarm passing through me.

"Well, it wouldn't have done much good just to hurt him a little. I mean, he was standing there with his semiautomatic phallic symbol. You know, the world would be a lot better off if men had semiautomatic phalluses instead of semiautomatic phallic symbols."

"Anne, did you kill him?"

"No. I pretended to choke on the food, and I stabbed him in the leg when he got close. He dropped his gun, and Imelda picked it up. She killed him. You should have seen the blood!"

"Blood is pretty."

"Yeah," Anne said. "Until it congeals."

"Look, uh, did they use you at all to, uh, relieve their frustrations?"

"No. I told them I had a yeast infection."

xx

When we got to the house, we found Rand sitting in the captain's chair in the study. It had been pushed up against one of the bookcases. Imelda sat on the glass-top desk, pointing an AR-18 at him. York, Anne had told me before we entered, was downstairs in bed. He was not in the best mental state. Roee called the Captain on his cell phone and told him to move in. Then we turned off the security and opened the front gate. That done, I confronted Rand.

"It's over. We have Batsarov, and he will testify against you."

Rand looked up at me. He had a smug look far exceeding any he had yet displayed. He was like a kid caught stealing cigarettes, refusing to look contrite for stupid old Mr. Whoever who clerked at the drug store. "Who are you?" he demanded to know, as if he, now, was Mr. Whoever.

"You can call me Fixxer."

It registered in Rand's eyes. It had meaning. "I thought you were a myth."

"Maybe I am. Maybe you're stuck in your own Veritas."

He laughed. "Well, if I am, for God's sake, unplug me."

"Not within my power, but I'm sure the State of California will happily plug you—in."

"I have many powerful friends," he said as if that answered the threat of institutional demise.

"What do you expect them to do? Form a Free Andy Committee?"

"Why are you doing this to me? From what I hear, you're nothing but a criminal. Join me. You know the power of Veritas. You know what we could do."

"I've done the criminal. I try to avoid the immoral."

"You've discovered a difference?"

I leaned into Rand. Close. I whispered into his ear. "Civil authorities decide on the one. *I* decide on the other." There was no better way to tell him I could not be his.

Rand turned his head to me. Our eyes met. His were questioning. Mine were unflinching.

"You—you really are going to turn me over to the police."

"If I don't let Imelda do a 'Miguel' on you."

Imelda jumped off the table and eagerly shoved the gun into Rand's golden gut. For the first time, fear crossed his eyes. For the first time, he was getting it. Imelda smiled and proudly puffed out her chest as she looked to me for permission. Her beauty had never shone as much.

"You know," I turned to Anne, "your crazy director may have had a point."

"Oh, shut up," she said with a smile.

We could hear sirens. "Imelda, you better give me the gun." Reluctantly, she gave it to me. "And you're to say nothing to the police about Miguel. I have friends in Immigration. I'll take care of you."

"And me, Imelda," Anne said, slightly competitive, "I'll be there for you."

Imelda nodded, reassured, but she probably remained cautious.

"Okay, Rand, let's go."

Rand stood up. "Last chance, Fixxer. There's much we could do with Veritas."

"That's a tabled issue."

Rand fell into resignation. His shoulders slumped. Pools of moisture began to form in his eyes. "Oh, God," he said, facing a hard truth he could not manipulate. Going from the top of the world to the bottom of the slag heap tends to yank your guts out. He turned away and faced the bookcase, taking a moment to recover some dignity. "You ever read Graham Green, Fixxer?" he said quietly among sobs.

"Yes."

"Great film critic. One of the reasons I went into film. And a great novelist." He ran his fingers along the spines of books as if they, strange non-celluloid, non-digital dreams, would save him. He stopped at a particular one. "Did you ever read this one? *This Gun for Hire?*"

I figured it out a micro-second too late. Rand pushed the book's spine and, through some clever mechanism, suddenly had a pistol in his hand and pointed it at Anne.

"Don't you love bootleggers?" Rand asked with a big wide grin. "They were so wonderfully paranoid. Not without good cause, I think."

I was not impressed. "Rand, that's a model 422 from Advantage Arms. Beautifully concealable with that two-and-a-half-inch barrel, but you'll have to be an awfully good shot to make much use of it in this situation."

Rand swiftly swung his arm in Imelda's direction, shot, then quickly turned back to point it at Anne. There was a groan from Imelda as she clutched her stomach and fell to the ground.

"Imelda!" Anne screamed and moved to her, Rand tracking her with the gun.

I wouldn't be surprised if Roee and I dropped our jaws.

Rand shrugged off our amazement. "Beverly Hills Gun Club," he said by way of explanation. "Now put the gun down, Fixxer."

I did.

"Anne, leave Imelda to her peace and come over here and push *A Thousand and One Nights*."

Anne coldly did so. The bookcase door opened. Rand walked over to her, grabbed her right arm, pulled it back, and jerked it up. The reality of pain showed on her face, but she refused to make a sound.

"Get anywhere near me, and I'll kill her and York. Understood?"

"Yes."

He moved Anne through the door.

"Fixxer!" Anne yelled back as they descended the stairs, her voice slightly echoing in the stairwell. "Now I'm a damsel in distress."

We could hear Rand laugh. He was enjoying this.

"Roee, get into that computer; it's linked to a camera down there."

It wasn't hard; the computer was only on sleep. An image of the lab came up quickly. Rand was forcing York out of his cell. He ordered him and Anne to unplug and gather all Veritas equipment. As we were watching, the Captain and many deputies arrived. Someone started to attend to Imelda immediately. The Captain came over to us. We could see Rand push Anne and York towards the backdoor.

"He's got a powerboat down there in an underground dock beyond the door," I informed the Captain and Roee.

"And probably some escape vehicles positioned around the lake," Roee said.

"Yes. Batsarov would have seen to that. Fully armed and with other provisions. Rand probably scoffed at the idea."

"Likes it now, I'll bet," the Captain said. "He could land anywhere, and he has two hostages. So there's a good chance he will make it off this mountain."

"Police procedure?"

"To follow maintaining a safe distance. Try to negotiate."

"That'll never work."

"Why?"

"You've never negotiated with a Hollywood executive, have you, Captain?" I ran for the stairs, and Roee followed.

The Captain, following good form, yelled after us, "Fixxer, stop!" But you could tell his heart wasn't in it.

As we ran through the lab, I explained, "Rand's got two water jets down there."

"They're not as fast."

"Then we'll have to get clever. Despite his demeanor, Rand is in a panic. So we need to use that."

The water was still lapping around the dock when we got there and mounted the two water jets.

"Oh great!" Roee exclaimed.

"What?"

"These are Yamaha WaveRaiders! These babies have 110 horses!"

"Really?"

"Yeah."

"I can't seem to get out of this damn Western!"

Coming out of the underground dock, we met the tail end of Rand's wake, but he was still well ahead of us, just leaving the cove and entering the main body of the lake.

"WILL HE SHOOT THEM?" Roee shouted as we gained speed, riding parallel to each other.

"CAN'T! WHAT DOES THAT LEAVE HIM WHILE HE'S VULNERABLE ON THE LAKE? BUT WE DON'T HAVE MUCH TIME!"

Looking up ahead, we could see that Rand had York at the wheel and Anne sitting next to him on the driver's bench, holding on as best as she could. Rand was forward in the scooped-out cockpit to the port side, pointing another AR-18 at them. Obviously, the boat accommodated more than just rods and reels. Even at this distance, we could tell he was nervous by his constant scanning of the lake shore, trying either to remember the landing spots or decide which one to use. Finally, he spotted us, and the AR-18 was up and firing in a second. We took evasive action, breaking away from each other, curving and coming back, crisscrossing every few seconds. I caught a glimpse of late afternoon boaters and skiers, shocked at the sounds and the chase, moving quickly to get out of the way.

As fast as the water jets were, we still weren't catching up. Our evasive maneuvers also slowed us. But we were confusing the issue, causing consternation in Rand. I could only hope that Anne would think to take advantage of that and do something, grab the throttle, bring it down, anything that would give Roee and me a chance at him.

Roee was passing again in front of me when a spray of bullets must have riddled his water jet, maybe a leg, for I saw him suddenly throw his hands up and kick backward off the craft, flying into the air. The water jet continued without him, exploding in a fireball. Momentum kept Roee flying forward, passing through the fireball, hitting the water just after it to skip along its surface like a stone. I slowed for a second, determined to return to him, a determination that waned quickly under analysis. I sped up again, pushing forward. I could only hope Roee survived. I could only hope the Captain had a force out on the water.

Rand's boat suddenly veered to the right, heading towards North

Bay. I followed, maintaining a zigzag, but I was losing the race, something Rand also knew, for he had stopped shooting.

Then Rand's boat hit the wake of a civilian's boat just getting out of the way. It bounced. Anne lost her grip and fell backward on the deck, grabbing one of the stabilizing rods of the jack plate to keep from going overboard. York tried to turn around to hold her, but Rand wouldn't let him, pushing the gun at him. Then suddenly, the whole powerboat shook and bounced. Rand lost his footing and almost fell overboard.

To save himself, he had to let go of the AR-18. It fell into the lake. I was catching up, and I could see why. Whether by plan or quick thinking, Anne had managed to hit the switch of the hydraulic unit on the jack plate and brought the engine's prop up out of the water. Rand was frantic. He jumped onto the back deck and kicked at Anne. She held onto the stabilizing rod, but the kick had forced her off to one side, and her legs were now hanging over the back end of the boat, just to the side of the engine. Rand reached down and pushed the switch, lowering the engine, the prop suddenly catching the water and sending the boat forward—but it was too late. I had gained enough to come up alongside just as the boat began to speed up again. I jumped off the water jet and onto Rand just as he stepped back into the cockpit. We fell together, and Rand was wedged between the instrument console and the side of the boat. He kicked and screamed and bit, but I managed to subdue him when I got one good shot at his head with my elbow, stunning him.

We were flying. The boat was up, out of the water, and slowly rotating upside down. I managed to get my head up. I could see York being thrown in the spin. Anne let go and followed, and I followed her. Rand was still wedged in the boat and went with it as it dropped down, hit the water, and capsized.

I was underwater, struggling to come up. I made it. There was Anne treading water. Behind her, I could see the ski jump ramp the boat must have hit the edge of, causing its flight and flip. I turned my head. The boat was bottom-up, strangely adrift, the engine still roaring, its prop sticking up in the air and chopping at it to little avail. I knew Rand was trapped. I dove, got under the boat, and found him still wedged, awake, his face full of fear. I grabbed him, pulled, yanked, put my foot on the instrument console, pushed, and got him loose. Pulled him out from under the boat and brought him to the surface, holding his head up. He took in a breath. I looked around—still only Anne.

"York?"

"Oh my god!" She looked around. Dove.

"No! Anne, don't!" I yelled, but too late.

Rand was beginning to struggle. Out of fight or flight, I wasn't sure. I held him tight but really wanted him to go away, to go away so that I could help Anne.

I got my wish. Rand managed to push a foot into my still-sensitive groin. There was a flash of pain. I let go of the bastard.

There was this stupid look of triumph on his face, and his manic eyes looked at me through his wet, oversize glasses, oddly still on his face. He was that puppet, that weird kids' show puppet gone mad, having to take one last moment to savor the pain of the loser, deluded opinion though it was. He turned to swim away, not hearing the engine, not seeing the stern of the boat that had drifted around towards us; he turned and took a stroke with his right arm, throwing his hand right into the spinning prop. The four blades caught him and sucked him up, chopping the arm up to the armpit, getting his head and mangling it into nothing but splattered bone, brain, and blood. The rest of the body was spun up, over, and away, then hit the water with a red-tinged splash and slowly sank.

Anne popped up with York, both gasping for air, much too close to the prop.

"Look out!" I screamed. She saw the danger and moved away, dragging York with her. The boat moved in the opposite direction.

Anne looked around her. Ragged flesh floated in red-stained water. "Eww! What's this?"

"Rand," I answered. "He met with a boating accident."

Anne looked around again and figured out the situation. "Eww!"

"Well—he said it was a mean prop."

CHAPTER 21

THE FINAL SAY

A small flotilla of Lake Patrol boats reached and surrounded us. I saw the Captain. "Roee?"

"He's okay. We picked him up. Just a flesh wound. He's back at the house now with the medical crew."

York was being pulled into one of the boats.

"And The Switch?"

"Well, Roee is done. We had to shoot the deputy in the leg to make a match, though."

"Double his pay and reimburse the county for medical."

"Okay—Here's yours."

A nude male deputy, approximately my height and build, jumped into the water beside me. Then a nude blonde female deputy jumped in close to Anne. I started to strip and instructed Anne to do the same.

"What?" Anne asked, disbelieving.

"These fine servants of the people will get the credit for stopping Rand. Strip, give her your clothes."

"Are you kidding? Do you know the publicity I could get out of this? Do you know what this could do for my career?"

"It would be bad publicity. Strip."

"Fixxer, there is no such thing as bad publicity."

"In your business. In my business, there is no such thing as good publicity. Strip."

"I'm not in your business."

"You are now."

"But...?"

"Loved every moment of it, didn't you?"

"Well, yes, but..."

"Strip."

We stripped and then handed our clothes to our surrogates, and they started the difficult process of dressing underwater.

We were pulled into the Captain's boat and quickly wrapped in blankets. Then, the flotilla headed back to the Chateau de la Lune. Once dry, we both put on the deputy uniforms of our doppelgängers.

"Captain?" Anne asked. "Imelda?"

"The maid?"

"Yeah."

"She's in critical condition but already on her way to the hospital. I'm sure she's being well taken care of."

"Keep us informed," I said. "We've decided to adopt her."

xx

At the house, they had Roee patched up.

"It's okay," he said. "Didn't touch the bone. But damn, that lake is cold."

"I'll send you to a hot spring for your vacation."

"Paid?"

"Of course. Generously."

"You're a good man, Charlie Brown."

"Please. I've told you never to use my real name." I started to walk away to confer more with the Captain.

"Fixxer," Roee said, stopping me.

I turned back to him. "Yeah?"

"You are a good man."

"Yeah. Good at what I do."

They had a Town Car for us with tinted windows. Anne offered to drive. "Neither of you guys is in the best of conditions. Why should I put my life in your hands? Roee, in the back, you can stretch out that leg. Fixxer, shotgun."

We did as she ordered without protest. It's not that long of a drive from Arrowhead to L.A., only about two hours. Roee and I slept the whole way like babies.

xx

Three days later, we all gathered at my place for dinner. Catered. Roee deserved a break.

"I never thought of that!" Petey was saying. "Someone going for your groin! Guess I'm just not vicious enough! Did it hurt?"

"I'd be happy to demonstrate."

"No thanks! I'd like mine to get a little more use before abuse!"

"Petey," the Captain said.

"What?"

"You are one sick puppy."

"Yeah, well—!"

"Petey," Roee got his attention.

"Yeah?"

"Eat your food. It's getting cold."

"Ahhh," Petey protested but dug into the goat cheese tart before him.

"Fixxer," the Captain asked. "Was Rand mad?"

"Mad? No. Just overly proactive, if I may use a God-awful current cliché," I responded. "What had fallen into his lap was what any man used to power in one aspect of life, used to having opinions of how things should be—which every human creature does—and used to having those opinions become fact—which few human creatures get to experience—what had fallen into his lap was what such a person truly desires: To have that same command over other aspects of life. Rand was the kind of man who didn't mind collaborating as long as he had the final say. That's not hard to understand. It's a description you could apply to me without error. Such a proclivity, though, demands an attendant arrogance that you can do well with that final say. Arrogance is not a rare commodity in Hollywood—or anywhere else, for that matter—but its justification is. People hate arrogant people who have never justified that arrogance with their actions. They hate even more, though, those who have."

"Rand had gotten tired of Hollywood quite a while back. Because of how he was, he didn't fit well in the corporate environment of the major studios, and he knew that that environment had taken too deep a root to change. He was lucky to have found a place with Engstrand, a good entrepreneurial immigrant who knew how to profit from Rand's arrogance. He treated Rand well, but it wasn't enough for Rand, he still had to answer to another, and no matter how big NewVue grew, it would never have a magical name or history like those of MGM; Paramount; 20th; or Universal. You've got to remember that Rand started as a film buff, a particularly virulent disease.

"How did EarthPeople figure in all this?" Anne asked.

"At first, it was just something to expend excess energy, a cause to give him recognition on another level. He was excited, like everybody else, about the fall of Communism and the New World Order. He wanted to be a part of it. It was trendy. But as he traveled around the world, talked to people, and saw the real problems out there, especially the breakdown of order in the former Communist states, putting that together in his mind with all the 'Business as usual' propaganda about Washington, he suddenly saw the value of, shall we say, decisive leadership, which was natural to his thinking. But being a good Hollywood liberal, he had previously had no idea you could seriously entertain a non-democratic outlook. He kept his feelings to himself, of course, and was probably just determined to build EarthPeople into a powerful organization that would give him a platform from which he could have at least some impacts on world affairs. After all, what more could he have expected?

"Then Veritas fell into his lap. And not just Veritas, it was York's treatment, V, based on a nightmare scenario Skinner had made up to show York what a huge responsibility they had. It laid out exactly how Veritas could be used not only to amass a fortune but also to control world public opinion by its direct connection to their minds. The rest of York's scenario had the good guys defeating the bad guys, of course, but Rand knew that that usually happened only in the movies. The core ideas in the treatment are what appealed to him.

"In his early days, when he was pushing to get ahead in this town, Rand used to secure drugs for people. He saw first-hand the impact of a product that, by its nature, created its own demand. The English had done it to the Chinese with opium. Philip Morris does it to kids with tobacco. It's the perfect business. Rand experienced Veritas on York's houseboat. He knew immediately that it could be addictive. Anything that provides an escape from most people's mundane, mean, short, brutish lives is naturally addictive—and a Midas money machine. Now combine that with its potential as a mind-altering 'drug.' If Veritas can get into your head and completely convince you of a truth, any truth, never needing to rely for even a second on suspension of disbelief or metaphor, then the people who manufacture these truths have ultimate power.

"His plan, I believe, was simple. Perfect Veritas; patent it; introduce it to the world consumer market as the greatest entertainment form ever; add just enough educational and therapeutic applications for goodwill; get masses of people addicted to it; amass a fortune. Then decide what opinions to feed your customers and what to dictate to their hearts and minds. I'm not sure Rand had that part all figured out yet. He was taking first things first. But he had thought ahead enough to know that if others got to know about Veritas, he would have to defend it with viciousness, for he knew that's how people would try to take it away from him. So he turned to Batsarov in anticipation and paranoia, paranoia inflamed when York reported that Finch had given V to Hinckley, and Hinckley was trying to buy it. It may have only been a movie treatment, but it revealed his hand. A revelation that he knew could hinder him. Then Finch was dead. And then he let Batsarov loose."

"But you got him, Fixxer! You fought the good fight, and you won the day," the Captain said.

"Did I? How do we know Rand would not have been a benevolent dictator?"

"What are you saying?" Anne seemed shocked. "He was vicious, condoning any method, including mass murder, to get what he wanted."

"Is that so unusual? It has often been done that way in the past. If the outcome would have been a peaceful world, efficiently run, might it not have been worth it?"

"No, of course not?" Anne protested.

"Why?" I challenged.

"Because, well, because...."

"Because such a world probably wouldn't tolerate a loud-mouth weirdo like me!" Petey piped up. "And that would be a woeful tragedy!"

I smiled at Petey. He was such a neat guy. "Thank you, Petey. For that grounding in reality, you may have the Bear Rug Program."

"Oh, thank you, Fixxer! You're my Santa Claus!"

xx

The rest of the evening was devoted to lighter topics, good food, and wine that Roee had presented to us with great enthusiasm, and which I was sad to have to report to him I didn't much care for. The others, though, seemed to enjoy it.

"One thing remains unanswered," I announced.

The assembled looked at me, questioning, wondering what it could be.

"Since about the same time this whole affair started, I've been trying to remember where Mae West had lived. I know it was a building on Rossmore, either the El Royale or the Ravenswood, but I can't remember which. It's been driving me nuts. I asked Finch; he didn't know. I should have asked George at Hollywood Book and Poster, but I forgot. Roee, you even failed me."

"And I fail you still. I still can't remember."

"And Skinner, a film buff, not to mention a genius, if ever there was one, couldn't remember. So it remains a mystery."

"Hey," Anne said rather pointedly. "You never thought to ask me?"

"Uh..."

"It was the Ravenswood."

"How do you know that?"

"Dad used to take me to revivals of her movies when I was a kid. I loved her. She was strong, sexy, independent, and nobody's victim. What a role model for a young girl who wanted to go to Hollywood! I wrote her letters. She wrote me back. Gave me a lot of advice. Especially about men."

"Really, such as?"

"Oh, no. Name, rank, and serial number, that's all you'll get out of me."

xx

The evening ended. The Captain left. Petey went to his room to pack. And Roee retired, leaving Anne and me alone.

"I'm not going to stay the night, you know," Anne informed me.

"You're not?"

"Nope."

"Why not?"

"This time of year, the morning sun comes in my bedroom window at just the most pleasant angle, kissing me awake. I love it. Hate to miss it."

"I understand."

"It's hard to explain. You must experience it yourself."

"I'm sure."

"Fixxer!"

"What?"

"If you don't beg me to take you home with me right now, I'll—"

The kiss was long, deep, and heady. When we broke, the aquamarine of her eyes seemed the critical element in a penetrating force that disturbed as it excited.

I'll give no account of the rest of the evening. I may not be a gentleman, but I do try to act like one occasionally.

END

ABOUT THE AUTHOR

Before publishing eleven critically acclaimed novels, award-winning and Amazon Bestselling author Steven Paul Leiva spent over twenty years as a writer and producer in the entertainment industry. He worked with such talent as Academy Award-winning producer Richard Zanuck; director Ivan Reitman; literary legend and screenwriter Ray Bradbury, and Star Wars producer Gary Kurtz. He even lent his voice to the Academy Award shortlisted (placing in the top ten) animated short, "The Indescribable Nth." https://vimeo.com/14857442

Leiva produced the animation for *Space Jam*, putting together an ad hoc animation studio for Warner Bros in three days over the phone.

During this time, he wrote novels and a play, *Made on the Moon*, which premiered at the 1996 Edinburgh Festival Fringe, receiving a four-star review from *The Scotsman*.

After *Space Jam*, Leiva decided to concentrate on writing novels. Since 2003, he has published ten novels, a novella, and a book of essays.

His work has been praised by literary great Ray Bradbury, Oscar-winning film producer Richard Zanuck, NY Times bestselling author and Pulitzer Prize finalist Diane Ackerman, and *Star Trek: Enterprise* actor John Billingsley, the greatest bookworm in Hollywood.

Leiva received the Scribe Award from the International Association of Media Tie-in Writers.

You can find more about Leiva and read his blogs at https://tinyurl.com/ydgpkps8

BOOKS BY STEVEN PAUL LEIVA

Blood is Pretty: The First Fixxer Adventure

Meet the Fixxer—with wit and aplomb, he works the fruitful fields of Hollywood, fixing the sins and correcting the stupidities of the denizens therein. In *Blood is Pretty,* he comes to the rescue of "the most beautiful woman I have ever seen" to extricate her from the grip of the soul-sucking sexual desires of a producer born in slime and takes on the task of buying off with money and muscle a film geek who won't cooperate with a director of minuscule talent who wants to claim "V"—the geek's "Holy Grail" of a film treatment—as his own.

Hollywood is an All-Volunteer Army: The Second Fixxer Adventure

What those in the know in Hollywood really know is that if they need a dark deed done, if they need a sticky personal or professional problem "fixed," they can call upon the mysterious and dangerous Fixxer. Whether you are a successful comedy film director whose "art" has never truly been appreciated because the country's most important film critic has held a grudge against you since college, or you are a neophyte and naïve screenwriter who resents the professional blackmail she has just suffered, you call upon the Fixxer.

Traveling in Space

A unique first-contact novel from the aliens' point-of-view.

The last thing the factfinders—who call themselves Life—expected to find while traveling in space in "The Curious" on a mission from their planet, The Living World, was otherlife. But one day, they stumble upon the third planet out from a backwater sun and find it teeming with a vast diversity of life, including one sentient and cognizant, if primitive, species that they dub: Otherlife.

Being not only from "The Curious" but inherently curious themselves, they begin to study the Otherlife and their alien culture, discovering such strange things as marriage, intoxicating drinks, weapons of minor and mass destruction, the gleeful inhaling of toxic substances, two-parent families, layered language, genocide, non-nude bathing, and—the strangest thing of all—religion.
This first contact between Life and Otherlife, disconcerting for both, has moments of humor and moments of horror—and neither escapes the encounter unchanged.

12 Dogs of Christmas - A Novelization

Winner of the Scribe Award from the International Association of Media Tie-in Authors

Based on the beloved independent family film.

12-year-old Emma O'Connor is sent to live with her "aunt" in the small town of Doverville, where Emma soon finds herself in the middle of a "dogfight" with the mayor and town dogcatcher. To strike down their "no-dogs" law, Emma must bring together a group of schoolmates, grown-ups, and adorable dogs of all shapes and sizes in a spectacular holiday pageant. The *12 Dogs of Christmas* is a fun, heartwarming story featuring a diverse canine cast and is perfect for all those who love dogs, kids, and Christmas.

By the Sea: A Comic Novel

A modern comic adult fairy tale with an ensemble cast of Cinderellas. Instead of a kingdom by the sea, our story takes place in and around a residential hotel by the sea. The architecturally eclectic Briers Hotel is situated on Leech Beach, a not particularly inviting beach, being often fog-bound and always scruffy. But it's the perfect setting for our Cinderellas, male, and female, who put up with the scruffiness of life while striving to make it through their various personal seaside fogs.

Theater; art; antiques; old movies; sex; more sex; death; fast and slow cars, chicken shit and cow poop; military bearing and erotic emissions—not to mention the wicked witch, the sea serpent by the seashore, the village ogre, the village idiot, and several Prince Charmings—all figure into this merry tale with a multitude of happy endings.

IMP: A Political Fantasia

Thomas P. Powell's political ascension was both unusual and yet very American. From traffic cop to Vice President of the United States, his climb up the ladder of public service was often due to the push of random acts and not-so-happy accidents—although Thomas held the opinion that it was due solely to his singular innate moral authority. What matters is what's within; that's the Powell political philosophy. But, then, on the cusp of his grasping the last rung of the American political ladder, something truly within suddenly appears. A horrible homunculus, a wild imp, climbs out of Thomas's right ear to bedevil his nights, confuse his days, and take him on a crazy, wild, nauseating, and nuclear journey. It's like The West Wing was done as a Twilight Zone episode. And you thought our last political nightmare was surreal.

Journey to Where: A Contemporary Scientific Romance

When a radical experiment into the nature of time is sabotaged, the scientific team finds themselves in an alternate universe where humans never became the dominant life force. Instead, dinosaurs evolved into intelligent bipeds, developing language and societal structures.
The scientists must learn to communicate with this alien species, who view them as unusual pets, and figure out how to recreate the original experiment in a non-industrialized world, so they can return home—assuming there's a home, or even a universe, to return to.
But the scientist who sabotaged them is trapped in this new world with them. And he's looking to rise to power, even if his quest means the death of his traveling companions. A contemporary scientific romance in the tradition of H. G. Wells and Jules Verne

Creature Feature: A Horrid Comedy

There is something strange happening in Placidville!

It is 1962. Kathy Anderson, a serious actress who took her training at the Actors Studio in New York, is stuck playing Vivacia, the Vampire Woman on Vivacia's House of Horrors, at a local Chicago TV station. Finally fed up showing old monster movies to creature feature fans, she quits and heads to New York and the fame and footlights of Broadway.

On her way, she stops to visit her parents and old friends in Placidville, the All-American, middle-class, blissfully ordinary Midwest small town she grew up in. But she finds things strange in Placidville. Kathy's parents, her best friend from high school, the local druggist, and even the Oberhausen twins are all acting curiously creepy, odiously odd, and wholly weird—especially the town's super geeky nerd, Gerald, who warns of dark days ahead.

Has Kathy entered a zone in the twilight? Did she reach the limits that are outer? Has she fallen through a mirror that is black? Or is it just—just—politics as usual?

Bully 4 Love: A Rather Odd Love Story

Adolphus Seruya is a happy, middle-aged, unambitious bachelor and History professor at a prominent community college. Then suddenly, SHE walks into his classroom. Lavinia Carson is beautiful in a unique yet compelling way. And radiant almost beyond description. Thus begins a rather odd story of love rejected, love ignored, love found—and cuttlefish pizza.

Extraordinary Voyages

What if a man wanted to go to the moon from when he was an infant? Not a toddler, not a child, not a young man, but a babe in his mother's arms?

What if Baron Munchausen traveled from 1790 to 1641 to take Cyrano de Bergerac to Mars?

What if the man who wanted to go to the moon from when he was an infant wrote some rude poems?

What if the author of this book wrote his own Wikipedia page? Which he was sure Wikipedia would never publish.

What if you bought this book and found out?

Includes the critically acclaimed novella *Made on the Moon.*

The Reluctant Heterosexual
A Tragicomedy in Four Movements A Prelude And An Interlude

With *The Reluctant Heterosexual,* Steven Paul Leiva concludes his thematic trilogy: **The Love, Sex, and Pursuit of Happiness Novels**. All three novels look at these essential aspects of the human condition, with each story focusing on one of the three. *By the Sea: A Comic Novel* looks at our unease when unhappy. *Bully 4 Love: A Rather Odd Love Story* takes a skewed view of this most revered emotion. And now, *The Reluctant Heterosexual,* as the title predicts, concerns sex, which is not always the same as love, nor is it always a happy situation. Subtitled *A Tragicomedy in Four Movements A Prelude And An Interlude,* each section of the novel, as in a musical composition, has its individual tempo, mood, and form as it tells the story—and stories—of Robert Leslie Cromwell and Sandy Smith—two *Homo sapiens sapiens* surviving and striving in the late 20th-Century.

Robert and Sandy are intelligent, creative, not unattractive, wealthy, married to each other, and in love. And yet their procreating bodies might as well be standing naked on a savanna in Africa in the late Pliocene Era. It's the sometimes comic conflict between ancient bodies and modern culture. Can there possibly be a happy ending?

The Definition of Luck
Or
The Post-Modern Prometheus

Khadambi Kinyanjui, a 6-foot-five Kenyan who grew up in London, is from a wealthy family. Joe Smith, quite a bit shorter, is a red-headed orphan who grew up with his Aunt Liz in a hole in the California desert. Both are brilliant scientists. One is a neurobiologist, the other an astronomer, who first meet in 2049 under the Tommy Trojan statue at the University of Southern California. They become the best of friends but a very odd couple. And yet, their brotherhood is more robust than most actual brothers.

Then tragedy strikes the pair. Death is near for one of them. What can fend it off? Can the mind, the *self*, be uploaded to some digital realm? Can one become more than a human and far less than an animal? Or will the fix be something unexpected and mysterious? Can this human survive? Can humanity? Can friendship?

Searching for Ray Bradbury: Writings about the Writer and the Man

Includes the title piece written for the *Los Angeles Times* and "The Man Who Was Himself," Leiva's memorial appreciation of Bradbury commissioned by the Science Fiction & Fantasy Writers of America for the Winter 2012/13 edition of their quarterly magazine, *The Bulletin*. Other pieces were initially written for *Neworld Review*, KCET.org, and Leiva's blog.

With a special foreword by Hugo and Nebula Award-winning author David Brin.

Blood is Pretty

www.ingramcontent.com/pod-product-compliance
Lightning Source LLC
Chambersburg PA
CBHW021212250626
47155CB00008B/2778